VICTORY

VICTORY

Book Three of the Legacy Fleet Trilogy

Nick Webb

Copyright © 2016 Nick Webb

All rights reserved.

www.nickwebbwrites.com

Summary: United Earth burns. The Swarm runs rampant across our space. We mourn the loss of thousands of ships and millions of fallen comrades. Billions of fathers, mothers, sisters and brothers-- all gone, all dead. It is time we end this, for our moment has come. But victory never comes without sacrifice. Heroes are not taught nor trained, but forged in blood and ashes. Our grandchildrens' history books will tell our story, and glorify the heroes and legends. The Swarm will be conquered; we will prevail. At any price.

Text set in Garamond
Designed by Jenny Webb
http://jennywebbedits.com

Cover art by Tom Edwards
http://tomedwardsdmuga.blogspot.co.uk

ISBN-10: 1530724678
ISBN-13: 978-1530724673

Printed in the United States of America

For J., L., and C.

Acknowledgements

Many thanks to Jenny, editor extraordinaire, without whom this trilogy would be a pale, Swarm-corrupted shuffling zombie of a book with plot twists to nowhere, zero-dimensional characters, officers who are discrete instead of discreet, and starships with altitude but no attitude.

And to the kids, for understanding that dad's odd hobby-turned career often takes him away during crunch month. Just remember that after book launch week comes boat launch week!

And to the incomparable Tom Edwards, whose stunning artwork for the Legacy Fleet Trilogy is ... stunning—there just isn't a better word for it.

And to Greg Tremblay, who narrates the audiobooks like a boss, and who now has to read this praise out loud and say anything, absolutely anything that I write. Banana.

And to my author friends who provided great advice and laughs along the way, and who all got to be redshirted throughout the series.

And to the readers and fans who made this trilogy possible and sent emails and messages of encouragement. Many of you made it into this trilogy, which pleases me to no end.

And also to the good folks at Grounded Coffee in Madison, Alabama—many thanks to Chris, Grace, Sarah (with an 'h'), and Gene for keeping me well hydrated and stuffed with the best blueberry muffins in the south while I wrote this book. Yes, the butt-groove on the couch is mine.

CHAPTER ONE

LIEUTENANT RODRIGUEZ stepped into a murky puddle in the middle of the street, wrinkled his nose, and swore. *Oh, for hell's sake.* It was the 27th century, technology had launched humanity to the stars, dozens of planets had been colonized, and galactic civilization had, up until four months ago, flourished on a scale few had ever dreamed of.

And now there was raw sewage flowing freely through the streets.

The refugee camp was bursting at the seams, having accepted over double the half million refugees from the Cadiz sector it had been designed to hold. As Lieutenant Rodriguez made his way down the muddy, sewage-infused street, the wails of sick babies rang in his ears. Small, dirty children huddled forlornly under their equally-harrowed mothers' arms, peering out the doors of their temporary shelters, looking for the next shipment of food and water from the city.

It wasn't coming, Rodriguez knew. The shipments had slowed to once every several days, then to once a week. The next one would not come.

Something else was coming instead.

They were coming.

Dusk began to color the sky. The sun had set several minutes ago—possibly for the last time, Rodriguez thought. Time was short. In spite of the crying children in the background the refugee camp was eerily quiet as he crossed the final hundred meters of mud, refuse, and sewage to reach his family's shelter. His own children would be waiting for him—hopefully with their bags packed, like he'd instructed.

As he opened the door to his family's shelter, the refugee camp's sirens began to sound, adding their urgent wail to the children's cries. That could only mean one thing.

They were here.

"Papa!"

His daughter Elsa ran up to him and hugged his lower torso. Tomas sat in the corner, hovering over his grandmother who was supposed to be taking care of them but instead had fallen sick with an illness that had left her feeble and coughing, lying weakly on the shelter's only bed.

Lieutenant Rodriguez peeled Elsa's arms off and approached his mother. Her face was ashen, but she managed a weak smile.

"Are they ready?" he asked, leaning down close to her. She gave a small nod.

"Are you?" he added.

Her shaking hand reached out to his. "Go," she said, with some effort, and descended into a fit of coughing. Her hand came away from her mouth, spattered red.

"I'm not leaving you, mom." He stooped over to pick her up, but the woman, with surprising strength, pushed him away.

"I said, go. They're ready. You're out of time. Get them to safety. I'll be—" she glanced at Tomas and Elsa, forcing out a grimaced smile for their sake. She always was a wonderful actress. "I'll be fine."

The sirens wailed outside. Crowds shouted in the dusky air.

Rodriguez breathed a silent curse, but sprang into action, grabbing the two bags sitting by the door. His own belongings were in his hangar at the fighter base on the other side of Gunaratana City. As a fighter pilot he, as a general rule, packed light. But there was no time to retrieve his own things. There was no time for anything. Except to run.

They were coming. In force. He'd seen the scans play out on the monitors of the hangar bay just over half an hour ago. Twenty Swarm carriers, plus something new: the unthinkably-massive super dreadnought that had made its first appearance the week before in the Swarm's invasion of the Mao Cluster.

Mao Prime no longer existed.

Eight billion people no longer existed.

Scouts reported that the surface, once the glittering cosmopolitan jewel of the Chinese Intersolar Democratic Republic, was now a sterile, fiery wasteland.

He pushed his children through the door and cast one last glance back at his mother, still on the bed, wan and pale. She mouthed, *I love you*. He blinked back tears and could only nod a curt reply before turning back out into the rank, muddy street.

The transport would be leaving soon; they had only minutes to spare. As they navigated the busy streets—which had erupted into a frenzied mob of panicked refugees now that the emergency sirens were wailing in force—he wondered if he'd be court-martialed for abandoning his post. *But really*, he thought, *what good would one more lone fighter craft be against the unstoppable force that was coming?* How could they court-martial a man just trying to get his kids to safety? Could one man really make a difference against such incontestable power? Such reckless hate?

Granger had. The Hero of Earth—he supposedly died, and returned, beating back the Swarm in the process. So the rumors said, though Rodriguez didn't quite believe them, video proof be damned.

It didn't matter. He looked up at the darkening sky, and his stomach clenched as he focused on a small cluster of bright lights above the eastern horizon that steadily grew clearer—twenty small dots surrounding the larger one.

They were coming.

So was the Hero of Earth. He'd heard chatter that Granger's fleet was on its way, coming to the rescue.

But he'd seen the tactical scans. There was no way he'd arrive in time. The man may have been a miracle worker, but it looked like his lucky streak was over. By the time The Bricklayer showed up, the entire world of Indira would be a wasteland, just like Mao Prime. Just like the Cadiz Sector. And the Veracruz Sector. Merida, New Oregon, and Calibri—all gone.

Five minutes later, they arrived at the local spaceport. After a few panicked moments of desperate searching for the transport he started to wonder if it had left without him.

"Are we too late, Papa?" asked Tomas.

Rodriguez swore under his breath, but breathed a sigh of relief as they rounded a corner and saw it: a small freighter, its captain waiting impatiently on the still-open ramp.

"Come along, Elsa," he coaxed his daughter forward. Tomas followed close behind.

He climbed the ramp, but not before glancing back up at the sky, looking for the cluster of bright lights that signaled their world's certain doom. They were bigger, closer, and more spread out. Several were still near the horizon while others had risen high into the sky overhead.

The ground shook, starting as a low tremor, and escalating into a moderate shaking that rattled panels inside the freighter. Rodriguez watched the horizon with a sickening feeling, and felt his face go white as he saw a mushroom cloud rise in the distance, hundreds of kilometers away.

"Stop gawking and shut the damn hatch!" yelled the freighter captain from the cockpit. Lieutenant Rodriguez hit the ramp retractor and ushered his kids to the rows of seats. All were full, except for three. They settled into them after fiddling with the restraints.

"Hey," said a teenage girl sitting across from him, "is that a pilot's uniform? An IDF pilot?"

He looked away, ignoring the girl, and busied himself with Elsa's seat restraint.

"Why aren't you out there? Why aren't you fighting for us?" The girl was visibly distraught—she shook, her eyes were wild, darting back and forth from the closed hatch back to Rodriguez and over to the cockpit. "They're coming! They're coming! Why aren't you out there? They're coming! They're—"

The woman next to her grabbed the girl's arm—her mother, or grandmother. "Quiet. He's getting his kids out. He's just the same as us."

"But he's a fighter pilot! He could stop them! He could—"

The woman shook the girl until she fell silent. "Nothing can stop them! One more won't make a difference. You just mind your own business."

Nothing can stop them.

Rodriguez pulled a necklace out from beneath his uniform and began thumbing the beads, whispering silent rosary prayers. He knew they were rising through the atmosphere now, well clear of any of the dreaded singularity weapons that were now ravaging the surface.

But making it through the perimeter of the Swarm fleet would be another feat entirely.

One more won't make a difference, the woman had said. But, besides the rosary, there was only one thought in Rodriguez's mind:

Granger, where the hell are you?

CHAPTER TWO

Bridge, ISS Warrior
0.3 lightyears from Indira, Britannia Sector

CAPTAIN TIMOTHY GRANGER paced the *Warrior*'s bridge. He was late, and it was killing him inside. Each second that ticked by was like a dagger twisting in his gut.

Because he knew that with each tick, another ten thousand people were likely dying.

"Initiating q-jump twenty-seven," said Ensign Prince.

The scene on the viewscreen shifted, and the central bright star grew slightly larger. And around that star, a planet. And on that planet, people. Millions of people. And drawing nearer to that planet, with a disconcerting head start....

"Any more word from CENTCOM about the Swarm fleet approaching Indira?"

Ensign Prucha slowly shook his head. "Sorry, sir. All outer system bases went quiet fifteen minutes ago. Last word was over twenty incoming vessels."

Damn. The Swarm had abruptly changed tactics the past two weeks, with deadly effect. Rather than slowly waltzing their way into a system, giving the population time to panic and scatter, they'd taken to striking as quickly as possible, with overwhelming force. Instead of three Swarm carriers here, four there, their enemy had entered a new phase of the war. A phase of extermination.

You ain't seen nothing yet, she'd said. That young pilot, Fishtail, had spoken those words after her life was saved by injecting her with Swarm matter. She wasn't lying. The scale of the new Swarm offensive was breathtaking. Three entire worlds destroyed in the past two weeks. Hundreds of ships lost. Billions of lives.

And the next target, Indira. Right in the heart of United Earth territory. Less than five lightyears from Britannia itself. Fifteen lightyears from Earth.

And Granger was caught with his pants down, stationed at Britannia, ready to defend against an attack that never came. The hammer was striking Indira instead.

"Ready for q-jump twenty-eight," he said.

"Sir, the *ISS Colorado* is reporting trouble with their cap bank. They need five minutes to lock down the problem and recharge."

He shook his head. "No. Leave them. Ready for q-jump."

Not having the *Colorado* there would hurt, but getting there five minutes later would hurt more. Plus, fighting with thirty-seven ships instead of thirty-eight ships wouldn't make much difference, especially if the Swarm had brought their newly unveiled super dreadnought.

While not quite as large as the massive Swarm orbital space stations they'd destroyed over Volari Three—the planet that had turned out to be the homeworld of the Dolmasi—the super dreadnoughts were formidable. Easily ten times the size of the run-of-the-mill Swarm carriers, packed with antimatter beam turrets and loaded with the singularity weapons the Russians had provided them with.

There were only three or four of them—the intelligence community hadn't come to agreement on that point—but whether there were three or three thousand, the result was the same.

Utter destruction.

"Ready, sir," said Ensign Prince.

"Initiate."

The viewscreen shifted again, and the central star, Indira Prime, grew even larger. Just two more jumps, nearly half a lightyear, and they'd be there, late, for the battle of their lives.

Or, they'd find a broken, empty, devastated world, depending on how late they were.

"What do you think?" Commander Proctor had been working doggedly at the science station, conferring with her new science team, immersed in a project that had consumed nearly all her time the past few weeks, but now she sidled up next to his chair and bent low to his ear.

"We're too late."

She nodded, apparently in somber agreement. "And if we really are too late? What then? Stay and fight? Wait until we've got backup? Wait for the Dolmasi?"

He grunted. "If we don't fight them here, then we fight them over some other world. Here is as good a place as any, and if the planet is already ravaged, best to limit the destruction."

She lowered her voice. "But if it's the case that the planet is lost, wouldn't it be more prudent to at least wait until Zingano shows up?"

Granger shook his head. "Weren't you listening earlier? He's dealing with a sudden incursion into the Maori System. Small raid of only four Swarm ships, but his fleet won't be here for hours, at least."

Only four ships. He inwardly chuckled that he now considered four swarm carriers to be a *small* raid. Four months ago, four ships had nearly destroyed Earth. While their defenses had improved since then, Zingano would lose at least a dozen capital ships and tens of thousands of men and women in that engagement with *only* four ships.

Proctor scowled. "I didn't hear. When was that?"

"Just ten minutes ago." He eyed her warily. "You ok, Shelby?"

She glanced around the bridge before dropping her voice to a whisper. "I think I'm on to something. The team and I."

"What?" He scanned the bridge as she spoke, watching the officers and crew. Proctor had subjected every crew member of the *Warrior* to the blood test that revealed Swarm infiltration, and though no one else had tested positive after Doc Wyatt and Colonel Hanrahan, Granger was still wary of speaking openly of either

IDF's strategic plans or Proctor's Swarm research. For all he knew, the blood test was incomplete and there could still be Swarm agents among them. Best to practice good OPSEC hygiene in the meantime.

"Just something about the fundamental mechanism behind Swarm communication. With the meta-space signals. It's quantum based. Using gravitons. Quantum particles."

"Right...." He wasn't sure where she was leading.

"But the singularities, they're not. All equations governing gravitational waves, gravitational singularities, gravitational *anything*, at least on a macro scale, is general relativity-based. Quantum mechanics, and general relativity—those two branches of physics just don't mix very well. We haven't reconciled them in the seven hundred years we've known about them, and here the Swarm is using both of them to devastating effect."

The viewscreen shifted as they made another q-jump. Only one more before show time.

"And?" he murmured.

"And ... that's it, mostly. Just a hunch. I've performed a few experiments I want you to look at later. Some of the results are ... interesting. To say the least."

Ensign Prince glanced back. "Ready for final q-jump, sir."

Granger nodded. Proctor retreated back to the XO's station where her deputy, Lieutenant Diaz, had been making preparations for the battle. Now that it was upon them, she took up her post, glancing at the tactical crew, who nodded back, indicating they were ready.

As ready as they'd ever be. Granger knew he was never ready for any battle. How do you prepare to lose tens of thousands of people under your command? It was something he hadn't grown used to, and hoped he never would, his nickname be damned. *Bricklayer? Bullshit.*

"Initiate," he said, sitting down just as the contents of the viewscreen shifted.

In place of the starfield centered on the distant sun of Indira Prime came the image of a planet.

A devastated, broken planet.

"Ensign...?" he whispered.

Ensign Prucha shook his head. "All planetary defenses are silent. Every other comm band is just frenzied chatter, both civilian and military bands."

Ensign Diamond at sensors worked his controls. "Most major cities destroyed. The Swarm fleet is spread out across an equatorial orbit, targeting the smaller population centers. Thousands of colonial transports and freighters are trying to break free of orbit but they're being intercepted by Swarm fighter craft."

Once again, he was left with the choice of who to save. Who to fight for. Who to die for. The hundreds of thousands of people in orbit who would form the next wave of refugee camps in the adjacent star system? Or the millions of people left on the ground, about to be either burned alive or vaporized in a singularity explosion under their feet?

He gripped his armrests, knuckles white. He'd had enough. A yell erupted from his throat, culminating in a balled up fist hitting the console swiveled in front of him, which snapped off onto the floor with a clatter that startled all the crew members around him.

All eyes were on him.

"Where the hell is that super dreadnought?"

Diamond scanned his console. "At longitude fifty-nine point two four, latitude—"

Granger cut him off, still staring at the wrecked planet below. "Send coordinates to the fleet. Prepare for maneuver Granger Omega Three."

Commander Proctor looked up suddenly, her face bunched up with concern. "Tim, we've only tossed that idea around. Never practiced it. Haven't even run simulations. Are you—"

"Now's as good a time to practice as any," he replied, maintaining his fiery stare at the screen.

To her credit, Proctor sprang into action, erupting into a flurry of orders. "Alert all crew on decks one through five to move to higher decks. Ensign Prince, full acceleration along heading fifteen mark eight. Prucha, coordinate fleet positioning behind us...."

Within a minute, preparations were complete. He could just barely feel the pull of the thrusters straining away at maximum, the inertial compensators struggling to keep up, pushed past their limit. The extra thrust, adding to the inexorable pull of the planet's gravity, was building their velocity up to a range that would take them far out onto a wide elliptical orbit after they swung around the planet.

But not before they blazed past the super dreadnought at a dizzying speed. With *Warrior* in the lead, shielding the rest of the fleet.

There was a good reason they called the maneuver Granger Omega Three. It could very well be the last thing Granger ever did.

"Time," he said. The bridge had fallen to a deadly quiet.

"Sixty seconds."

Granger nodded. "Cut thrusters. Rotate us with aft lateral thrust. Show them our belly."

"Done, sir," Ensign Prince said after a moment.

"All ships," Granger lifted his head to the inter-fleet comm, "prepare to fire on my mark. Keep your heads, and remember the pattern." He glanced up at Proctor, who nodded once, confirming all was ready. "And if we don't make it out of this one ... it's been an honor serving with you. However—" he nodded toward the tactical station, where ten officers were staring at him, grim-faced, "—I do not give you permission to die until that piece of cumrat shit is destroyed. On my mark ... fire!"

CHAPTER THREE

Star Freighter Lucky Bandit
Low orbit, Indira, Britannia Sector

ELSA AND TOMAS both jumped nervously against the restraints as the freighter lurched again. It was clear to Lieutenant Rodriguez that the captain was repeatedly changing their heading, to avoid either Swarm fighters or debris pluming up from the dozens of singularity impact sites on the battered continent below.

After calming the children down, he glanced toward the passenger compartment's lone viewport, a round thing less than half a meter across. Indira's atmosphere looked like a thin shell wrapping around the fragile, besieged planet—a shell that was rapidly turning from a vibrant, living blue to a sickly brownish gray over the dozens of spots where the ground had erupted outward. Too numerous to count, the mushroom clouds seemed to extend up past the edge of the atmosphere and into space itself.

The planet was bleeding.

How many people had just died? The last sounds from his hurried walk through the camp still rang in his ears—the sick, crying babies. Were they silent now? Probably not—the Swarm would target the major cities first, and only make it to the smaller refugee camps once the larger population centers were smoking craters. But other babies were silent in their place.

Rodriguez wished he could cry, but the magnitude of the loss was too great to comprehend. Besides, he'd already mourned his own planet, Merida. He'd already mourned his extended family, his hometown, and everyone he ever knew.

He'd already mourned his wife. How could he have anything left to mourn?

The freighter lurched again. And again. A third time.

He knew what that meant—they were under attack. The captain was flying a merchant freighter. He'd have little experience evading Swarm fighters. Hell, *no one* had experience evading Swarm fighters.

But he wasn't going to trust his kids' fate to some merchant freighter pilot. He ripped the seat restraint away and maneuvered around the rows of seats, tripping over passengers' legs as he ran to the cockpit.

When he got the door open he found the pilot and his copilot arguing heatedly. Just a glance through the viewports told him what he needed to know—the Swarm was all around them. Looking down at the sensors he grimaced as three contacts approached from three different directions.

They were being hemmed in.

"I'm telling you, Avi, we're no match in speed for those things, we can't just blaze past one and think they'll ignore—"

The copilot shook his head and swore. "Raf, all I'm saying is doing *something* is better than doing *nothing*. We can't just go back and land for god's sake—"

"And what, are you just going to pick a random direction and hope it doesn't take us past a fighter? For hell's sake, there's three of the bastards zeroing in on us right now!"

Rodriguez squeezed the shoulder of the co-pilot. "Gentlemen, if you'll allow me?"

The co-pilot, a short, stubby man with a close-cropped black mustache, shot him a dangerous look. "Get back in your seat, sir. I'll get around to the cabin beverage service after we figure out how to not die."

Rodriguez scowled. "Look, I—"

The co-pilot twisted around suddenly in his seat, and pat a bulge under his vest. "I'm not going to ask you again. Sit."

Lieutenant Rodriguez glanced at the bulge—could be a firearm, but probably just a canister of chew—and swore as the freighter bucked again as the pilot chose another direction.

"Look, see these?" He pointed to a a pair of small medals pinned near his flight suit's shoulder, just under the epaulette. "This one here. Wings on fire. Any idea what that means?" Before the copilot could answer, Rodriguez did it for him. "Fighter combat. And the one next to it, the one with the number fifteen on it? Any guesses?"

A proximity alarm went off as the nearest Swarm fighter closed in. Raf, the pilot, swore and punched it off. "Are you going to go sit down, fly-boy, or do I need to—"

"It means I've been in orbital fighter combat bloody fifteen times against the cumrat bastards out there." He jabbed a finger toward the viewport. The distant Swarm fighter was quickly becoming visible to the naked eye. "So if you want to live, give me the controls. *Now.*"

Avi looked like he was about to jump up and try ripping Rodriguez's arms off. "Why you little ignorant piece of AWOL shit." He reached into his vest and pulled out the firearm. Rodriguez grit his teeth—he had been sure the man was bluffing. "I'm giving you to the count of *one* to get the hell—"

"Avi," began the pilot, "stand up. Give him your seat." He jabbed his thumb toward the cockpit door. "No, don't give me that look. You're half drunk anyway. Go. Get up." When Avi hesitated, looking from his gun to Rodriguez to the co-pilot controls, Raf repeated himself. "Go. Before you put a hole through the hull. *Now.*"

Avi grumbled as he thrust himself from the seat and stalked out of the cockpit. The pilot glowered at him as he left. "Don't worry," he said, watching Rodriguez take Avi's place, "the gun was empty. He just carries it around for show. Micro-dick compensation, most likely. Now are you going to show me your fancy flying, or what?"

"That's the idea...." Rodriguez studied the controls. It was similar to his fighter cockpit, but just different enough to give him a moment's pause. "Time to intercept?"

The pilot glanced at the sensor readout. "That bogey'll be here in twenty seconds."

"What's the maximum acceleration on this thing?"

"Staying within inertia-canceling limits, about two point five—"

"I didn't ask about inertia-canceling limits. Tell me. Maximum acceleration?"

The pilot considered a moment. "Five g's. But that'll give our passengers quite the scare, I don't know if—"

"They'll live." Rodriguez pushed the control stick to maximum and flipped off the acceleration governor. "Maybe."

The thrust nearly took his breath away. He heard his kids scream behind him as everyone was thrown violently against their restraints and he could swear he heard Avi fly through the air and crash into the bulkhead, but all that mattered now was getting them all to safety. Wherever *that* was.

"They're still gaining on us, and our trajectory is straight at the planet—" the pilot's face turned white, "—straight at that plume coming from what used to be New Bangalore...."

"We'll just skirt through the top. Hold on...."

The billowing debris cloud loomed in the viewport ahead of them. From far away it had looked static, but now that they approached, Rodriguez realized the cloud was expanding at what was probably a supersonic rate. He wondered how good the freighter's shielding was.

The pilot apparently read his mind. "If there is any debris in there bigger than a grain of sand, we're goners."

"We're goners anyway. Here we go...."

They plunged into the cloud, and the freighter began to lurch violently as the turbulence from the debris plume buffeted the ship. After a few seconds Rodriguez shifted the controls, veering the craft hard to the left, still at maximum acceleration, staying in the turn until he'd nearly completed a full-about.

The pilot nodded his understanding. "Hoping they keep a straight course, and meanwhile we pop out of the cloud right where we entered it?"

"That's the idea...."

A moment later they cleared the plume and the violent shaking ceased, but Rodriguez maintained the gut-churning acceleration. A quick glance at the sensors told him the gambit had partially worked—the Swarm fighters trailing them were nowhere to be seen. Probably on the other side of the massive debris plume by now.

But ahead of them loomed a new nightmare.

The Swarm super dreadnought, flanked by two regular-sized carriers. Green antimatter beams lanced down toward the planet, raking across towns and smaller cities, even as a half dozen bright points shimmered around the giant ships—growing singularities readying for their imminent launch.

"We're screwed," breathed the pilot.

An odd reading on the sensors. Rodriguez studied the anomaly. A large mass approaching at a dizzying speed. No, not one large mass. It was broken up into several discreet pieces, approaching as one large clump. Had one of the Swarm carriers broken apart?

Raf's eyes widened as he studied the readout. "Is that what I think it is?"

Rodriguez scanned the transponder frequencies. They were IDF ships. Packed together into as tight a formation as he'd ever seen, moving faster than any fleet had a right to.

He grinned. "Yep."

The Hero of Earth had arrived.

CHAPTER FOUR

X-25 Fighter Cockpit
Indira, Britannia Sector

Lieutenant Tyler "Ballsy" Volz gripped his controls. If he wasn't wearing flight gloves, he imagined his knuckles would be white with tension. With good reason—they'd never practiced the Granger Omega Three maneuver before. Lately, he hadn't practiced much of anything.

All he could think about was Fishtail. He visited her every day. Or rather, visited what had taken her place. A smug, over-confident Swarm agent—at least, when she wasn't under full sedation. Gone were Fishtail's mild-mannered wit and sarcasm. Her easy-going charm. In its place was ... something alien. Utterly foreign.

"All craft, prepare for launch. Watch yourselves, people. None of you have ever launched at this speed before, and you most certainly have not launched all at once like we're trying today." The CAG, Commander Pierce, listed off the instructions one final time. Each fighter, in its turn, would launch exactly one third of a second after the one before it. All one hundred and fifty of them. The accelerations would be gut-churning. The distances between fighters uncomfortably small.

There was no room for error on this one.

And the giant osmium brick tied to the undercarriage of each fighter more than doubled each craft's mass. Maneuvering would be difficult.

The Granger Omega Three maneuver. Omega: an appropriate term. It would most likely be the last thing they ever did.

He glanced to his left, down the line of fighters with their engines idling. Spacechamp. Pew Pew and his brother, Fodder. He'd sure miss them. Commander Pierce's voice cut through his headset. "Standby ... five seconds ... three, two, one, NOW!"

To his right, the line of fighters started shooting out the giant bay door, one at a time, every point three three seconds. Much of it was computer-controlled, but not the actual maneuvering. When his time came, the engines roared to life automatically, and he barely had time to steer the nose of his fighter out toward the exit and space beyond.

Fifty seconds later, they were all in position, forming a vast halo around the *ISS Warrior*. Thirty-some-odd heavy cruisers bunched up tightly behind the giant tungsten-armored carrier. All of them blazing toward the planet ahead of them. In orbit above that ravaged world stood the largest Swarm ship any of them had ever seen. It was still a tiny dot, but it grew larger.

"All craft," came Pierce's voice, "brick launch on my mark."

Volz checked the computer calculations one more time, ensuring his thrusters were linked appropriately to the targeting computer. All clear.

"Launch."

He flew back against his seat as the fighter leapt forward and to starboard, and moments later he felt the tell-tale clank as the osmium brick detached. A moment later he reversed thrust, aligning his nose with the edge of the *Warrior*'s bulk and maneuvered his fighter around the ship. There was no time for all of them to land in the fighter bay, and staying out to fight during the flyby was pointless. All they could do was hide in the shadow of the *Warrior* like the rest of the cruisers.

Hide, and pray.

CHAPTER FIVE

Star Freighter Lucky Bandit
Low orbit, Indira, Britannia Sector

SOMETHING SEEMED dreadfully wrong. "They're coming in way too fast. This doesn't make any sense...." Rodriguez studied the sensor readout even as he pointed the nose of the freighter on a trajectory that would eventually let them break orbit and make their first q-jump.

"Whatever," said the pilot. "As long as they keep the bastards distracted while we make our getaway. And it's not just us—there's thousands of other freighters and colonial transports trying to make a break for—"

Thousands of tiny explosions leapt out from the super dreadnought.

"Hot damn!" Rodriguez watched the scene unfold in amazement. Granger, with his fleet coming in close behind, had oriented the *Warrior* so the bottom face of its hull was fully exposed to the super dreadnought and its two smaller companions. But peeking out from the shadow of the *Warrior* were hundreds of mag-rail turrets from the tightly-packed fleet of cruisers, each ship positioned such that its hull was protected by the *Warrior*, but with a clear enough view of the super dreadnought that it could fire several steady streams of ultra-high-velocity mag-rail slugs.

Which they did. Thousands of impacts erupted all over the massive super dreadnought. It, along with the two escort carriers, opened up a devastating volley on the rapidly approaching *Warrior*, raking the underside of its hull with dozens of antimatter beams. Rodriguez could only imagine the destruction on the lower decks.

"Pretty gutsy, but they're flying past in less than ten seconds. I still don't see how much good it'll do," said Raf, shaking his head.

"Watch. I see it now," interrupted Rodriguez, pointing at the sensors. They just barely detected over one hundred small projectiles which rocketed away from the *Warrior*. Small, but thousands of times larger than the standard mag-rail slug.

And traveling at fifty kilometers a second.

The incoming IDF fleet, still sheltered by the *Warrior*, continued pummeling the super dreadnought, some ships even turning their attention to the two Swarm carriers, but Rodriguez understood it now—the conventional fire was a ruse. Moments later, his suspicion was confirmed with a violent, eye-piercing explosion.

One hundred and fifty eye-piercing explosions.

"I don't believe it." Raf couldn't take his eyes off the disintegrating super dreadnought. From the hundred and fifty massive, gaping holes erupted a hundred and fifty streams of debris, smoke, and fire, all up and down the hundred kilometers-long spine of the ship. "I don't believe it," he repeated breathlessly.

"That's Granger for you." Rodriguez pushed hard on the accelerator. Now that the Swarm ships in the immediate vicinity were focused like a laser on the IDF fleet, it was the perfect chance to high-tail it out of there.

"They still can't win. Even without that super dreadnought there are over twenty Swarm carriers in orbit, and Granger only has thirty-six ships. Plus, he came in so fast that he'll be flung out toward the outer solar system unless he can miraculously arrest his velocity in the next two minutes."

Rodriguez shook his head. "He'll figure something out. He always does."

The pilot regarded him for a moment in disbelief, like an atheist skeptically eyeing the firm faith of a sincere believer, but he shrugged and began plotting their course toward a point where it would be safe to make the q-jump. Or at least, that was his intention. Instead, he gawked at the sensor readout again. "Yes, but what is he going to do about *that*?"

Rodriguez's eye followed the pilot's outstretched finger.

The sensor readout had more bad news.

CHAPTER SIX

Bridge, ISS Warrior
Indira, Britannia Sector

GRANGER WAS BEGINNING to regret his order—the Granger Omega Three maneuver was wreaking havoc down on the lower decks. The ship trembled and shook violently. The super dreadnought and its two accompanying carriers were unloading everything they had straight into the *Warrior*'s gut, tearing their lower hull to shreds.

But the results spoke for themselves—after twenty seconds of fleet bombardment, the super dreadnought was beginning to show signs of extreme duress, to put it lightly.

"Massive power fluctuations coming from the dreadnought!" Ensign Diamond yelled over his console.

Granger nodded, and inclined his head toward Commander Proctor. "Brick status?"

"Launch in ten."

He studied the sensor readouts coming from the super dreadnought, then waved over to the comm station. "Send to fleet: retarget accompanying vessels."

"Aye, aye, sir," said Ensign Prucha. Moments later, the IDF fleet protected under the shadow of the *Warrior* redirected fire toward the other two Swarm ships hovering near the super dreadnought, which also began to erupt with thousands of small explosions where the mag-rail slugs ripped into their hulls. *These three buggers are toast,* Granger thought.

But he was paying for it. Dearly. The bridge jolted to starboard violently as several of the incoming antimatter beams connected with one of the main inertial cancelers. Those things were embedded at least five decks within the lower hull. Damn—they were cutting deep. The bridge jerked again, and out of the corner of his eye he saw the marines stationed near the bridge entrance sway and struggle to remain on their feet.

Granger counted silently in his head the remaining seconds, and moments later Proctor announced, "Brick launch. Impact in five. Prepare for attitude realignment."

"Put it onscreen," said Granger, gripping his armrests ferociously to steady himself against the violent buffeting of the incoming storm of antimatter beams. "At least we'll get to enjoy the show."

Just moments after the viewscreen focused on the Swarm super dreadnought, which had redirected its fire to the incoming osmium projectiles in a vain attempt to destroy them, the gaping holes appeared in blinding explosions as large chunks of the hull were blasted away. Each osmium brick, though only a few tons, was moving so fast that it slammed into the massive vessel with the energy of over a hundred megaton-class nuclear warheads.

And even though the ship was dozens of kilometers long, it was no match for explosive energy on that scale. As *Warrior* and the rest of the fleet flew by at nearly fifty kilometers per second, reorienting itself so the smaller cruisers would remain in the shadow of Granger's ship, the super dreadnought shuddered as it disintegrated into hundreds of smaller smoking pieces.

Excited whoops and cheers erupted on the bridge, and Granger, for the first time that day, allowed himself a small smile. "Full reverse. Two times safety limits. Settle us into an orbit that will take us to the next cluster of Swarm carriers."

Commander Proctor looked up from her status board. "Heavy damage on the lower decks, sir. Main inertial cancelers are out. Numerous casualties on decks six and seven." Her face tightened into a pained expression. "They nearly cut all the way up to main engineering, Captain. Just a few more seconds and we would have been goners."

"How much thrust can we sustain?" They *had* to arrest some of their speed, otherwise they'd fling out from the planet, hundreds of thousands of kilometers away from the battle, leaving the ravaged planet to its doom. From the looks of his planetary sensor readout, the Swarm had already devastated dozens of cities with singularity blasts, likely killing millions. Tens of millions. But there were still a handful of major cities left, and hundreds of smaller towns that had to be defended.

"Auxiliaries are only rated at half the safety limits of the primaries."

"Then full reverse—double the safety standards of the auxiliaries." He punched the internal comm. "Hold on, folks, we're about to have a rough ride." He noticed Proctor shoot him a raised eyebrow. "Again," he added.

As the reverse thrusters engaged, they were thrown back against their seat restraints, then forward, then backward again as the inertial cancelers struggled to keep up, swinging like a pendulum between the extreme acceleration vectors they were trying to balance. The deckplate seemed to groan, and Granger could hear the screeching of twisting metal deep within the walls. How much more could the Old Bird take?

He shook his head. *Dammit.* The Old Bird was dead. Still sitting on the main boulevard in South Salt Lake City, where it had crash-landed and skidded to a halt, leaving a trail of destruction in its wake. IDF engineers had decided to leave it there, building up a giant scaffold around the broken hulk as they performed a refit—the goal was to restore her, though she wouldn't be ready for months yet. But he still hadn't shaken the habit of calling the *Warrior* his *Old Bird*.

He heard a groan from the sensor station, and almost simultaneously he heard Proctor mutter a curse. He glanced over at her. "I'm almost afraid to ask...."

She looked up, her face taking on an almost resigned expression, as if she knew this battle would be their last. "Two more super dreadnoughts just q-jumped in. They'll intercept our course in five minutes."

The math was starting to weigh on Granger's mind. Twenty Swarm carriers still orbited the planet, pummeling its already-ravaged surface. Less than a third of the planet's population likely was still alive. Two new dreaded super dreadnoughts to deal with. The *Warrior* was a wreck. Admiral Zingano, with his fleet, was occupied with its own invasion, lightyears away.

"Sir?" Proctor said, eyeing him.

He sighed. "Prepare for q-jump."

CHAPTER SEVEN

Bridge, ISS Warrior
Indira, Britannia Sector

THE BRIDGE FELL QUIET in the aftermath of his order to q-jump. From the way they eyed him it was clear that they were expecting to make a strategic withdrawal. To stand and fight another day. Somewhere else. He saw in their eyes that it pained them, but that they were prepared to do it. To run.

But Granger had never retreated. Ever.

And he wasn't about to start. "Prepare for q-jump to these coordinates," he said, punching in a set of numbers and sending them to the helm. Ensign Prince looked at them, finally understanding Granger's meaning.

"We're making another pass?"

"You got it, Ensign." He looked around the bridge. "Any objections?"

No one spoke. Before he could continue, Commander Proctor cleared her throat. "We're all behind you, Captain—" she began, but he could see in her eyes what she was going to say—that strategic withdrawal was smarter. But he wasn't going to have any of it. He'd lectured her, and Zingano, and all the other captains more times than he could count. Stand your ground and fight, make the Swarm pay for every single system they took. Never retreat. Show no weakness of will. It was either that or fight them—and retreat from them—at the *next* world. And the next. And the next.

No. The Swarm needed to be taught that humanity would never, ever, ever back down. Eventually, they would learn, calculate their own losses and realize that they would never truly win until every last human outpost was utterly obliterated.

"Good," he said, leaving Proctor with her mouth left half-open.

"Sir, if I may, our lower hull is breached in three dozen locations. Engineering is a mess. Our fighters are all back in the bay and none has been reloaded with a brick yet, and you're sending us into another Granger Omega Three against *two* of those super dreadnoughts? Surely there's something else that can be done at this point."

He sighed. She was right, of course, but there simply was no alternative. He held up his hands. "If you have a better idea, Commander, I'm all ears."

With any other officer, he'd have them removed from the bridge. But Proctor had saved his ass more times than he could count. Still, their relationship had been strained over the past two months. Ever since that fighter pilot, Volz, had returned with Fishtail, claiming that he'd just escaped from a Swarm-controlled Captain

Granger on the other side of the singularity. She'd defended him—hell, Zingano had defended him—against
General Norton, the chairman of the joint chiefs, and
though he'd kept his command, suspicions around him
were high ever since.

"Split the fleet. Send everyone in threes and fours
and engage the carriers—they're all spread out singly in
various orbits. We'd last longer that way, and take out
more of their fleet. And if we're lucky, Zingano will
show up before we're all dead."

Admiral Zingano to the rescue. Dammit, that was
Granger's job.

But she was right, of course. And he wasn't going to
let his pride get in the way of the best outcome. That was
something a politician would do, and, dammit, he was *not*
a politician. He was not an Avery. Or worse, an Isaacson.

"Do it." He pointed to the tactical station. "Assign
targets. Focus on those heading toward the remaining
large population centers. Commander," he said, turning
back to her, "make the fleet assignments."

She nodded, focusing her attention to splitting up
the fleet and informing the other captains. She looked
back up. "And where will we be going, sir?"

"My previous order stands. When our fleet has
dispersed on their assignments, we make the q-jump."
He watched the viewscreen as the planet began to pull
away—they were still on their highly elliptical course.
"Straight down the throats of the two super dreadnoughts."

Proctor hesitated. "Alone?"

"Alone."

CHAPTER EIGHT

Star Freighter Lucky Bandit
High orbit, Indira, Britannia Sector

LIEUTENANT RODRIGUEZ could hardly believe his eyes. Just minutes ago he was watching the largest warship he'd ever seen begin launching its horrifying rain of fire down onto his homeworld, razing vast swaths of a continent, and the next moment that same ship was in pieces.

It was impossible. He'd always suspected that the stories surrounding the Hero of Earth were embellished and shaded with hyperbole, that the crew around Granger and the people he'd saved tended to be over-the-top in their praise of him.

If anything, those stories were cheap, fanciful lies compared to what he'd just witnessed.

"You know, I think that maybe, just maybe, we might make it out of this," he said.

Raf, the pilot, nodded slowly, his eye still wide at watching the ongoing destruction of the super dreadnought.

"Yeah. I think you might be right." A moment later, he came out of it and cranked on the controls. "Watch out for those fighters."

Rodriguez nodded. "Look." He pointed toward the pieces of the dreadnought, which were starting to break up into smaller red-hot chunks. "The fighters are high-tailing it out of there. Let's thread the needle."

"You mean fly into that storm of wreckage coming off that thing?"

"No, no. Not through it, just close enough and around it so we can avoid these fighters."

Raf shook his head, but then seeing the cloud of Swarm fighters approach, he relented. Rodriguez steered the freighter toward the fragmenting dreadnought. Soon, the hundreds of bogeys faded into the background behind them as they approached one of the large pieces of wreckage—a section of hull nearly a kilometer long.

"We're too close," said Raf, nervously.

"We're fine." He pulled up on the controls and whipped them around the side hull section.

Which, to Rodriguez's surprise, disappeared in a flash. Not an explosive flash, but a bright, white flash.

He'd seen that light before.

"Be on the lookout for—"

He was about to warn Raf about the singularities—they could be so small that you'd never see one until right on top of it, but he didn't have time.

It was right in their path. Shimmering. Deadly.

The cockpit turned brilliantly white for a split second, and Rodriguez felt as if his head had just taken a direct hit. He fought against the rising sleep with its promise of peaceful oblivion. He knew he was close to passing out, but he needed to stay awake to steer the freighter to safety. His life depended on it. His kids depended on it.

The view through the windows had changed. Instead of giant pieces of the shattered super dreadnought, set against the backdrop of Indira, he only saw one piece, falling.

Falling toward a swirling maelstrom of material. Rocks, ice, debris, dust—all falling into and colliding with a central mass.

They were falling too. Their engines were out. He felt his consciousness slipping away. The last thing he saw was the surface of the giant ball of material looming up, filling the entire window. Hundreds of rocks struck the outside hull like a million hailstones in a hailstorm. Even their relentless cacophony could not keep Rodriguez awake.

CHAPTER NINE

Bridge, ISS Warrior
Indira, Britannia Sector

"Time?" Granger asked.

"Still two minutes until we've matched the velocity of the incoming dreadnoughts, Captain," said Ensign Diamond.

He nodded. "Q-jump in one. We'll decelerate the rest of the way once we've made the jump. That'll give us some time to assess the tactical situation."

Proctor eyed him warily. *What is there to assess?* her eyes wondered. Even though she said nothing, he answered her unasked question.

"We still have no idea what tactical advantages these things have—"

"You mean, other than the fact that they're a hundred times our size, sir?"

The remark was accompanied by a wink, indicating humor, but he continued as if he didn't hear. There was no time for humor, even gallows humor. "And for all we know they have a weakness that can be exploited if we just took the time to scan them properly and study their ship layout."

"You think we'll be able to study their ship schematic enough in one minute and figure out a way to destroy them? What, like fly into their exhaust port and blow up their main power reactor?"

"Something like that."

"Seems a little cliché." She studied his face. "Do you remember anything like these things? The super dreadnoughts? No fleeting memories?"

Lately, Proctor had been questioning him more about his Vacation—his missing three days aboard the *Constitution*. The memories were still foggy, especially after Vishgane Kharsa, the Dolmasi admiral, had tampered with Granger's mind, making him think he'd been peering down at the Swarm homeworld. Afterwards, he'd thought he was remembering the Swarm's point of origin, but the memory was false. And by thinking, wrongly, that he'd seen Volari Three, the Dolmasi's homeworld, he had inadvertently liberated them thinking he was striking down the Swarm.

For all the good it had done them—ever since then, the Dolmasi had rarely shown up to any battles when called upon. Some allies they were.

He shook his head. "Nothing. I remember nothing of them."

Ensign Prince caught his attention. "Sir?"

Granger noticed the time had elapsed. "Initiate q-jump."

Prince engaged the drive, and Granger felt the tell-tale momentary sway as the change in the starfield on the viewscreen indicated the jump was successful. Quantum effects such as the q-jump were always a little more unpredictable close to large gravity wells like planets.

"Continue deceleration," he said. "Full scan of the ships as we approach. All bands. All fields. Neutrons, gamma, RF, meta-space, quantum signatures—everything."

"And tactical?" Proctor stood near her post in the rear of the bridge, the eyes of the tactical crew were on her and Granger.

"Show them our belly again. That section of the ship is already dark. The crew is evacuated from decks one through five, correct?"

"Yes, but—"

"Extend the evacuation to deck eight."

Proctor looked flustered. She never looked flustered. The battle was getting to her, or, more likely, *he* was getting to her. "Sir, Engineering starts on deck seven. Are you going to evacuate Engineering?"

"No, Engineering crew stays."

"Tim, this is highly irregular—"

"There's *nothing* regular about this, Shelby, why would you expect it to start getting regular now?" Why was she calling him out in front of the crew? If she pushed any harder he'd have to relieve her—he couldn't have this kind of public questioning of his orders, especially not in the middle of a battle.

But deep inside, he knew why. Ever since Lieutenant Volz had come back through that singularity. Ever since a Swarm-controlled Fishtail had woken up, and started

fingering Granger as a former Swarm agent, confirming what Volz was saying—that the pilot had talked to
Granger on the other side, acting for the Swarm.

It was getting to her, that much was obvious. It was
making her doubt his orders, wondering if every action
he took was *still* controlled by the Swarm. He needed to
figure out a way to regain her complete trust. She was
too valuable an asset to lose, and if she didn't shape the
hell up, he *would* lose her.

That word lingered in his mind. *Asset.* Was she only
an asset to him? Another human brick to hurl at the
enemy? Another tool in his mission for complete and
total victory?

But it was true, wasn't it? He himself was a tool.
They were all tools. When it came to the survival of
the species, none of them mattered, individually. Each
of them, as a member of the pack, as a carrier of the
precious genetic instructions that made the human race
viciously fight for survival, was expendable. Including
Proctor. Including Granger. She had to understand that.

"We're all bricks, Commander."

He looked her in the eye. The pain behind her gaze
told him she understood.

"Very well, sir," she said with a curt nod.

"And send word to the CAG. I need some more
human bricks."

CHAPTER TEN

Fighter Combat Operations Center, ISS Warrior
Indira, Britannia Sector

COMMANDER PIERCE stared at the roster. The list of one hundred and fifty men and women who'd committed their lives—and their deaths—to the safety of the *Warrior*, and by extension, the safety of all of humanity. *They signed up for this*, he thought to himself. *All of them.*

Except, had they? Had any of them *really* signed up for this? Sure, fighter pilots weren't drafted. But humanity had not signed up for this war. It was thrust upon them. It was a gift from the Russians, or the Dolmasi, or Avery and Isaacson, or whoever else the conspiracy theorists insisted were involved in starting the war.

He'd signed up. Because of his father. All the Pierces go military, for three hundred years, ever since the First Colonial War. His father had insisted. The old man had hinted that any Pierce that did not graduate at the top of his or her class at the Royal Fleet Academy on Britannia was a waste of space. So, with a combination of guilt and familial duty, Tyler signed up and graduated at the top of his class. It was what Pierces do.

But this Pierce wasn't happy about it.

And he wasn't happy about the decision staring him in the face. Finally, after another ten seconds of indecision, the voice in his ear erupted again.

"Commander, we need those fighters *now*. Pick thirty and be done with it."

"I—I can't pick who lives and dies anymore," he whispered into the comm.

"Tyler," began Commander Proctor, in a softer voice, "you can do this. I know it's hard. Thirty will die, but they'll save thousands. Maybe millions. And those pilots will be heroes."

He sighed. "Will they? Or will they just be victims?"

"If you don't act now, Commander, we'll *all* be victims."

"Fine," he said, his voice hoarse. He selected thirty, starting with the A's and ending with the H's. Alphabetical. "Sending orders now, sir."

"Thank you, Commander," she said. "Proctor out."

He keyed in an instruction to the computer to open a commlink to the selected fighters and their pilots. He cleared his throat. "If you can hear this, you are receiving an order for an Omega run. Launch immediately. Accelerate to maximum toward the super dreadnought at fifteen mark two. Unload your torpedoes and all your guns on the target before final impact."

He flipped the comm off and slumped back in his seat. His assistants, Lieutenant Schwitzer and Ensign Spiriti, gave him grim, significant looks. They all knew that they would have lost at least thirty pilots anyway in a normal fighter battle. But this way felt far, far worse. It felt inhuman. It was like he lost his humanity with every Omega run order.

He glanced at the picture of himself and his wife, their two children draped over their laps as they posed for the camera in some forest on York. It's what he fought for. What kept him alive.

With a miracle, they might win the war. But the greater miracle would be keeping their souls.

CHAPTER ELEVEN

Bridge, ISS Warrior
Indira, Britannia Sector

GRANGER WATCHED the sensor readout, waiting for just the right moment. The fighters raced out of the bay, all thirty of them targeting the heart of one of the super dreadnoughts. Once they had formed up into a regular pattern, the *Warrior* could commence firing, but for now they risked hitting one of their own birds.

Not that it mattered: they'd be dead anyway in a matter of thirty seconds. He felt awful for thinking it, but it was true.

They formed up into a ring and Granger gave the order. "Open fire!"

All the functioning mag-rails on the *Warrior* surged to life, blasting the slugs out at another twelve kilometers per second in addition to the fifty kps speed of the ship itself.

In response, the two super dreadnoughts unleashed their own hell on the *Warrior*, raking her underside with dozens of antimatter beams. The ship shuddered. A moment later a blast several decks below threw the entire bridge crew up against their restraints. One officer who'd removed his and forgot to refasten it was thrown up against the ceiling where his head hit a light fixture. Granger could tell the man was dead before he hit the floor.

"Hull breaches up through deck seven!" yelled Proctor. "One of the Engineering compartments is compromised—if we lose main power there's no way to restore it!"

He could tell the targeted ship was already starting to move laterally, and as a result over two thirds of their mag-rail slugs missed, but it didn't matter: the other ship couldn't evade them—they were coming in too fast. A few moments later the dreadnought lit up with brilliant explosions as some of the slugs found capacitor banks or auxiliary power lines.

In a few more seconds it too would be destroyed. Two super dreadnoughts down in only one battle. *Not bad,* he thought to himself. Another explosion ripped through the lower decks, this time manifesting as power overloads at several junctions and terminals, resulting in dangerous electrical flashes and fires across the bridge. *And all it took was me destroying the* Warrior, he thought grimly.

But a moment later, the view on the screen made his stomach lurch. Thirty shimmering points of lights appeared suddenly right in front of the super dreadnought. They only lasted for a second, because almost immediately after they appeared, all thirty winked out as each fighter slammed into one, disappearing in a flash.

Shit.

Another explosion.

"Tim," Proctor began, "we've lost main power. We're not getting it back. Rayna is not responding down in Engineering. It's over."

He closed his eyes.

"Ensign Prince, how much thrust can you give me?"

The young man, his face white, looked at his console. "Mains are out, but I can give you half lateral thrust and one quarter aft."

"Steer us in. Clip them on their side—with any luck, whatever's left of us will ricochet into the other one."

Five seconds left. The massive ship grew quickly on the screen as the *Warrior's* incredible velocity propelled it toward a direct collision.

So this was goodbye, he thought. *For real, this time.*

Two seconds.

One.

The super dreadnought disappeared. Did they hit it? Were they all dead? He looked around at his dazed bridge crew. He imagined death would be a lot more painful. And fiery.

"Where the hell did it go?"

Ensign Diamond at tactical studied his sensor display. "Unknown, sir. We flew by the other one. But the target itself just ... disappeared." He brow furrowed. "Oh. Sir, I'm reading a q-jump signature. The target q-jumped away. Location unknown."

Granger pounded on his armrest. Proctor's voice cut through his disbelief with more bad news. "And sir, the one we passed is accelerating, catching up to us. It'll match our speed in less than a minute. Weapons range in eighty seconds, if they maintain this acceleration."

Dammit. I can't even get suicide right today.

CHAPTER TWELVE

Bridge, ISS Warrior
Indira, Britannia Sector

"WHAT'S OUR VECTOR? What kind of orbit are we in?"

Ensign Prince, a little dazed at being still alive, shook his head a few times before responding. "Uh, looks like we're coming in toward the planet on a highly inclined orbital plane, though, uh, we're far above escape velocity. Should take us just above the atmosphere before spitting us out into open space."

Commander Proctor added, "And we'll fly right by a few of the Swarm carriers on the way past. By the time we pass them that other super dreadnought will have caught up to us."

"How long?" Granger watched the planet grow larger as they approached. The billowing mushroom clouds had almost completely shrouded the view of the surface. He wondered how the rest of his fleet had fared against the remaining Swarm carriers.

"Fifty seconds," said Proctor.

"And the fleet?"

She glanced at her task force tactical display which Lieutenant Diaz had been using for fleet coordination. "Holding their own, for the most part. Five Swarm carriers destroyed. We've paid for it with nine lost cruisers."

Doing the math in his head he came to the grim conclusion. The Swarm was going to win this one.

"Thirty seconds until dreadnought intercept. Around the same time we'll pass three carriers." Proctor looked up. "If we angle ourselves *just* right, we might be able to take out all three...."

He flashed a wry, gallows humor grin. "A chance to redeem our previous failed suicide attempt? Very well. Do it."

Another dread silence fell over the bridge as the crew at the navigation station made their calculations, and Ensign Prince reoriented the ship and adjusted the orbital vector slightly to plow them right into one of the carriers. With any luck they'd careen right through it and into a second one on the same path. Hopefully the blast front would take out the third hovering just out of the flight path.

It was as good a death as any, taking out three whole carriers.

"Uh, sir," began Ensign Prucha. "Incoming transmission."

Please say Admiral Zingano finally showed up, thought Granger. "Source?"

"I may be mistaken, but it looks like it's coming from the dreadnought."

Granger spun around. "It's coming from the *Swarm*?"

"Looks like it, sir." He blinked in surprise at his console. "And it's visual."

Granger, his head half cocked toward the front viewscreen, nodded incredulously. "Put it through."

The image of the devastated planet disappeared, replaced by another image. That of an alien. Not Swarm. Not Dolmasi. A third alien race. Vaguely human, but with tighter skin. Almost a blueish tint.

"Captain Granger. Will you make alliance with us?"

Granger's automatic reply sounded surreal in his mouth. "We will." They were the only words to say, really. "And who do we make alliance with?"

"The Fifth House of the Concordat of Seven. You've shown us we can throw off our masters, just as you did with the Dolmasi."

Granger cut his hand across his throat, eyeing Ensign Prucha, who muted the audio. He shot a glance at Commander Proctor. "It's got to be a trick. They have us at their mercy."

"Maybe," she said. "But what choice do we have?"

He shrugged, and nodded toward Prucha, who restored the audio. "Very well. To prove your sincerity, would you mind neutralizing the Valarisi carriers that are just now coming in range?" he said, using the name the Swarm used for themselves.

The alien, to Granger's disbelief, nodded once. "By all means, Captain. Please maneuver your ship around ours to shield yourselves—we detect that you cannot take much more damage."

Granger signaled Ensign Prince, who maneuvered the *Warrior* as the alien had suggested, putting the dreadnought in between it and the three incoming Swarm carriers.

"Captain, the dreadnought is opening fire on the carriers," began Ensign Diamond. "Full spread of anti-matter beams."

The viewscreen split, half still displaying the new alien, and the other half showing the carnage. The dreadnought had at least ten times the number of beam turrets as the carriers, and within fifteen seconds of the flyby, the targets were in ruins, breaking apart and blazing through the upper atmosphere.

"Captain," said Proctor, her voice betraying her disbelief, "receiving word from the fleet: the rest of the carriers are pulling back. One already made a q-jump out." She looked up at him. "Shall I order pursuit?"

He nodded quickly, still paralyzed by disbelief himself. The new twist of events had happened so suddenly, so ... illogically, that he was still trying to process it.

"New contacts, sir," said Ensign Diamond, who broke out into a grin. "It's Admiral Zingano and his fleet."

The dreadnought broke off from their escort vector and accelerated toward another Swarm carrier that was blasting away from the planet, trying to make its escape. Over a hundred green beams lanced out from the dreadnought, overwhelming the carrier. The dreadnought eclipsed the fiery death throes of the much smaller ship.

"Maybe they detected Zingano's imminent arrival and decided to make their move?"

"Maybe," said Granger. "I suppose we'll get their explanation shortly." He watched as the dreadnought reoriented itself and rejoined *Warrior*'s flight vector. He couldn't help but feel he'd cheated. Or that *someone* had cheated. It was too easy. They were about to die. Twice.

That alien had better have a damn good story.

CHAPTER THIRTEEN

Senator Joseph P. Hill Memorial Shipyards
Athens, Alabama, Earth

VICE PRESIDENT ISAACSON smiled as widely as his strained, exhausted cheeks would allow him to. As the hovering cameras nearby zoomed backward into the air and panned wide, he relaxed the rictus-grin a bit, knowing that the actual crowd assembled on the street below wouldn't be able to see him as closely as the ever-present cameras. Wouldn't be able to see him sigh ever so slightly.

They would never see him like *she* saw him. She saw everything. She was always there. In his every waking moment. Governing his thoughts, his feelings. And of course, his actions, and to a lesser extent, his words. At least, his spoken words. But he had to tightly govern his running mental commentary.

He couldn't even call her *bitch* anymore. Not in his mind, at least. Not without suffering ungodly agony—an unfortunate side-effect of having thirty mind-

and-emotion-reading implants capable of delivering fifty-four millijoules of brain-bending pain apiece.

In certain moments, talking with certain senators or Russian agents with whom he was still trying to uphold the facade of agitator-in-chief, he allowed himself to unload on President Avery, calling her every filthy name his frenzied mind could grasp at. With those people, he had to maintain appearances of a murderous traitor and so she allowed him to play the part. But with everyone else, with the public, he was to be the cheerleader. Avery's number one surrogate.

"Thank you. Thank you. You're too kind," he said, his voice amplified by a microphone hovering just a meter in front of him. Thousands of people had crammed into the plaza and neighboring streets to see him in person. It was just another ribbon-cutting ceremony for the newest heavy cruiser coming off the line at the nearby shipyard, but the people of Athens, Alabama were proud of their contribution to the war effort.

It was their fifth ship completed since the start of the war. All four of the previous ships had been lost, of course, just like over sixty percent of all newly-built ships these days. But the pride of the crowd was palpable. "You know, back when I was interning for *Senator Hill*," he paused for dramatic effect, "I guess some of you may have heard of him." The crowd roared. The late Senator Hill was, in fact, an Alabamian native. "Back when I interned for old Joe he told me, he says, 'Eamon, the people in my senatorial district are simply the best people in the galaxy.'"

More roars from the crowd.

Isaacson continued. The crowd was putty in his hand—he may have hated his forced servitude at the scheming hands of President Avery, but this part—the adoration of a war-weary crowd—this part he loved. "He says to me, 'Eamon, the people in my senatorial district are simply the best in the galaxy,'" he said again, expertly knowing that the key to any good political speech was repetition, repetition, repetition. "'And you know why they're the best, Eamon? It's because they never give up. They never give up. They're the most bad-ass, unbreakable people on the planet. They never give up. And you know what, Eamon? You know what? If the Swarm ever comes back, the shitheads—I'm sorry folks, Senator Hill was pretty colorful, if you know what I mean—the shitheads will never know what hit 'em.'"

He paused to let the crowd scream ecstatically again. Old Senator Hill was an Alabama legend, especially here where he grew up. It didn't matter that Isaacson was making up the story about the old bastard, one hundred percent blatant fabrication—the crowd ate it up. "When old Joe died a few years later," he continued slowly, adding a note of heaviness to his voice. The crowd hushed. "When old Joe died, I found a letter in my mailbox the next week. He'd included it in his will. Imagine little ole' me, just a snot-nosed intern, getting a personal letter from a United Earth senate legend. I opened it. Hands trembling."

The crowd was utterly silent.

"I pulled out the letter. I read it. I read it again. Tears came to my eyes." He continued, filling in with meaningless words as he racked his brain for what he'd say next. There was no letter. He'd only interned for the old codger for a week before the man died suddenly of a heart attack during a blowjob from some prostitute, and Isaacson had never even met him. But he needed a good line for the crowd. "And through my tears I saw the firm, hand-written signature of that patriot, that giant of a man." He cleared his throat, summoning a good show of emotion. "The words he wrote are these. And I quote: 'A sacrifice made in the service of your fellow countrymen is no sacrifice at all.'"

Brilliant, Eamon, he thought, as the crowd went wild. He held up a hand. "Thank you for your sacrifice. I know you've seen hunger, pain, loss, and seemingly endless war. And through it all, you've persevered. You've given us a fighting chance against our mortal enemy. You've given us *this*," he said, indicating the giant cruiser in dry dock about a kilometer away.

He slipped in a few more anecdotes, some good old fashioned folksy homespun wisdom, pumped up the crowd with a bit more cheerleading, and finally called it a day. Three speeches in a row. Three starship naming ceremonies. Three ceremonially broken bottles against tungsten-iridium hulls. Hundreds of local dignitaries and factory chiefs and shift managers. Thousands of handshakes. His hand ached. His back ached. His head ached. And when he finally collapsed on his bed at the end of the day, he groaned when his comm card alarmed, indicating *she* wanted to talk to him.

He couldn't mentally swear at her. He couldn't slather her with creative insults and curses. All he could do was take a deep breath, and tap his fingers against his leg in the same rhythm as the syllables of one particular insulting vulgar phrase. He couldn't think the words—she'd hear that. And she'd punish him severely for it. But he tapped the rhythm. *Tap, tap-tap, tap. Tap, tap-tap, tap.* It was his only release. The only way he could impotently strike back at her.

The alarm sounded again, and one of his thirty implants buzzed slightly. Not painfully, but as a warning: *Don't keep me waiting, Mr. Vice President, I'm not a patient woman.*

He pulled his comm card out and tapped it. "Yes, Madam President?"

"Good work today, Mr. Isaacson. I trust you're not too exhausted? *Three* naming ceremonies. Three! That sounds downright tiresome!" She laughed.

Tap, tap-tap, tap.

"Don't worry, I'll let you sleep soon. Any word from Ambassador Volodin?"

"Not yet. He says an audience with Malakhov is highly unlikely, but that he'd pull all his strings to arrange it."

"Good," said Avery. "We need to get you in there. Much depends on it."

"If I may ask, Madam President, why not just meet him yourself? If the message you want delivered to him is that important, wouldn't it carry more diplomatic force if it was the President of United Earth delivering it?"

She laughed. "Oh, Eamon. You're so incredibly naive sometimes."

Tap, tap-tap, tap.

"Oh?" he couldn't help but let a hint of sarcasm seep into his voice. Luckily, she let it slide—his implants remained silent.

"Mr. Isaacson, the message I want delivered is one that is suited uniquely to you." She laughed again, then added, "Besides, it wouldn't look good at all if *I* were the one to negotiate with Mr. Malakhov. Just think of the optics! I'm the bad-ass no-nonsense take-no-prisoners President of United Earth. I can't be seen talking to war criminals."

He'd been halfway through sitting up to walk to the bathroom, but he froze. "I beg your pardon, Madam President?" *Was she* actually *thinking of sending him off alone, outside her influence, to talk to her mortal enemy?*

"You heard me, Eamon," she said, using his first name for the first time in two months. "You're going to negotiate with President Malakhov. In person. In his own office. You need to get inside his head. See what he's thinking. Otherwise, we don't stand a chance."

He heard her take as sip of a drink she was holding, the clink of the ice rung against the glass. She continued, "And if that doesn't work, then you'll sabotage his secret computer network. Preferably with a bomb or something. In full view of live television cameras. The whole galaxy will see it live." She laughed again. "Should cause quite a stir, don't you think? People will see that we're finally striking back against the Russian bastards. Oh, don't worry, I know what you're thinking. I'm sure you'll escape the blast. Well, reasonably sure. Ha!"

Tap, tap-tap, tap.

CHAPTER FOURTEEN

Sickbay, ISS Warrior
High Orbit, Britannia

VOLZ WATCHED HER through sickbay's window. She was asleep, and still bound to the bed by thick straps and cuffs. They weren't going to take any chances with her—Commander Proctor had done some tests involving meta-space signals and determined that while Fishtail was unconscious the Swarm was not able to control her or send and receive signals though her, but even so it was safest to keep her chained.

When she could transmit the Swarm virus with the touch of a single finger, it was the only thing that made sense. A transparent panel had been set up around her to prevent medical staff and other patients from inadvertently brushing up against her skin, but otherwise sickbay still made the most sense as the place to keep her. This way she could be easily kept under sedation, and under constant monitoring.

He watched her. Just as he had almost every evening for two months. When he wasn't flying his bird, or training his squad, or sleeping and eating, he was here.

Was she in there somewhere? Could she be saved? Proctor had assured him that she could be saved. Just like Granger. But he had trouble believing his XO when he passed away the long hours watching her.

"If you keep watching her this much I think I'm going to rename you Stalker. Tyler "Stalker" Volz."

Volz gave a short, gruff laugh. "What do you know about stalking, Spacechamp?"

She stood next to him, watching the former pilot sleep. "Clearly not as much as you, Ballsy. Though, if a guy were to stalk me, I think I'd want him to at least leave me some chocolates or something. Maybe some small talk. If I was really drunk maybe a quickie."

He looked at her aghast.

"Kidding, Ballsy." She turned to him. "Seriously, man. You're obsessed. What's up? You can't go on like this, pining over her. You guys weren't even an item, right? I mean, she was married, has a kid...."

He waved a hand, dismissively. "No, nothing like that. It's just ... she was on my team, and she threw herself into that thing to save the ship. And she made me promise to go tell her kid that everything would be ok, and I just, I don't know. For awhile she was dead, and then, miraculously, she was alive. And I rescued her. But now she's in limbo, and ... I'm just hung up, Space-champ. It's hard to explain."

He wasn't even sure why he was there.

"Are you just scared that you'll end up the same way?" Spacechamp folded her arms, studying the sleeping pilot. "That you'll go into the void and then come back ... changed? Different? That you'll lose yourself? Demon possession?"

He rolled his eyes. "This isn't some *B*-movie space horror show."

"And yet, there she is. Changed. Taken over by an alien race. Sounds like a horror show to me," she said.

"Yeah," he rubbed his arms—he'd clasped his hands behind his back for so long that they had started to prickle. "I guess this is a horror show. It could happen to any of us, at any time. Dogtown? Taken by the Swarm, then killed. Those other two pilots? And Hanrahan? Doc Wyatt?"

She pat his shoulder. "Don't worry. At least there won't be any aliens bursting out of your chest and dancing on the bar. And remember, Granger came back. If he can, so can Fishtail."

"Yeah, I know. I keep telling myself that."

Spacechamp turned to leave, then paused. "You know why they call me Spacechamp?"

"Uh ... didn't you just pick it because it sounded cool?"

"Pfft. You know you don't pick your own callsign. No, they called me Spacechamp when I was first assigned to the *Oregon*. I wore my hair in a bun, and the guys said I looked like that cartoon character from when we were kids. Remember her? Spacechamp? The zany happy-go-lucky nerd girl turned space pirate? Robbed from the rich inter-solar plutocrats and gave to the poor?"

Volz shrugged. "I played basketball. Never watched many cartoons."

"Well," continued Spacechamp, "the thing with that cartoon was, Spacechamp was a goon. A total gamer girl with bad grooming habits and crazy hair that she wrapped up in a bun. When those jocks called me Spacechamp, it wasn't a compliment, believe me. Behind my back they called me, and I quote, "Eterna-virge," referring to their belief that I'd never get laid in my entire life. That first week was horrible. But you know what I did? I got in that cockpit, and I decided that I'd be the best goddamned fighter jock any of those bastards had ever seen. I put up a friggin' full-size poster of Spacechamp on my locker. I plastered her name on my helmet. I owned it. I wasn't going to let them define who I was. And, by the time a month had passed, I *was* the best. Ya know why?"

"Why?"

"Mainly because the rest of them were killed by the Swarm. They had it coming, the bastards, god rest their souls," she crossed herself. Volz had forgotten she was religious. "But I lived. I survived. I fought my way through and clawed my way out when those other wankers got themselves killed. By the time I left, Spacechamp was my badge of honor. It was my title that said, *Suck it, bitch, I'm better than all your sorry asses.*"

She turned and pointed to Fishtail. "She survived. Both because she's a kick-ass pilot, and because you risked everything to bring her back. She had the lady-balls to put her life on the line for all of us, throwing herself into that thing to save the ship. Something tells me she's going to fight this thing, and win. You just watch."

Volz shook his head, finally turning to face her.
"You haven't talked to it, Spacechamp. You don't know.
You don't know what it's like. It's completely taken her.
When she talks, it's all Swarm. All hate and malice and
chest-thumping and dick-wagging about how they'll overcome us all and make us all *friends*, or kill us if we resist. I
just ... I just worry that in spite of her bravery, in spite of
me bringing her back, that we've lost her after all." He bit
his lip. "And that I'll have to go back to that house, *again*,
and tell them that their daughter and his mother is dead,
again. I don't know if I can handle that."

He was looking her in the eye, but she seemed
distracted. Following her gaze, he scanned sickbay for
what Spacechamp was looking at, and gasped.

Fishtail was awake. And staring right at him, with dead,
glassy eyes. A joyless smile curled the edged of her lips.

He put his hand on the window. One of the nurses
noticed the monitor beeps announcing Fishtail's return
to consciousness, and raced over to the transparent
enclosure, jabbing a few times at the automatic IV to
dispense a new dose of tranquilizer.

A few moments later, she closed her eyes again and
fell asleep.

That look. That look on her face. He shuddered. The
expression had horrified him. But there was still hope,
wasn't there? *She's got to be in there.* He pulled his hand
back from the window, and made a decision.

He needed to talk to her. Break past the monster and
reach Fishtail. And bring her home.

Again.

CHAPTER FIFTEEN

Conference Room, ISS Lincoln
High Orbit, Britannia

"SHE CALLS HERSELF Vice Imperator Scythia Krull. Says her people, the Skiohra, have been servants of the Swarm for thousands of years. She claims that once they realized the Dolmasi had managed to throw off Swarm influence, it inspired the Skiohra to do likewise."

Admiral Zingano scratched his facial stubble as he studied the schematic of the super dreadnought displayed on the conference room wall. "Sounds damn suspicious if you ask me, Tim."

And even as he said the words, something stirred in the back of Granger's mind. Something someone once told him about the Swarm. But the words eluded him. Was he remembering something he learned during his Vacation?

On the opposite wall of the conference room was a video feed displaying the image of President Avery

surrounded by General Norton and a handful of her
military and intelligence advisors, seated in the command center of her new presidential starship, *Galactic
One. Interstellar One* had been destroyed two months
ago by unknown saboteurs—somehow the woman had
managed to avoid an impressive number of assassination attempts.

"How convenient for them," she said with a snort,
"that their come-to-Jesus moment came right as Bill's
fleet was about to show up."

Granger nodded in agreement. "The optics are unsettling, I agree. And Krull did tell me that she didn't decide
to make her move until she received intel that Bill was on
his way with the fleet. She—or he, I've discovered you
really can't tell very easily with the Skiohra—thought that
switching sides during a major battle would be a lot more
devastating to the Swarm than to do it all by themselves,
alone. Basically she wanted to desert when she was
assured that she'd have the cover of our fleets. If she did
it alone, she reasoned the Swarm would have destroyed
every single Skiohra ship."

"Bastards," muttered Avery. "Just like that shithead
Kharsa. Using us for their own gain. Using us like a
shield, or in Kharsa's case, a spear, and risking our lives
instead of their own to free his planet. I'm telling you,
gentlemen, if we ever get out of this thing with the
Swarm, we're going on a nuke spree with these other
bastards—things were so much simpler when all we
had to worry about were the Russians and a long-dead
Swarm threat." She seemed to notice Commander
Proctor's eyes widen a bit and chuckled. "Not to worry,

Shelby, I'm not as cutthroat as that. Still, I'm getting sick of the politics. I know, politics is my game. I'm good at it. Hell, I thrive on it. But intergalactic, interspecies politics where I don't even know the motivations of all the players is a bit much for even my tastes."

Admiral Zingano's brow furrowed as he studied the dreadnought's layout on the schematics displayed on the wall. He gestured toward Proctor: "And what do you make of this, Commander? These super dreadnoughts are basically extremely large copies of the regular Swarm carriers. Similar interior design. Same weaponry. Nothing like the Dolmasi ships."

Proctor nodded. "It sure does look like one of two things. Either the Skiohra are using ships supplied by the Swarm, or perhaps building their own based off designs supplied by the Swarm...." She trailed off, her brow furrowing, as if realizing something.

"Or...?" Zingano prompted. All eyes turned to her.

"Or, the Skiohra gave the designs to the Swarm, or even built the carriers for them. Think about it—the regular carriers have corridors, consoles, even door handles, though the Swarm themselves are essentially liquid. Why? Well look at the size of those corridors, consoles, and door handles. Everything matches the dreadnought. The dreadnought which happens to be a perfect match for Skiohra ergonomics. They're a little shorter than us, it seems. Smaller hands." She turned to Avery. "I think we've finally solved the mystery of where the Swarm gets their ships, and why they're designed how they are."

Avery leaned in toward the camera. "Do you think that the Skiohra are the Swarm's shipbuilders? Could it be possible that they've just lost their ship-building capabilities with the Skiohra defection?"

Proctor shrugged. "It's just speculation at this point, ma'am."

"And they could be playing us," said Granger. "This still gives me a bad feeling."

"Playing us?" Zingano shifted uncomfortably in his seat. "They destroyed five carriers before the Swarm high-tailed it out of there. Doesn't sound like a particularly effective strategy—feign friendship and destroy Swarm carriers? Look out, here come the humans! Quick, let's pretend to be their friends while we blast our real allies to hell?" He sniffed. "Cynical cloak-and-dagger false flag tactics like that work great in novels, but in real-life military strategy? I'm not buying it."

Proctor shook her head. "You're forgetting that the allies of the Swarm are not independent individuals," she said with a glance at Granger. He knew what she was insinuating, consciously or not, and it grated on him. Even if his annoyance was unfair. "The Dolmasi, before they managed to throw off Swarm control, were completely and utterly controlled by the Swarm. Likewise with the fighter pilot we recovered. Fishtail. She *is* Swarm. Same with Doc Wyatt and Colonel Hanrahan. They weren't Swarm allies, they *were* Swarm. So saying it doesn't make sense for the Skiohra to shoot up a few Swarm carriers to pretend to be our friends is missing the point."

"And the point, Commander?" Zingano looked impatient.

"The point, is if they are playing us, it's not the *Skiohra* who are playing us, it's the Swarm. Assuming the Skiohra haven't broken Swarm control over themselves. Every action they take is not *their* action, it's *Swarm* action."

Avery nodded in agreement. "And the implications of that? What do you think, Shelby?"

Proctor shrugged heavily. "Just that as we try to decipher the Skiohra's motivations, we can't look at it from *their* point of view. We still need to look at this from the *Swarm*'s vantage point. They certainly could be capable of executing a false-flag attack on their own ships if they think it could give them a strategic advantage over us in the long haul."

Granger shook his head. "The Swarm has overwhelming firepower and numbers. In all our battles they've never relied on anything but sheer blunt force. Their tactics have been, shall we say, lackluster. They're slow to adapt to quickly-changing orbital battle conditions. It's like they have two modes: attack with overwhelming force when they think they can win, or retreat when it looks like defeat is imminent."

Zingano nodded. "You're right. I don't buy it. This is totally out of character for them. My experience with them matches yours, Tim. Why would they suddenly use subterfuge in a misdirection like this?"

President Avery glanced at them all in turn before pursing her lips. "Right. So we take the Skiohra at their word. At least until we have reason to believe otherwise. But in the meantime, be careful, gentlemen. Just as with the Dolmasi, we do not share intelligence about fleet movements or capabilities. By the way," she turned to Granger, "how big *is* their fleet?"

"Ah yes, that's another interesting point. According-ing to Vice Imperator Krull, the only ship the Skiohra deploy is the super dreadnought, and they have six of them. Up until yesterday, that number stood at seven. And we were just moments away from destroying a second one before it q-jumped away."

Avery nodded. "Brilliant work, by the way. Those dreadnoughts out-power you, what, two hundred to one? And you took it out within a minute? Brilliant."

"Thank you, ma'am."

"And putting your own life on the line to do it, shielding the rest of your fleet. Very admirable, Mr. Granger. There are those who toss brick-laden epithets your way"—her eyes darted to General Norton, whose frown stiffened—"but I think you've shown you're will-ing to throw your own life away to stop these bastards. You've got a spine. You have my *full* confidence, in spite of recent events."

Her eyes moved around the room again, laying her eyes on the assembled admirals, generals, and captains. Her meaning was clear. Ever since the fighter pilot, Volz, had reappeared with Fishtail, claiming that a Swarm-con-trolled Granger was on the other side of the singularity they'd traversed, it seemed the top brass trusted Granger even less than they did before, Admiral Zingano being the lone exception. Some days it seemed that if Zingano were gone, Granger would find himself in a solitary cell deep inside CENTCOM Intel, or worse, airlocked.

"Speaking of recent events," Proctor began, "has IDF Science come to any conclusions about Volz's trip?"

Avery glanced at a man seated next to her. The head of IDF Science, Commander Rome, cleared his throat. "As far as we can tell, Volz's fighter was gone for about half an hour, judging from his shipboard computer. We can detect no tampering with the records. From the *Warrior's* perspective, he was gone for less than an hour. So whatever time dilation was present with The Event is markedly less in Volz's case," he said, using the more neutral The Event for Granger's disappearance rather than Vacation, as everyone else called it behind Granger's back.

Rome continued, "However, Lieutenant Miller had been gone, from our perspective, for over two months. Obviously, we don't have access to her fighter, but we analyzed her DNA, looking at telomere length and a few other markers, compared it to her last physical, and came to a rather remarkable conclusion—from her perspective, she'd only been gone a few minutes at most."

Proctor nodded knowingly. The others looked perplexed. "Strange," she said, connecting the dots for the rest of them. "Tim was gone for fifteen seconds, which for him was three days. Volz was gone for half an hour, and from what we can tell that's how long he thinks he was gone for. But Fishtail was gone for two months, and for her the time dilation wasn't stretched, but instead it was compressed somehow, since for her she was gone only a few minutes." She turned to the chief scientist. "Has IDF Science run any more simulations of matter traveling through a micro-singularity connected wormhole?"

"Nonstop," he said. "Of course, we know little about them, other than the fact that we've indirectly observed their existence not once but *three* times now. But in all our simulations we've run up against the hard truth that in essence we are physical matter, which is governed by quantum mechanics. And inside the event horizon of a singularity—even an artificial micro-singularity—the rules are set by general relativity. All our models break down and we're left with guesswork. I mean, it's a miracle the three of them came out in one piece and not creamed into a soup of atomic particles."

Avery cleared her throat. "Shelby? You look like you're hiding a secret. Spill it. What do you think is going on with these trips through the singularities?"

"Oh, nothing certain. But the timing of those three singularity events seems to suggest one of two things. Either the time dilation component is completely random, or it's being precisely controlled. From the other end."

General Norton rolled his eyes. "Precisely controlled? How would whoever is on the other end know where and when to send everyone back if they're in the past?"

Commander Rome held his hand up. "Or the future. Honestly, until four months ago I would have thought if time travel was possible, the *only* direction one may travel is into the future. Although, I concede that based upon what Vishgane Kharsa has told us, along with Commander Proctor's groundbreaking work on Swarm detection through blood test, it's undeniable that Granger went to some point the past during The Event. I mean, he clearly has blood markers for former Swarm influence."

Granger tried to stifle a grimace at the reminder that he was once under Swarm control, but Proctor only nodded again, seeming to catch more of the chief scientist's meaning than Granger did. He made a note to ask her about it later—perhaps it had to do with her secret Swarm matter research she'd been conducting with her new team when time allowed. She *had* said she'd made a minor breakthrough, though since the battle yesterday he hadn't had time to bathe, much less grill her on the results.

Silence fell around the table as everyone was reminded about the possibility that Granger could still somehow be under the influence of the Swarm.

"So now what?" said Avery. "I want a plan. We've been on defense ever since the Volari Three incident. For now we can count on not having to fight the super dreadnoughts, at least. But the Swarm has pulled out all the stops and we're getting our asses handed to us. Bad. Give me something, gentlemen. Something audacious. Something bold."

Zingano shook his head. "We still, after four months, have no idea where their *real* homeworld is."

"What about the Skiohra captain. What's her name, Vice Imperator Krill—

"Krull," corrected Proctor.

"Whatever. Did you ask her if she knew the location of the homeworld, Tim?"

Granger shook his head. "We only talked for about five minutes. It didn't come up. But we established a schedule for regular communications and decided on a location in open space where we'd meet two days from now and discuss matters further."

Avery locked him in her gaze. "If they've been slaves of the Swarm for thousands of years as they say, I can't

see how they'd not know the location of the homeworld, especially if they're the Swarm's shipbuilders.
How can you build a fleet for your masters and not
know where they're filling it with all that Swarm shit
goo? Get that information, Tim. Even if you have to
blast your way onto her ship and rip the information
from her computer yourself. Hell, we've got twenty
million marines just itching for their chance at real
combat. I'm afraid all this space warfare has them a bit
disappointed and restless. Got cabin fever, all of them.
A little close quarters hand-to-hand combat with these
midget douche-weasel Skiohra folks might be just the
way to blow off the steam that they need." She chuckled a dark laugh.

"I don't think a hostile takeover of one of their ships
would be prudent at this—" began Zingano.

"Kidding, Admiral. But only half kidding. Prudent
my ass—if they don't cooperate with us, we treat them
like the enemy they are, and use them as a war asset.
Don't kid yourselves, gentlemen, until we win this war,
the Skiohra, the Dolmasi, the Russians—hell, *especially*
the Russians—are our enemies, no matter how much
we pretend we're still one big happy family."

She turned to General Norton, who'd been whispering furiously with an aide that had tapped him on the
shoulder. "General? Something wrong?"

"Yes, ma'am. We've received a meta-space distress
call from the planetary defense command on York in
the Britannia Sector. York is under attack."

CHAPTER SIXTEEN

Wellington Shipyards
Gas Giant Calais, Britannia System

W‍HEN THE ORDER CAME, Rear Admiral Littlefield wasn't expecting it, of course. Such orders are never anticipated. One never plans for them. All he knew was that one moment he was signing requisition orders for fifty-three new q-jump engine manifolds from the industrial center on Novo Janeiro, and the next moment, he had a moment of clarity.

These ships are all faulty. They need to be restarted from scratch.

Littlefield paused, shaking his head. What an odd thought. He stretched his back from the customary hunched-over position he always adopted while in his cramped office chair, and craned his neck to look out the window. Over sixty gleaming new heavy cruisers floated nearby, perched against the umbilicals coming off the shipyard nacelles, scaffolding still enclosing

about half of them, all waiting for their freshly com-
missioned and conscripted crews.

And all of them were *faulty*, somehow. How did he
know that? He shook his head, and made a mental note
to himself: get more sleep. Drink less coffee. Maybe,
just maybe, start that exercise regimen ordered by his
doctor. Ok, maybe he wasn't all *that* bad—if things got
worse he'd resort to such desperate measures. But definitely the sleep and the coffee.

These ships are all faulty. They need to be restarted from scratch.

The thought was stronger this time, and he nearly
jolted out of his chair. *What the hell?*

And yet, on the other hand, it made perfect sense.
He'd been forced to cut some corners recently. The war
against the Swarm was getting desperate. There was no
time for the usual six-hundred-point long safety checklist
that had been the standard before the war. He'd cut that
down to the essentials. Basically, make sure the damn
things don't explode at the first q-jump. Explode on the
two hundredth q-jump? That wasn't as critical. Most of
these ships weren't expected to make it past their fiftieth
q-jump. The life expectancy of an average ship was about
one month from launch. Such were the times.

These ships are all faulty. They need to be restarted from
scratch. Not only that, the shipyards itself could use a refit.

He stood up and paced his small, narrow office. He
was a *rear* admiral. An entire career of ship-shape clean-
liness, meticulous adherence to orders, and occasional,
strategic ass-kissing had led him to this, the pinnacle
of his career, and here he was, in a tiny closet that had
been refurnished into an office, in an orbital installation

floating over the god-forsaken gas giant in the Britannia solar system that should have been mothballed last century. Wherever the thought had come from, he was right. This place was downright obsolete.

Out the window, the red and orange sulphur dioxide and ammonia clouds swirled almost imperceptibly on Calais, the gas giant below. The upper atmosphere was a veritable gold-mine of helium-3, which was necessary for a properly functioning q-jump drive, so it made sense to him why the Wellington shipyards had been originally located here.

But what he didn't understand was the layout. The scale. In fact, every detail about the giant structure trailing off into the distance now made no sense to him. Why were there thirty separate scaffolding structures, each building an entire ship? It would be far more efficient to have a hundred smaller structures, or two hundred, or two thousand, each building the same component of a ship, and then piece the whole thing together on down the line. Ford was onto something seven hundred years ago—had they strayed so far?

The shipyards could use a refit. Why not start from scratch?

He weighed his options. It *was* a bold plan. Start from scratch. He'd be an innovator. A disruptor. The entire military needed a paradigm shift, he realized. And lowly Rear Admiral Littlefield was just the man to do it.

And his *friends* would reward him handsomely.

His friends? Who the hell were they? He had no friends. Just superiors who thought they knew more than him. Subordinates who grudgingly followed his orders, but he knew, just knew, that they secretly detested him. His real friends understood him. He was one with them. With the great family.

He shook his head again, and sat back down to approve more requisition orders. Seventy-two fusion power plants from Earth. Two thousand mag-rail turrets from Novo Janeiro, five hundred pallets of power conduit from Brunswick. Eight hundred and thirty-two tons of bonded—

He dropped the datapad and swiveled back to the window. It all didn't matter. They were going to lose, unless he could revolutionize the ship-building enterprise here, and then replicate that success across the other five shipyards. If IDF didn't double, or triple, its production rate, they were goners.

These ships are all faulty. They need to be restarted from scratch. The shipyards needs to be rebuilt from scratch. Only I can do this. Only I—only we can save humanity. The Adanasi cry out for our help. Our guidance. Our friendship and fellowship. They need us. Only we can save them.

It all made perfect sense to him now, where, just moments before, it had only been a fanciful thought.

We'll fix this, he pledged. For a moment he wasn't sure if that was *his* thought or *our* thought, but the next moment the confusion passed. *My, I, we, us, our—it's all the same. Whether by my own voice, or my servants, or my family, or my friends, it is the same.*

His command terminal against the wall would do. It was connected to the secure network—only ten such terminals even existed, and two were in this very shipyard. He logged in, giving the appropriate security credentials, presenting his retina for a scan, and giving a verbal passphrase for a voice match. The Special Armaments Command System required rigorous security. Anything less was dangerous—they couldn't risk the enemy ever getting access to antimatter armament control.

He scanned through the list. Not optimal—only half of the ships at Wellington were stocked with antimatter torpedoes. They were behind schedule. Avery had been insistent that every single ship be stocked with at least a thousand, even though the admiralty doubted they'd ever be used. Far too slow to be effective. But it would do for his purposes. Even one torpedo would do nicely.

As he entered the command, the thought crossed his mind, *my mind, our mind—we will prevail, after all. None shall hurt, or fear, or make afraid, or divide. We will be one.*

The command entered, confirmed, reconfirmed and locked, he swiveled back to the window. Ten second countdown.

Ten.

Nine.

This should be glorious, he thought. *We'll bring order. We? What the hell...?*

Eight.

Seven.

Why are we counting down? Why am I counting down?

Part of his mind was fuzzy. But he remembered clearly what was going on.

Six.

He jumped out of his chair and raced back to the terminal. There was still time. Still time.

Five.

Four.

He furiously brought up armament control, his fingers shaking.

"Abort. Authorization Littlefield alpha-omega-pi-zero-zero."

Three.

Two.

The computer chimed in with a compassionless voice. "Authorization denied. Initiation process is locked."

One.

He spun toward the window. Simultaneously, thirty ships exploded. The fire lasted just seconds, but the debris flung outward at terrifying speeds, engulfing the sections of the shipyard nacelles the former ships had been connected to. He squinted—dozens of kilometers away, the antimatter armament depot vanished in a haze of fire and wreckage.

He collapsed to the floor. *It's over*, he thought. If they can infiltrate this far, this high ... it's over.

Crawling, fumbling toward his desk, he reached in the lowest drawer, withdrawing the pistol.

It's over. It's over. *I can't let them work through me again.* He raised the pistol to his head. *How many others?* was his final thought.

A pop, some spray, and Rear Admiral Littlefield slumped to the floor.

CHAPTER SEVENTEEN

Intergalactic Safari Expeditions Company Nature Preserve
Tanzania, Earth

ISAACSON PEERED DOWN the sights of his high-powered
rifle, keeping the crosshairs steady on his target. He
considered himself an expert, of course, and so had
foregone the electronically stabilized version of the firearm. *Why rely on electronics when I can rely on myself?* There
was no one to trust in the whole world, he knew, so may
as well trust the only person who made sense. He was
all that mattered. He was the only real thing.

I am god. With an ironic chuckle, he lowered his rifle
and pulled out a handkerchief and wiped his brow. It was
midwinter in the northern hemisphere, but here in Tanzania the summer heat was oppressive. And even though
he'd taken Volodin on a big-game hunting expedition
to "oligarch's playground," as the nature preserve was
called, complete with all the amenities the galaxy's elite

would need on such a hunt, he'd shunned the personal air conditioning devices in favor of a more natural setting.

He was a man. He'd rely on himself, his own wit, his own brawn. It was just Isaacson, his fortitude, and his high-powered Thiessen & Wells grav-assisted automatic-trajectory-correcting rifle.

"Why are you laughing, Eamon?" asked his friend, Ambassador Volodin, who was looking through his own sights at a target far off in the distance, across a savannah plain. Their targets weren't live, of course. This was just the practice session required of all the patrons of Intergalactic Safari Expeditions Company. Most of the galaxy's elite—politician and oligarchs and wealthy scions of "old money" families—were not the most accomplished hunters. They came here in order to indicate their status, not their skills. And so they invariably needed lots of handholding and guidance, as well as comprehensive insurance policies.

"I'm laughing at me, Yuri."

"What's wrong with you? You never laugh at you. You're Eamon Isaacson, Vice President of United Earth, the least united government in the known galaxy."

He raised the gun back up to his shoulder and looked down the sights again. The target was elephant-sized, about one hundred meters away, with concentric rings around a bullseye. "I'm laughing at my ridiculous situation. Here I am, with Avery enjoying record approval ratings now that we're in the middle of a two-front war with both the Swarm and the Russian Confederation, and _you_, trying to figure out not how to decide on a cease-fire, not how to convince both sides to train their guns on the Swarm and at least hold off on shooting each other. No. When we get together, what do we talk about?"

"The only thing worth talking about, Eamon," Volodin said, tightening his grip on the gun. "Ourselves."

"But what about your good friend Malakhov?"

Isaacson fired. A split second later a hole appeared in the center of the bullseye, even though he was sure the shot had gone wide. Thank god for automatic-trajectory-correcting technology.

"He's a useful tool, Eamon." He fired off his own shot. "As am I. As are you. We're all tools. All instruments and means to someone else's end."

Not me, he thought bitterly, even as he knew he lied to himself. He couldn't face the fact that he was the biggest tool of all. First he'd been a Russian puppet and then he'd become Avery's bitch, all the while thinking he'd been advancing his own self interests. And now here he was, trying to maintain the self-interested charade for Volodin, all while doing Avery's bidding.

"Malakhov? Tool? Are you telling me you've got your president wrapped around your little finger? What's he doing for you? What's his angle?"

"Doing for me? Malakhov does nothing for *me*. But his angle is the same as Avery's. It's the same for all of them. World domination. Galactic domination. And knowing that gives us power over them. We see the whole chessboard while they only see the squares right in front of them. We know what makes them tick, and so we can channel their efforts for ... more worthy purposes."

Isaacson took another shot, then tossed the gun down. The instructor nearby cringed when he saw that, but stayed where he was, safely by the open bar. The Vice President had instructed him that they weren't to be disturbed, under pain of being forced to listen to a political speech.

"And your worthy purpose? I've never known you to be so noble, Yuri. For years we've been plotting Avery's death, and now you want to serve a higher purpose?"

Volodin smiled, and set his rifle down carefully, like a practiced, trained marksman. Isaacson remembered he'd served in the Russian infantry as a young man. "Removing Avery *was* a higher purpose. Though now that I've seen her in action, maybe she, too, can be part of the higher purpose. As some of us are making Malakhov serve a higher purpose."

Isaacson strode toward the land vehicle that would take them out to the "wild" part of the preserve where dozens of cloned elephants were waiting, semi-drugged so they wouldn't run away. United Earth law forbade hunting big game animals, but by a small quirky loophole of the law, elephants that had already been shot and killed were grandfathered in. Someone figured out you could clone one of the dead ones and stay within the law by exploiting the loophole. But, drugged or not, Isaacson didn't care. He just wanted to kill something. And elephants were something.

"And just what is this *higher purpose* you have in mind, Yuri?"

"Simple. Save humanity, of course. Not only save it from the Swarm, but save it from itself. Look around you, Eamon. Even if United Earth wins, what exactly has it won? And if the Russian Confederation wins, it will have won a pyrrhic victory, for Avery and the United Earth government and top brass will not go quietly. Once the Swarm is gone, there is nothing to stop full-scale civil war. You read the reports. You know what happened at Volari Three."

Isaacson snorted. "Of course I did. Fifty Russian cruisers almost turned the tide during the largest space battle in history. Nearly gave the Swarm their final victory."

"And three weeks later, IDF bombed the shit out of New Petersburg."

Isaacson smiled. "Payback, my friend. Plus, I managed to convince Avery to attack New Petersburg instead of Smolensk, just like you wanted." It was half true, at least. Volodin *had* asked him to try to influence Avery, and Isaacson had told her so. And she, wanting to ensure Volodin absolutely trusted her human tool, allowed him to tell Volodin that he *had* convinced her, and the attack happened exactly as the Russians wanted.

"Well, that still hurt us, but not as much as Smolensk would have. Still," he said, stopping outside the vehicle as they approached, "You've been a good friend, Eamon. Both to me, and to the Russian people. And to your own, for taking actions that will increase the goodwill between our people, when the time comes. *If* the time comes."

The ambassador sounded distant and hopeless. "You think it might already be too late?" said Isaacson.

"It's possible. If the Swarm wins, we lose. If the Russian Confederation wins, half of humanity loses. If IDF wins, the other half of humanity loses. Take your pick."

"And what is there to do about it? I can't help it that your government has sided with the Swarm in the war. What logical choice is there for us to take? Just bow down to joint Russian-Swarm hegemony?"

"No, Eamon. There is a third way. And, being the man I know you to be, you'll jump at the chance."

The driver came over, interpreting their presence by the vehicle as their signal to start the hunt. They paused the conversation as they piled in. The drive out to the cloned elephant habitat only took fifteen minutes, and along the way they could see various other enclosed savannah environments, each presumably holding collections of cloned animals. Isaacson saw several lions packs, giraffes, a rhinoceros—animals that a well-heeled oligarch from high society might want to hunt.

They arrived at the habitat, and the driver set them up on a pad outside the perimeter. A shimmering screen rose up a dozen meters in the air, forming a transparent barrier that would presumably keep the animals from reaching over or crossing through to harm their hunters. "It's transparent to you," said the driver, "but to them it's reflective and angled such that they only see sky. You are invisible to them, my friends."

The driver retreated back to the vehicle while Isaacson unpacked the rifle from the case. Volodin watched him, and Isaacson didn't notice the other man hadn't unpacked his gun until he was himself already leaning through the screen, elbows resting on the wooden railing. "Aren't you going to hunt?"

"This is no hunt, Eamon. I prefer my kills to be ... more well deserved."

"Suit yourself." He scanned the savannah setting, catching a glimpse of a large elephant drinking from a small pond near a tree. "So? You were saying? What's this third way you were alluding to?"

Volodin smiled. "Tell me, Eamon, for years we've worked toward Avery's death, and for you to replace her. Tell me. What would you do in her place?"

Be president, he thought at first, before flinching. He'd almost forgotten she was listening. "The opposite of everything she does," he said, putting on a good show for both Volodin and Avery. Volodin needed to hear he was committed to taking out Avery. Avery needed to hear that he was playing Volodin convincingly. Damn, this was getting hard to keep track of.

"Oh, come now, Eamon, she doesn't do *everything* wrong. Really, what would you do?"

Isaacson sighted the elephant, and aimed for the head, which was bent low to the water, oblivious to the perilous situation it was in. "Before the war broke out, she was the worst president in recent memory. Nearly gutted the military. Raised taxes. Took on the families and companies that *mattered*. Tried to destroy our way of life. She's been a disaster." He ran through the litany of political complaints her opponents leveled at her, the same issues that Avery and her party would have claimed as accomplishments. In reality, he didn't care a bit about the particulars. He just hated her as a person, and wanted the job for ... well, he just wanted people to call him *President Isaacson*. To be top dog. The person everyone in the room deferred to.

"And I just want my country to survive, Eamon. Tell me, what do you think would happen if you were the president of United Earth, and I was the president of the Russian Confederation?"

Isaacson pulled the trigger. The bullet sheared through the elephant's skull, and he saw a cloud of red emerge from the other side. The huge animal bolted instinctively, but then fell a few steps later and collapsed.

"You're kidding, right?"

"Humor me, Eamon. What would happen?"

Isaacson shrugged and sighted another animal. He knew the price would go up astronomically with every elephant he killed, but he didn't care. The bill was on Avery's administration anyway. "Well for one thing, the Swarm wouldn't stand a chance against both of us. Then, after the war, I suppose we'd finally have peace and cooperation. No more endless suspicion and working at cross purposes. Humanity would be safer than ever."

"Exactly, Eamon. Do you really think that the Swarm is all there is out there? Suddenly, out of the blue, come the Dolmasi. And we've just received intelligence about your meeting with the Skiohra. Hell, just the *name* of the Concordat of Seven suggests there are at least seven intelligent alien races out there. And if there's seven, there's most likely many more. And do you really think the Swarm is the worst out there?"

Another shot rang out. Another elephant slumped to the ground. Isaacson saw a third animal a hundred meters away. Its jaw moved steadily as it ate a mouthful of leaves, unconcerned about its neighbor's plight, too drugged to care about anything. "I suppose not. But one mortal enemy at a time. I would have thought that your government knows everything there is to know about the Swarm and the Concordat of Seven."

"And you'd be mistaken. You're right about us, Mr. Vice President. My government has only thrown in with the Swarm out of self-preservation. But that doesn't mean we know the first thing about it. We learned about the Dolmasi after you did. Same with the Skiohra. Just because we're in the family doesn't mean we know all the siblings. We only know the drunk, abusive father, who we suspect wants us dead as soon as he gets what he wants from us."

A third shot. A third dead elephant. Isaacson saw a fourth a long distance off, perhaps three hundred meters. He wondered if the automatic-trajectory-correction system would be enough to let him bring it down. He set himself up into position. "Are you telling me you have buyer's regret, Yuri? Wishing your government had stayed loyal to its own? To United Earth?"

Volodin lowered his voice, glancing to his left and right, even though they were completely alone, except for the driver who'd already retreated to the car. "Of course we have buyer's regret. We've been regretting for months. We completely underestimated the Swarm. And furthermore," he paused again, looking up toward the sky as if searching for surveillance drones. "Most of us in the political sphere have buyer's remorse with Malakhov. It's his fourth term, you know."

"Pushing for an early election?"

"In a sense. Eamon, I need your help. If we succeed, it could mean we, the two of us, save our entire race."

The fourth shot cracked the air. A moment later, the fourth elephant fell, drawing a grin from Isaacson. "Oh? Help with what?"

"Eamon, I need you to help me kill Malakhov."

CHAPTER EIGHTEEN

Bridge, ISS Warrior
High Orbit, Britannia

"YORK IS JUST seven lightyears from Britannia," said Proctor as they raced to the bridge. "They must know Zingano keeps his strike force based here. I'm worried this could be a decoy. Draw us away from Britannia and then strike one of our main worlds."

"The thought had crossed my mind. I wouldn't be surprised if Bill stays here and sends the *Warrior* with its own force, maybe supplemented with some of the newer ships in the third fleet based at Wellington shipyards in the Britannia System. We'll know soon enough."

They quickly maneuvered their way past a crew of workers installing the back end of a new mag-rail turret that had just been replaced. "Shelby, what about that research you've been hinting at? You've been holed up with your new team for weeks."

She caught up with him around a corner. "Remember our resupply at Earth last month? Well, I brought on board a little piece of equipment that didn't show up on any shipping manifest."

"Oh?" He turned and raised his eyebrows, but kept his brisk pace down the hallway.

Ever since Ballsy had returned with Fishtail, albeit with a foggy memory, his report of talking to a fully-Swarm-controlled Granger had unnerved her. That, combined with the admission from Granger himself that when he'd confronted Colonel Hanrahan, he'd somehow been able to convince him, mind-to-mind, to lower his weapon. It added up to something suspicious, but she didn't have hard evidence. At least, not yet. *That should change soon,* she thought.

"Remember Engineering on the Constitution? After you came back from The Event? How I carried you down there as we fell from the sky?"

"Still hazy, but sure," he replied.

"You might not remember, seeing how you were passed out for a lot of that time, but there was a bunch of new equipment installed in Engineering."

He nodded, twisting to the side as he rushed past a herd of fighters making their way down to the fighter deck. The alarms were blaring, signaling everyone to battle stations. "I remember. Haven't had much time to think about it. Did we ever get the report of what it was? I presume it's of Russian origin?"

"Of course. The voices we heard on the sickbay voice recorders: Russian. You obviously were in their hands for at least a little while. And it turns out that equipment is Russian, too. Jury-rigged and duct-taped—it sure looked like they installed it in a hurry."

He stopped momentarily, and his shoulders hunched. "Are you telling me you brought it here?"

"I am."

"When were you going to tell me about it?" He kept walking, but sounded annoyed.

"When I figured out what it did. Sorry, I had to be sure."

"Sure that I'm not, in fact, still under Swarm control?"

"I'm ninety-nine percent sure you're not under Swarm control. Well, ninety-five percent sure, at worst."

He shot her a look. At least he could still take a joke—he'd seemed particularly on edge the past month, ever since the Swarm attacks had intensified.

"Anyway," she said, dodging the original question, "the techs down at IDF Science suspected it had something to do with singularity production. And they're right."

He stopped again, and turned. "Are you telling me...?"

"It's in my lab now. We tested it. Nothing too big, of course—"

His eyes grew wide. "You made a singularity onboard the *Warrior*?"

"Barely," she said. She held up two fingers. "A micro singularity. Femto. Like a billionth of a billionth the size of the ones the Swarm throw at us."

He glowered at her, but resumed his brisk trot to the bridge. "That's your big result you wanted to tell me?"

"Not quite. What's *really* interesting is that we tested it on Swarm matter. I sent a small sample of Swarm matter through the pair we made. When it came out the other side, it was changed. Fundamentally changed.

Many of the complex protein encoding structures were broken apart. It no longer responded to manipulation with meta-space signals."

"Dead?"

She shook her head. "Not sure. I'd say no, as I still detect marginal electrical and chemical activity. But I can no longer coax it into producing Swarm virus. The stuff that actually controls people."

"Interesting," he said, as they walked through the doors to the bridge. The two marines saluted at the entrance. "And your conclusion?"

"I can't conclude anything yet. But I suspect," she lowered her voice, subconsciously noting how the crew stiffened their backs slightly as their superior officers walked onto the bridge. "I suspect that it has to do with the conversation we were having earlier, and what the IDF Chief Scientist was talking about. Quantum mechanics and general relativity. They're like oil and water. But since it seems that the Swarm matter responds strongly to meta-space signals, which are general relativity-based, they must be, I don't know, general relativity-based beings? Whatever they are, sending them through the very indefinable intersection of QM and GR—a quantum singularity—could be like the solvent that neutralizes them. Or at least their effect on regular matter."

He leaned in close. "That sounds highly speculative."

"It is," she agreed. "If we had a team of a thousand scientists working for a decade we could do the proper science. Peer review, conferences, research papers, the works. But I'm doing cowboy science here, and sometimes speculation, duct tape, and a good hunch are all I've got."

A flurry of readiness reports were starting to come in from all the department heads. Granger nodded at her. "Keep it up. I think we need to understand this if we want to have any hope of defeating the Swarm for good." He sat down in the captain's chair and then looked back at her. "And Shelby, next time you plan on making a quantum singularity onboard the ship, I'd appreciate it if you let me know."

She retreated back to the XO's station. *That went about as well as I could expect....*

Most of the departments were not as ready as she would have liked, owing to the widespread destruction from the previous battle over Indira, but it would have to do. Her head snapped up to see a flashing red message pop onto her screen. A priority one from Zingano. She read it, letting the news seep in. Just when it seemed like things couldn't get worse.

"Sir," she said sharply, wrenching Granger's attention away from the navigation officer. "Emergency at the Wellington shipyards."

He raised an eyebrow. Little seemed to phase him anymore. "Oh?"

"Rear Admiral Littlefield is dead, and about thirty ships are either destroyed or disabled. The shipyards is in shambles."

Granger nodded calmly, taking in the news and reanalyzing the new tactical situation. "Looks like our little fleet's on its own. Again." He turned back to Ensign Prince at navigation. "Q-jump in three minutes."

Proctor scowled. "Aren't we going to wait for orders from Zingano? Surely they've been revised—we were supposed to be accompanied by at least twenty new ships from Wellington."

He shrugged. "Why? I know exactly what he'll say, because they're the orders I'd give myself." His eyes were deeply lined; heavy bags sunk low underneath. To Proctor, it seemed like age, fatigue, and constant stress were all competing to see which could destroy him first. "We're expendable, Shelby. If we don't stop them at York, the road to Britannia lies open and uncontested. And if Britannia falls, the only other major defensive center of all United Earth is, well, Earth itself."

Her console beeped softly, indicating new orders from Zingano. Granger was right. *Proceed to York asap without escort. Godspeed.*

CHAPTER NINETEEN

Tyler Volz was dreaming. He knew he was dreaming because every time it happened it felt like he was flying his bird through the middle of a firefight.

Regular, real-life firefights always felt like a dream—his actions became automatic, instinctual—so it made sense that when he actually was *dreaming, it would feel like a life-or-death battle.*

Space twirled around him. Like he was perched on a spinning top. Stars wheeled over his head. He couldn't remember what was happening, or what he'd just done. Or what he was looking for.

He was looking for something.

Sleep overcame him again, but when he awoke, it was to a voice. He recognized it—it sounded familiar, but he couldn't quite remember who it was. Looking out his cockpit viewports he saw ships—he knew he was surrounded by enemies. One was coming toward him.

He maneuvered and dodged and veered, though he couldn't remember why, but he knew he had a goal. And up ahead, there they were.

They?

There were two of them. Two fighters. Both in danger. He had a choice to make—a terrible choice.

More maneuvers. He fired off a few shots. The Swarm was there, he knew it. And the voice in his ears again told him they'd all been betrayed.

But he still had time to make the choice. To save one.

And kill the other, before the Swarm got to them first.

CHAPTER TWENTY

Pilot's Locker Room, ISS Warrior
York, Britannia Sector

VOLZ WAS HALF-ASLEEP when the klaxons started blaring. *Dammit*, he thought. Another engagement. They weren't ready. He rolled out of his bunk and, still groggy-eyed, slid into his flight suit and pulled on his boots, clicking the magnetic air seal into place between them. The boots were still ripe—he'd run his crew through the wringer today, practicing new maneuvers using tow cables, carbon-composite nets, and new targeting algorithms that would allow them to fling debris into singularities instead of osmium bricks, or, barring those, broken-down fighters, along with their helpless pilots.

Morale was low. The pain and shock at the loss of the Lucky Thirty—the nickname Pew Pew had given to the sacrificed pilots—was still fresh on everyone's minds. It was normal to lose that many during an average engagement with the Swarm. But to lose them like *that*, chosen because their last name happened to start with the wrong letter ... it just felt so ... mechanical and inglorious and ... wrong.

They all—all the pilots—knew it was necessary. It was what they all signed up for. They signed up to die.

But that didn't mean they had to like it.

"What do you say, Ballsy, is it your lucky day?" said Pew Pew. "We just replaced all the A's through H's. Maybe today it's the R's through Z's." The other pilot pulled his flight gloves on and engaged the air seal.

Fodder snickered. "Every day is my lucky day. I just officially changed my last name. Say goodbye to Dave "Fodder" Zavaleri. Say hello to Dave "Fodder" Asterisk-One-Big-Unit."

Volz rolled his eyes. "Big Unit?"

"Yeah. I'm the Big Unit, didn't you know?"

Pew Pew grabbed his deodorant before glancing up toward the blaring klaxons, shaking his head, and tossing the stick back into his locker. "He's just compensating. Also drives a big-ass truck back home. Classic small-man compensation."

"Asterisk-one?" Volz asked, a little absentmindedly. He had little patience for the locker-room joking lately.

"Yeah. Except not spelled out. Just the symbol. Asterisk-One-Big-Unit. That way I'm strategically placed in the alphabet in case Pierce has any more bright ideas for dishing out the less desirable assignments."

"How the hell is Asterisk-One-Big-Unit going to help you, dipshit?" Pew Pew struggled to pull his boots on.

"It's obvious, Vacuum-Dick. Asterisk ain't a letter. Next time he says something like A's through H's, go ahead and fly your sorry asses into that singularity, I've got an out."

Pew Pew snorted, but Fodder pulled his flight helmet out of the locker and pointed to a label that he'd taped to the side. In bright red letters it read, *Dave *1BigUnit.*

The other pilots around them in the locker room laughed. Volz and Pew Pew were still waiting for Fodder to finish dressing when Spacechamp poked her head through the door. "Oi! Briefing room! Now! Pierce is starting."

They jogged down the hall to the pilot's briefing room where Commander Pierce had already launched into his pre-engagement pep-talk. Except his pep-talks these days were more somber affairs. Not that Pierce had ever been anything even approaching a cheerleader, but the weeks and months of sending pilots to their deaths were obviously wearing on the man.

"—won't know until we get there. Alpha Wing, you run interference for Beta Wing for package delivery." He looked up at the late arrivals. "Untouchables, nice of you to join us. Lieutenant Volz, I want your crew ready and available for special maneuvers—"

"Save those for F through K," grumbled Pew Pew. The uneasy silence was punctuated by a few gallows-humor chuckles.

"And save the sass for your mom, Lieutenant," said Pierce, but his face was white. "Like I said, we won't know the tactical situation until we get there in—" he glanced at the status board, "—eight minutes. Just remember, York is small, only a few major cities. Over half the population is scattered across the main continent in smaller towns and villages. Very few orbital structures to make use of in our engagements. Most of the action will take place close to the capital ships, but pay attention to fleeing transports and freighters—offer them cover until they make their q-jumps. And—" he paused, and looked down before continuing. "Let's save this one, boys. Our record has been spotty the past few weeks. Let's save this one."

He manner was a bit off—forced, even. With his patrician accent he often came across as stiff, but this was backed by a quiet, underlying sense of emotion that seemed out of place for the unflappable CAG. Volz glanced at Spacechamp seated next to him, questioningly. She leaned in and whispered, "His family's down there."

"Launch in five. Dismissed."

The crew of pilots broke up into their squads and rushed into the fighter bay through the double doors on the side of the briefing room. Techs and flight crew members were in a frenzy, making last-minute adjustments, clearing the launch paths, removing restraints on the fighters. Volz climbed up into his bird and clicked his restraints in place. His body on autopilot, he ran through the pre-flight checklist—it was the same almost every day for the past four months. Confirm ammunition levels. Check. Osmium brick release hydraulics. Check. Find Fishtail.

Check.

Check check check check except she was not dead, and not alive. She wasn't Fishtail. And it was Granger's fault. Volz's memory of the other side of the singularity was still hazy—Commander Proctor guessed that was a side-effect of traversing a relativistic quantum singularity—but the memories he had were unambiguous. Granger had, at one point at least, been a Swarm agent, he was sure of it. He remembered seeing that same, huge dreadnought. And a station. And the *Constitution*. And Russians were involved somehow. But Volz had eluded him. Found Fishtail, and somehow, miraculously, found the exact singularity he'd left, and went back in. How did he find her again? It was so hazy. He remembered space. Debris. Floating. Gasping for air. But against all odds, he'd rescued her.

And now, in spite of all his efforts, Fishtail was just like Granger had been. Gone, but still alive.

The kid, Zack-Zack, had sent messages, the grandma had sent requests to vidcom every time the *Warrior* made it to Earth for resupply and crew transfer, but he'd ignored it all. He couldn't face them. He couldn't give them the news. Not only because the information was classified, but the truth was too horrible, too painful, to share with them. That their daughter, the kid's mother, was a monster. Not dead. Not alive. And definitely not human.

"Ready for launch," came Commander Pierce's voice. Volz looked out the cockpit, giving a thumbs up to his team. Spacechamp, Pew Pew, and Fodder all nodded back at him. He watched his tactical screen. A green indicator message popped up. They'd arrived. The final q-jump had placed them just fifty thousand kilometers out from York. Their velocity would take them into a close elliptical orbit, which meant they needed to be ready to launch within minutes.

Except....

Spacechamp swore in his headset.

"Bloody hell," breathed Fodder. Volz switched over to planetary view.

York was already hit hard. They were too late.

A voice came over his headset. Lieutenant Schwitzer. Commander Pierce's assistant. "All pilots, stand down. Please remain on standby. Schwitzer out."

Pierce usually gave both the engage and disengage orders. Volz glanced out the cockpit toward the command center. Through its window he could see Schwitzer at the command station. The CAG, Commander Pierce, sat nearby on a bench.

Holding a framed picture in his hands. Staring blankly ahead.

CHAPTER TWENTY-ONE

Bridge, ISS Warrior
York, Britannia Sector

CAPTAIN GRANGER stared at the bleak view on the screen. Dozens, hundreds, of mushroom clouds had billowed up into the blue atmosphere, rendering the entire planet a gray, desolate, swirling maelstrom of dust and lightning.

"Ensign? Final sensor report?"

Ensign Diamond nodded. "Nearly there, sir." He pointed to a few of his sensor crew members, indicating that they finalize their scans. Moments later he continued, "Destruction is nearly total, sir. All major cities and towns gone. A few outlying settlements still there, along with ... perhaps a few thousand single houses scattered out on farms and ranches, and up in the Bolen mountain range and the Huxley Hills."

He paused, to either catch his breath, or to let the enormity of the destruction sink in. "We estimate about

one hundred and twenty-five singularities were fired
into the crust. Atmospheric dust coverage is at ninety-nine percent.

"Any sign of the Swarm fleet?"

"None, sir."

No. *No you bastards, you're not getting away that easily.* "Continue scanning. Scan toward the other inner solar system
planets. Athena is the next one out, and there's a few
orbiting mining colonies out there in the asteroid belt."

"Aye, aye, sir."

"Tim," said Proctor, who'd been talking to the Science Station crew. "We estimate about two billion tons
of material billowing around, screening out most solar
radiation. With the sun completely blocked out, the average planetary temperature will start to plunge within
days. Recommend we request a relocation fleet to set
out from Earth immediately."

"Do it," he said.

Relocation. Perhaps twenty thousand people left, out
of tens of millions.

He was tired of this. It was time not only to take
the fight to the enemy, but to turn their own weapons
on them.

Hanrahan. Colonel Hanrahan. Back when Granger
had confronted his Swarm-compromised security chief,
he'd used the Swarm's own communication method
against them. *Somehow.* He still had no idea what he'd
done, or how he did it. All he knew was that, at some
point, he'd been tied into the Swarm's communication
network, and had somehow tapped into it to convince
Hanrahan to lower his weapon, even if only for a second.

He closed his eyes.

Where are you? Where the hell are you, you miserable rat bastards?

No, he wasn't going to find them that way. His state of mind was too angry. When he'd influenced Hanrahan, it wasn't with anger. He breathed deeply, and slowly, calming his mind.

Where are you? Where are you, my friends?

He searched his mind, grasping at any stray thought, any hint of Swarm presence. They *had* to still be there somewhere. There was no reason for them to stick around after the fall of York, but part of him raged against the idea that they could simply swoop in, destroy a world, and not stick around for the consequences. There had to be consequences. He needed to bring justice to them.

Where are you, my friends?

We are here, our friend. We never left. We will be with you, always.

He opened his eyes.

"New course. Distribute this heading to the fleet." He keyed in a set of coordinates and sent them to Ensign Prince.

"Sir? These ... these are in the asteroid belt out past Athena."

"I know, Ensign."

"But sensors show nothing there. Nothing but asteroids."

He glanced up at Prince. Then Proctor. The entire bridge crew was staring at him. "Regardless. That's where we'll find the bastards that did this. When we're clear of York's gravity well, engage q-jump drive."

"How do you know, Tim?" Proctor had stepped forward. Everyone was now looking at her. Then back to him. Like there was a showdown of wills. Not that she was challenging him, but she was voicing all their doubts. All their unspoken suspicions about him.

"I just know. That's where we'll find the cumrat ships that destroyed York. Anyone got a problem with this? We're going there to destroy them. Anyone got a problem? I imagine Commander Pierce doesn't. His family is buried down there. I imagine the *ISS Lancaster* doesn't—their entire ship was crewed from York. They're in our fleet right now—I imagine they'll lead the charge."

"But sir, there's nothing *there*," said Proctor. She held up a datapad. "Here. Look for yourself. All visual scans—"

"Are over thirty minutes old," interrupted Granger. "It might not look like they're there now—the light from their ships won't hit our sensors for another thirty minutes—but they are. I know it." He stood up, taking in the gazes of the bridge crew. "Anyone else want to speak up?"

Silence.

"Right, then. Maximum thrust."

Warily, the crew moved into action. Five minutes later, they were sufficiently clear of the gravity field to safely initiate a q-jump.

"Signal to the fleet. Q-jump on my mark." He paused until Ensign Prucha at comm indicated everyone was ready.

"Now."

CHAPTER TWENTY_TWO

Bridge, ISS Warrior
York, Britannia Sector

A MOMENT LATER, the screen shifted and the swirling, lightning-filled dust clouds disappeared, replaced by a star field dotted with asteroids.

"Scanning," said Ensign Diamond. "Nothing showing up on visuals. Scanning the rest of the EM band."

Granger tapped his fingers. They were *here*. He knew it. "Keep at it, Mr. Diamond." He raised his head. "Mr. Pierce, are my birds ready?"

A woman answered. "This is Lieutenant Schwitzer. Commander Pierce is indisposed at the moment, Sir. But yes, we're all ready down here."

Granger understood. "Tell him we're on the hunt." He remembered the picture of his CAG's family sitting on Pierce's desk. "They're not getting away this time."

Another minute passed. "Still nothing, sir."

Granger balled his fists. Where the hell were they?

The time ticked by. Every sensor band came up clean. Nothing but asteroids, and open space.

"Tim," began Proctor, leaning in close so no one else would hear. "We should go talk."

He shot her a look, eyes sharp as daggers. The tone of her voice said only one thing. *You've gone off the deep end, old man.*

With teeth clenched, he closed his eyes. *I'm here. I'm here, my friends. Show yourselves.*

Another minute. Proctor bent low next to his chair, crouching. "Tim," she whispered. "It's time to call it off."

He kept his eyes closed. Another minute.

Her hand rested gently on his arm. Finally, he let out a deep sigh, opened his eyes, and stood up. "Very well. Set a course back to York and commence rescue operations." He started walking toward his ready room. He noticed Proctor following him. "Lieutenant Diaz, you have the bridge. Let me know when—"

"Sir!" shouted Ensign Diamond. "Ten Swarm carriers, out of nowhere! Q-jumped in right on top of us!"

CHAPTER TWENTY-THREE

Bridge, ISS Warrior
Asteroid Belt, York System, Britannia Sector

THE SHIP SHOOK as the hull was pounded with antimatter beams. Granger grabbed onto an outstretched hand from one of the marines at the door to steady himself. "Evasive maneuvers," he shouted.

"Full about! Launch fighters! All ships form up into attack wings and engage!" Proctor had run to tactical and began to direct the battle. There was no escaping from this one, not that Granger wanted to. He'd hunted the Swarm to this point. Hell, he'd summoned them.

He stumbled back to his chair and monitored the battle. They were taken by surprise, but the odds were even—he had twenty-four ships to the Swarm's ten. It would be close—the casualties would be horrific, but they'd pull out a victory. Especially if he could outthink them. His eyes glanced toward the tactical readout and the display of the surrounding asteroid-filled environment.

Most were small, but there were a few larger ones that might come in handy.

"Helm, move us in toward that asteroid. The one at fifteen mark eight."

"Aye, aye, sir."

The tiny dot grew larger very quickly, and soon the *Warrior* and the dozen ships of its attack wing swung around the giant rock. "Now, new course. Use the shadow of that rock, and redirect us toward that dwarf planetoid." He pointed to his tactical display, indicating the hundred-odd kilometer wide rock in the near distance.

The ship rumbled in the background as four Swarm carriers continued their hot pursuit.

"Sir, just lost the *Michigan*. The *Budapest* is losing power," said Lieutenant Diaz.

"Just get us to that rock. Swing around the backside, accelerate, and come at them with some speed."

The planetoid grew larger, its cratered, pockmarked surface gleaming white in the distant sunshine. On the far side, Ensign Prince kicked in the thrust, well past the recommended limits of the inertial cancelers, and as a result the ship shuddered with the violently alternating momentum swings as the systems tried to keep up, adding to the growing rumble of the explosions in the rear decks.

"We're not shaking them, sir. They've kept up this whole time." An explosion cut off Lieutenant Diaz. "Just lost engine four."

He closed his eyes again. He summoned them here. Maybe he could send them away. Maybe he could send them off course. Maybe he could control them.

Friends, stop.

Friends, stop. We need to talk.

In response, only laughter. Or its equivalent. He didn't hear it, but he could feel it. They had played him, and he'd fallen for it, and now they scoffed at him.

But now there was something else. Another voice. Something discordant. Angry and howling. *We're coming,* it said. There were no words—never any words, but he felt the feeling and knew the meaning and the meaning was unmistakable.

He opened his eyes and was not surprised in the slightest when Ensign Diamond announced, "New contact. It's a Dolmasi ship. No, it's fifty Dolmasi ships."

They had flashed into existence right next to the small planetoid, already traveling straight toward the incoming enemy. Without pause they opened fire on the four Swarm carriers pursuing the *Warrior* and its fleet.

"Help them out, tactical."

"Full mag-rail spread," said Proctor. "Laser banks, target where the Dolmasi's antimatter beams hit. Open up those holes."

Within a minute, they'd made quick work of the four ships. Granger watched the tactical display and sighed in relief as he watched the remaining six carriers disappear, fleeing before the Dolmasi reached them.

"About time," he said out loud. They'd come. They'd finally come. In the two months since he'd helped them regain their homeworld, they'd never once helped in any battle. Never once come when summoned, desperately, to help repel an invasion. He had begun loathing the idea that he'd helped them liberate their world, loathing the idea of being made a tool, an unwitting instrument in someone else's plan.

But they'd finally come. They came when they didn't have to. When they had nothing to gain.

Leaning back to Proctor, he wondered, "Think we can trust them yet?"

CHAPTER TWENTY_FOUR

President's Stateroom, Frigate One
High Orbit, Earth

"HE WANTS TO TAKE ME to a planet called Penumbra
Three, presumably because Malakhov is scheduled to
do an inspection tour there in a few days."

Avery was jabbing and typing furiously at her computer terminal pad in her lap, but glanced up at Isaacson's mention of the planet. "Penumbra Three. Now
why does that name ring a bell?"

Isaacson shrugged. He was dour. Sullen. From her
other computer monitor nearby she could see the
constant readout of the man's emotional state, and
even view words and phrases as they appeared in one
of the boxes on the screen. She'd been able to read his
thoughts from his face since the beginning. The implants made the process more ... literal, but he'd recently
been developing a troubling self-discipline that made it
increasingly difficult to see what he was truly thinking.

The emotions, of course, were laid bare to her. He couldn't hide those from the thirty-odd implants tucked deep into his skin. And he was always bad at hiding his feelings from her. The revulsion for her pulled at his eyes, made his nostrils flare, tugged at the corners of his mouth. His left eye twitched ever so slightly on the occasions when the emotion indicator on the screen suggested barely-concealed anger and disgust. This was tearing him apart, and she loved every minute of it.

"No idea, ma'am."

She leaned back for a moment before nodding. "I remember now. Granger's fleet stumbled into a Russian settlement there two months ago, presumably in Swarm space. Were chased off pretty quickly, if I remember right. Why? What's there that Volodin wants you to see?"

"Malakhov? Maybe he thinks killing him somewhere far from Earth will—"

Avery snorted. "Oh, don't be so naive, Isaacson. Do you really think Volodin wants to kill his boss?" She held up a hand. "Yes, yes, I know there are plenty of lower-level politicians around who've wanted to kill their bosses, you don't need to remind me. But ... no. This is a trick, somehow. He wants to get you out there for another reason, and we need to know why."

"Are we going to keep me here then? Draw it out of him? Convince him to tell me what's so special about the place?"

"Of course not. We're sending you. That's the easiest way. Plus, it will further convince him you are absolutely on his side. I'll protest, of course, and complain to some of the senators and blowhards that you're leaving on some damn-fool diplomatic mission in the middle of hostilities with the Russians, and that will leak back to him and reassure your allegiance is real. Then, when he reveals his true intentions, you'll continue on with the original plan. I need that peace treaty. Our fleets need some breathing room— we can't keep patrolling our Russian border.

"And then?" said Isaacson, carefully.

Too carefully. She laughed again at him, and just for a moment she saw the anger indicator spike on her terminal.

"And then, Mr. Isaacson, you'll be free. Do this task for me, and I'll let you go. I'll disable the implants. Hell, if you trust me enough, I'll arrange for them to be taken out completely. Or you can do it yourself. Either way they'll be disabled and harmless if you choose to take them out."

He looked flabbergasted. "Really? You'll take them out?"

"Of course, Eamon. You've made a noble effort at atoning for your sins. You are not clean yet, but this peace treaty with Malakhov will go a long way toward regaining my trust. And the trust of all the top brass, and the people. Public opinion of the Russian Confederation is at an all-time low, Eamon, ever since their betrayal at Volari Three. They'll hate me for making a peace treaty, and consequently they'll love you more. Never mind the fact that once this is over, we'll nuke the Russian bastards to kingdom come. But for now, seeing you negotiate a temporary peace with the despised leader of the new Russian empire will make you a hero in the eyes of billions."

His eyes flashed, just for a moment. Oh, god, he was so easy to play. Just one mention of public adoration and he basically gets a boner. She tried hard not to roll her eyes.

"Are you sure, ma'am? I mean, sending me out there, out from the influence of your ... monitoring?"

She raised an eyebrow. "Oh, don't worry, you'll be adequately monitored. My team in charge of your implants has been busy writing a firmware program that will be uploaded to your implants very shortly. It will keep you from thinking anything *too* treacherous, and keep a running log of your thought and emotional parameters that I'll have access to when you return. Any deviation from the script, and...." She gave him a knowing shrug and lopsided smile as she reached for her coffee. Can't let him forget the consequences. He rubbed a temple at the reminder, and she wondered just how intense the pain could be. She should test that sometime.

"And what if he's dead set against it? What if we can't make the concessions that he wants? What if I can't—"

"Eamon, Eamon ... I can't solve all your problems for you. It'll require some improvising. You're brilliant at that. Honestly, how in the world did you make it to this point if you can't think for yourself?"

"I—"

"Dismissed, Mr. Vice President. Be a dear and send General Norton in when you see yourself off the ship."

Isaacson stood up, paused a moment as if he wanted to say something else, but chose not to and left. Avery, however, read his intended thought on the screen nearby. *And what if the program fails, and I betray you out there?*

The door shut, leaving her alone.

"Don't worry, Eamon, you won't. Nothing you do can betray me now."

CHAPTER TWENTY-FIVE

Bridge, ISS Warrior
Asteroid Belt, York System, Britannia Sector

"CAPTAIN, INCOMING SIGNAL from the main Dolmasi vessel. Asking for you by name."

Granger waved a hand up toward the screen. Moments later, Vishgane Kharsa appeared, looking as triumphant as he supposed a Dolmasi could look. The alien had dropped all pretense of mimicking human social cues like laughter and shrugging and frowning, but Granger knew smugness when he saw it.

"Vishgane. It is good to see you again. You are most welcome."

"Granger. You should not be here."

"How did you know we were here? You must have been pretty close to have come so quickly."

Kharsa held a single hand out. Granger did not quite understand the motion, but the words made it clear.

"You summoned us, Granger. We were close, within a few lightyears, monitoring Valarisi movements near Britannia, and we heard your voice."

"We?"

"We. All of us. We are just like you, Granger. Once one has been under the influence of the Valarisi, one retains the link. They can no longer control you, or us, and we must be careful that they do not see through our eyes, but the fact remains, we all heard you. And the decision was made, out of gratitude for what you, Granger, have done for us, to come to your aid."

The open discussion of his link to the Swarm made Granger uncomfortable, but there was nothing helping that now. The secret was out in the open. Proctor had known, and the bridge crew had suspected. Now it was fact. May as well acknowledge it. Own it. Make it, publicly, for the benefit of his people, part of his arsenal.

"Can you control them? Can I?"

"In some ways, yes. In most ways, no."

Granger waited for an elaboration to the cryptic response. Before it came, Proctor interrupted. "Sir, incoming meta-space transmission from Admiral Zingano. Sending it to your terminal."

He glanced down to the readout. *Warrior* and her fleet were to return to Britannia as soon as the battle was over to begin something Zingano was calling, Operation Ground War.

"You must leave, I know," said Kharsa. How he knew that, Granger had no idea. Could they read his thoughts? "You project them too loudly at times,

Granger. It is how we all heard you, lightyears away. I'm surprised every Valarisi ship and every other asset of the Concordat of Seven within a hundred lightyears didn't converge on this location."

"I'll be more careful," assured Granger. The thought was unnerving, that this whole time, out of sheer carelessness, he may have been telegraphing his own intentions to the Dolmasi, to the Swarm, to the Skiohra. Hell, even to the Russians.

"Before you depart, Granger, a warning. You are about to engage in negotiations with the Skiohra."

"Yes," he said, confirming what should have been highly classified information. "You know them?"

"No. No direct contact, that is. As I told you before, the Valarisi keeps the Concordat of Seven highly com-partmentalized. We knew them from a distance, but that is all. By reputation."

"Explain," said Granger.

"Each member of the Concordat of Seven has their strengths and weaknesses, as any race does. When the Va-larisi conquered my people, they used us for our ability to procure resources. We were experts at it. We had spread across thousands of lightyears, harvesting raw materials and energy from countless protostars, dead brown dwarf bodies, and asteroid fields. That infrastructure largely remains in place, and controlled by the Valarisi."

"You haven't retaken your former worlds? Just the homeworld?"

"We simply don't have the resources. All our fleets have been recalled to the homeworld, and there they stay, until we can be sure the Valarisi pose no threat. Otherwise, for us, it is extinction. A fear you know all too well. That is one of the strengths the Valarisi see in the Adanasi. In you. The Russians. You fight to survive, at all costs. But perhaps the greatest tool the Valarisi have absorbed and adapted from the Russians is the ability to deceive. Duplicity. Subterfuge."

"What about the Skiohra?"

A low grumble from Kharsa, which Granger interpreted as either wary anger, or fear, or deep concern. "The Skiohra. Great shipbuilders, of course. But fearsome warriors. You might not see it, looking at them. They are physically small. But what they lack in size the make up for with both formidable strength and technological prowess. When they attack, they come with deadly force. The antimatter beams? They are a Skiohra innovation, copied onto all our ships. They built the Valarisi's fleet, scaled down significantly from their own ship size. It is them you must be very careful of, Captain Granger."

"Do you suspect they're duplicitous? That they'll betray our truce?"

"Hard to say. We do not have contact with them. But regardless of whether they are controlled by the Swarm or not, if they desire it, they will destroy you. Before the Valarisi brought them into the Concordat, no fewer than five other races met their end at the hands of the Skiohra. It is perhaps from them that the Valarisi learned their ruthlessness. Their utter focus on destruction and mayhem, even as they pursue their main goal of unification."

"That sounds somewhat contradictory, don't you think?"

Kharsa held out another hand. The gesture must mean agreement, Granger supposed. "That is true. The Valarisi, or rather, the Concordat, is, fundamentally, a contradiction. You well know, Granger, that they consider us *friends*. They consider all life to be part of them—all life is destined to be united with them, subsumed into them, and ultimately, controlled by them. Is that friendship? You know the answer. They have absorbed from the Skiohra the ability—if one can call it that—to project overwhelming and terrifying force. Fortunately, they still lack much of the Skiohra's tactical abilities. You may also have noticed that the Valarisi ships, once set upon a world, are not the most innovative of fighters. That alone is our most significant advantage."

"And the others? What of the other four races? We know of you, the Swarm themselves, the Skiohra, and the Russians. There's three left."

"We know little of them. Two are races you have little to fear. They are on the other side of the galaxy, and will most likely keep to themselves, only coming to their own defense if attacked."

"Are they peaceful?"

"I wouldn't say that. Rather, they are artifacts. They were the first races the Valarisi conquered. From one, they learned interstellar travel, and nothing more. From the other, they absorbed their life cycle. The pattern of expansion, and rest. I think you're aware that the Valarisi were not supposed to have emerged from their lifecycle for another seventy-five of your years?"

"We'd worked that much out, but have no idea why."

"For that, you'll need to ask your own kind, Captain."

The Khorsky incident. He knew it. He'd suspected Russian involvement with the Swarm ever since that day, ten years ago. "The Russians?"

"I think you know the answer to that." Kharsa held out a hand one last time, indicating affirmation. "The question is, why?"

CHAPTER TWENTY-SIX

President's Stateroom, Frigate One
High Orbit, Earth

NORTON STALKED through the door, motioning to his marine guard to wait outside with the secret service officers. "Madam President," he said in greeting as he sat down. "I assume your meeting with Isaacson was fruitful?"

"Very. My team uploaded the new programs while he was sitting here."

"Does he suspect anything?"

She chuckled. "Oh, he suspects a *lot* of things. But his greatest suspicion will be his undoing. He suspects that I'm telling the truth. That I'm sending him out there to make a treaty with Malakhov, and that when he gets one I'll truly let him go."

"Why would he think that, Madam President?"

"Because he's a narcissist, General. He's at the center of his world. We—me, you, the rest of us—we only exist as shells of skin and flesh to him. We don't exist as human beings in his mind, at least, not self-aware, feeling individuals. He's a true psychopath. He can't empathize. He's incapable of it. And so, when I dangle the chance in front of him of being worshipped by the masses, of being in a position of true power, he can't resist."

Norton scowled. "Is he really that naive?"

Avery expression was clear: *are you kidding?* "General, this is *Eamon Isaacson* we're talking about. The oligarchic buffoon with the nice smile and boyish good looks who, in spite of his family, connections, wealth, and power managed to spend three whole years of his vice presidency trying to kill me with nothing to show for it except for making me late to a hair appointment once. The man wouldn't know his own dick from a hot dog if it was wrapped in a bun. His mind is so prodigiously empty that my technicians had to invent a new sensitivity setting for the inter-cranial monitoring system I put inside him," she said, patting the terminal nearby that gave her the readout of Isaacson's thoughts and mental state.

The general nodded. "Well sure, he's a few tines short of a pitchfork, but don't underestimate him, Madam President. Once Volodin got involved in the assassination attempts a few months ago he very nearly succeeded. Don't forget about *Interstellar One*. And the *Verso* and *Recto*," he added, referring to the president's former starliner and its two military escort frigates.

"Yes, Volodin," she sighed. "Did we ever grab a sample from him?"

"No, Ma'am. CIA is still working on it. But until they do I think it's safe to assume he's Swarm, like the rest of the Russian high command."

"Agreed." She sipped her coffee. "What's our ETA at Britannia?"

"Two hours. Zingano is already there. The *Hero of Earth* is on his way," he added with a snort of derision.

Avery gave him a sharp look. "You need to get over him, General. Focus your anger on the enemy, not our best weapon."

"I *am* focusing on the enemy, Madam President. I think it unwise to place so much trust in him. He's been compromised. By his own admission, for god's sake."

"And *that's* why I trust him, General. The very fact that he's so unsure and hesitant about his own loyalties, so anguished about once being under Swarm control—that alone tells me he's on our side. Plus, if he were still under Swarm control, the Swarm must be the worst tacticians in the galaxy. They could have destroyed Earth months ago. Earth, New Dublin, Marseilles, Johnson's World, Tyr ... they all would have fallen were it not for Granger. The man has spine, and even if he's rough around the edges and borderline insubordinate, so be it—he's the best we've got."

"Then god help us all," said Norton. "I don't trust him. Not since the Khorsky incident. Not since he demonstrated he's willing to disobey direct orders, *and* throw his superior officers under the bus during congressional questioning."

"This is not the playground, General. Just because he told on you once doesn't make him evil or the teacher's pet or unpopular or whatever your problem with him is. Man up, and win me this war without all the catfighting. Got it?" She'd started glaring at him. He glared back. It

129

was clear he detested being told by a civilian how to do
his job, but to his credit he nodded stiffly. "Yes, ma'am."

"What do you make of Granger's report?"

"Troubling. The Skiohra add a new wrinkle to the
patchwork of threats we face. Those super dreadnoughts are overwhelmingly powerful—the battle of
Indira is the first time any of our commanders has
defeated one—"

"And yet you *still* distrust Granger," she said derisive-
ly. "Go on."

Norton scowled again. "His initial report claims that
there are six of them—"

"Six? I thought IDF Intel said there were three. Four
tops."

"They could have lied to Granger. In either case, the
meeting they requested with Granger is tomorrow."

She swiveled her chair and stared out the window
at the numberless stars and empty interstellar space.
"We need something big, General. We're losing. Losing
badly. We need to do something daring. Completely unexpected. We can't continue to rely on outside events to
save us. Just like what I'm doing with Isaacson, we need
to do something that will result in our gain no matter
what the outcome of the tactic is. We've fought bravely,
we've fought desperately. It's time we started fighting
intelligently. Ruthlessly."

"You have something in mind, Madam President?"

"Of course I do. Send a meta-space message to General Palmer."

"Army chief?" said Norton in surprise. "Ground
troops?"

She nodded. "We're going to do something that, whatever the outcome, will leave us in a stronger position. Just like with Isaacson."

"I'm afraid I'm still not following on how allowing Isaacson to go out to Penumbra Three with Volodin will result in anything but headaches. Once outside your immediate control, there's no way he'll do what you want. He may not even return."

"Doesn't matter. I'm finally playing smart, General. He'll go out there, and whether he chooses to follow through with it or not, the programs I've uploaded into his implants will accomplish our goals."

"Are the scientists sure? Are they absolutely certain it will work?"

"Nothing is certain, General. This is a gamble. And in a game of chance like war, what else do we have?"

CHAPTER TWENTY-SEVEN

Bridge, ISS Warrior
High Orbit, Britannia

As soon as the *Warrior* q-jumped into the Britannia system, a message from Admiral Zingano appeared on Granger's terminal.

Meet me on the Victory, *as soon as you get in. Bring Proctor.*

"Diaz, you have the bridge. Commence resupply and general repair ops."

"Aye, aye, Captain."

He left the bridge and headed for Proctor's lab. It was on the way to the shuttle bay anyway, may as well tell her in person. Plus, it would let him get a peek at that singularity equipment she'd hauled over from the *Constitution*.

They'd only left the devastated York system two hours before, but she was spending every waking moment he didn't need her on the bridge stowed away in her lab. He suspected she slept there. With his permission, she'd reassigned a fifteen-person science team from fleet headquarters. Ostensibly, this was merely a satellite lab of IDF Science Division. A mobile lab that could be on the front line, the first to take data or draw samples or make observations. But in truth, Proctor was the main show. At least, that was what Granger suspected. He'd met the eggheads at IDF Science. All hat, no cattle, he believed the saying was. Most of the best scientific minds these days went to either medical or materials and weapons science.

"Tim. Good, you're here. Come look at this."

He sat down next to her at one of the molecular imaging scopes. She gestured to the eyepiece, and he looked inside.

"What am I looking at?"

"Not entirely sure, but I think I've isolated *three* separate strains of Swarm virus."

"Swarm matter comes in three flavors, huh?"

She selected the next sample and moved it into the scope's field of view. "Not quite. If you'll remember, a few months ago I discovered that Swarm matter itself was just a precursor to virus, not a virus itself. It can manufacture billions of different types of proteins, enzymes, and structures with so many functional groups that I don't even begin to know what to call them. But then I hit the Swarm matter with a focused meta-space field, and voila, virus. Highly transmissible, but not through the air, thank god. Mainly mucus membranes. Saliva, blood, etc."

"So, you're saying you want my dating history?" He deadpanned the joke as he watched the sample change yet again through the eyepiece when she dialed in the next one.

"Actually, the more research I do, the more I'm convinced you're completely safe. Recent evidence to the contrary be damned ... really, Tim, do you have to go around flaunting your newfound mutant telepathic skills? I'm sure it unnerved the hell out of the bridge crew."

He nodded, still peering at the sample. "You're right. I'll be more discreet."

"And speaking of the crew...." She paused, and out of the corner of his eye he saw her bite her lip, hesitating. "We've been going nonstop for four months, Tim. From the original *Constitution* crew, only about two thirds have survived. Lots of people are on their last leg."

"We're at war, Shelby," he said, still gazing at the virus.

"I know, Tim. But it wouldn't hurt to pay attention to their mental state on occasion. Rayna is on edge— she babies those engines like, well, her baby, and she hasn't gotten more than four hours of sleep a night since Lunar Base."

"She'll be fine. She's made of tougher stuff than you or I."

"I agree," said Proctor. "But even more troubling is Commander Pierce. He might hide it well, but he's been at breaking point for weeks. And now he's lost his family—"

"We've all lost family, Shelby."

"Not like him, Tim. Neither of us are married with kids."

"Other people have lost spouses and kids. They're still fighting."

"Barely, Tim, barely. They're barely fighting. You don't see them the rest of the time. I do. I'm the XO. When I'm not in here with the science team or up on the bridge, I'm down in the galley or on the rec deck." She sighed. "Look, all I'm saying is, maybe make some time to have a few heart to hearts with Pierce and Rayna and Prince and Diamond and Diaz. Make some appearances down on the rec deck. Let the crew know that you care."

"Caring's not my job, Shelby. Keeping us all alive is my job."

"Caring will help them stay alive, Tim. That makes it your job."

Dammit. She was right. *Again.* "Fine. I'll see what I can do. Now tell me what I'm looking at."

"You'll do fine, Tim, just like you have with everything else. We wouldn't be here if it weren't for you." She rested a hand on his arm—what was she doing? But rather than pull the arm away, he kept it there. Not that he had anything even approaching romantic inclinations—he simply didn't have the luxuries of time nor circumstance for that. It was just nice to have a friend. He'd missed Abraham Haws so damn much after he died during the battle of Earth—it was good to know he wasn't alone.

She cleared her throat and continued on. "But what we've got here are three strains. The first matches the ones I pulled from Hanrahan and Wyatt. Fishtail too. All of them were—and in Fishtail's case *is*—completely under Swarm control. The second is a similar virus, but it has far fewer functional groups than the first. The first had something like two thousand bonding possibilities. The second one has just eight."

"Sounds promising. Eight beats two thousand." He looked up. "Anyone we know have this?"

He nodded. "I took the liberty of getting access to a sample of Admiral Azbill's blood. Remember him?"

"The one who almost lost us the battle of New Dublin. How could I forget? How did you convince him?"

She shrugged suspiciously. "I had one of my new techs accidentally bump into him before she left Earth. Forged orders from Zingano. I'm sure he won't mind. Bill hates Azbill anyway."

Granger looked back into the scope. "You're telling me that John Azbill is infected with Swarm virus?"

"I'm calling it, the *backdoor virus*. It seems to lie inert. Dormant, in a person's body, unless activated by a very particular meta-space signal. The main virus responds to all kinds of signals. The backdoor virus only to a handful."

"Just like the functional groups, right?" he said, connecting the dots.

"Exactly. The backdoor virus can only perform a few functions, responding to only a few meta-space signals. I assume once we examine Admiral Littlefield's blood, it'll become pretty clear why Wellington Shipyards blew."

"You think the Swarm had backdoor entry into his mind? Influenced him, just enough, to destroy the ships?"

"I wouldn't be surprised. And the third," she said, bringing up the final sample on the scope. He peered inside.

"Anyone I know?"

"Yes. *You.*"

He pulled back to glance at her, frowning. "Mine's detectable?"

"Of course. Once I knew what to look for."

"And what are you looking for?"

"This sample matches the one I sent through the micro-singularity I made. The singularity inactivated the main virus. The *first* virus. But something about the shock of traversing a singularity pair disrupts most of the virus's response functionality. It only responds to one waveform of meta-space signal now. But this means that you were, at one point, infected with the full virus. It tells us that Lieutenant Volz is probably right— you were on the other side of his singularity, and you were acting for the Swarm."

He peered at it, with its hundreds of protrusions and cilia-like extensions and arms. One part of it was labeled with its molecular makeup. Words like *ketone* and *methyl* dominated the word-soup, but several stood out to him. "Lanthanum trioxide? Iridium? Thorium? Uranium 238?" He pulled back to glance nervously at her. "I've got uranium pumping through my blood, Shelby?"

"Oh, calm down. It's the non-radioactive isotope. And it's less than a femto-gram. You're fine. Better than stage ten thousand cancer, wouldn't you say?"

He shrugged. "So. We have proof. Actual physical data, that I'm not a crazy time-bomb waiting to go off." He stood up and stretched his neck after having hunched over to peer through the scope. "Maybe that will calm Norton down and half the top brass. I swear the've been calling for my head from day one. God help us all if Zingano ever kicks it."

Proctor shut the scope down and stowed the samples in her desk. "Proof? That's a stretch. It's compelling evidence, but still not proof. I doubt this will sway General Norton. Honestly, if it weren't for Avery, Norton would have had you tossed out an airlock by now."

Granger motioned to the door. "Come on. Zingano wants to see us. Let's keep him happy. I prefer to be on this side of the airlock."

They walked to the shuttle bay where a pilot stood outside his craft, waiting for them. Once inside with their restraints attached, the shuttle glided out the bay doors, revealing the deep blue atmosphere below, and, beyond that, green continents. Britannia was the most Earth-like planet humanity had settled so far—more Earth-like even than Earth—and one of the first habitable planets discovered. As such, its population was burgeoning, rapidly dwarfing the cradle of humanity. Since it was slightly less dense, but more massive, the land area was nearly twice as large as Earth, and hundreds of cities peppered the coastlines along every continent.

"Shelby," said Granger, after he'd sealed the hatch to the cockpit so they'd have another moment alone. "We need to be able to block the Swarm's meta-space signal. They do it. Since the first contact, four months ago, they've been doing it to us. They come in, and any ship within a certain range of a carrier loses meta-space comm until the carrier is neutralized. I want that. We need that."

She closed her eyes, as if running through the possibilities, modeling who-knows-what in that brain of hers, immediately trying to attack the problem. That was Proctor. She never blinked in the face of an insurmountable problem. She just ... figured things out, and then implemented solutions, managing people and resources so expertly that his superiors had wanted to snatch her away from him. Hell, her ship, the *ISS Chesapeake*, was nearly ready. It had taken longer than planned to retrofit it, but it'd be ready within weeks. Yet there were already rumblings at IDF to make her an admiral, skipping the captaincy altogether. Half the push was to spite Granger, sure, but half came from sheer admiration for her abilities. If she wasn't careful, she'd end up as head of IDF someday, and would have his condolences.

"And one more thing. We need to be able to shut down an active Swarm virus."

She opened her eyes. "We've been trying desperately. But we can't seem to move beyond the cure I injected into Wyatt. As it stands, the cure kills."

"What about something temporary? Don't cure, but block. If the cure kills, then forget it. Just focus on blocking. Or target just a few of those functional groups on the virus, and maybe give the victim a fighting chance. Let them fight Swarm control."

"Interesting." She turned to stare out the window as they approached the *Victory*, a carbon-copy replica of the *Warrior* and *Constitution*. "I hadn't thought to do a half-measure like that." She glanced over at him. "No offense."

"None taken. You never were one for half-measures."

"I'll work on it. Both ideas."

Zingano met them in the shuttle bay and immediately handed Proctor a small briefcase.

"What's this?"

"Blood."

She and Granger eyed each other. "Whose?" he said.

Zingano thumbed toward his chest. "For one, mine. As well as every other admiral and captain based here at Britannia. Turns out, Rear Admiral Littlefield committed suicide. Bullet straight though his own brain. *After* he self-destructed every antimatter bomb present at Wellington Station."

"You suspect the chain of command has been infiltrated?" said Granger.

"Well it obviously has. Look at you."

"And Admiral Azbill," added Proctor.

Zingano smirked. "Bastard. I'll send word to IDF CENTCOM at once. Have him detained."

Granger shook his head. "The Swarm doesn't know we can detect their influence. Maybe for now it would be best to allow them to think they've got us fooled?"

Zingano weighed the options. "For now. But this means our circle of trust is closing. We need to test me, General Norton, Admiral Chandrasekhar—my deputy."

"And Avery?" said Proctor.

Zingano shook his head. "If Avery's got it ... well, god help us all."

Proctor nodded in farewell and hefted the briefcase. The shuttle door closed behind her, and the craft took off, leaving Granger and Zingano alone.

"You know," Zingano said, thumbing in the direction of the departing shuttle, "she's been due at the *Chesapeake* for a few weeks now."

"I know. I just don't think it's wise to lose her right now."

"Lose her? Heh. Putting one of the best commanders in the fleet at the helm of one of the best ships isn't what I'd call *losing* her."

"Dammit, you know what I mean, Bill. Plus, something tells me we need her doing the science more than we need her doing the commanding."

"IDF Science is making steady progress. She's not the only one doing Swarm research, Tim."

"Yes, but she's the only one who knows what she's doing."

Zingano shrugged. "I wouldn't be surprised if Avery has a secret army of scientists somewhere working the problem. Wouldn't put it past her. She's got more pots boiling than anyone has a right to." He fished in his pocket for something, producing a small datapad. "Speaking of which, she's got something for us."

Granger examined the pad. "antimatter torpedoes?"

"The *Warrior* is to be outfitted with an entire bay of them, with launch capabilities tied in directly to the bridge. Seems she wants to avoid the fiasco that some mid-level tech caused with the antimatter bombs during the battle of Volari Three. No more remote control. All direct."

"But why?" asked Granger. "We tested a few of the prototypes in battle. They're just far too slow to do any good—the Swarm zaps them before they make it a hundred meters from the launch tubes."

He shrugged. "If you ask me, I think this has more to do with the Russians than the Swarm. We're not openly at war, officially, but I suspect we'll be ordered to carry out some bombing runs on the side. Make a few of their worlds pay for the betrayal. antimatter torpedoes would do just the trick."

Granger shook his head. "Good god. It's like we're as bad as the Swarm now. Bombing our own worlds just because their leaders are on the wrong side."

"War is messy, Tim. I thought you would have learned that by now."

"I guess my humanity doesn't wash off very easily," quipped Granger.

Zingano grunted. "I tend to agree with you, Tim. But either way, a team will install the equipment on your bridge while you're here at Britannia. Tomorrow morning Avery's called a top-level meeting. To discuss something she's calling Operation Ground War."

Granger raised an eyebrow. "Ground war? We don't have any Swarm worlds to target. Russian?"

Zingano shrugged. "No idea. I guess we'll find out tomorrow. All I'm told is it will be big."

"Big?"

"A game-changer."

CHAPTER TWENTY-EIGHT

Bridge, UESS Albright
High Orbit, Penumbra Three

"WE'VE ARRIVED in the Penumbra system, Mr. Vice President. Now approaching high orbit over Penumbra Three," said the navigator aboard the United Earth State Department Frigate *Albright*. The Russians would never have allowed an IDF military vessel to approach the planet, but Volodin assured him that if he arrived in a diplomatic ship he'd be permitted to dock at the main station.

"What are the scanners picking up?" said Isaacson, sitting in the captain's chair. The captain of the ship, an old freighter pilot who'd been drafted to serve in the State department during the war stood nearby, visibly glowering at the intrusion. But he didn't care what she thought.

"The planet is mostly water, filled with high concentrations of long chain proteins and amino acids, plus lots of other exotic organic material I don't recognize," said the officer manning the sensor station. "The star it orbits is actually a binary—a main-sequence orbiting a thirty stellar-mass black hole. But the hole itself is pretty quiet. No danger of it consuming the star for another billion years or so."

"Interesting," said Isaacson. "Are we in any danger?"

The captain chuckled, as if she was used to suffering through space-newbie questions. "They're actually quite common, relatively speaking. Galaxy has millions of black holes, and most of those are in binary or trinary star systems."

"Millions?"

"Black holes aren't some dangerous juggernauts that roam the galaxy eating up stars and planets and shit, Mr. Vice President. It's just a star, basically, but without the light. Just like you'd never dream of flying straight at the actual star right next to it, you wouldn't do the same with the black hole. And with either one, you can orbit it safely, just like Penumbra Three is doing. It doesn't just magically reach out and suck you in. We're perfectly safe, Mr. Isaacson."

"I knew that," Isaacson huffed. It was a lie, of course—he didn't know the first thing about galactic composition, much less black hole dynamics, but he hated it when people assumed he was an idiot.

"Of course, sir," she said, rolling her eyes. She turned back to the sensor station. "Any sign of the station, Wu-Jin?"

"Coming up on it now, ma'am. Looks like it used to be a major asteroid, but it's been caved out."

Isaacson nodded. He remembered Volodin telling him that, back when the Russians thought it was they who had the Swarm under their control and not the other way around: they'd had the Swarm cave out a large asteroid for them as a proof-of-principle that they could direct the Swarm to do simple tasks. Looks like they'd gone beyond simple tasks—the space station was massive. On the viewscreen, he saw dozens of Russian warships docked at the large rock, which here and there was dotted with patches of metal peeking out from the crater-marked surface, hinting at the vast, cavernous structure underneath the surface.

"Also reading thousands of ... well ... gravitational anomalies, I guess you could say," said Wu-Jin, the young man at sensors.

"Where?"

"Surrounding the station. Orbiting the planet. *Inside* the station. Really, they're scattered everywhere. There's what looks like a small moon beyond the station, in the middle of a debris field. The anomalies seem to be concentrated in that area."

The captain stood up and walked over to examine the monitor at the sensor station. "Thousands of them. Hmph. Steer clear, just in case." She turned back to Isaacson. "Now, you said you were expected? I don't like the thought of hanging around here with all those warships. The *UESS Albright* has no defensive capabilities, you know."

"Don't worry, Captain Hall, we're *perfectly safe*," he said, mimicking her earlier assurance, in the same tone, but with an added edge of condescension. "Ambassador Volodin assured me safe passage here for secret peace talks."

"You really think you can convince the Russians to end hostilities and join us against the Swarm?"

Isaacson rolled his eyes. "*That*, Captain Hall, is none of your business." He stood up and walked toward the comm station. "Open up a secure channel. Diplomatic code fifteen. Inform Ambassador Volodin that we've arrived."

A few moments later the young man at comm nodded. "Receiving confirmation. The ambassador sends his greetings. Says the Russian Premier is here waiting for you—"

"Malakhov himself is here?" said the captain with a sharp gasp of surprise.

"I told you, Captain Hall, it's none of your business." He noticed the fear in her eyes. "You can't talk peace with an empire without talking to the head," he added reassuringly. Not out of concern for her emotions, of course, but to make sure she carried on with the mission to deliver him to Penumbra Station.

The comm officer continued. "The premier is waiting. We're being given docking coordinates."

"Change course, Jill," the captain said to the navigator. "Intercept course with the Station. Line us up with the docking coordinates."

"Ma'am," began Wu-Jin. "There is a large debris field in between us and the Station. We'll need to adjust our orbit by about a hundred kilometers and rise up again before we attempt docking."

Captain Hall nodded. "Very well. Make the adjustments."

The navigator entered the instructions into the nav computer as Isaacson watched the planet grow larger on the viewscreen as they descended into a slightly deeper orbit.

"Oh my god," muttered Jill. "Emergency course change! Hold on—"

Everyone was thrown to starboard as the ship lurched to port with an acceleration that momentarily overcame the ship's inertial cancelers. "What the hell happened?" demanded the captain.

"Another debris field. Just came in out of nowhere. I'm sure we scanned that orbit before we descended."

The captain turned to the sensor officer. "Wu-Jin?"

He shook his head. "I scanned it, ma'am. It must have been moving fast enough that we didn't pick it up. Or maybe it was aligned between us and that first debris field such that our sensors couldn't distinguish the two."

"We're clear, Captain," said the navigator. "Resuming course."

The captain nodded. "Keep a full sensor sweep going. I don't want to run into anything else unexpected."

CHAPTER TWENTY-NINE

Volz knew he was dreaming again, but it was getting harder to distinguish dreams from waking life. Because he knew this wasn't just a dream. He'd been here. He'd done this. He was flying, racing other ships, hearing voices—impossible voices—and knew he had a terrible choice to make.

Both of them were friends. Both deserved life.

But fresh on his mind was Dogtown's fate. The Swarm had taken him. And Hanrahan. And the Doc. Made them do horrible, unspeakable things. The Swarm was coming—the ships were all around him now. He wouldn't let them get his friends. Not this time.

He made his choice.

The dream raced ahead, jumping to the point where he was floating, in space, just him in his pressurized flight suit, dangling at the end of his tow line. He reached, stretched—he knew there was a good chance he'd miss, and they'd both be lost forever.

But he grabbed on, keying in the emergency open code into the pad and yanked the hatch open.

She was dying. Bleeding and delirious and dying.

But there was still time to save her.

CHAPTER THIRTY

Sickbay, ISS Warrior
High Orbit, Britannia

HE AWOKE with a start. The dreams were becoming clearer, but it was still difficult to remember the specifics. When he came out of that singularity, holding Fishtail in his lap, trying to make the landing on the *Warrior's* fighter deck without passing out, he felt sure he knew what had happened.

Just like in the first waking moments after a dream—you know exactly what you dreamed about, all the details firmly in place. Sometimes you dream about a great idea—a new squadron maneuver, or a witty insult, but as soon as you reach for something to write it down, the idea fades, lost to haze and uncertainty. When he'd landed, he was certain of so many things—he'd *seen* the *Constitution*, and a large Swarm carrier—far larger than any he'd ever seen. And he'd heard Granger's voice. And another voice. An impossible voice.

That's where it started getting hazy. Why was it impossible? And was he even sure now that he'd heard Granger's voice? And he rescued Fishtail—that much he was sure of, but how had he done it? It was getting harder to separate dream from reality, even as he was remembering more while in the dreams. But somehow, he knew he'd been confronted with a terrible choice.

And there she was, the result of that terrible choice, laying in that sickbay bed. He rested his head against the window, standing vigil in his customary spot in the hallway outside sickbay, watching her breathe. Watching *it* breathe. Was she in there?

He walked into sickbay and stood next to the transparent enclosure that kept them all safe from Swarm infection. The monitor next to her bed indicated her heart beat, her breathing pattern, all the rest of her vital signs— many of which had edged beyond normal human ranges now that the Swarm virus roamed her system, changing her, for all intents and purposes making her stronger, healthier, better. But simultaneously stealing her away.

The machine also monitored the level of tranquilizer in her system, and he saw that it was getting low. He waited, waited, waited for the beeping that would commence once the sedative wore off completely. Glancing up, he saw that the nurses on duty were busy with other patients, but for the most part sickbay was empty.

His finger was poised and ready. The monitor beeped. With a quick tap of his finger—a trigger impulse learned from dozens of life-or-death battles with the Swarm—he switched off the sound. He looked up again. The nurses hadn't noticed the abortive beep.

Fishtail started to stir. Soon, her eyes fluttered, and she looked at him.

The smirk returned. The cold, dead, glassy eyes. *Shit. They really had her.*

"Ballsy, how nice of you to watch over me." Her tone was mocking. "I've seen you watching me. Almost every single day." Her voice lowered in register to a dark, mock-sultry tone. "Are you in love with me?"

He ignored her taunt. "We're going to destroy you, you know. You may as well give up now."

She rolled her eyes. "Please. You're weak. Disjointed. Scattered. One leader undermining the other, one nation scheming against the next. You lack focus. You have no purpose. For humans, it is every man for himself, at the expense of everyone else."

"You're wrong. We help each other. We lift each other up. If you knew Fishtail at all, you'd know that."

Her cold eyes drilled into him. "Help each other? Lift each other? You don't fool me, fly-boy. You help your own tribe. That's it. Humanity is tribal. Always has been, and left to its own primitive devices, it always will be. That's where *we* come in. We will elevate you. You can join the family, become our friends, and take your rightful place in the Concordat."

He leaned over the top of the enclosure. "We don't want a place in your Concordat. And you're wrong. We're not just tribal. We've come far from those days. We're—"

"Ballsy," she interrupted with a scoff, "humanity hasn't changed in a hundred thousand years. You're just a handful of spear-shaking jingoistic tribes that fight for that coveted spot on top of your tiny, insignificant hill. Believe me, we know. We've been watching. The Russians are trying to destroy you. You're trying to destroy the Russians. The Caliphate wants both governments destroyed, but they don't dare say it since your last war with them nearly destroyed them. And even in your own government, the factions squabble and fight, scheming to kill each other, obtain power over the other, each fighting for his own little group of like-minded and small-minded sycophants. The shrillest, most profane leaders win, and the reasonable, quiet voices are squashed. We are not like that, Ballsy. You'll see. It'll be better with us. In the Concordat, you'll know harmony. Unity. Peace and prosperity."

It was hard to argue with her. Mainly because she was right—he hated the political class. Even more, he hated the oligarchic plutocrat class that pretended to be above the political fray. Pretending to be outsiders when in fact they were the most deeply inculcated of all of them, protecting their money and their status. But the Swarm's solution was unthinkable. Forced freedom was no freedom.

"Look, Fishtail, let's change the subject."

"Yes, let's," she replied with another smirk.

"You remember that hair-raising maneuver you pulled? Against that Swarm turret? Spiraling in against who knows how many gees, knocking it out, and then flying through the fireball?"

"What of it?"

He tried to smile, genuinely. Maybe he could reach her, connect with her, if he could just punch through the Swarm cloud. Maybe reach her with real emotion.

"Child's play. You should see the shit I'm doing now. Unbelievable shit. They even changed my name from Ballsy to *Oh-my-godsey*." He threw in a wink for good measure. Something, anything to reach her.

But her face remained stoney.

"Look, Fishtail ... I—well, I did what you wanted. I took the ring to your parents. I played with Zack-Zack. Gave him a toy. Hugged him. I just wanted you to know that he's ok. And that he misses you. Terribly."

Her eyes changed. They widened. A brief, choking noise came from her throat, as if she was struggling to say something, but couldn't bring herself to say it. And, at the corner of her eye, he could swear he saw water building up. Not enough to form a tear.

But he'd reached her. He was sure of it.

In a moment, it was gone. The haughty face returned. "Ballsy, Ballsy, Ballsy. You've been a dear. A huge help, in fact. Where is the *Warrior* right now? On time for its appointment? I hope you don't run into any surprises while you're there."

Shit. He'd made a huge mistake, he realized now. Once awake, the Swarm not only could speak through her, but apparently they could track her. At least, that was the impression she was giving. He jabbed the monitor with his finger, and the beeping rang out, indicating the low sedative levels in her blood.

The closest nurse looked up, swore, and rushed over, punching buttons and controllers to get the next dose of tranquilizer queued up.

"See you soon, Ballsy," she said as her eyes fluttered shut.

CHAPTER THIRTY-ONE

Presidential Command Center, Frigate One
High Orbit, Britannia

"The plan is called Operation Ground War. After tomorrow, the Swarm will have learned that you don't mess with the marines," said President Avery. "This has gone on too long, gentlemen. It is time we take the initiative. We tried it, two months ago. Granger did a commendable job with that attempt. But even then, we were *reacting*. We thought we were taking the initiative, taking the fight to the enemy, but for all our efforts, they expected us. It is time we do something completely unexpected. Something so ballsy and dramatic, that it will change the course of the war, and deliver us a steaming pile of dead Swarm shit that we can flush away and get on with our lives."

She waved a hand toward General Norton and leaned back in her seat. He stood up and approached the front of the conference room, and on the table in front of him, a three dimensional holographic display of the Skiohra's super dreadnought bloomed from a single point in the air.

"Our target. Tomorrow, Captain Granger has a rendezvous scheduled with the Skiohra vessel." He turned to address Granger. "You will keep your appointment. You will play along, and squeeze as much intel out of them as you can. Stall for as much time as possible. Your tactical crew will begin intensive scanning of their vessel. The Skiohra will expect this, of course, as we expect they will do to you. When you have a lock on their position and drift vector, you will relay their precise coordinates and velocity to my fleet, point one lightyears away." He turned to a trim gray-haired man behind him. "Colonel Barnard?"

Barnard stepped in to replace Norton and waved the holographic display forward. It zoomed in on a section of the vast ship, and a tiny holographic image of a troop transport shimmered into place. A chart of data, troop numbers, and transport capabilities appeared next to it.

"Standing by in the boarding fleet will be roughly five thousand troop transports, each carrying one hundred and ninety-five marines. Five hundred thousand soldiers total, including logistics, engineers, and support crew. Analysis of the scans taken by the *ISS Warrior* during the last encounter have revealed that the Skiohra ship contains, at most, two hundred thousand life individual life readings. And it's most likely that a large portion of them are not soldiers, but crew members necessary to keep a ship that large functioning. If all goes well with the docking, we should outnumber them over two to one."

"That's a big *if*," said Granger, and the plan was already sending off alarm bells in his mind. Attack, when they didn't even know the Skiohra's true intentions?

"Your scans revealed that our docking ports are compatible with theirs, with minor adjustments." At a raised eyebrow from Granger, Colonel Barnard elaborated. "We will magnetically lock as best we can, then blow through their hatch doors with projectile-based explosive charges. When the door is breached, we'll throw out a cylindrical umbilical, made out of a special flexible composite material that will be shepherded by a cluster of miniature bots. The umbilical will expand, and the bots will automatically find the small crevices and notches where air continues to escape, and seal them, with double fail-safes if—"

"Get to the good part, Colonel," said Avery. "The part where we steal a big-ass ship and point it down the throat every Swarm fleet we detect."

"Ah—yes, ma'am. Took the words right out of my mouth. As the marines progress deck by deck, we'll rapidly take over their command and control structure, occupy key sections of the ship, and neutralize any effective opposition." The holographic display of the dreadnought expanded again, and thousands of bright red points erupted all along the edge of its hull spreading inward like an infection. "We anticipate that, with moderate losses, we can be in control of the entire ship within eight hours."

"Sounds like fun," said Admiral Zingano. "What's the catch?"

General Norton stepped forward again. "No catch. Using standard ship-based combat models, we calculate the risk of failure at twelve percent, which the president has deemed to be an acceptable level."

"Bullshit," said Granger.

Everyone turned to him. Avery's eyebrows rose high up on her forehead.

"My apologies, Madam President, my comment was not directed at you, rather to the modelers."

General Norton took a threatening step toward him, and looked like he was about to call for the marines at the door to escort him to the brig, but Avery waved him off. "Explain, Captain."

"First of all, we've never met a Skiohra in person. We don't know their capabilities, their strength, their speed, their ability to fight—everything about them is unknown, except for the fact that they're bipedal and can probably carry a gun."

Norton raised a hand. "Our modelers have taken every uncertainty into account. Even with all that not completely understood, due to our numbers and adapt-ability we calculate that one standard deviation of risk still gives us a seventy-five—"

"And furthermore," interrupted Granger, "you're forgetting one thing. We still have no idea if the Skiorha are truly liberated from the Swarm or not. If not, we've got a problem on our hands, don't we? Two hundred thousand highly trained warriors, all communicating with a hive mind that we can't disrupt or take down. It doesn't matter if you block their comm links—they'll still be able to coordinate the defense of their ship. And that's assuming we can even dock. For all we know, the Skiohra are playing us, and as soon as our transports show up, fifty Swarm carriers q-jump in and vaporize a tenth of our ground army in one fell swoop."

"Captain Granger, you will show some respect—"

"And, last, but certainly not least, there's the issue of the communication even if they *are* liberated from the Swarm. We've recently learned, after a little trial and error, that it is in fact possible for an individual to tap into the Swarm communication network, even after they've been liberated. We don't understand it, but we know this as fact."

"And how do we know that, Granger? Did you contact your Swarm buddies and tell them to meet you at York?" General Norton was back on his feet now, pointing angrily at him.

To everyone's surprise, Granger nodded. "As a matter of fact, I did."

Silence.

"To clarify, this was not until after they left. After the destruction of York. But when I got there, I summoned them back. And they came. I also, unwittingly, summoned the Dolmasi. And they came, too, saving our asses in the process, and giving me vital intel on the Skiohra in the process."

Norton turned to President Avery. "Ma'am, it's clear what we're dealing with. I've warned you about him time and again. We can't continue on with this security threat in our midst, I mean, for god's sake, he just admitted to communicating sensitive fleet movements to the Swarm!"

Avery eyed him suspiciously. "Captain? Anything else you'd like to say? I've half a mind to quarantine you for the duration of the war, until we either win, or the Swarm come in and break you out of prison and carry you home as a conquering hero."

"One more thing, Madam President. After the incident at Winchester Shipyards, you yourself authorized Commander Proctor to conduct blood tests on all senior level defense officials and officers. Obviously, she has only scratched the surface, but she's managed to test a number of them. Upwards of thirty captains, admirals, generals—the like. I'm afraid she has some disturbing news."

All eyes turned toward Commander Proctor. "It's preliminary, of course—"

Avery snorted. "Out with it."

"They tested positive for one particular form of the Swarm virus."

It took Avery a moment to put together what she said. "When you say *they*...."

"I mean, *they*. All of them. Every captain I test. Every admiral. I tested the late Rear Admiral Littlefield's blood too. Same thing. All of them carry the backdoor virus. And all of them, potentially, could be used against us like Littlefield."

CHAPTER THIRTY-TWO

The cold, bright lights glared overhead. He tried to focus on them, but fell asleep.

Then he was at the window. Just moments earlier, he knew he'd been laying down, staring at the light fixture above him, hearing the presence behind him. Someone stood there, just out of sight. Now, at the window, he couldn't take his eyes off the planet.

The planet—oh, the planet. It was beautiful. It was a deep green, dappled with lakes and clouds and it called to him—

No, wait. It was not green and full of lakes. It was a deep blue, bolder than water but not icy like the swirling clouds of Neptune. This was deeper and warmer and bluer, and alive.

The presence behind him had returned. It opened the door, then shut it firmly.

He didn't turn around, there was no need. The presence would speak, eventually. All he cared about was that planet. And beyond the planet....

CHAPTER THIRTY-THREE

Captain's Quarters, ISS Warrior
High Orbit, Britannia

GRANGER AWOKE with a start. He'd spent over an hour tossing and turning, worrying about Operation Ground War, and when he'd finally fallen asleep, the usual dream returned—what he was sure was the actual memory of being held by the Russians and Swarm four months ago.

His sheets were wet with sweat, but he'd kicked the blanket off and he was shivering. A glance at the clock told him he'd gotten three hours, and with a sigh he rolled over and heaved himself to his feet. Three hours was considered good sleep these days. A cold shower helped wake him up, and he was glad he finished quickly because as he finished dressing the door chimed.

"Come in," he grumbled.

The door slid open, and outside he could see the two marines standing guard, flanking Shelby Proctor, who poked her head in. "You dressed?"

"Barely. Come in." He waved her through and pulled up a chair.

"Sorry, no time to chit chat," she said, refusing the chair. "I just wanted to let you know ... well, I've got good news and bad news."

"Hit me," he said, applying shaving cream to his stubble. In the mirror, under the harsh light of the vanity, his eyes looked bruised, but that was just the deep shadows cast by his fatigue.

"The bad news—I'm sorry, Tim. I've tried everything I can think of and ran through test after test with my team, but we just can't seem to block the meta-space signal like the Swarm can. I'm sure we'll figure it out, but not yet."

He grumbled. That *was* bad news. Especially in light of her findings yesterday with the blood tests. With most of the admiralty and ship captains infected with the backdoor virus, he didn't know who he could trust. Zingano was clean, fortunately, but he couldn't very well quarantine every single one of his infected admirals and captains. The fleet would fall apart.

"Please tell me the good news makes up for it."

"It might. I had a few team members do some tests, and they've collaborated with their counterparts at IDF Science, and we might have a pharmacological solution. A temporary one, at least."

"Pharmacological? You're going to drug them all?" He ran the razor across his cheek, revealing clean, wrinkled skin underneath the stubble. Time to do something about those wrinkles, too. *Aw, hell, who am I kidding?*

"I am. It turns out that one of the many things the backdoor virus does when triggered is increase the levels of oxytocin and serotonin in the brain. Those influence our feelings of love, friendship, and similar bonding emotions, making it easier for the virus to do the rest of its work—influencing the host to do certain acts. But if we simply block those chemicals, suppress them, then the virus can't work as well as it usually does."

"So basically, make us all assholes. Great. You've tested this?" His face was clear, and he moved to his neck, drawing the razor carefully across his adam's apple.

"On a lieutenant at IDF Science that we discovered was infected. I first hit him with a meta-space signal that I suspect mimics a Swarm signal and he showed elevated levels of oxytocin and serotonin. Then, after I injected him with the suppressant, and hit him again with the signal, the levels stayed the same."

"Will it work?"

"No way to tell without an actual Swarm signal telling someone infected with the backdoor virus to go do something. At the very least, when the signal comes, the drug may give that person pause—may give them some moments of clarity where they realize what they're doing, and may even delay action long enough for someone else to see them and realize what's going on."

He finished up, and wiped his face clean. "Sounds risky, but I guess it's all we've got. Besides," he sat down and pulled his boots on, "risk is our calling card."

She followed him to the door when he stood up. "I've distributed the suppressant in pill form to the top brass, and every captain and commander in the fleet participating in Operation Ground War."

"Good. As hair-brained as that mission is, it won't do us any good to have captains with loose screws. Zingano messaged me—we're to leave in three hours. You all ready?"

"Well, after I spent the night working on the suppressant, I huddled with my science team to work on the quantum field versus relativistic gravitational field theory I mentioned to you earlier, and—"

He stopped and grabbed her arm. "Wait, Shelby, are you telling me you didn't sleep last night?" He looked into her face when she turned back to him. She looked exhausted, and almost as old as Granger, even though she was at least thirty years younger.

"I dozed in between test assays," she said defensively. "Look, Tim, sleep can wait. Don't worry, I had plenty of coffee. And a few energy pills. And then some more coffee. Believe me. I'm fine."

He let go of her arm and grumbled as they continued. "I'm warning you, one more day like this, and I swear I'll order you to bed." He'd been kidding, of course, but he softened his tone further. "I worry about you, Shelby. I worry you're working yourself too hard."

She smiled back at him. "I'm touched, Tim. Really I am. Now go show the same concern to the rest of the crew. They need it."

Before they walked on to the bridge, he gave a lazy salute to her. "Yes, ma'am."

CHAPTER THIRTY-FOUR

Bridge, ISS Warrior
Interstellar Space, 2.4 Lightyears From Sirius

"HOLD THE NEXT Q-JUMP," said Granger. "Distance?"

"Point one lightyears, sir," said Ensign Prince.

Doubt gnawed at him. He was uneasy with the plan put forth by President Avery and General Norton. He supposed he was hesitant because the plan was, put bluntly, utterly cutthroat. Take advantage of a potential friend, before they'd even determined the nature of that friend. Use them as a tool against the Swarm, before understanding them, or knowing anything about them.

And yet, Avery's logic was sound, in a brutal sort of way. The human race was on the brink. And when it came to the basic survival of the race—something to ensure that humans would always be found, somewhere, in the universe—they could stop at nothing, *nothing*, to prevent total annihilation. Even if betrayal meant giving up their souls in exchange for their lives.

But Granger didn't care about his life. And he supposed neither did Avery. They cared about the future. And yet, he had to be sure they weren't walking into a trap.

"Alter the final q-jump. Take us most of the way in, but stop ten million kilometers short. We need to see what's going on before we jump all the way in."

"Aye, aye, sir."

Moments later, the starfield on the viewscreen shifted again. "Full scan, Mr. Diamond. Optical, EM bands."

Ensign Diamond nodded. "At ten million kilometers, the light is about thirty seconds old, sir."

"Understood, Ensign."

The sensor crew performed the scans. "Picking up the super dreadnought, sir. Right at the rendezvous point."

"Is it alone?"

"Yes, sir."

Granger stroked his chin, finally smooth after that much-needed shave. His body was protesting the ungodly schedule, but there would always be time to sleep on the beach when this was all over. Or when he was dead, which, if he was being honest, was a more likely scenario.

"Extend scan to all directions. Anything?"

The sensor crew busied themselves, and a minute later Diamond shook his head. "Nothing, sir. We're in the middle of interstellar space—nothing around for lightyears. Or, at least light-minutes, that we can tell."

"Of course," said Granger, "there could be a Swarm fleet waiting just a light-day away. They could've been waiting there for half a day and we'd never know it."

"Yes, sir," agreed Diamond.

Granger paced a few times across the bridge before deciding. "Very well. Take us the rest of the way in. They've probably detected us by now. This was probably good for them too. Let them see from a distance that we're coming alone."

Even though a five-hundred thousand strong army is right behind us.

"Q-jump in five," said Ensign Prince.

Granger glanced back at the XO station, and caught Lieutenant Diaz's eye. The deputy XO nodded back, indicating his readiness. Proctor was holed up in her lab, continuing her cowboy research, as she called it, right up until the last minute before battle operations were scheduled to begin. Granger was supposed to keep the Skiohra talking for at least an hour.

The screen shifted one final time, revealing the immense mass and mind-boggling length of the super dreadnought. It stretched off into the distance, its hull mostly dark and invisible due to the lack of sunlight, except where it was punctuated by thousands of lit viewports.

"I just can't used to how massive that thing is," said Diaz.

Granger paused his pacing in the middle of the bridge. "And that there's six of them." He turned to tactical. "Begin scans. Go through the checklist provided by Colonel Barnard of things to confirm. Ship layout, atmospheric conditions, numbers of life signs, automation systems. All of it. I'll buy you as much time as possible."

"We're being hailed, sir," said Ensign Prucha.

"Patch it through."

The familiar form of Vice Imperator Scythia Krull filled the screen. One of her deputies stood nearby, another Skiohra woman who eyed Granger carefully. "Captain Granger. You've come. We were undecided of whether you would arrive or not."

"Of course I've come. We owe you a great debt. To not come would have been disrespectful to you."

And you have no idea how much we're about to disrespect you.

"Thank you, Captain Granger. I've summoned my people's ... I believe a close translation to your language would be ... Bonded Council of Seven—our leaders and matriarchs. They come for a council of war. A war to finally liberate all of the family from its master."

Granger raised an eyebrow. "You have your own Concordat of Seven?"

"The Swarm appropriated the social structure from us. Almost ten thousand years ago. They don't have original ideas, Captain: that is their failing. I've debated with my sisters as to whether they are truly alive or not. Living beings must create to survive. The Swarm does not create. It appropriates. It infests and corrupts and controls. And so when the Swarm came to our world, they took what they thought would serve them, and destroyed the rest."

"And yet here you are," said Granger. He weighed the benefits of putting up a skeptical front this early in the conversation. But he supposed if he had entered into the dialogue under the pretenses the Skiohra assumed, he'd most likely sound doubtful at first. Either way, Vice Imperator Krull took it in stride.

"Over the millennia, the Swarm permitted us to retain those parts of our culture they found useful. And now, finally, we have discovered the key to thwarting their control over us."

Granger was becoming more skeptical by the second. How could a species, after millennia of control by the Swarm, suddenly figure out a way to break free, when the Swarm's control extends so completely over every individual they dominate? How does one suddenly just spontaneously cast of complete control? Though, he remembered, the Dolmasi had already proven it was possible.

"And how is that? How was it that you suddenly found yourselves free of Swarm influence? To be honest, it seems suspect."

The Vice Imperator's face sagged a little. Granger couldn't even guess what the expression meant.

"Captain Granger, we are here, all of us, all of my people, because of *you*. What you see here, this ship—and five others like it—contains all that remains of the once proud race of the Skiohra. And we are here, and free, because of you."

CHAPTER THIRTY-FIVE

Russian Singularity Production Facility
High Orbit, Penumbra Three

"WELCOME TO PENUMBRA STATION, Eamon," said Ambassador Volodin at the exit of the docking hatch. The crew had been instructed to remain with the ship. Only Isaacson's secret service escort was allowed to accompany him, though Isaacson had half a mind to dismiss them, too, given their inability to protect him during the bombing attempt on his life two months ago and the fighter attack immediately after. The Swarm had penetrated deep into the bureaucracy: he couldn't even trust his security folks.

"Yuri, this is incredible. Is this the rock that was caved out by ... you know?"

"It is. Actual construction took far longer of course, but the excavation only took a few months." He started walking down the hallway. "Come. President Malakhov awaits."

Volodin took them deep into the complex, passing first by a series of bays holding equipment, large containers, and storage boxes which merged gradually into a section of the station devoted to experimental work, with gleaming high-tech labs, high energy power sources, and gas chambers, and then through what appeared to be the administrative area. The desks and cubicles gave way to a large expanse filled with what looked like natural light reflected in from Penumbra's sun. The space in the middle stretched up at least fifteen levels, each floor bordered by a railing that wrapped around the free expanse in the middle.

It wasn't crowded, but the occasional worker glanced their way, sometimes recognizing Isaacson with wide eyes, but no one stopped to say anything. Instead, Volodin led them to an elevator shaft near the central railing on their deck. Its walls were clear, and Isaacson felt a moment of vertigo as they shot up through the empty space.

At the very top, at least a hundred meters above the ground floor, they arrived at the executive offices. Lush carpeting covered parts of the floor of the atrium, and the fine surfaces of marble, granite, and crystal glittered everywhere. There was even a giant fish tank with coral and exotic, colorful fish that could be seen in another reception area nearby.

The walls were lined with giant pictures of President Malakhov in various, manly situations. One showed him at the top of Everest, shirtless, no oxygen tank in sight, looking through binoculars at some unseen sight off in the distance. Another was of him doing what looked like a pull-up, dangling two kilometers from the famous Wittingham suspension bridge connecting two towers in Britannia's capital city. Frame after frame boasted of his physical and testosterone-filled exploits, occasionally softened by a random image of him caressing a poor, wrinkled grandmother's face, or of the president sitting on a tree trunk in a picturesque setting, with children on his lap and surrounding him, fawning over him playfully, yet worshipfully. They reminded Isaacson of the old kitschy christian paintings of Jesus showing him in similar settings, all unbiblical, but inspiring to the simple people that needed such unrefined and simple-minded inspiration in their lives.

Oh, the poor masses. Taken in by such tripe and propaganda. And yet Isaacson couldn't help but admire it. *Crude, but brilliant*, he thought. *If I ever knock Avery off, I should keep something like this in mind....*

He automatically cringed, expecting the usual shock that accompanied the treasonous thoughts whenever they slipped through his guard. And sure enough his head felt like it contracted and twisted in pain. It only lasted a moment, but enough to make him sway and nearly lose his footing. Surely Avery couldn't monitor him from this far away, could she? Had the reaction simply become automatic on his part?

"Eamon? Are you all right?"

Isaacson waved him off. "Fine. Just dizzy from the ride up."

A door opened nearby. Isaacson expected to see a security contingent come in and escort him to the Russian President. But instead, just a single man walked through, dressed in a simple business suit with an old-fashioned red power tie, clicking along the marble floor in sensible but fashionable black shoes at a confident pace, gazing straight ahead toward Isaacson, his hand extended for a greeting.

President Malakhov.

CHAPTER THIRTY_SIX

Bridge, ISS Warrior
Interstellar Space, 2.4 Lightyears From Sirius

BECAUSE OF ME?

The words began to dawn on him, the gravity of their meaning finally weighing on him. "Are you telling me, that your ship is full of your entire society? Families? Children? This ship and the other five contain your entire civilization?"

"That is correct, Captain."

Which meant, he, Granger, was guilty of a genocide. Or at least, one seventh of a genocide. "And the ship I destroyed? Over Indira?"

"The *Harmony* held the once-great house of the Trell, fifth family of the Bonded Council of Seven. Vice Imperator Tyree Trell, my third cousin, was their matriarch."

Granger stumbled to his seat. "How many?"

"Excuse me, Captain?"

"How many of your people were on that ship? The *Harmony*?"

"It doesn't matter, Captain Granger. All that matters is that we make plans—"

Granger waved a hand dismissively. "It matters to me. How many?"

Vice Imperator Krull hesitated. "Approximately fifty billion."

The words pierced him to the core. He felt hollow, and distant, like he was observing the situation from above his head.

"But ... how is that possible? Our scans of your vessel reveal only around two hundred thousand life readings. Does your ship carry similar numbers?"

"As the *Harmony*? No. Not by far. We only number fourteen billion here in the House Krull on the *Benevolence*. The life readings you see are accurate, Granger. But most of us are mothers. And our Children are already born, inside us, waiting for us to give them the Exterior Life. I still hold over twenty-two thousand of my Children within me."

"Twenty-two *thousand*?" breathed Granger, incredulously. "How is that possible?"

"They are embryos, of course, and mostly composed of brain tissue. But even though they lack the rest of their bodies, each is a fully developed individual. A person."

"And they will all be born later? To the Exterior Life?"

"Some will. Most won't. Most will live the Interior Life for their whole existence. And they are linked to me. They are part of me. I hear their thoughts, their passions, their fears, and their hopes. Each of them has memory, and some are suited to remembering certain things, certain concepts. The majority of mine are suited to remembering communication, diplomacy, and relationships, and so I was chosen as Vice Imperator of my house at the moment of liberation."

"When was that? When were you liberated?"

"You don't know?" Her face stretched. Surprise? "This happened two days ago. During the battle over your world. Indira, you called it. One moment, we were thralls of the Valarisi. Then you came. You destroyed the *Harmony*, coming with such speed and destruction that it was ripped into pieces. Some of those pieces broke off and collided with singularities. Those were the first to be liberated, and from them, it spread. And through our meta-space link ... a good translation might be ... the Ligature, the effect spread to us all. Something about what you did saved us all, in spite of the ... unthinkable destruction."

Finally, Granger understood. The singularities. The Swarm matter. When those doomed Skiohra fell into the singularities, they emerged cleansed from the virus ... somewhere.

Just like Granger.

And, through the meta-space link, the effect spread to their whole race. Yet the Vice Imperator seemed to have no idea of how it actually happened.

Which was good—the fewer people who knew about the effect, the better. If they could keep the Swarm in the dark about their knowledge, it would give them more of a tactical advantage.

But he was still wary. Was this a trick? The Swarm could be feeding her what to say, drawing him in, gaining his trust, waiting for him to lower his guard.

Except ... why? The super dreadnought—the *Benevolence*—out-powered and out-gunned the *Warrior* over a thousand to one. If the Swarm wanted a shot at Granger, they didn't need subterfuge to get it. Just a scant minute in battle with that monstrosity of a ship would be enough to finish him off.

Unless—he paused, weighing the possibilities—the Swarm wanted something else.

CHAPTER THIRTY-SEVEN

Bridge, ISS Lincoln
Interstellar Space, 2.5 Lightyears From Sirius

"GENERAL NORTON, we're at one hour, sir."

The general paced the bridge of the *ISS Lincoln*, circling the captain's chair, where the ship's commander waited for the order that would take them into battle.

"And no word from Granger?"

"None," the comm officer replied. "No meta-space transmissions. Nothing except the constant background noise of Swarm communication, right at the frequencies and phase patterns you gave to us, sir."

Norton chuckled. *Ah, Commander Proctor. At least you're good for something besides being Granger's lapdog.*

He turned back to the Science Station, where Commander Alonso, IDF's Associate Chief Scientist and Director for Intra-Swarm Communication stood monitoring the progress of his science crew. "Commander, any progress in actually breaking down what they're saying out there?"

"No, sir. But we've definitely built off of Commander Proctor's work. She was never able to achieve such tight phase discrimination as we have."

"Overconfidence, Commander Alonso. Overconfidence, arrogance, and hubris. They're Granger's callsign. And it's rubbed off on his XO. If she would simply collaborate with IDF Science more instead of striking out on her own, trying to be the hero, thinking herself special and above the rules, we may have won this war months ago. But she's just like the Bricklayer. Just like Granger."

Commander Alonso shrugged. "She *has* given us perfectly good data. A little rough, some of her conclusions are a little hasty, but really, she's done ... adequate work...."

"And yet, if she had have collaborated with you, she'd be scanning for the backdoor virus frequency on the proper phase configuration. But it's obvious why she's not doing that. I don't believe it's that she *can't*, Commander. It's that she *won't*. She knows that if she lets that knowledge out, it'll compromise Granger's ability to work, because I'll catch him in the act. Talking with the Swarm. Collaborating. Just like he's doing now."

The science chief shuffled uncomfortably. "Well, sir, that is *one* interpretation of the data we're seeing...."

Norton turned to face him, threateningly. "What other valid interpretation is there? Granger is there, with the Swarm dreadnought. Talking to them, virus to virus. Mind to mind. Sharing our secrets. We clearly see the meta-space signals. What the hell are they doing if not that?"

Silence. Commander Alonso had no answer.

"Exactly." Norton turned to watch the viewscreen. The camera was panned wide, out toward their fleet. Thousands of troop carriers. Hundreds of thousands of marines. And half of Zingano's fleet, just in case.

And one other thing, floating just beyond the fleet.

None of the vessels were lit, except for a few visible viewports that cast pale, weak light on the hull around them. But even without the light, enough stars were blocked out to make it obvious that this was the largest fleet of ships IDF had ever assembled.

"Give them ten more minutes. If we don't hear from Granger by then, we're going in. Relay the orders to Zingano and Colonel Barnard."

Commander Alonso made one last attempt. "But General, if what you say is true, if you think Granger is being played by the Swarm, or even colluding with them, then he already knows our battle plans. Our secrets. Wouldn't it be wiser to pull back, regroup, and think this through?"

Norton snorted a harsh, short laugh. "Well, it's a good thing I didn't tell Granger all my secrets." He glowered at the scientist. "Stick to numbers and data, Commander. Leave the tactics to me."

CHAPTER THIRTY_EIGHT

Bridge, ISS Warrior
Interstellar Space, 2.4 Lightyears From Sirius

GRANGER GLANCED at the countdown timer. He'd promised General Norton and Admiral Zingano he'd keep
the Skiohra talking for at least an hour. Enough time for
Warrior to take more detailed scans of the dreadnought,
compare the readings to the originals and the projections
from Norton's tactical modeling crew, and pass any cor-
rections on to the invasion force when it finally arrived.

Thirty-nine minutes.

And now Granger wasn't even sure he wanted the invasion force to show up. The entire Skiohra civilization
was on those six remaining ships. Could he participate
in a genocide of a people that was itself in thrall to the
Swarm? Even if it meant deliverance of his own?

Too many questions. "Excuse me for one moment,
Vice Imperator."

He signaled to Ensign Prucha to mute, and thumbed the comm open to Proctor in her lab. "Have you been listening in, Shelby?"

"I have. In between assays. Very interesting. Do you believe them?"

"Don't know. I think you'd better get up here. I want some meta-space scans of the vicinity around their ship."

"I've been scanning. Absolutely silent, as far as I can tell. I'm no meta-space expert, of course, but—"

Granger glanced at the muted image of the Skiohra matriarch on the screen. "I'd still like you up here."

"On my way." The comm cut out. And Granger motioned to Prucha, and turned back to Krull. "Vice Imperator, I hope you can appreciate the difficult position I am in. On the one hand, I recognize the dire need we all have to trust each other and work together to defeat the Swarm. The Valarisi. And yet, you must realize that I need evidence that you are not under Swarm control. It would be foolish to put our fate in your hands by taking you at your word so blindly. Normally, a relationship like this would require time. But time is running out."

Krull held up both palms, revealing three long, delicate fingers and one beefier thumb on each hand. "The same is true for us, Granger. The Valarisi guard knowledge of the other friends very jealously. We know little of the Dolmasi, for instance, only that you've been in contact with them. We were there when they became friends and entered the Concordat of Seven, but have not seen them for thousands of years. Similarly, we know little of the Adanasi, the part of your race that has been made friends. We have no idea who among your crew are communing with the Valarisi, or even if you, Granger, are one with them. Through the Ligature I sense that you were once a friend, at least. But now?"

"I assure you, I'm not. But I propose a test, Vice Imperator. We have the ability to detect the presence of Swarm matter in the blood. I assume you have blood?"

"Of course."

At that moment Proctor walked through the doors. Granger waved her over. "My associate here has developed a test that will reveal whether one is under Swarm control or not. Will you submit to the test? I think just your blood will suffice. At the same time, you can watch us test my blood. Or, if you prefer, we can pass along the method and your scientists can try it themselves."

Proctors eyes widened almost imperceptibly. It was a huge gamble to tell the Skiohra that they'd figured out how to detect Swarm influence. If the Swarm were playing them, they were giving up one of the few intel advantages they had.

"We accept," said Vice Imperator Krull. "And seeing the results from your lab will be sufficient, if you'll permit me to verify them. I will board a shuttle immediately. Shall we meet shuttle to shuttle, or shall I come aboard your ship?"

Granger had no idea what she meant by *verify*, but he nodded his agreement. "Meet me in our shuttle bay as soon as possible—my superiors have given me a deadline that I must adhere to, or there may be unpleasant consequences. We'll relay coordinates momentarily."

He inclined his head toward Ensign Prucha, who began entering in the shuttle bay coordinates into the comm to send to the Skiohra.

The screen flickered off. Proctor raised her eyebrow. "Risky."

"I know."

"But I think they're telling the truth."

"Me too." He motioned toward the doors. "Let's go." He glanced over at the deputy XO. "Have Sergeant Washington set up in the shuttle bay. Guards at the doors, and at least twenty more in the hallway beyond. And sharpshooters. But tell him to keep it discreet."

"Aye, aye, sir," said Diaz.

As they walked out the doors he called back to the tactical station. "Time, Mr. Diamond?"

"Forty-five minutes, sir."

"Damn," he mumbled. "We're cutting this a little too close."

CHAPTER THIRTY-NINE

Shuttle Bay, ISS Warrior
Interstellar Space, 2.4 Lightyears From Sirius

THEY RACED TO the shuttle bay, making a quick detour
to Proctor's lab to pick up a few sample vials and a
blood draw meta-syringe. When they arrived, the Skiohra shuttle was already passing through the force field
holding the air in. Granger noticed three men, including
Sergeant Washington, perched up on the second level walkways spanning the perimeter of the room. No
weapons were visible, but if they were doing their job
they could get set up for a shot within two seconds.

The shuttle landed—it was almost like a miniature
version of a Swarm carrier—and as the ramp descended Vice Imperator Krull didn't even wait for it to lock
into place as she quickly descended. She was short, no
more than five feet, but walked almost disconcertingly
fast for such a small person.

The viewscreen hadn't done her justice. Though lithe and thin, a powerful muscle structure flexed noticeably behind her taut, faintly blue-beige skin. He began to wonder if perhaps Vishgane Kharsa was right. These people didn't sound like vicious warriors, and they didn't look it, but watching Krull's gait and the way she carried herself, he started to suspect that she could be deadly in a close quarters fight.

"Granger." She outstretched her two hands out above her shoulders and to the side, palms toward the two wall. A greeting. He mirrored the motion back to her. She responded with an unexpected laugh. How interesting—facial expressions, gestures, these all varied, but the laugh seemed to be universal. At least for humans, Dolmasi, and Skiohra. "You honor me by returning my greeting after what you suppose is our custom. But among us, the male reaches forward, not to the side."

"My apologies," said Granger, bring his arms forward toward her.

"No need to apologize. No need even to honor our customs. If I knew yours I would participate."

"A simple handshake is customary," he said, before pausing, thinking better of it. He remembered what happened the last time he'd shaken hands with an alien he'd just met. Vishgane Kharsa had implanted the false memory of seeing the Swarm homeworld, leading to near disaster.

Her hands, still extended to the side, started to quiver. Realizing what she was doing—shaking her hands—he grunted a laugh as well. "No, I mean we clasp each other's hands. But that can wait. Until we know each other better."

"I understand." She lowered her arms.

He waved Proctor forward. "My second in command. Shelby Proctor." They nodded at each other.

"I and all my Children greet you both, and thank you."

"Your Children," began Proctor. "You say they are alive, already individuals. Are they self aware? Conscious?"

"Of course," Krull replied. "I know them all, individually. If they ever attain the Exterior Life their knowledge and personalities will develop further as they grow. But they are intelligent. I wouldn't be a fraction of what I am now without them. Most of them will never see the light of the Exterior Life, but the Interior Life is a full and beautiful one."

"You rely on them?" asked Proctor.

"Yes. I store memories in them. I confer with them. They help me reason and make judgements and work out problems. Even under Valarisi control. In a sense, being under their control was almost second nature, as it was just one more voice in my mind, albeit an all-powerful, overriding voice that I could not disobey. And now, for the first time in millenia, my thoughts are free of them. Just me and my Children in here now," she said, touching her head.

"If you'll excuse the question, Vice Imperator, exactly how old are you?"

"Measured in the time cycle of our home ships, one thousand and seven. Seven hundred and fifty of your years. I am one of the oldest. My Children are on every ship. Thousands of them. I've mated with tens of thousands."

Granger and Proctor exchanged significant, uncomfortable glances. But it was fascinating. He had no idea that a species could be so vastly different from themselves, though he supposed it shouldn't come as a surprise, given the extreme biodiversity even on Earth. He wanted to interview her for hours. Days. Her people and her culture were beginning to be beautiful to him.

But time was running out.

"Vice Imperator, if you'll permit Commander Proctor to extract a sample," he said, indicating the meta-syringe Proctor held. Krull held out a long arm, the muscles rippling subtly beneath the skin. No sagging, no wrinkles. Granger wondered just how old an individual Skiohra could get. Or how age manifested itself in one of their bodies. So many questions. So much to learn, and so little time.

The sample vial filled quickly with blood, which, surprisingly to Granger, came out just as red as his. For some reason he was expecting it to be blue, or green, or some other alien color. Red. Just like him. Even Skiohra blood flowed red.

Proctor nodded. "All done. I can get this analyzed in minutes." She pulled out a datapad, brought up a display, and handed it to Krull. "Here are the results of Granger's test. I'm sure the two of you can discuss them further. Now, if you'll both excuse me...."

She raced out of the shuttle bay, toward her lab. Granger turned back to Krull. "As you can see, the virus is still present in my blood, but it has been effectively deactivated. I can still use it to ... how did you put it ... use the Ligature? But otherwise it has no sway over me."

Krull examined the data displayed on the chart. She appeared to have a decent grasp of English, but he wondered how much of the written language she understood. "I see," she said.

"You mentioned something about verification?"

"Yes. Through the Ligature. I can do it mind-to-mind, but physical contact is more precise. All I need is your hand."

He was worried about this. She wanted to do exactly what Kharsa had done. Get in his head, sift around. Could she alter memories too? Could she control him? He hesitated.

She seemed to sense his uneasiness. "You have nothing to fear. I can not control you. I can not even control my own Children. Even the very youngest, at just ninety cycles, has such a ferocious will of his own that I can not even say good morning to him without getting an ear-full, so I'm sure an old man like you is in no danger of influence from me."

The youngest is *ninety*? He decided not to tell her he was sixty-five, and had nearly died four months ago.

"Is touch necessary?"

"No. I can communicate with all my Exterior Children through the Ligature—the one and only good thing that has come from our subservience to the Valarisi. And I can communicate with you as well, through the Ligature. But the Interior Children, since they are in physical contact with me, I have immediate access to whatever they want to show me. And while in that communion, one can see through deception. Such it is with the Valarisi—there is no lying to them. So it is with my Children. If they attempt to deceive, I know it." She laughed. Somehow, despite her alien appearance, the laugh was endearing. "A mother always knows. And while we commune, in essence, you will be my child. You can not lie to me. And I will be yours. I cannot lie to you."

There was no other way. At least, no other timely way. He was sure the hour had elapsed already. Norton and the invasion force would be here soon. With a start, he extended his hand to her. She reached out to his. They clasped each other.

He felt her. There, inside of him. Not as an intrusive presence, but almost as a neighbor, standing patiently on the front porch of his mind. At first he didn't know what to do, but as she was just standing there, waiting, expectantly, making no effort to in any way push herself into his thoughts, he projected his own thoughts out at her.

With some effort, he brought up the image of Proctor extracting a sample of blood from his arm. She collected the vial and inserted it into the imaging scope in her lab. He wasn't there for the actual analysis, and had no mental imagery to project to Krull of that process, but he remembered Proctor summoning him back and showing him the results. The virus, broken down and inactivated. He projected his relief that he felt as Proctor explained that the Swarm had no influence over him, that whatever had happened to the virus had made it completely benign. Harmless, but still useful."

With another jerk, he stopped. The explanation of *why* the virus was inactive had started to come to his remembrance, and so he shut it down. There was still no reason he needed to let that slip. That traversing a quantum singularity somehow had the effect of neutralizing Swarm virus. He let his hand drop.

"I understand," she said slowly—he wasn't sure if she'd noticed his unwillingness to share everything. "You speak the truth. You truly fight the Valarisi, and your blood is cleansed of them. But there is some knowledge you deliberately withhold from me." She looked down at her feet, as if considering her words. "No matter. I feel your intent. It is not to harm. It is to save." She held her arms out to the side, as she did in greeting. "I trust you, Captain Granger."

He mirrored the motion, before remembering what she'd said earlier, and brought his arms forward as was customary for the males in her race. She laughed again. "No, you had it right the first time. Arms forward for greeting in a male. Arms to the side for expressions of...."

"Friendship?" he asked, as she trailed off.

"Family," she said. "With the Valarisi, we were friends. Or at least their corrupted version of that. But with you, you are family." She paused, and closed her eyes momentarily. "I've communicated this to the other matriarchs and vice imperators of the Bonded Council of Seven. It is agreed. We will wage war alongside you. For freedom, and for family."

Granger smiled. It was time to send a meta-space signal out to the fleet. With much better news than he'd hoped.

Proctor's voice cut through the silence in the shuttle bay. "Captain, just finished the analysis. She's clean. Has

a similar inactive virus that you do. Slightly different—
that's to be expected since the Skiohra biology is not
the same as ours, but it's clearly inactive."

"Any idea why it's different?"

"Probably a species difference. I mean, she's Skiohra
and you're human. I'd expect difference in the way the
Swarm virus interacts with—"

Her voice cut out abruptly, replaced by Lieutenant
Diaz's. "Captain! The fleet has arrived, with no warning.
And they've started firing on the dreadnought."

CHAPTER FORTY

Executive Command Center, Russian Singularity Production Facility
High Orbit, Penumbra Three

"MR. VICE PRESIDENT, it is good to finally meet you,"
said President Malakhov. Isaacson noticed that his
handshake was frighteningly firm, though not painfully
so. After seeing all the propaganda, news vids, and listening in on all the intelligence reports from IDF intel
on the Russian strongman, it was almost surreal to see
him there in person, as a real flesh and blood individual.
Someone real, and not a rumor, a caricature, or a terror,
as popular culture in the west tended to depict the man.
His accent was obvious, but not too thick. He clearly
had a good command of English.

"Mr. Malakhov, the feeling is mutual. President Avery
sends her ... regards," he chose his words carefully.

"I'm sure." Malakhov turned to Volodin. "That will
be all, Yuri."

Isaacson felt Volodin stiffen next to him. He clearly hadn't expected to be dismissed—that was not part of the plan. They'd discussed the possibilities for how the meeting could play out. Isaacson wasn't quite sure how they'd get the President into a vulnerable enough position to take him out, and they'd rehearsed various scenarios together.

Being alone with the President was not one of them.

"But, Mr. President, I thought we were going to discuss—"

Malakhov waved him off. "Later." He pointed to the elevator. "Go. Now."

Uneasily, Volodin edged toward the door, glancing tentatively at Isaacson, who wanted to protest, to say something to keep the ambassador there.

"Mr. Isaacson, you'll notice I have no security here with me. I have no need of it. Neither do you. Your men will wait downstairs with Mr. Volodin."

Red flags were going off in Isaacson's mind. The secret service chief protested. "Sir, we're not going to leave you here alone with Mr. Malakhov."

Malakhov turned toward Isaacson. The expression on his face was clear: *are you a man, or not?* The look on his face, his stance, his upturned eyebrow, they all said the same thing, daring him to dismiss the guards, questioning his resolve. His manhood. Dammit, Isaacson wasn't going to stand for that.

"No, no I'll be fine. I'm perfectly safe here. Wait downstairs."

"But—"

"Go!" shouted Isaacson, pointing toward the elevator door where Volodin waited. He was not going to be second-guessed, have his authority questioned in front of the Russian president, who seemed more than in control of his own situation. He could be in control too, dammit.

The secret service guards reluctantly filed into the elevator, and a few seconds later, he was alone with President Malakhov, who, to Isaacson's surprise, burst out into a boisterous laugh. "Ha! Did you see the looks on their faces? Sycophants. Pretenders and attention-seekers. All of them. Including good old Yuri. Come on, Mr. Isaacson, let's go discuss matters in my observatory."

He started walking toward the door he'd come out of, though Isaacson stayed put, confused.

Malakhov paused and looked back. "You don't trust me, do you, Mr. Isaacson?"

"I don't *know* you, Mr. Malakhov. Plus, we're at war. How can I possibly trust—"

"Because, Eamon—can I call you Eamon? Because, my estimable opponent, even though we are at war—I do acknowledge that—we are actually on the same side, though you might not realize it."

"Oh?" Isaacson raised an eyebrow and crossed his arms. "How so?"

Malakhov paced back to him and put an arm around his shoulders, guiding him toward the door. "Because, we are both human. We both fight to survive. Individually, nationally, and, more importantly, as a race. A civilization."

"You fight the Swarm?"

"I use the Swarm, Eamon. I'm not to be controlled or taken advantage of by some race of vile raw sewage. I shit more intelligent sludge than the Swarm. I've played for fools many people in my career, Eamon. The United Earth Senate, President Avery, her predecessor, all the governors of all the United Earth worlds and the worlds of the Confederation. But the ones I've played the worst are the Swarm. My finest accomplishment. The pinnacle of my career."

Isaacson rolled his eyes, even as he allowed himself to be led through the door into a large room that looked more like a science laboratory than an office or ... what had Malakhov called it ... an observatory? "Please, Mr. Malakhov. You're not claiming to have been on our side all along, are you? Just pretending to be allied with the Swarm so you can stab them in the back when the stakes are at their highest? I'm a little smarter than that."

"*Your* side? You and Avery and the United Earth government and senate? No. I'm not on *that* side. But I'm on humanity's side. I'm humanity's best friend."

Isaacson stopped midstride. "I've heard *that* language before. The Swarm wants to make *friends* of us all. You're one of them, aren't you? You've been infected. I'm talking to the Swarm right now."

Malakhov laughed.

And laughed.

"Eamon, my man, I'm the one of the few people you've talked to in the last few days that is *not* infected by the Swarm."

Isaacson's jaw hung upen. "Yuri?"

"Swarm," confirmed Malakhov.

"My secret service detail?"

"Swarm. Though in their case they've been infected with the backdoor version." He pointed up to an electronic device on the ceiling, and another one above the door frame. "Meta-space detection grid. No Swarm communication happens anywhere on this station without my knowing about it. I read your security detail's Swarm control the moment they stepped on the station. Not day-to-day control, but should it be necessary, the backdoor can be ... potent. As you no doubt discovered with the incident at Wellington station."

The implications ran through Isaacson's mind as he connected the dots. "So ... the assassination attempt. In Moscow, with the car—"

"Obviously set up by your own men. Not consciously, of course. But it's true. And the incident with the two fighters over North America on your return trip the next day—also due to your men. Same with Avery's detail, though at least she had the sense to turn most of her security over to the military. And not *all* of the secret service is compromised. But enough. Believe me, the Swarm wants nothing more than to decapitate both governments."

Isaacson squinted suspiciously at the other man. "How do you know all this? How can I believe you?"

"The main reason is because it makes sense, and you trust your gut," said Malakhov, as he strode confidently over to a table with a large opaque enclosure resting on top. "You're a politician, Eamon. A good one. And very bright. You have a good sense for these kinds of things, and you know I'm telling the truth." The enclosure had a few electronic controls on it, and Malakhov pressed a few of the buttons, presenting his finger for an identity scan. "But another reason is this."

One half of the enclosure turned transparent, almost as clear as glass. Resting underneath it was a naked man. He looked to be awake, but his stare was constant and glassy as if he were in a daze. Metal rods and electrodes stuck out of his head, and out of his half-open mouth trailed an oxygen tube.

"Who is he?"

Malakhov saluted toward the prone man behind the enclosure, to Isaacson's surprise. "He's a patriot. Warrant Officer Igor Pavlenko. He gave his life to the motherland ... though," Malakhov glanced up at Isaacson with a grave look on his face, "he did not know it at the time. Thought he was volunteering for a special mission. He wasn't aware that mission would be to lie here for ten years."

Isaacson, seeing the forest of electrodes, tubes, and rods protruding from the skull, started to understand, putting the pieces together. "This is his *mission?*" He wasn't sure whether to feel horror or awe. He supposed he felt both. "He's your Swarm experiment. See how the Swarm matter affects the body. You learned how to control it from him."

Malakhov shook his head. "No. Not quite. By the time he volunteered for this mission, I already knew roughly how the Swarm communicated and controlled. No, Warrant Officer Pavlenko's mission was not to be an experiment, but to be a backdoor into the Swarm itself. He's fully infected. Fully under Swarm control. But

I've had him heavily sedated, and tied in electronically directly to his brain stem, the temporary lobe, and the hippocampus. Through those areas I not only have him immobilized and disabled, but I can decode what he hears through his Swarm link, and how his brain interprets those signals."

"You're spying on the Swarm? Why do they let you do this?" Isaacson was completely befuddled. He knew that Malakhov was either playing him—but why?—or feeding him false information that he would take back to Avery, or ... maybe, just maybe ... he was telling the truth. A politician? And one at war, no less, giving the truth to his enemy?

"I can see the doubt in your eyes, Mr. Isaacson. You don't trust me, and I understand that. What I tell you is true, and I'll tell you why it is true. I make no secret of my aspirations for my culture, my people. I tell you this freely. I do not wish the west to fall, but I want to come out of this war on top and the west humbled and willing to finally accept friendship with my people, not as superiors, but as equals. And so I tell you the truth because, though lies can be potent tools, the truth is the most powerful weapon of all."

Isaacson stood up straight from having stooped to peer at the glassy-eyed Russian soldier. "And, Mr. President? What is the truth? Why have you brought me here today?"

"Mr. Vice President, my aim is not to control the Swarm. Not to use them to cow and intimidate the west. My goal, for my entire career, has been to destroy them, once and for all."

CHAPTER FORTY-ONE

Shuttle Bay, ISS Warrior
Interstellar Space, 2.4 Lightyears From Sirius

GRANGER DASHED to the control station in the shuttle bay and brought up a tactical display on the main panel. *Damn.* Norton hadn't just brought his boarding ships and a few escort cruisers, he'd brought an entire fleet. Admiral Zingano's by the looks of it, as the *Victory* hovered in the background. The cruisers were already pounding certain points on the dreadnought, softening it up for the boarding parties.

"Dammit," he muttered, and set up a commlink to the *Victory*. "Bill, what the hell is going on? I didn't send a signal to attack!"

Zingano's voice sounded out from the panel. "Sorry, Tim. General Norton has operational authority for the mission, by order of the president."

"But Bill, the Skiohra are the real deal. They're *allies*. I'm absolutely sure of it."

A new voice blasted over the speaker, interrupting a response from Zingano. "That's what they might want us to believe, Granger. And it might be what *you* want us to believe. But we've been monitoring meta-space transmissions from you for the past hour, and it's clear you're collaborating with them."

Meta-space transmissions? He spun around to Krull. "Are you in contact with the Swarm? Don't lie to me...."

Her eyes were closed. All she said was, "My Children. They are dying." The deep blue eyes opened. "We are betrayed. Are you prepared for the full force and fury and the combined might of the Skiohra?" There was a new menace to her voice.

The four marines by the door readied their assault rifles. Granger held out a hand to restrain them. "Wait. Not until she poses a threat." He regarded her—the depth and wisdom in her eyes was gone. Replaced by a deadly fury. "I can convince them to stop. But the meta-space communication—I need to know. Was it you? Are you still with the Swarm?"

When she didn't immediately answer, he strode over to her and reached out to grasp her hand. "Tell me!" he said, gripping her hand tightly until his own skin turned white.

He gasped. A rush, a flood of emotion washed over him. He felt the pain at a billion deaths. Thousands more were dying by the second, and he felt every one of them. The image, the thought, the impression floated up before his eyes, though he saw nothing, but he knew it all the same. She was telling the truth. It was undeniable. He knew Swarm—he knew what the felt like, their heartless, almost mechanical will to dominate, and this was not it.

He jerked his hand away, and even after physical contact was broken he could still feel the terror of billions. "They're dying."

The rage in her eyes smoldered. "I know. Because I trusted you."

He dashed back to the terminal and re-established the link to Zingano. "Bill, I'm telling you, this is madness. These people are our allies. They can help us win this goddamned war! Hold your fire!"

Zingano's heavy sigh greeted him. "Tim, listen. We knew this was a possibility. But Avery decided that regardless, we would take their ship, and point it straight at the heart of the Swarm fleet—"

"But we don't even know where that heart is! Dammit, Bill, can't you see that? She's wrong on this one."

Norton's voice interrupted again. "You're too late, Granger. Save it. The Swarm just showed up. In force. Now let's get this show on the road. Direct the *Warrior* to run interference against the Swarm fleet for our boarding ships. We've got one shot at this, Granger. Don't blow it. And if you disobey orders, I've given Lieutenant Diaz authority to put a bullet in your head and command the *Warrior* himself."

Granger glanced at the tactical display and saw a fleet of Swarm carriers converging on their position. At least fifty. *Shit—they knew we were here.* He turned to the marines. "Restrain her," he said, reluctantly.

The four men bounded forward. Another group of marines burst out of the service room door nearby. As the first dove for Krull, she, somehow, caught him in midair, and despite being half his size flung him around into the second group of marines. Three more men tackled her. With a yell she elbowed one in the face, knocking him cold. Another she kicked with a free foot, sending him flying up into the faces of two more marines.

Her strength was incredible—Kharsa wasn't exaggerating. In a way, she looked and sounded like a mother bear, cornered with her cubs, as she bellowed and shouted, struggling against the crowd of soldiers attempting to take her down. Two more went down, unconscious. A third flew across the room into a wall, blood trickling from his nose.

Finally, they managed to get her arms behind her back and manacled together, using not one but two sets of heavy composite-steel handcuffs. Another pair clamped around her ankles. One last marine went down as she snapped her spine backward and whipped the back of her head into the chest of the man, tossing him back five meters, clutching his chest.

"Keep her there in the service room," he said, pointing to the open door to the small room off the shuttle bay. "Twenty men are to guard her until I say otherwise."

The soldiers saluted, and, satisfied she wouldn't escape, rushed to the bridge.

Proctor was in his chair, directing the initial maneuvers. The battle was just spinning up. Zingano and his fleet had already taken out a few carriers, under the cover of the dreadnought, which was firing at Swarm targets seemingly at random—it seems their main attention was drawn inwards, as hundreds of marine transports had already docked. In short, it was one, giant mess.

But Granger was in the middle of it. And he had a duty to perform.

Save the fleet. Save the dreadnought.

Save humanity's chances against the Swarm.

And, somehow, not participate in a genocide.

CHAPTER FORTY-TWO

X-25 Fighter Cockpit
Interstellar Space, 2.4 Lightyears From Sirius

VOLZ LOOPED AROUND a small group of Swarm fighters, firing at the ones he could manage to line up in his sights and leaving the stragglers to Pew Pew and Fodder who were backing him up. At the center of the cloud, flying slowly enough to encourage the cloud of bogeys to track her, but fast enough to just barely avoid getting hit by the overwhelming fire, Spacechamp zipped around like lightning, distracting the enemy while Volz and the two brothers took out her pursuers.

"Next time, you're the bait, Ballsy," she yelled through the headset. When the last of the fighters disappeared in a puff of debris and goo, she shot forward and leapt into the next horde of oncoming Swarm ships.

"Hey, Ballsy," Fodder's voice blared in his ear, "any word on when we get to dump our bricks? Getting tricky to maneuver with all this mass."

He veered left to avoid a formation of bogeys that was flying to intercept them and looped around to take them out but they scattered before he could squeeze off a shot. "There haven't been any singularities yet, so we hang onto them for now. Don't worry, you'll get your chance, Mr. Asterisk-one-big-unit."

A quick glance out the window as he completed the loop gave him the layout of the battle. The IDF fleet had broken up into two attack groups, each taking on about twenty-five Swarm carriers, on opposite sides of the dreadnought. The Skiohra ship occasionally fired at the nearest Swarm ships, but for the most part seemed occupied with the thousands of IDF boarding vessels latched on to its hundred-kilometer-long hull—the invasion force led by Colonel Barnard would be slogging through, deck by deck. Though, strangely enough, the entire front section of the ship—at least five kilometers—was clear of IDF troop carriers.

The nose of his fighter ended up pointed toward the *Warrior*. It was taking a pounding from three Swarm carriers that had flanked it, skewering it with beam after deadly beam of antimatter ions. "Come on, team, let's go take out some of those turrets, or else we won't have a deck to land on when we get back."

They zipped toward the nearest carrier, and, once again, Ballsy held his breath as Fodder and Pew Pew seemed to disappear into a cloud of Swarm fighters guarding one of the turrets. Every single time they did this he knew their luck would run out. There was no possible way they could keep coming out of these suicide runs alive.

But, once again, they both emerged from the other side, taking out the turret with a few well-aimed torpedoes.

Pew Pew laughed over the comm. "That was a close one, bro. Hey, Ballsy and Spacechamp, you gonna let that one stand? Bet you can't do better."

He heard Spacechamp mutter something under her breath, something about best god-damned pilot ever, and he remembered her pep talk to him in sickbay. She was right. He needed to stop pining. Get in the here-and-now and blast as many Swarm fighters to hell as he could.

"Suck it, Pew Pew, Watch this. Spacechamp? Let's go. Turret at sixteen mark three."

Fodder snorted over the comm. "We've got your back. But remember, don't fly like my brother."

"And remember," came Pew Pew's customary answer, "don't fly like my brother."

Ballsy smiled. This was their element. He and his Untouchable crew. They could handle this. He stared forward, almost with tunnel vision, even as he concentrated on all the bogeys flitting around in his peripherals. With Spacechamp right in front of him, softening them up, he danced around her, trusting Pew Pew and Fodder to pick off any strays coming in from the rear.

One long, eternal minute later, he emerged from the other side, locked a torpedo on the turret, and fist pumped the air as he watched it explode.

"Fodder? Where are you, man?"

Silence.

"He'll turn up. He always does," said Pew Pew. "Trust me, we had to keep a cowbell around his neck when were kids—you never knew when he was going to sneak up on you."

In the distance, the *Warrior*, in spite of the massive destruction erupting out from its hull in dozens of places, was accelerating toward the nearest carrier, pelting it with thousands of mag-rail slugs.

Volz pushed on the accelerator. "Come on, let's go ease her passing. Last one there is—" He glanced at his scope and did a double take. A fighter was flying up and down the length of the carrier targeted by the *Warrior*, taking advantage of the lack of Swarm bogeys due to the hailstorm of mag-rail slugs. "Fodder? Are you already there?"

The other man laughed. "Lost an engine. Finally got it back online but my momentum took me over here so I thought, why not?"

"Why not? Ten thousand high-velocity why-nots! Get the hell out of there! You're right in line with the *Warrior*'s line of fire!"

But, in spite of the storm of slugs, Fodder managed to flip around and make one more pass, ripping apart two more antimatter turrets before peeling off, joining Ballsy, Pew Pew, and Spacechamp where they'd been hitting the carrier on the other end, safely away from the *Warrior*'s onslaught.

A flicker in his peripheral vision drew his eye, so he craned his neck up and around. A ship—a large ship, had just q-jumped in, and it was aimed straight at the forward section of the dreadnought on a collision course. He squinted to try and see the nameplate on the hull, but in his gut he knew exactly what it was.

"Oh, you've got to be kidding me."

CHAPTER FORTY-THREE

Bridge, ISS Warrior
Interstellar Space, 2.4 Lightyears From Sirius

"CAPTAIN, THREE CARRIERS coming in hot pursuit!" yelled Lieutenant Diaz.

"Maintain fire on target," said Granger, monitoring the progress of their assault on the Swarm carrier they were pummeling in tandem with the *ISS Tripoli*. "Show the incoming carriers our belly—it's already damaged beyond repair, may as well use it as a shield."

The *Warrior* twisted, keeping its forward mag-rail turrets focused on the bleeding carrier, exposing its underside toward the incoming ships, which opened up a full spread antimatter beam barrage. The walls and deck trembled all around them.

Granger gripped the armrests, planting his feet firmly on the deck, willing his ship to hold together. He lost the *Constitution*. He wasn't going to lose the *Warrior*. Not if he could help it.

"Reading widespread power failures in the target. All antimatter turrets are quiet," said Ensign Diamond.

"Flip us around, but maintain course. Target the carrier on the left, and swing us around the husk of the carrier we just walloped. Use it as cover. Relay to *Tripoli* to loop around from the other side and come out firing. We'll cover them."

"Aye, aye, sir," came several voices as the bridge crew relayed his orders.

The battle was a mixed bag so far. Not a complete disaster yet, as they'd managed to take out a dozen carriers, at a loss of only fifteen of their own—IDF's and Granger's best record yet. But the dreadnought was under heavy assault by the legion of troop transports under the command of General Norton and Colonel Barnard. Thousands had already docked, presumably including Colonel Barnard himself, and the hundreds of thousands of marines were doubtlessly locked in deck-by-deck bloody melee combat with the Skiohra.

Pointless violence. Needless blood.

And the Skiohra's was as red as any of theirs.

But Granger had no time to focus on that. Norton was uncompromising and rigid in his mission of taking over the dreadnought at all costs. And Zingano's fleet needed all the help it could get against the surprise appearance of the Swarm force.

"Ask Captain Dillman on the *Venokur* for help keeping this other two busy while we pick them off one by one," said Granger, noticing that the Swarm carriers they'd managed to shield themselves from were angling for a better attack vector. He nodded in approval as, moments later, the *Venokur* moved up from a deadly flanking angle, making the other two carriers stop in their tracks.

"Target is neutralized. All turrets quiet, but heavy damage on the *Venokur*," said Diamond.

"Good man, Dillman," he murmured. "Move on to the next."

Granger took a moment to survey the wider battle taking place. Admiral Zingano on the *Victory* was right in the thick of things, rallying a strike force of twenty of his new heavy cruisers, relying on their ultra-thick hull plating to provide cover from the Swarm carriers as the *Victory* shot them full of tens of thousands of mag-rail slugs.

One of the IDF fleet's attack wings was in bad shape. Half of the cruisers of Delta Wing were belching debris as green Swarm beams sliced into them. The other half were gone, disintegrated in expanding fields of wreckage. He saw General Norton's ship, the *ISS Lincoln*, far in the background beyond them, acting as a command center for the ground army now moving through the decks of the dreadnought. If that attack wing crumbled completely, the *Lincoln* would be vulnerable to the Swarm ships in that vicinity.

"Swing out. Full acceleration toward the Swarm formation at coordinates thirty-two mark five. We need to relieve pressure on Delta Wing. Keep all guns trained on that third carrier as we pass it."

The *Warrior* swung wide, out from the cover of the broken Swarm carrier they'd used as cover. In the intervening space, a full fighter battle played out, with thousands of IDF birds taking on tens of thousands of Swarm bogeys. There hadn't been any time to take out the main fighter bays of the Swarm fleet, so they had no choice but to engage the full force of the Swarm fighter wings. Seventy-five years ago, that's where the Swarm got its dreaded name. Tens of thousands, hundreds of thousands of fighters. Overwhelming and incontestable numbers. The IDF fighters were holding their own, but it was a blood bath.

Curiously, the Swarm had not used any of their singularity weapons. No shimmering points of light to hurl osmium bricks into. Consequently, all of IDF's fighters were over twice the mass they needed to be.

"Why do you think they haven't used the singularities, Shelby?"

"Maybe they don't want to risk hitting the dreadnought?"

Granger stroked his chin. "Possibly. Maybe they just ran out of singularities."

"Unlikely," she replied. "I made my own here on the *Warrior*. No reason they can't just keep churning them out."

The ship rocked again as explosions rang out from the lower decks. He supposed the mystery would have to wait. Still, if all those osmium bricks were only slowing things down....

"Commander Pierce, this is Granger," he began, speaking to the open air.

A moment's hesitation. "Pierce here. What is it, Captain?" His tone was heavy. He remembered Proctor's lecture from the other day, and he chided himself that he had yet to make time to do what she suggested.

"How would you like to relieve yourself of a hundred and fifty bricks?"

"They are slowing us down quite a bit, sir."

Granger nodded. "If we don't see any singularities in the next five minutes, I want you to come up with a plan to launch them at the carriers. Full acceleration—at least twenty seconds. Get them up to over two kps before they hit. That should punch a few big holes through the bastards."

"I'll see what I can do, Captain."

"And Tyler," Granger added, "we may need a few Omega runs before this is all over." He thought maybe the CAG could use a warning. The last few times seemed to have affected him quite a bit more than they should have. But losing his family at York—that should have strengthened the man's resolve. No man was more deadly than one who'd lost everything, and was fighting out of sheer desperation, revenge, and a sense of common survival for the entire race. He supposed they all had come to that point: no one alive had escaped tragedy; all had lost something.

And some had lost everything.

"I ... I understand, sir," said Pierce.

"Good man. Granger out." He turned to tactical. "Time until firing range on our targets?"

"Ten seconds, sir. But that third Swarm carrier still has operational antimatter turrets," said Diaz.

"Leave it to the *ISS Venokur*. Focus all fire on the nearest ship of that formation hitting attack wing Delta."

The mag-rail turrets all swiveled in concert, those that remained undamaged, and aimed squarely at a straggling carrier whose attention was focused on an IDF cruiser shuddering under the impact of dozens of antimatter beams.

"Sir, incoming fleet-wide transmission from General Norton," said Ensign Prucha. "All ships near the forward section of the dreadnought are to withdraw to a, quote unquote, *safe distance.*"

Granger turned to Proctor. "Now what is that supposed to mean?" she said.

It didn't sound good, whatever it was. "Patch me through to the *Lincoln.*"

Moments later, Norton grumbled out of the comm. "What the hell do you want, Granger?"

"Why are we moving away from the dreadnought, General?"

"Sorry, Captain. I won't divulge that information to someone clearly under the influence of the Swarm."

"Dammit, Norton, what are you playing at? Can't you see I'm taking it to the Swarm even as we speak? We're laying our asses on the line out here for you, or haven't you noticed? If Delta Wing falls, you're exposed, and won't last more than a few minutes against that Swarm formation."

Norton hesitated. "The invasion is going poorly. The Skiohra have mounted a much more formidable defense than even the pessimists expected."

"How much of the ship do you control?"

A pause. "Less than five percent. But we've gained valuable intel on their ship layout. We're about to hit them in the nerve center. Where their main ship population is."

"General, I strongly object. Get them all out of there. Retreat. The Skiohra are peaceful, and can be powerful allies. You don't know what—"

"Can it, Granger. Stand back and watch the fireworks. This maneuver should be familiar to you."

What the hell did he mean by that?

But he didn't even have time to voice the question. The comm cut off. Moments later, commotion came from the tactical station.

"Holy *shit!*" yelled Diamond.

Granger shot to his feet, reflexively. "What?"

"It's the *Constitution*, sir. What's left of it."

"Onscreen!"

The view on the screen shifted from the ongoing battle with the Swarm formation besieging Delta Wing to a wide-panned shot of the front of the dreadnought. Off in the distance, his old ship. The Old Bird. Still broken and hobbled from its final battle and descent to Earth.

Closing at lightning speed, straight for the dreadnought.

CHAPTER FORTY-FOUR

Executive Command Center, Russian Singularity Production Facility
High Orbit, Penumbra Three

"YOU? DESTROY the Swarm?" Isaacson scoffed.

"Complete eradication," replied Malakhov, nodding.

"That's ... ambitious." Isaacson eyed the president, his head cocked, wondering what the game was. The man was clearly either delusional, or playing him.

"I am a man of ambition, Eamon. When I see something I desire, I take it. When it is out of my reach, I plan, meticulously, how I may obtain it. And when there is a trophy that everyone claims is unreachable, it only makes me want it more. And I achieve it."

From the very public, macho exploits of the president, Isaacson knew he meant every word. He had something to prove, for sure. The man had a very high opinion of himself, though in this case, Isaacson suspected he'd bit off more than he could chew—the war was going very badly for humanity, even considering the Russians were temporarily safe and supposedly on the same side as the Swarm. But he knew that wouldn't last. Once United Earth fell, there would be nothing stopping the Swarm from turning their attention to the Russian Confederation, and unless Malakhov knew something about the state of their military that Isaacson didn't, they wouldn't last long.

"Mr. President, what makes you think you can eradicate the Swarm? They can control us, infiltrate us up to the highest levels, their fleets seem endless, they've got the Skiohra under their control and supposedly at least *three* other races that we haven't even heard of. What happens when *they* show up? Have you even considered this?" He parroted the list of concerns he'd heard from Avery and her senior commanders during the strategy sessions he'd been allowed to participate in.

Malakhov touched the enclosure's electronics and the clear material turned opaque again, shrouding the naked soldier from view. He motioned to another door leading to a smaller side-room containing some other scientific equipment. "Let me tell you a story, Eamon." He pulled a chair up to one of the machines and began touching a few spots on the computer screen next to it.

"The story begins seventy-five years ago," Malakhov began, still touching certain areas of the screen and shuffling through several menus. Unfortunately, Isaacson didn't read a word of Russian and didn't even recognize half of the Cyrillic alphabet. "It actually started ten thousand years ago, but seventy-five is where *we* show up, and that is all that matters. The Swarm awoke from its cycle, which, decades later, our scientists determined was about one hundred and fifty years long. They came, they devastated Earth and dozens of other worlds. But they encountered unexpectedly fierce resistance from humanity. Though they probably would have won had the war continued, their period of wakefulness was near its end, and they knew they would not be able to complete the invasion before they needed to rest. To enter their refractory period."

"So, it really was just luck that they disappeared?"

"Basically, yes. Their plan was to return in one hundred and fifty years, rely on their client races—the Dolmasi, the Skiohra, etcetera—to improve Swarm technology and ships to the point that, when the Swarm awoke again, they'd conquer humanity with ease."

"But they came early," said Isaacson.

"They came early."

"Was it something humanity did? Or was it spontaneous?"

Malakhov laughed. "Of course it was humanity. Or, more precisely, it was *me*."

"*You?*" Isaacson couldn't believe his ears. Why would the Russian president, knowing the destruction that would likely await it, awake humanity's mortal enemy? "Why? Seems like an incredibly foolish thing to do."

"Oh, I didn't do it on purpose, of course. My top scientists were devising a new weapon. Something we could use against the Swarm when they returned, as well as against ... less friendly elements of human civilization. Here. Let me show you." He finished typing commands in—he'd apparently done this before, and Isaacson thought it strange that the other man was so well versed in the operations of such technical equipment.

The top of the machine, which before had been just as opaque as the enclosure covering the soldier, turned transparent, and Isaacson peered inside. A white, shimmering light glowed in the middle, just barely visible. Occasionally it would flash, but most of the time Isaacson had to squint to see it properly. "Is that what I think it is? Mini-singularity?"

"Yes. The very first one, in fact. And its sibling. They are so close to each other that your eyes can't separate the two."

"And how do you keep them stable? How do you prevent them from gobbling up the entire station?"

"Proprietary information, Mr. Vice President. But I will tell you that the popular understanding of black holes is simplistic and mistaken. For instance, this singularity weighs less than a femtogram. You'd need a billion billion of these to equal a kilogram, and your average *natural* black hole is a million billion billion billion kilograms, give or take a billion billion. Needless to say, it's quite easy to use our regular gravity plates to manipulate these—modified gravity plates, of course. But we discovered something even more interesting. You can only create them in pairs. And furthermore, what goes in one, will come out its sibling sometime later— the exact timing depending on our gravitational input parameters. And so I thought: what if we could use this to destroy the Swarm's homeworld, even as they slept? Ensure they never come back?"

"But they came back early," Isaacson repeated.

"So they did, but I merely adjusted the plan. I gave them the singularity technology, in exchange for my autonomy. All my top commanders, most of my top leadership, they were all infected with Swarm virus. But this technology was so valuable to them, they agreed to let me keep control over myself and my government, as well as to monitor what the Swarm network was telling my people to do—through the patriot soldier you saw earlier in that pod."

"But why give them the technology they could use to destroy humanity?"

"Because, Mr. Vice President, I figured I could hit two birds with one stone. Two enemies with the same arrow. Your United Earth Senate and the previous administration was so perversely anti-Russian, that it became clear to me: if *I* wasn't going to stick up for my people, no one was. The only answer was for the west to be humbled. And what better way to do that than to have the Swarm do it for me? I'm never one to do my own dirty work, Mr. Vice President. I don't do my own laundry, I don't scrub my own toilets. I'm certainly not going to fight my own wars. Why do that when I can get my enemies to destroy each other for me?"

Isaacson stroked his chin, regarding the shimmering light in the vacuum chamber. The occasional flashes must have been when the occasional stray air molecule got too close to the minuscule event horizon and vaporized. Or at least, that's what he reasoned—he supposed an actual scientist would say something similar, but with larger words. "Still, Mr. Malakhov, surely you'd realize that once the Swarm finished with United Earth, they'd turn the weapons back on you. Did you really think they'd let you keep your autonomy?"

"Of course, that was a possibility. But, you see Mr. Isaacson, that would require them to still be alive at the end of the war with United Earth. Something that won't happen. In fact, I've brought you here to witness the end of the Swarm."

"*Here*? The Swarm will be eradicated here? I don't see any fleets, and shipyards, any bases." Isaacson turned back to look through the giant viewport at the end of the observatory. Just the planet below, turning serenely and slowly. Its vibrantly blue surface pock-marked by a few clouds. The small moon, with its field of dust and rocks, hovered in the background in a higher orbit. "Unless ... is *that*...." He pointed out the window, toward the planet.

"It is."

Was it possible? Could it be true? Had the Russians known the location of the Swarm homeworld this whole time, and sat on the information until United Earth had been sufficiently broken that Malakhov could end the war and destroy the Swarm, assured in the knowledge that Russian hegemony over humanity would never be seriously challenged for centuries? Millenia?

Impossible. The Swarm would never have entrusted Malakhov with knowledge of the homeworld's location. Even they weren't that stupid. They were probably lead-ing Malakhov along, letting him believe it was their home.

"So, you're just going to shoot your own singularities down there? Is that what this station is for?"

Malakhov waved a hand. "Of course not. I told you, I don't do my own dirty work. I'll let the Swarm do it for me. You're forgetting, Mr. Isaacson, the singularities come in pairs. What goes in one, comes out the other. The Swarm have been using these things for months, ravaging the surfaces of dozens of worlds. Sucking up billions of billions of tons of material. But, here's the secret, Mr. Isaacson. I only ever gave them *half* of the singularities. The other half—all the siblings—I kept here. Or rather, *there*," he said, pointing out the viewport.

Toward the moon.

Isaacson stood up and walked toward the glass, following Malakhov's finger. And then he finally noticed something odd. It wasn't a moon, drifting distantly in its orbit, hundreds of thousands of kilometers away. It was much closer than he'd realized.

Now that he focused on it, he could see it was enormous. It seemed to have its own hazy atmosphere, though Isaacson supposed that was just dust and debris colliding with each other, grinding down to ever smaller particles, clinging tentatively to the ball of rocks through their weak gravitational pull.

But that wasn't all. It was growing. Right before Isaacson's eyes he saw a flash, and another giant ball of material appeared a few kilometers away, tumbling and swirling as it fell down into the maelstrom of rock and debris.

"Have you ever wondered what a small moon striking the surface of a planet looks like? They say that's how the Earth's moon was created—a large planetoid struck Earth with such terrifying force, that enough material was sloughed off to form a satellite, leaving a molten hellish planet behind. Of course, *this* moon isn't quite as big, but it should do the trick."

"Haven't the Swarm seen this? Surely they'll try to stop it."

"That's the thing with the singularities, Eamon. I've timed them all to arrive here, at this moment, no matter their place or time of origin. The debris moon has only been forming for the last few hours, and is nearly complete. And has the Swarm noticed it? Will they do something about it? What can they do? By the end of the day that debris moon's orbit will decay and the whole thing will slam into Penumbra Three, eradicating every living thing within a hundred kilometers of the surface."

Isaacson stared at the ever-growing cluster of rocks and debris in awe. He could only imagine the utter destruction such a large mass would trigger when it collided with the planet below. The atmosphere would ignite, the upper crust would liquefy into an ocean of lava. Nothing could possibly survive.

He really was going to eradicate the Swarm.

CHAPTER FORTY-FIVE

Bridge, ISS Warrior
Interstellar Space, 2.4 Lightyears From Sirius

THERE WAS NOTHING he could do but watch, helplessly. Impact would be in seconds. No time to call Norton, to plead with him. No time to move the *Warrior* to intercept.

No time.

The explosion was tremendous. Spectacular. Blinding.

And just like that, the Old Bird, which he had thought was being repaired and retrofitted back on Earth, was gone.

Again.

The dreadnought was belching flame, molten metal, debris, wreckage, twisted metal and solid, glowing chunks of hull. Even though the massive ship was nearly a hundred kilometers long, it began to list and rotate as it absorbed the momentum of the *Constitution*, which had come in with terrifying velocity.

And he felt someone screaming in the back of his mind. Someone nearby.

It was Krull, he knew. She was feeling the death throes of her people. Not just the tens of thousands aboard the dreadnought, living their exterior lives, but the billions of Skiohra still living their interior lives inside the mothers.

Genocide.

"Get me Norton back," he said, almost in a whisper.

"You're on, Captain," replied Prucha.

"Norton, you bastard, what have you done?"

"What have I done, Granger? I'm winning."

"You've killed billions of innocent Skiohra lives—"

"*Innocent* Skiohra lives? You're delusional, Tim. They've got you. They're in your head. Think about it. Why have the Skiohra only barely fired on the Swarm? They haven't destroyed a single carrier, and the reason why is obvious. They've been playing you." There was crosstalk on the other end of the comm, and then Norton continued, "there, see? Now the dreadnought is firing on us. How do you explain *that*, Granger?"

Granger glanced at the tactical display—it was true, several antimatter beams shot out from the dreadnought toward Delta Wing.

"It's clearly self-defense. We were the aggressors here, not the Skiohra."

"Bullshit, Granger. Treasonous bullshit. Now, your orders are to continue—"

The transmission cut out. On the display, several beams stretched out from the dreadnought toward the *ISS Lincoln*, though at such a large distance the beams were more diffuse. Still, the damage probably knocked out Norton's commlink for the time being.

It was a disaster. The front twenty kilometers of the dreadnought was utterly devastated, with a *Constitution*-sized hole in it. The remains of his old beloved ship had blown out the back, in the form of dozens of chunks of molten tungsten. The Skiohra, as evidenced by the still-screaming presence of Krull in the back of his mind, were enraged, the Swarm was pounding Delta Wing and Zingano's efforts with Alpha Wing had started to go south.

Pure, utter disaster.

"We're going to lose the war," he muttered. He no longer cared who heard him.

Proctor had come up behind him. "The marines might still take the ship...."

Granger shook his head. "No. They won't. You didn't see Krull fight. It took half a platoon to restrain her. And she was unarmed. Our boys don't stand a chance, no matter how many of them the Old Bird took out."

The *Warrior* had been pounding the nearest Swarm carrier with mag-rail slugs, and now that it was in the midst of the formation locking down Delta Wing, the IDF ships had a chance to regroup. Half of them went to the aid of the *Lincoln*. The other half formed a two pronged trident line that Zingano favored in his engagements, and re-engaged the Swarm formation of carriers.

"Tim," Proctor said. Her voice had changed. Whereas before she'd sounded like she was trying to keep hope alive, this time she was resigned. "Look. Zingano and Alpha Wing."

While the *Warrior* had been busy assisting Delta Wing, the tide had turned for Alpha. Ship after ship exploded. The rest were flanked by fifteen surviving Swarm carriers, who'd backed them up into the dreadnought, which was shooting out the occasional antimatter beam as well. *Victory* was getting hammered.

Warrior bucked beneath them. Its underside was a wreck, with hull breaches reaching all the way up to engineering. Half its mag-rails were gone. None of the laser turrets were operational. They'd never even had the chance to try out the new experimental antimatter torpedoes that IDF Armaments had stocked them with on Avery's orders, as all the launch tubes were destroyed.

They were on their last leg.

Granger punched the comm. "Mr. Pierce. It's time for some fancy brickwork from our pilots. Are they ready?"

Silence.

"Mr. Pierce, please respond."

The comm link was open, and he even thought he heard background noises, possibly heavy breathing, but there was no response. He glanced up at Proctor. *Now what?*

"Get down there, Shelby."

CHAPTER FORTY-SIX

Fighter Bay, ISS Warrior
Interstellar Space, 2.4 Lightyears From Sirius

PROCTOR RAN. Even as the hallways shook, buckling under the sustained fire from the Swarm carriers, she sprinted to the fighter bay, leaping over fallen girders, strewn battle debris, and even two injured crew members, bloody from being tossed against bulkheads.

Less than a minute later she burst into the fighter bay. The deck chief looked up in surprise from haranguing a young tech who was refueling a fighter. She dashed toward the CAG's office, but nearly collided with the door when it did not open automatically for her. The door control was unresponsive.

Cursing, she looked up to the window, just above her head, where the CAG and his crew could look out at deck operations as they directed traffic and tactical operations. "You!" she called to a tech nearby, who was busy opening a new container of fighter ordnance. "Roll that over here. Now!"

Flustered and red-faced, the young woman pushed the large wheeled box of rounds toward. the window. Proctor joined her, pulling on it, guiding it into position.

She jumped on top, craning her neck to peer up into the fighter deck operations center.

Commander Pierce was alone. Sitting in his chair next to the console. She could barely hear Granger's voice yelling out of the comm speaker.

On Pierce's lap was a photograph.

In his hands was a gun. He stared at it.

"NO!" she yelled. Pounding on the window.

His head jerked up toward her. His eyes were swollen and red. His face tormented and twisted.

Oh god, she thought. She saw in his eyes only one thing.

Hopelessness. He'd given up. The pain had consumed him.

He'd made his choice.

"NO!" she shouted again, pounding on the window. "Pierce, we need you!"

But it was too late. His hand trembled as it brought the gun up to his mouth. His eyes shut.

Even from behind the window the shot rang in her ears. A stream of red followed the bullet when it came out the top. He jerked, and slumped. Blood poured from his nose.

She leaned her forehead against the window, still pounding on the glass with a fist, and, for the first time since the first invasion of Earth, she cried.

Granger is right. We're going to lose.

CHAPTER FORTY-SEVEN

Bridge, ISS Warrior
Interstellar Space, 2.4 Lightyears From Sirius

GRANGER HEARD THE GUNSHOT through the comm
speaker and knew immediately what it meant, without
having to ask Proctor.

"Pierce?"

The rumble of distant explosions answered him.

"Tyler?"

He should have listened to her. Should have taken
her advice more seriously. Paid attention to his crew.
He was so consumed with winning, with victory, with
saving the human race, that he forgot about the humans
around him. They were people.

And people could break.

"Shelby," he began, his voice low. "Can you hear me?"

The comm crackled as the computer automatically
patched him to the nearest comm receiver. "Yes, Tim."

"Is he dead?"

"Yes, Tim."

Another explosion, this time throwing all of them against their restraints. The *Warrior* didn't have long to live, either.

"Shelby, we need a CAG. Someone the pilots trust. Who's the most senior?"

After a moment, she answered. "Ballsy."

He almost protested, not wanting to trust such a huge responsibility to someone so young, so full of adrenaline and testosterone. Plus, the kid had had it in for him ever since he came back from the singularity claiming to see a Swarm-infested Granger on the other side.

But he'd been with the crew from the beginning. For some reason, Granger considered the formal decommissioning ceremony of the *Constitution* the beginning. That was when his crew was born. When the fire started raining down. The champagne bottle breaking at the ship's christening was the pleasant baptism of water. The baptism by fire was what really made a person. Made a crew.

"Is he there?"

"No, sir. He's out in his bird."

He motioned over toward Prucha. "Put him on."

Could he do this? Could *Granger* do this? It felt hopeless at this point. So pointless. Why continue, why keep on fighting, if the cold death of space awaited them all in just a few minutes?

He noticed the bridge crew staring at him despondently. They were used to seeing the Hero of Earth in action, sure and confident in himself and his crew. *Dammit, they still need their hero.*

Could he pull things together one last time?

"Here, sir," came Volz's voice.

"Ballsy," he said, using the semi-vulgar callsign. He'd act a swaggering hero, if only for a few more minutes. "I hereby appoint you CAG. Your mission: kick ass."

"Uh ... yes, sir."

"And your first assignment as CAG is to take out ten Swarm carriers in the next five minutes. Can you do that, Lieutenant?"

Volz flustered. "Sir? I don't think that even a thousand fighters—"

"Ballsy, I gave you an order. I didn't ask for excuses or hesitation. Now by my count, you've got over a hundred fighters with osmium bricks slowing them down, and no singularity targets to hurl them at. The *Warrior* is about to make an Omega run to end all Omega runs against the Swarm formation harassing the *Victory*, and I want to see some epic ball-busting on your end. Got it?"

"Yes, sir."

"Commander Proctor will stay in the Fighter Combat Operation center and direct things until you manage to get back in. But don't come back without blowing up a few cumrat ships. Granger out."

CHAPTER FORTY-EIGHT

Fighter Bay, ISS Warrior
Interstellar Space, 2.4 Lightyears From Sirius

ONE OF THE FIGHTER DECK technicians managed to wrest the door open to the combat operations center, and Proctor took the steps three at a time. The CAG's assistants followed him in—they'd been sent away for whatever reason by the late Pierce, and when she finally saw the body, surprisingly, it didn't faze her so much as anger her.

As much as she wanted to respectfully pick up the body and lay it gently in the corner, there was no time. She unceremoniously shoved Pierce out of the chair, and in spite of the blood soaked into the fabric and pooled on the floor beneath him, Proctor sat down and pulled herself up to the console.

She took in the tactical situation. Ninety-eight fighters left. She breathed a quick sigh of relief when she saw that the Untouchable crew was still alive. That meant their new CAG wasn't dead yet, at least. That would have been a new record—two CAGs within ten minutes.

She keyed herself into the whole fighter wing. "This is Proctor. Ballsy is the new CAG, people, but until he gets back to the nest, I'm it. Form up into your squadrons. Ignore the Swarm fighters. New target is the Swarm formation currently picking apart Alpha Wing of the fleet. Two fighter squadrons per carrier. Full acceleration until you reach maximum safe breakaway speed, then release bricks. Target...."

She paused. She knew eight osmium bricks wouldn't be enough to disable a Swarm cruiser, at least not at these speeds. But they could at least neutralize ninety-eight antimatter turrets, which would at least buy *Warrior*, *Victory*, and Alpha Wing a few more minutes.

"One brick per antimatter turret. My lovely assistants will make individual squadron assignments," she glanced at Lieutenant Schwitzer and Ensign Spiriti. *Damn, they look too young to even be in flight school, let alone have graduate.*

Granger's voice blared out of the comm. "Shelby, you ready down there?"

She watched the tactical layout as the fighters started to respond, and winced as two more birds blinked out as they were caught in a Swarm crossfire. "Fighters moving into position, sir."

"Good. *Warrior* will head out now, and hopefully distract their attention away from your people." The comm channel stayed on, and Proctor heard Granger give the order for full thrust toward the Swarm formation, now at eighteen carriers. On the tactical display she saw that Alpha Wing was just barely hanging on: only

234

fifteen ships, half of those disabled, but their fighters still fought desperately. They'd apparently caught onto the lack of singularities, too, as they'd begun launching their osmium bricks at the carriers as well. In such close quarters and with low speeds, though, the bricks were significantly less effective. Time to ramp things up.

The *Warrior* started to pull away from the remains of the battle near Delta Wing, and accelerated up to half a kps, then three quarters. Soon they'd reached a full kilometer per second, and they were over halfway there, guns blazing. *Warrior*'s—and Granger's—signature move.

She noticed they were aimed at one of the carriers. Not dead center, but at an angle such that the underside of the *Warrior*, already devastated from multiple battles using it as a shield for the rest of the ship and other IDF vessels, would bear the brunt of the glancing collision. Not quite an Omega run, but the experience would not be a joy ride.

The fighters were in position, lined up by squadron and already accelerating toward their targets.

Showtime.

CHAPTER FORTY_NINE

X-25 Fighter Cockpit
Interstellar Space, 2.4 Lightyears From Sirius

VOLZ AND HIS UNTOUCHABLE CREW were lined up in their brick-launch formation. Not a static line—no sense in providing the Swarm fighters with easy targets—but they'd settled into a near-maximum acceleration vector alongside the *Warrior*, making occasional evasive maneuvers to avoid the stray bogey, while lining up their sights on the assigned targets.

Two kps, two point five kps, three kps ... at this speed the explosive energy from the osmium bricks tearing through the Swarm's hulls would be unstoppable. The carriers might be huge, but a solid chunk of metal the size of a fighter slicing its way down the entire length of a ship was something else entirely.

"Launch in ten," said Commander Proctor through the comm.

Volz was still trying to wrap his head around being the new CAG, but he pushed it from his mind—he didn't need to think about that until he got back. "Look sharp, people," he said. "Keep an eye out for bogeys as you launch." He kept the nose of his bird lined up on the assigned carrier, and centered an antimatter turret in his scope—may as well make sure he at least took one of those out.

"Three ... two ... one ... launch!" Proctor shouted.

Volz pressed the release trigger after one final burst of acceleration, then immediate kicked in his reverse thrusters and veered away from the carrier before he slammed into it.

Blazing by the Swarm ship at breakneck speed, he craned his neck around to see if he could catch a glimpse of the aftermath, making sure the auto-deceleration subroutine was engaged. Sure enough, the carrier his crew had targeted suddenly had four gaping holes from where the remains of the osmium bricks had shot out the backside. Secondary explosions erupted all over the ship. The carrier wasn't destroyed—it still hobbled along and even attempted to veer out of the way of the *Warrior*, but the guns all fell silent.

"Yee haw!" shouted Pew Pew.

Fodder's outburst was less positive. "Aw, shit."

"What happened?" said Spacechamp.

"Release mechanism malfunctioned," said Fodder. "My brick is still attached."

Pew Pew snorted. "Well, Mr. Asterisk-one-big-unit, we can always help you get it off."

"That's what she said," Fodder quipped.

"Here, let me shoot it out from under you. Turn around and hold still."

"I hate it when other men tell me that."

"Guys, another time, please?" Volz was watching out the viewport at the aftermath of the modified Omega run. The *Warrior* was coming in fast toward a carrier that was still actively firing. Destructive green beams lacerated the *Warrior*'s already devastated hull. "That's not just an intercept course, people."

Spacechamp swore quietly. Fodder and Pew Pew swore less quietly.

"She's coming in for an actual Omega run," said Volz. *Damn. That dreadnought had better be worth it.*

CHAPTER FIFTY

Bridge, ISS Warrior
Interstellar Space, 2.4 Lightyears From Sirius

"TIME?"

"Ten seconds," said Ensign Prince.

Granger tightened his seat restraints. This would be a wild ride, if they survived it at all. "All hands, brace for impact." And again, to Ensign Prince at helm, "Look sharp, Mr. Prince. Just a graze. Slide along the surface and take out as many turrets as we can."

"Doing my best, sir."

Granger nodded. "I know you are, son. And a damned fine job you're doing too," he added, remembering Proctor's recent lectures. He'd failed Commander Pierce. He wouldn't fail the rest of them. At least, not in the few minutes they had left.

The distance separating them from the carrier shrunk at an alarming rate, and before he knew it, they hit, grinding across the surface, their hulls scraping together. The ten meters of tungsten armor plating served the *Warrior* well, preventing the Swarm hull from gouging up into it too deeply.

But the energy of the collision shocked them all. He was thrown against his restraint so hard he was worried he'd snap his neck. He knew there were injuries among the bridge crew as some of the officers didn't have the full restraints he did, and he knew in his gut that many in the lower decks had perished.

They shed velocity quickly, and when they'd flown past the carrier, the *Warrior*'s lower hull glowed red. "One more, Mr. Prince. Slide us along the carrier just ahead."

They repeated the modified Omega run, thrusters pushing them into position until they started grinding across the hull of a second Swarm carrier, knocking down turret after turret. antimatter beams from a dozen other carriers ripped into the upper hull, flashing green across the viewscreen until their view was almost completely washed out.

"Fighter bay reports brick deployment. Ninety-five launched. Over eighty-five antimatter turrets destroyed across ten carriers," said Diaz.

The viewscreen flashed with green beams, but noticeably fewer. The remaining Alpha Wing cruisers were regrouping, concentrating their fire on the Swarm carriers that still had full guns.

"Cap'n," came a tired voice from the comm.

Granger had been waiting for this call from his chief engineer.

"Yes, Rayna?"

"That second run cut through our main coolant line."

"Did you shut down the plant?"

Silence. "It's ... it's stuck, sir. The automatic shutoff is damaged, and the manual controls are ... well, the compartment they're in is open to space at moment."

He grit his teeth. "How long?"

"Less than five minutes until we lose reactor containment. After that, we'll have less than a minute until we go boom. Let's ... just make it an even five?"

She sounded oddly calm about losing her second ship. If he remembered correctly, her grandfather had been the assistant chief engineer aboard the *Warrior* in his time.

He hoped it had been worth it. "Understood, Commander Scott." He flipped on his general alert comm. "All hands...." He glanced over at Diaz, who nodded gravely. "Abandon ship. All hands to escape pods. Ship destruction in less than five minutes. Repeat, abandon ship."

The bridge crew ripped off their seat restraints as they began to exit. The bridge was deep in the core of the ship, and the nearest space pods were a good two minutes away. He eyed the tactical display, noticing a third carrier ahead of them that was still firing, and intercepted Ensign Prince before the young man stepped away from the helm.

"One more thing, Mr. Prince." He pointed down at the tactical display on the helm's console, and tapped his finger on the image of Swarm ship ahead of them. "This carrier's fighter bay doors are open. I want the nose of the *Warrior* stuck in there before we leave."

A minute later, Ensign Prince nodded as the ship swayed again. "Done, sir. We're lodged pretty firmly in there."

"Good. Go. Get to your escape pod."

Prince ran out the doors. Only himself and Proctor left—she'd run up from the fighter bay when he'd called for the evacuation. "I need to pick up a few things from my lab on the way. And Fishtail—she might still be a valuable link to the Swarm if we need it."

A voice called out in the back of his mind.

Dammit. He'd forgotten Krull in the last few minutes. She was still down in the shuttle bay, restrained, angry, despondent at losing so many of her Children and her people.

"Go. I've got one more thing to do. Get to the *Victory*."

They both raced out the doors. The customary marine guard had left, and the hallways were empty. At the intersection, they parted, and Granger rushed toward the shuttle bay, three decks down and toward starboard. He took the stairs two at a time, counting down silently in his head the remaining seconds they had left. Less than three minutes, he figured.

The shuttle bay was empty, except for Krull's shuttle still parked on the landing pad next to the *Warrior*'s shuttle. He opened the door to the control room, expecting to see the Skiohra still bound with cuffs around her wrists and ankles and tied to the chair.

A dead marine lay slumped against the wall. The chair was empty, the handcuffs lying broken on the floor.

CHAPTER FIFTY-ONE

Executive Command Center, Russian Singularity Production Facility
High Orbit, Penumbra Three

"WHY ARE YOU TELLING ME all this?" said Isaacson, though in his gut he knew there were only two possible answers. Either the Russian president was monologuing before he struck, satisfying his inner super villain, or....

"Because I need you, Mr. Vice President. Together, after all this is over, we can build a better world. You're someone I know I can work with."

Or ... Malakhov was looking for another tool. He was planning on using Isaacson for his own purposes. Just like Avery. Just like, he supposed now, Volodin.

Dammit. Just like every politician and military commander he'd ever met. In all his interactions with any person in a position of power or influence, that's all he ever was to them. A tool. A means to an end. Avery with her thirty implants she'd injected into him. Volodin and his Swarm masters with his flattery and scheming,

243

helping Isaacson with his initial attempts to kill Avery all while avoiding IDF defenses during the first foray against Earth. To all of them, Isaacson was not a partner, not a colleague. He was an instrument to enable the aspirations of others. Nothing more.

Anger boiled up inside of him. *Not anymore. Not anymore!* He resolved to start using others—make *them* his tools. Use *them* to boost himself, use *them* in his own plans. Stop being the pawn and be the queen. Or ... king. No, queen. *Dammit.*

"I agree, Mr. President. What do you need me to do?" Isaacson smiled eagerly. His first tool: Malakhov. Convince him that Isaacson was an eager and willing partner. Do what it took to gain his trust. Then, turn the tables. Make the other man a pawn in his own schemes.

Malakhov looked surprised, just for a moment. "Well, I admit, that was easier than I thought it would be. Are you so eager to turn on your own government, Eamon?"

"Just like you said, Mr. President, I don't see it as turning on my government. I see it as saving our civilization. Finally achieving peace between east and west, after all these centuries." He turned away from the window, away from the massive ball of gathering debris and faced the Russian strongman. "How can I help? The sooner we can end this, the faster I can take over for Avery, make an alliance, and start rebuilding."

Isaacson hoped playing up the Avery-replacement angle would convince the man. He *had* been trying to kill her for years, after all. Malakhov would certainly believe his sincerity.

"Of course," replied Malakhov smoothly. "In fact, that's part of why I brought you here. I have a recently-acquired tool in my possession that I think you can make use of to both take out Avery, and possibly even some of the Swarm's most deadly allies. The Skiohra's ships are ... well, gargantuan. They've been one of the uncertainties in my plans. I never knew how they'd feel once the Swarm were destroyed. But recent developments will make that less of an uncertainty, and more of a bond between us, Eamon. You see, I'm going to give you the means to destroy the Skiohra, at the same time I destroy the Swarm and Avery. All of humanity will be so grateful to the both of us that ... well, let's face it. We'll be presidents for life."

"And just what is this most recent development?"

"Come." Malakhov shut off the viewscreen to the singularity enclosure, and the walls became opaque once more. He strode off toward another door on the other side of the giant viewport covering the wall. It slid open, revealing what looked like a medical examination room. A tall window was set into one wall, while the other walls were covered with monitors and medical equipment, cabinets, and diagnostic equipment showing the steady pulse of a person laying on the only bed in the room.

Isaacson passed the threshold, staring at the man on the bed. "Impossible."

"I was expecting him, given events over Earth four months ago."

The blanket covered most of his body, leaving his head exposed. His face was white and haggard, as if sick from a deadly disease.

Captain Granger. From another time. Alive, but only just.

CHAPTER FIFTY-TWO

Fighter Cockpit, ISS Warrior
Interstellar Space, 2.4 Lightyears From Sirius

VOLZ GASPED as he watched the *Warrior* grind across the surface of the carrier. It happened so fast, with the ship moving at such a high velocity, that he almost didn't believe what he was seeing. The carrier's hull wasn't as tough as *Warrior*'s, and vast chunks of the Swarm ship flew off like glowing white-hot embers from a piece of flint struck by steel. All the antimatter turrets on that side of the carrier were ground off, and the rest fell silent too as the *Warrior* careened into the second carrier.

By the time *Warrior* had slowed and slid off the edge of the other ship, she was in bad shape, hardly even recognizable anymore as one of IDF's greatest warships. Gouts of flame erupted from a thousand holes before they reached the quenching vacuum of space. Half the hull glowed red, almost white-hot.

And a minute later, escape pods began shooting out from her like explosive seeds.

"*Warrior*'s toast, people," yelled Volz into his headset. He would have expected notice from Proctor in the operations center, but the comm equipment was probably down, or everyone on the flight deck dead. Either way, it was their job to escort those pods to safety. "Intercept the bogeys out amongst the pods." He looked and saw that most of the pods were aiming toward Admiral Zingano's ship, which hovered near the *Warrior*, like a nervous twin watching its sibling die. "Get them to the *Victory*."

They plunged back into the fray, targeting the Swarm fighters that were harassing the escape pods. Luckily there weren't that many of them, and just a few pods were lost to bogey fire. But that was a few too many.

A brilliant green light illuminated his cockpit. "Holy shit!" he yelled into his headset. His eyes followed the green beam back to the last remaining Swarm carrier in the vicinity that was still unscathed. It had approached, and was targeting the escape pods, picking them off one by one. As the pods lacked any armor, each beam only had to maintain contact for a split second before the escape vessels exploded.

"All fighters," he began, flipping his comm over to wide-band broadcast to not only *Warrior*'s fighters, but any other IDF ships in the area. "Target that carrier's turrets. Give our people some cover. Move!"

"Disregard that," said a voice. *Fodder?*

Volz glanced around him, and saw Pew Pew and Spacechamp's fighters nearby. Fodder was nowhere to be seen. "Fodder, where the hell are you?"

Fodder breathed heavily into his headset. "I believe this situation calls for an Asterisk-one-big-unit," he said, adding an odd chuckle. Volz craned his neck around, and finally saw it.

Fodder had peeled out into a wide loop, accelerator pressed beyond safety-limits. Volz could only imagine the g-force pressing on the man. "Fodder, don't," said Volz.

"I finally found a good use for this brick of mine," he said, breathing even harder, apparently straining against the immense acceleration. His loop crested, and he'd begun swinging back toward them.

Straight toward the remaining Swarm carrier. Straight down its throat.

Volz heard Pew Pew mumble something, before he cleared his throat. "Don't fly like my brother," he said. His voice sounded solemn. He was saying goodbye.

Volz watched his sensor screen—Fodder's velocity climbed high fast, reaching over four kps. Just before he hit, Fodder chuckled one last time, though this one sounded less forced than before. "See you on the other side, boys," he said.

And then Fodder, with the osmium brick, plunged right into the nose of the carrier. A second later, a glowing fireball leapt out the rear of the ship, and a split second after that, multiple explosions ripped out from a dozen spots all along the kilometers-long hull.

The green beams fell silent. In their absence, the remaining escape pods raced over the empty gap between the ships and started landing on the *Victory* wherever they could find a berth.

"Goodbye, Fodder," said Spacechamp.

Volz wiped an eye with the back of his glove. *Hotbox.*
Pluck. Dogtown. Fodder. Fishtail.

Fishtail. Had she made it off the *Warrior?*

CHAPTER FIFTY-THREE

Shuttle Bay, ISS Warrior
Interstellar Space, 2.4 Lightyears From Sirius

"LOOKING FOR ME?" came the gravelly voice from behind him. He turned. She was there, standing on the ramp of her shuttle.

Pointing the dead marine's assault rifle at his chest.

"Krull. We need to get out of here," he said urgently.

"*We* do. I, and my remaining Children. You, however, will die here." She stepped down the ramp toward him, gun still trained on his chest. He noticed that her shoulder was damp with blood, the cloth soaked through and still spreading.

"Take me with you. I can help. We can still win this. We can still salvage—"

She made a strange guttural noise, as if dismissing him or scoffing. "We can salvage nothing. You have betrayed us. Billions have died on the *Benevolence*. Tens of thousands are still dying. Your men are still moving through the ship, hunting us down. Fortunately, they are weak. And slow. We are not. Soon, they'll all be dead, your fleet destroyed, the Valarisi carriers disabled, and we will be on our way."

"Where will you go? After the Swarm destroys us, surely they'll come after you," said Granger, eyeing the assault rifle as she stepped closer to him.

"They will. But we will be long gone. We're leaving this galaxy. It will be lost to the Valarisi within a few decades. They will spread across the galaxy from one end to the other, from the core to the ends of the spiral arms. And then they will move on to the next galaxy, and the next. But we will outrun them."

"But you're free of their influence. Surely, when they enter their next regeneration cycle, you can find them, hunt them all down and destroy them while they sleep?"

She scoffed again. "You still do not understand, do you? Your people, the Adanasi, the ones you call Russian, they have broken the cycle. Never again will the Valarisi sleep. For centuries I helped manage the interim periods. Keeping their ships hidden and safe, moored safely to our own as we harvested asteroids and comets, building new ships, maintaining and growing their ability to conquer during the next cycle. But that is over now. The Valarisi are here to stay. And we must run."

He held up his hands. Toward her, as she had taught him. "Krull. We can defeat them. I know we can. We're missing part of the puzzle, but once we find it, we can free ourselves of them. I know it."

The gun stayed pointed at his chest. Both of them held each other's gaze. He could sense her rage, through the Ligature, and feared that her anger was too great, too overwhelming for any reason to creep in.

And really, she was absolutely correct. His race *had* betrayed them. There was no reason whatsoever for her to trust him.

Especially not now—he tried to keep his eyes straight ahead of him, even as he noticed Proctor creep up behind Krull, brandishing a twisted piece of metal.

"It's over, Captain Granger. They've won. Even now, the Adanasi think they have the Valarisi fooled. They are experts of deception. But the Valarisi have learned, and have turned the schemes of the Adanasi against them—"

The steel rod hit her head, and the next moment she was on the floor, at Proctor's feet.

"She was right about to tell us what the Russians are up to!" he said, breathing heavily, glad he was alive and yet dismayed Proctor couldn't have waited just five seconds.

"Ship's blowing in twenty seconds. You want to stick around?" she said, rushing to the control panel on the wall and raising the bay door, revealing the shimmering force field keeping the air in—luckily the field's auxiliary batteries were still full, though that wouldn't last much longer.

But it was all the time they needed. Granger lifted Krull up onto his shoulders. Even as he touched her skin, he heard the voices of thousands scream in his mind. Her Children. The ones living the Interior Life, still inside of her. She may have been knocked out, but they were still very much awake. He climbed the ramp, Proctor right behind, and she shut the hatch behind them after the ramp swung up.

"What about Fishtail?" said Granger

"I got her in an escape pod with a nurse and three marines." Proctor squeezed into the tiny chair at the helm.

"Can you fly this thing?"

"We're about to find out," she said, studying the controls, pushing what looked like the engine initiator.

Nothing happened.

Thirty seconds were up. The *Warrior*'s power plant would blow at any moment. His hand was still in contact with Krull, holding her on his shoulders, and suddenly he felt the Children in his mind. *We hate you, traitor and oathbreaker*, he felt them say, thousands, all at once, each in their own way with their own emotions.

We hate you we hate you we hate you, but we need you. For now. Learn from us. And as he stared at the controls, he know what to do. They were instructing him, in spite of their anger. He pressed several buttons, in the order they indicated to him, not with words but with images and impressions, and moments later the engine roared to life.

"Go!" he said, and she pulled up on the controls, bringing the nose of the shuttle toward the force field, and squeezed hard on the accelerator.

The shuttle shot out of the bay, and he breathed a grim sigh of relief. Before they'd gone two hundred meters, the *ISS Warrior* exploded.

CHAPTER FIFTY-FOUR

Bridge, UESS Albright
High Orbit, Penumbra Three

CAPTAIN HALL of the *UESS Albright* paced nervously, her eyes flicking between the clock, the Russian fleet docked at the massive space station, and the growing cloud of debris surrounding the giant ball of rock and ice that floated in the distance. Every so often, a flash of light announced the arrival of a new chunk of rock, often glowing red, as if part of it was more magma than rock. The new arrivals would careen toward the central mass and slam into it, sending more dust and debris out into the maelstrom of swirling clouds surrounding it.

She'd read the reports—even though her security credentials weren't all that high, she could clearly see what was happening. The Swarm weaponry used against the United Earth worlds seemed to be sucking up material, and transporting it lightyears to this point, where they were collecting it.

For what purpose she could not fathom.

"Keep scanning that debris cloud. We should be gathering as much intel as we can to bring back to IDF."

"Yes, ma'am."

He was late, she thought. She glanced at the clock again. He was supposed to have checked in by now. Or at least, his secret service detachment. They'd heard nothing from either Isaacson or his security for over two hours. "Still nothing?" she asked the comm officer.

"No. Nothing."

On the viewscreen, something flashed white again, amid the debris field. Or rather, dozens of somethings, all at once.

"What was that? Wu-Jin, get us a closer look."

"Zooming in," said the woman at sensors.

On the viewscreen, the image was unmistakable. IDF fighters, all tumbling end over end through the debris field, straight for the giant ball of rock.

"I'm reading exactly thirty of them, ma'am."

"Retract docking clamps. Jill, maximum acceleration. Move in to assist."

With a distinct clunk, she heard the docking clamps release. The *Albright*'s nose pointed toward the spiraling fighters, and Captain Hall wondered if they'd even get there in time, or what they could even do to help once they did.

An explosion arced across the bridge, engulfing the helmsman in fire. Other bridge crew members screamed.

"What the hell...?"

The color drained from her face as she watched the viewscreen, and three Russian cruisers descended on the *Albright*, weapons firing. The ship shook, and another explosion rang out, knocking her to the deck.

The last thing she saw was the thirty IDF fighters colliding with the ball before another explosion ripped through the bridge.

CHAPTER FIFTY_FIVE

Skiohra Shuttle
Interstellar Space, 2.4 Lightyears From Sirius

"WHERE TO?" said Proctor, after they'd emerged from the shock of seeing their ship disappear in an inferno of destruction, less than an hour after watching their beloved Old Bird die a similar death. Luckily, the Swarm carrier in whose fighter bay the *Warrior* was lodged got caught in her fiery death throes, and though still intact, drifted harmlessly away from the carnage.

"*Victory.*" He realized he'd forgotten to tell the crew their destination, he'd been so focused on getting them all out to the relative safety of the fighter battle still happening all around them. He reached inward, still holding Krull's hand though he'd placed her on the floor, and asked for the wide-band comm controls. Reluctantly, the Children responded, showing him in his mind how to operate the controls.

"This is Captain Granger, to all *ISS Warrior* escape pods. Get to the *Victory*. I repeat, all *Warrior* personnel get to the *ISS Victory*. Wherever you can find room to dock. Fighter bay, shuttle bay, empty escape pod hatches. Commander Diaz will coordinate," he added, hoping that his deputy XO was still alive. The Skiohra shuttle wasn't equipped to interface with all the escape pods, and there would be no way to coordinate all two hundred from there—only another IDF shipboard computer could do that.

"Aye, aye, sir," came the man's voice, steady and sure, through the speaker. The man was a rock, unflappable. If Granger didn't make it through, Proctor would have an excellent XO on her hands.

"*ISS Victory* fighter bay, do you read me? This is Captain Granger." he fiddled with the comm controls, trying to remember the exact frequency band for intra-ship comm lines.

"Yes...?" asked the voice, apparently surprised to hear directly from him.

"I hereby transfer all *Warrior* fighters to your command and control. Please inform Admiral Zingano. Granger out." He cut out before they could respond— he had no idea what garbage General Norton had been feeding the rest of the officers in Zingano's fleet, but he didn't have time to listen to any protests.

"Almost there," said Proctor. Out the front viewport the fighter bay of the *Victory* loomed ahead. Dozens of escape pods already littered the deck. She guided them carefully in, finding a space off to the side that just barely fit the Skiohra craft. With all the pods, plus all the surviving fighters from both the *Warrior* and the *Victory*, space would be tight.

He hoisted Krull back onto his shoulders and followed Proctor down the ramp which was still descending. The fighter deck was utter pandemonium, with hundreds of *Warrior* crew members streaming out of escape pods, many of them injured, all of them wild-eyed, having just escaped the destruction—for the second time—of their home in space.

Krull was still bleeding. The voices of the Children were like an enormous stadium of people shouting in the background of his mind. She was critically injured, he knew, from the tone and emotion of their voices.

And she had critical information. She had been about to expose some secret about the Russian motivations before Proctor had nailed her on the head. "I'll be in sickbay—we need to find out what she knows," he said to Proctor. "Get to the bridge and find Zingano. Try to convince him to call this madness off. He may listen to you."

She nodded her agreement and they both rushed out the fighter bay doors, in opposite directions.

Luckily, the ship layout was identical to both *Constitution* and *Warrior*, with just a few exceptions. When he arrived at sickbay, he was dismayed to find it overflowing with wounded. Bodies lay in the hallway outside, where they'd been placed, lining the walls, presumably because there was no time to properly store them in the morgue, which he supposed was probably full. When your ship is about to blow up, hygiene and sanitation is the first to go.

Heads turned toward him. Usually, in the past few months, heads turning his way meant that people were craning their necks to see the Hero of Earth, and he almost acted on habit by giving a stern, resolute nod and a quick salute.

But then he realized they were staring at the alien on his shoulders. The existence of the Skiohra was still a tightly guarded secret, known only to the President, the top brass, and now, five-hundred thousand marines. He supposed the sight of a blue-hued, hobbit-sized alien on his shoulders was sure to draw attention.

"Doctor," he said, approaching the woman wearing the sickbay chief's uniform, "this individual needs urgent help."

Her eyes grew wide as she saw Krull. "Is that—"

"Swarm? No. But national security depends on this individual being treated and revived. In fact, I'm pretty sure we will all die if you don't."

Her eyes widened further, if it were possible, and she pointed to a private examination room off to the side. "In there. You'll need to see who's in there anyway."

Granger carried Krull through the doors to the examination room and looked down at its occupant.

"Bill?" he said, horrified. Blood oozed from the admiral's forehead, which was clearly fractured. More blood seeped into his uniform where his abdomen was obviously torn open in several places.

The doctor whispered in his ear. "He's got massive internal bleeding. His organs are shutting down—there's just nothing we can do, Captain."

Admiral Zingano roused from a daze at the sound of Granger's voice and waved him forward with a bloody hand. He whispered. "Norton."

"You want General Norton in command of the fleet?" asked Granger, unsure of what he meant.

"Nor—Norton. P—p—possibly compromised," he forced through labored breath, licking his lips with a bone-dry tongue. Then he turned to the doctor. "IDF protocol. Standing ... standing order ... ten. Command transferred—"

His eyes glazed, and closed, but his hand stayed up.

His lips moved. "*Victory* transferred to Timothy J. Granger. In ... in ... inform the co—"

He trailed off.

Dead.

CHAPTER FIFTY-SIX

Executive Command Center, Russian Singularity Production Facility
High Orbit, Penumbra Three

THE SIGHT OF A sickly Granger, feeble and white, shocked him.

Isaacson spun around toward Malakhov. "But everyone in IDF and Avery's senior staff agreed: he went to the past. The Dolmasi confirmed it. Vishgane Kharsa said that Granger *used* to be a friend. That he'd been compromised by the Swarm in the past, but no longer was."

"Vishgane Kharsa ... is lying," said Malakhov.

"So he's still aligned with the Swarm?"

"No. But he's not aligned with us either. Or Avery. Or Granger. The Dolmasi care about the Dolmasi. They intervene only when it benefits them. And in Granger's case, they used him. He's been their most effective tool, convincing him that he was destroying the Swarm homeworld while the whole time he was liberating the Dolmasi homeworld. Brilliant, if you ask me."

"But why allow Granger to think he went to the past?"

Malakhov shrugged. "Think about it from the Dolma-si's perspective. You've just used Granger to liberate your homeworld. You know that at some point in the future, the *old* Granger is going to show up, then return to the past to a point before you've liberated your home. Do you tell current-day Granger about that? In the Dolma-si's case, no, you don't. Kharsa won't risk anything that will threaten his homeworld. Now that he's liberated it, he'll stop at nothing to keep it. Even if it means the destruction of humanity, for all he cares. No, Kharsa lied to Granger about The Event—his Vacation—because if he didn't, he risked current-day Granger rushing off to intercept himself when the old Granger arrived in the future, potentially messing up the timeline and Dolmasi plans for their homeworld's liberation."

"How do you know all this?"

Malakhov tapped his head. "I don't. But it's the only thing that makes sense. It's what *I* would do. Plus, I've had the benefit of eavesdropping on the Swarm for the past few years and I have some insight into Dolmasi thinking. In fact, I predicted their liberation years before it happened. The Swarm never saw it coming. But I did."

Isaacson turned back to Granger. "So? What are you going to do with him?"

"Keep him here, for now. My doctors have kept his cancer in check, at least temporarily. He's in no danger of dying in the next few days. Come. Let me show you your part in all this."

Isaacson, still slightly in shock at seeing the old Granger, allowed himself to be led out of the medical room, out of the observatory, and back out to the atrium by the elevator where the heroic pictures of Malakhov hung on the walls. Rather than take him into the elevator, the Russian president led him down the hall, framed pictures of himself on the left, and a massive hundred meter drop-off on the right behind the wall of glass. They walked for several minutes, Malakhov pointing out various features of the station as they passed.

Finally, double doors opened up to reveal a giant bay. Not just giant. It was monumentally huge. Isaacson had thought that the interior space of the station they'd just left—the hundred meter tall open-air space lined with glass and railing and offices, topped by Malakhov's observatory—he'd thought *that* was what the Swarm had hollowed out of the asteroid.

He was mistaken. Now he saw what a monumental task it must have been—the interior space, lined mostly by craggy rock and thousands of spotlights, was not only large enough to hold a ship, it was large enough to hold dozens of ships. Several were moored to scaffolding, including one Swarm carrier. But Isaacson's eyes were drawn to the center.

The *ISS Constitution*, battered and scarred from its battle over Earth, floated near some scaffolding that served as a docking port.

"There, Eamon, is my gift to you."

Isaacson gawked. "You're giving me the *Constitution*?"

"Of course. It's not mine. If anyone should have it, you're it. Though when you're done with it, we *do* need to send Granger back in it, otherwise ... well, there's no telling what happens to the timeline if he doesn't."

Isaacson shook his head. "This is crazy. What happens if we don't? Does the universe implode or something?"

Malakhov scoffed. "Of course not. We don't know for sure, but my top scientists tell me *nothing* will happen. In some universes that are mostly parallel to ours, Granger doesn't return. Their timelines will look different from ours, from the moment that Granger disappeared. But for *us*, he *did* return. That's all that matters, or so my scientists claim. But you're right to be concerned, and that's why I've decided to send him back—to be on the safe side." He grinned at Isaacson. "Just not quite yet."

Isaacson's eyes followed the path of several work crews as they walked the surface of the ship in gravity boots, carrying tools and boxes containing what he presumed was repair equipment. "How long has it been here?"

"Two and a half days."

So, he thought, *if everything happens like it did four months ago, the* Constitution, *and Granger, will go back through the same singularity he came out of in less than one day. Now, what do I do to take matters into my own hands? How to throw off Avery's domination? How to not be played by Malakhov? By Volodin? By Granger and Norton and—shit—all of them?*

Malakhov leaned over the low railing, holding loosely to a bar that connected the railing to the ceiling. "And in that time, we've cleaned up engineering—it was flooded with radiation from the damage it sustained with the Swarm— and I've installed some equipment you'll find very useful in your mission. Ten singularities should do it. One for each of the six remaining Skiohra dreadnoughts. One for Avery. And three extra, just in case you need them."

"You trust me to take the *Constitution*, fire singularities at the Skiohra dreadnoughts, send Avery into another, and then return in time for you to patch Granger back up and send him on his way back to Earth?"

"It's not a matter of trust, Mr. Vice President. It's a matter of interests. I know you. This aligns with your interests. You want to replace Avery. You want peace with me. You want to be rid of the Swarm. This accomplishes all three."

He was right, of course. This *was* something Isaacson wanted. All three of them.

But he was tired. Sick and tired of being the tool. Of being the pawn in someone *else's* game. That Isaacson was dead. Gone. He wouldn't stand for it anymore. Malakhov was playing him, using him for his own purposes, just like Avery was doing. No more.

Malakhov grinned at him, and turned back to watch the work crews scurry over the *Constitution*. "I take from your silence that you're in. Good. Preparations have already been made, and within—"

He was still leaning over the railing, and, surprising even himself, Isaacson grabbed the President and thrust him outward with all the strength he could muster.

Malakhov was surprisingly strong. The epic photographs of him weren't exaggerations—before he could fall down three hundred meters into the cavern, he grabbed firmly onto the support bar that held up the railing, swinging out, and then toward the ledge, grabbing at the support railing with his other hand, dangling there, his face overcome by shock. This was clearly the last thing he expected.

Isaacson channeled his anger, all the bottled-up rage and violence he'd been suppressing over the months he'd been under Avery's thumb. Every violent thought, every feeling of vengeance and malice he'd been pushing deep down within himself and away from Avery's all-seeing view finally burst out. He screamed, kicking at Malakhov's stomach and lunging out to punch the man in the face again and again.

In spite of Isaacson's assault, Malakhov was managing to pull himself back onto the ledge. *Shit*, he thought. If the other man stood up, Isaacson was a goner. He kicked at the leg Malakhov had managed to swing up onto the ledge, and without even thinking pulled the pen from his pocket and rammed it straight into the man's eye.

Malakhov screamed. He reached up to pull at the pen. Isaacson kicked at the remaining hand holding the rail.

And President Malakhov fell. Three hundred meters. Screaming, all the way down.

A final crunch confirmed he was gone. Isaacson felt a thrill of something he hadn't felt in a long time.

Control. Victory.

He was free.

CHAPTER FIFTY-SEVEN

Sickbay, ISS Victory
Interstellar Space, 2.4 Lightyears From Sirius

GRANGER LOOKED DOWN at the admiral. His friend. No—friend was too strong a word. But the man had stood up for him among the top brass when no one else would.

Now he was alone, with a General Norton who was possibly under Swarm influence, at least according to Zingano.

"Doctor, please inform the bridge of the Admiral's wishes," he said, looking sternly at the woman.

She nodded slowly, still in shock at seeing her first alien and losing her commanding officer within the span of a few minutes. "Commander Oppenheimer, this is sickbay...."

"Go ahead, Doctor," came the reply. "Make it quick, we're in a bit of a situation here...."

It wasn't until then that Granger became aware of the ship shaking all around them as it was pounded by enemy fire. The battle had continued without him this whole time, but he hadn't even noticed.

"Sir, Admiral Zingano is dead. And he invoked standing order ten."

"Thank you, Doctor. I understand. Oppenheimer out—"

"No, sir," she interrupted, "you don't understand. Admiral Zingano named Tim Granger the commander of the *Victory*."

Silence. Granger was sure he heard a muffled curse on the other end. "Is ... uh ... is he there now?"

"I am, Commander Oppenheimer. I'll be up to the bridge shortly."

Another pause. Granger supposed it involved more swearing. "I understand, sir. Orders until you get here?"

"Continue battle operations. You've done an excellent job so far, Commander. Please keep it up." Krull issued a low moan. "Expect me shortly. Granger out."

He motioned toward Zingano's body, and the doctor called in a nurse to carry it away. Granger moved Krull onto the examination table.

"Captain...?" began the doctor. "What ... exactly ... is it?"

"She is a matriarch of the Skiohra people," said Granger. Krull moaned again, softly. "Can you help her?"

"I don't even know her anatomy, Captain. The only thing I can tell is that she bleeds, is bipedal, and has a similarly shaped head as us. Does it contain a brain? Does she breathe? I assume so, because of the nostrils. Does she—"

"I don't know, doctor. Just start ... scanning her or something. Surely you'll see something wrong."

The doctor grimaced again, and pulled out a device, waving it slowly over Krull's head, chest, and abdomen.

"Also, you should know, she has ... well, she has about twenty-two thousand Children inside her." He forced a brief smile. "Don't let that throw you off."

The doctor shook her head. "This is all gibberish to me. I mean, I see organs. There's a brain. But I don't know what an appropriate blood pressure would be, I don't know if these cells are anti-bodies or—"

"Hold on," he said, reaching down to grab Krull's hand. The Children helped him once. Surely they'd help him save their own mother.

He reeled backward. A flood of images assaulted his mind, They were crying out, in a frenzy.

Because she was dying.

Slow down, he thought at them. *Too much, too fast*. He glanced at the images coming up on the display being fed from the doctor's diagnostic device. Error messages flashed on the screen as the medical algorithms struggled to decipher the alien's physiology. *Just tell me what to do. Slowly*.

The flood stemmed to a trickle. The image of blood came into his mind, then numbers, then a few other simple procedures. "You need to raise her blood pressure up above..." he began, relaying all the information they were giving him. The stream ended with an image of her head injury, a bleeding brain, and a chemical formula. "Her brain is bleeding from where Proctor hit her. You need to stop the bleeding with ... something." He was no chemist.

"With what?"

He strained at the formula, trying to remember his basic chemistry class at the academy. "Two carbons with hydrogens coming off ... a few nitrogens ... phosphorus...."

"That's not helpful."

He threw his hands up in the air. Krull was dying. And only she had the secret of what the Russians were up to, and how the Swarm was going to exploit it. "Just fix the brain bleed, doc. Do what you'd do for me. For him," he pointed to Zingano's body which lay near the wall. "She bleeds, she walks, she talks, just like the rest of us. Just give her what you'd give me."

The ship lurched violently to the left, nearly throwing Krull off the bed. The doctor reached down and strapped restraints over the alien, swearing as she ranted about chemistry and anatomy and why the hell doesn't anyone take basic science anymore and all this wouldn't be necessary if only they'd give her proper equipment and....

"Doctor, I've got to go to the bridge. Keep her alive. Fix her. That's an order, and your highest priority right now, even if your next patient is me. Understood?"

And with that, he ran out of sickbay, heading to the bridge and to what he knew would be a testy confrontation with General Norton.

If he, the military chief closest to the president, was compromised by the Swarm, then god help them all.

CHAPTER FIFTY-EIGHT

Bridge, ISS Victory
Interstellar Space, 2.4 Lightyears From Sirius

THE MARINES THAT WERE supposed to guard the entrance to the *Victory*'s bridge were sprawled unconscious outside the doors, victims of the violent shaking and explosions rocking the ship. Every head snapped toward him as he strode onto the bridge. Commander Oppenheimer stood up. His face betrayed his feelings—it was clear what he thought of Granger. Admiral Zingano may have trusted the Hero of Earth, even amidst the rumors that he was collaborating with the Swarm, but Oppenheimer looked to be more skeptical.

"Commander Oppenheimer, I relieve you, sir," said Granger.

Silence. Even amidst the shaking and rocking and distant booms and yells, every head on the bridge stared at Oppenheimer, to see what he would do.

"General Norton—before we q-jumped in—announced to all of us that you'd turned. That you'd been corrupted by the Swarm."

Granger stared at him. There was nothing he was going to be able to say to convince them otherwise. Nothing to do but wait and see what they decided.

"But ... the Admiral trusted you. After Norton signed off, all Bill said under his breath was 'bullshit.' And Doc tells me he transferred command to you right before he passed."

He stepped aside from the chair. "I stand relieved, sir." He retreated to the XO's station. "Please don't get us all killed," he said under his breath.

Granger smiled grimly, and took the captain's chair. "We're still alive, Commander. And while we're still alive, we've got a fighting chance." He examined his tactical readout at the command station to his right. The battle was a mess. The remaining Swarm carriers were pounding the surviving IDF ships, who fought back under the seemingly random fire from the dreadnought, which appeared to be shooting at both Swarm and IDF targets.

A green antimatter beam lanced out from the dreadnought and ripped into the nearest Swarm carrier, hitting it in a weak spot and piercing it through. But moments later the same turret focused its attention on the *ISS Panikkar*, one of *Victory*'s escort ships. The *Panikkar* fired back.

It was a free-for-all.

And he supposed the marines were still slogging through the ground war all along the hundred kilometer length of the dreadnought.

"Get me General Norton," he said toward the comm station. The comm officer worked the controls. Granger turned around slowly, looking for a familiar face. *Where the hell was Proctor?*

"You're on, Captain."

"General Norton, this is Captain Granger commanding the *ISS Victory*. I strongly encourage you to call off—"

Norton's angry voice interrupted him. "What the hell? Granger? Commander Oppenheimer, what is the meaning of this?"

"General, I'm the commanding officer of the *Victory*, by the express command of Admiral Zingano. I ask you again, sir, call off the attack and regroup to—"

"Like hell. Look, Granger, we're doing well over there. We control about ... ten percent of the ship. But now that it's started firing on us ... and these Swarm carriers are still hounding us...."

Why was the dreadnought firing on both sides? He reached out in his mind, calling to the Skiohra on the *Benevolence*, thinking the question to them.

You are all a threat. You must all be neutralized, came the furious chorus of a reply. And he saw their strategy as they thought it: attack both the Swarm carriers, and IDF, keeping them on equal footing, such that neither would have the advantage over the other until it came down to the last two ships, most likely the *Victory* against one of the least damaged carriers. Then the *Benevolence* would lay into both of them, even if it meant sacrificing one of their own matriarchs.

Wait, he told them. *I can save your matriarch. We can still destroy the Valarisi together. Just give me a chance.*

Prove it.

He had to get that army of marines to stand down. There was no negotiating with the Skiohra until they did. "General," he began, "if I can convince the Skiohra to destroy the remaining Swarm carriers, will you order a ceasefire? Give us a chance to figure out what's going on?"

Norton didn't immediately reply, though he heard muffled discussion on the other end.

"General, too many lives are at stake. If we don't act now, hundreds of thousands of IDF soldiers and officers will die."

"Fine, Granger," said Norton. "If you can get them to turn on their own ships, then fine. Give us a breather, and we'll talk to them. For all the good it will do us."

"Thank you, General. Granger out."

He closed his eyes. This would require all his powers of persuasion. *Please*, he began. *Please stop firing on us. If you destroy the Valarisi ships, I can convince my superiors to withdraw all the soldiers on your ship.*

Lies.

Believe me.

Your people are not to be trusted. They have already demonstrated that.

But we can learn. We can learn from you. You are an honorable, ancient people. We have much to learn from you. Please grant us that chance.

He could feel them debate amongst themselves, even as every few seconds another tens of thousands of voices disappeared as another mother perished. The argument swayed one way, then another, and all the while, as more voices disappeared, the side in favor of taking a chance on Granger started to win out.

"Captain," said someone at tactical, "the dreadnought has ceased firing on the fleet. They're ramping up the assault on the carriers.

Granger opened his eyes. On the viewscreen the sight was incredible. The dreadnought opened up all of its antimatter turrets, raining terrible green fire upon the more vulnerable Swarm carriers. One exploded. Then another. Then three more. Soon, there were only five left.

The guns of all of the survivors of Alpha Wing combined with the deadly onslaught from the *Benevolence* finished them off quickly.

Norton's voice sounded over the comm speaker. "Well, Granger, impressive, to say the least. You're a goddamned hero. Now watch as we finish this." The channel cut out. On the viewscreen Granger watched, seething with anger, as the IDF fleet opened fire on the dreadnought.

Granger pounded on the armrest. "Dammit!" *That swaggering, lying fool.*

Maybe Zingano was right. Maybe Norton really was compromised. Controlled by the Swarm. And not just with the backdoor virus, but the full-on usurpation strain.

And if so, maybe he could be manipulated. Maybe Granger could exercise the barest, momentary control over him, like he had Hanrahan. He closed his eyes, and reached out, toward the *ISS Lincoln*. Reaching for Norton's mind through the Ligature.

Friend, stop.

He tried to think of how he could convince the Swarm to cease their operations. If Norton really was under Swarm control, then they were using the IDF army to retake the dreadnought for themselves. The reason why was obvious—the ships were deadly, worth at least fifty Swarm carriers each.

Friend, I have information the Skiohra are hiding from you. Stop the attack, and I can convince them to tell us what they know. Everything depends on it.

Nothing. No response from the Swarm through Norton. Or any other potential Swarm-compromised person on that ship, or anywhere in the immediate vicinity. Meanwhile, the Children were screaming again. The soldiers continued their assault, and the voices continued to dwindle in number.

Dammit. "Helm, is the q-jump drive operational?"

"Yes, sir..." began the officer, confused.

"Initiate a q-jump to these coordinates on my mark," he said, entering in a set of numbers on his console. At the same time, he broadcast the thought to the Skiohra. *Jump. Come with me. I can stop the soldiers if you come with me.*

They had no choice. In spite of the chorus of Children calling for attack and denying Granger's request, the majority, fearful and weary of battle, overcame the voices of mistrust. Not due to any trust in Granger or what he was saying, but due to desperation.

We come.

"Mr. Oppenheimer, are all *Warrior* escape pods aboard?"

"Aye, sir."

"Recall the fighters. Both *Victory*'s and *Warrior*'s. And the ones from every other destroyed Alpha Wing ship we can fit in here. They have three minutes to land, and then we're out. If they don't all fit in the fighter bay, send them to the shuttle bay and the cargo bay. Pack 'em in."

Norton would try to stop them, he knew. This was basically mutiny. Not just insubordination. This was a one-way street, a path there was no coming back from. General Norton would go back to President Avery and the top brass and say he'd turned, that Granger had joined the Swarm openly.

This had better be worth it.

Two minutes later, they were all in. "Jump," he said, while simultaneously thinking the order to the dreadnought.

The screen shifted, the remains of the fighter battle replaced by empty space.

Moments later, the dreadnought snapped into existence, debris still streaming from the massive hole gouged out by the former *ISS Constitution*. A battle still raging all across its thousands of decks, in effect, one large ground war, in space.

"Get me on the invasion force channel," he said, and waited until the comm officer nodded toward him. "IDF invasion force, this is Captain Granger. Cease fire, and lay down your arms. I repeat, cease fire. All battle operations are hereby suspended, on orders from the Commander in Chief herself." He supposed if he was going to lie, he may as well go big.

It took a few minutes for the orders to propagate through the command structure, but he knew the results faster than anyone, as the Children's voices began to change, from dread and fear and confusion....

To glee and triumph.

Then righteous anger, tinted with a thirst for revenge.

CHAPTER FIFTY_NINE

Bridge, ISS Victory
Interstellar Space, 2.3 Lightyears From Sirius

IT WAS OVER. At least for now. The antimatter turrets on the dreadnought were quiet. Proctor relayed reports from Colonel Barnard that the marines had stood down, and either retreated back to their docking ships or barricaded themselves in different sections of the dreadnought.

But the *Victory* was a mess. Granger hadn't noticed it before, but there was dried blood smeared all over and around the captain's chair, and nearby a beam from the partially collapsed ceiling lay on the floor, pushed to the side. Probably the beam that killed Zingano. He looked up—sections of the deck above them were visible through the ceiling.

"Status summary," he said, glancing at the XO's station where Commander Oppenheimer and the ship's XO were conferring with each other.

"We have q-jump drive, life support, and the main engines. But the power plant has been damaged. Not critically, but they're short-handed down there as it is. We lost half our engineering crew in the attack."

The bridge doors slid open and Proctor finally walked through. He supposed she'd been coordinating rescue operations for the *Warrior* crew, getting all the escape pods to safety and accounting for who was still alive.

Granger motioned over to her. "Get Rayna and her crew down to Engineering." He turned back to Oppenheimer. "Your chief engineer—is she good?"

"He's dead, but—"

"Then Rayna Scott is the new chief. Please inform the deputy chief of the change," he said, not pausing to address whatever concerns the Commander was going to bring up. They were out of time. Krull had information, and from what she had been saying it sounded time-critical. "Sickbay, this is the Captain," he spoke to the open air.

"Sickbay here," said the doctor.

"Status of our patient, Doc?"

"Still unconscious, but stable. I think. Believe me, Captain, I'll make sure you're the first to know when she wakes up."

Still unconscious. For all he knew, the Russian plan she'd alluded to was already in progress, and they'd never even get to Earth or Britannia or whatever the target was in time.

"Thank you, Doc. Granger out."

Now, the would wait, and hope that Krull would wake up again. Looking around at the ruined bridge,

Granger knew there was plenty to do in the meantime. Even if they knew exactly where they needed to go in the next hour, they'd never be able to get there with the ship in its current state. And then there were the quick glances and the outright distrust on the faces of half the bridge crew. He knew they had good reason to look at him that way.

He was a renegade.

In spite of Zingano's confidence in him, the rest of the top brass hated him. And he'd just fled an active battle with known collaborators of the Swarm. IDF knew he could communicate with the Swarm and their allies through his mind, and that naturally created distrust. Hell, even *he'd* mistrust himself if he didn't know any better.

And he'd disobeyed direct orders from General Norton. In theory, any of the top officers aboard the *Victory* would have solid legal standing if they ever decided to mutiny. Any court martial worth its salt would decide that they'd acted rationally if they chose to topple him and toss him in the brig, or even put a bullet in his head.

"Commander Oppenheimer, casualty report," he said. For what lay ahead they'd need a smoothly running ship, and a crew he could trust. At the moment he had the survivors of two crews, all of whom had just lived though one of the most traumatic battles he'd ever seen.

And he'd seen many.

"During the engagement we lost, at current count, two hundred and thirty-eight souls. Including Admiral Zingano, Chief Engineer Ryu, the entire bridge ops crew on duty at the time, my deputy XO, and over half our fighters."

"Wounded?"

"Still too early for exact numbers, but the most recent estimate from sickbay is ninety-one crew members too wounded for duty. A dozen of those are critical and may not even make it."

He turned to Commander Proctor, who'd been hovering near the empty science station, apparently lost in thought. "Shelby?"

She shook her head, regaining focus. "Yes, Captain?"

"What's the status of *Warrior*'s crew? How many made it?"

After a moment of confusion, she brought up her data on a science station terminal. "We lost a handful of escape pods during the flight over from *Warrior*, but most made it. I count eight hundred and two crew members. Many wounded, but most not critically so."

"We need to integrate the two crews. Can you do that?" He noticed her head had drifted off to the side again, as if lost in thought. "Shelby?"

"Sorry, Tim, I've just been thinking. Trying to put it all together. The Swarm. The two viruses. The Skiohra. The Dolmasi. The meta-space signals. What it all means."

Granger nodded. He understood—she needed to work on the *real* problem. Someone else could handle the drudgeries of command. "Commander Oppenheimer. My Lieutenant Diaz is now your deputy XO. You and he will handle the integration of the *Warrior*'s crew aboard the *Victory*."

"How long will your old crew be staying, sir?" Oppenheimer's gaze was neutral, but the question dripped with meaning. *How long will you be here, Granger? How long will we be on the run from IDF?*

"As long as it takes to save our civilization, Mr. Oppenheimer."

Oppenheimer squirmed in his seat. Something had happened. Bridge crew officers were whispering amongst themselves. Granger glanced from Oppenheimer, to the tactical crew, who was also eyeing him uncomfortably. Finally, the comm officer spoke up. "Captain, we just picked up a meta-space signal from General Norton. You are to be apprehended, and we're supposed to return to his location."

Granger sighed. It was inevitable, of course. "You should all know that, right before Admiral Zingano died, he told me he suspected Norton was under Swarm control. Your own doctor can verify this. And I think the disastrous results of this hair-brained mission speak for themselves. So think long and hard before you make your call, Mr. Oppenheimer."

It was mostly true. Of course, in the minutes after Zingano had suggested as much, Granger had reached out to Norton through the Ligature, and determined that, in fact, the man was just being a stubborn jackass. No Swarm-control needed for that. No need to ascribe to foreign influence the ability for an officer to be a moron.

"But I'll tell you this, Mr. Oppenheimer," he began again, and turned to look around at the entire bridge crew. "I'll let you all in on a little secret. They call me the Hero of Earth." He paused. The bridge was silent. "Bullshit. I'm no hero." He pointed up toward Proctor.

"There's your hero." He pointed down in the direction of the shuttle bay. "More heroes down there on the fighter deck and shuttle bay. And here's another secret. When I was floating above Earth, in the *Constitution*, broken and hobbled, I knew with certainty that we'd win. Even as those first carriers closed in on us, battering the shit out of us, breaking our noses and kicking our asses, even then I knew. We would win. And do you know how I knew that?"

He rested his gaze on the navigational officer at helm. He hadn't had to give a good rah-rah speech in awhile—his old crew had gotten to the point where they performed expertly in every battle even when all he said was *go get 'em*, but this crew was on the cusp of turning on him. They needed their hero.

And the best hero was a reluctant hero.

"I knew we were going to win, not because *I* was the hero, but because I was resting on the shoulders of heroes. We won that battle, Mr. Oppenheimer, not because of me, but because of my crew. In fact, I literally rested on the shoulders of Commander Proctor when she carried me to safety as the *Constitution* blazed through the atmosphere and crash landed in Utah. Came to rest almost nose to nose with the monument to the old *ISS Victory*, in fact. It was why this ship was named what it was. Zingano thought it was poetic or some shit. But the fact remains, it's not the guy in charge that's the hero."

He turned back to Oppenheimer. "It's you. And by god, Commander, Earth needs us. Britannia needs us. Novo Janeiro needs us. Marseilles needs us. All of humanity is depending on us, and the decisions we make right now. One wrong move, and it's over."

He stepped away from the captain's chair and made for the exit. "You all have a duty. What that duty is is your own decision, and I won't stand in the way of it. Let me know what you choose." He motioned for Proctor to join him, and silently prayed that Oppenheimer wouldn't call the marines on him before he managed to leave the bridge. "But for my part, I hope you choose to be heroes." And with that, he passed through the bridge doors which opened to receive him.

After they'd rounded the bend, Proctor whispered behind him. "That was pretty good."

"Think they bought it?"

"If they don't, this'll be the shortest mutiny on record." She smiled, even if briefly. Good—her old sense of humor was intact. "Where are we going, by the way?"

"Sickbay. We need that information that Krull has. Unconscious or not, I'm going to get it out of her."

CHAPTER SIXTY

Sickbay, ISS Victory
Interstellar Space, 2.3 Lightyears From Sirius

SICKBAY WAS STILL CROWDED and busy, possibly more
so now that the wounded from the *Warrior*'s crew had
begun trickling up from the fighter deck and the shuttle
and cargo bay. Though, fortunately, the *Warrior*'s medical staff had also transferred over, so at least there was
care, if not space, for the patients.

On one of the beds he saw Ensign Prince, half his
head wrapped in a bandage, tinged with blood. He must
have had a mishap either during the evacuation or the
flight over to the *Victory*. He recognized a few more injured crewmen from his old crew, and the conscious ones
gave him small salutes as they were able. He was still *their*
hero. Their symbol of survival. And it showed in their
eyes. Just seeing him seemed to give their eyes life.

In the private examination room Krull lay unconscious on her bed, and to his credit the doc was still

there, taking life-sign readings. "I've got nearly a hundred of your people out there, Captain. One of them already died for lack of immediate care. This alien had sure better be worth it."

"She is. She and all twenty-two thousand of her Children."

The doctor nodded. "Yeah, I found them. In her abdomen, lining her bones, her ribs, embedded in fatty tissues all along her arms and legs. Not terribly large, but definitely embryos. Highly developed embryos—I've never seen anything like them. I can't even fathom how they get out."

"Most of them never do," said Granger. He wondered what it would be like to live the Interior Life, never knowing mobility, choice, independence.

But immediately the Children corrected him. *We do have choice. One does not need the Exterior Life to make choices.*

He realized he'd been thinking ... forcefully, for lack of a better word, and exposing himself to the Children through the Ligature. He wondered how sensitive it was. Was there some threshold below which they had no chance of hearing his thoughts? And how far did it extend? Could the Swarm, dozens of lightyears away, hear him? So many questions.

Questions that could wait.

"Wake her, Doc."

The doctor protested. "But Captain, that could be dangerous. Coma is a natural mechanism for the body to repair itself. Presumably for these people as well. You can't just wake someone up and expect them to be ok."

"Do it anyway. I need to talk to her."

Reluctantly, the doctor pressed a meta-syringe up to Krull's neck. "What if it kills her, Tim?" said Proctor.

"It's a chance we'll have to take. We need what she knows."

"Can't you just talk to the Children?"

He shook his head. "No, it's not quite the same. When she's unconscious, they are more disorganized. Like thousands of discordant voices. When she's awake, they were more like a choir. She gives them focus and order. They don't always agree on everything, just like most children, but not having her there makes it difficult to communicate."

Krull stirred. Granger heard her in his mind. He reached out to her through the Ligature. "Krull, I'm here. I need to know what you know."

She opened her eyes. "And why should I trust you?" Her voice was weak, barely above a whisper. "Your people have demonstrated their inability to be trusted," she said, weakly. "It's not just the Russians. You might think you're special, that you're different, but you're all the same. You all lust for power and control."

"No," said Granger. "It's not true. All I want is to save my people."

"It's what all of you say. It's what your president says. It's what Malakhov says. It's what every tyrant says."

Granger looked up at Proctor. Strange, wasn't it, that she mentioned the Russian president. "Do you know Malakhov?"

She slowly nodded. Her face had turned from a light cream-blue to a more greenish shade. From her mind it was clear that she felt terrible. Her chorus of Children hadn't calmed, and in fact, seemed to be getting more discordant and agitated. "I was the one to make the deal with him. Over ten of your years ago. It was under Valarisi control, of course, but I still remember it."

"The Khorsky incident," he muttered, to which she nodded. "And? What did he want?"

"He claimed he wanted to join us, of course. But we knew better. He wanted only to destroy us, but to do so on his terms, as part of some grand plan for Russian hegemony. He told us he had new, terrifying weapons that we could use to subjugate humanity quickly, without the need for a long, protracted war. We agreed, and helped him set up the production facilities over Penumbra Three. Construction took nearly a decade."

"And what did he want in return?"

"To survive, of course. He sold out humanity for his own survival. We agreed to leave his people—the Russians—alone, in exchange for the rest of humanity. That, and ... he wanted his own personal freedom."

Freedom? "Explain."

"I didn't understand at the time, since I was thrall to the Valarisi. I had no conception of even what he was asking for, or why he would ask for it, but of course it makes sense to me now. You see, Captain, he wanted to join the Swarm, but without being ... made a friend. Most of his top commanders and generals and politicians were made friends. But not Malakhov. He stayed outside the family. His mind, and his alone, was silent to us."

Granger and Proctor exchanged significant looks. So, out of all the Russian political and military structure, Malakhov stayed truly independent. The Russians were under Swarm influence at a tactical level, but not a strategic level. Malakhov was still in control.

"But he was wrong," she continued, coughing, then wincing. "We knew exactly what he was doing. You see, when we absorbed the Adanasi—the Russians—when we brought them into the family, we absorbed all their knowledge, their expertise, their skills. The Adanasi—and your people are no exception Granger—are experts at deception. At double dealings. At artifice and subterfuge and lies. And in the moment that the Valarisi absorbed the Adanasi, we understood them, and came up with our own subterfuge. We recognized what Malakhov was aiming to do, so we turned the tables on him."

"And what was that?" Granger asked urgently. She looked terrible, and worried that she'd pass out again soon.

"Malakhov planned the destruction of the Valarisi, using the new weapons he gave us. The singularities come in pairs. What comes in one side, goes out the other. We deployed the weapons on the carriers, but the other sides were all kept above Penumbra Three, near the production facility. Malakov claimed they needed to be there to maintain their stability, but we saw through that lie. His real goal was to collect all that matter, all that debris, enough mass to form a small moon. And then he would hurl it down to the surface."

"The surface?"

"Of the planet. Over which the production facility orbited."

"Why? What's on the planet?"

"Captain, it's obvious. When the Adanasi were absorbed, the Valarisi gained their penchant for subterfuge. And one of the first lessons of politics is that you keep your friends close, but your enemies closer."

"Are you saying...?"

"That Penumbra Three is the Valarisi's homeworld?" She coughed again. Blood tinged her lips. "Of course, that knowledge was kept from me, even for all the time I served the Valarisi. But isn't the answer obvious?"

"And Malakhov was going to bombard the surface of Penumbra Three with all the debris sucked up by the singularities that he's been collecting for the past four months?"

Proctor nodded. "It's a pretty effective way to eradicate the Swarm matter. It can most likely seep into the crust of whatever planet it's on, so you'd have to be thorough. A moon-sized mass hitting the planet would not only destroy all life, it would heat up and liquify the crust down to the mantle. There would be no way any Swarm matter would survive."

"Yes," said Krull. Her voice was faint. "But the Valarisi won't let that happen. In fact, the pieces are already in place. All that mass, instead of striking Penumbra Three and destroying it, will all be intercepted by another singularity. One outside of Malakhov's control."

Granger felt his blood run cold. "And where is that singularity's pair?"

"Over Earth, of course."

CHAPTER SIXTY-ONE

Sickbay, ISS Victory
Interstellar Space, 2.3 Lightyears From Sirius

"WHY DIDN'T YOU TELL ME this earlier?" asked Granger.

"We didn't know if we could trust you. And that hesitation on our part was vindicated," she said, wincing in pain. "But you *are* different, Granger. Maybe *you* can actually do something about it."

She brought her hands to her head and closed her eyes, almost seeming to pass out for a moment. The doctor scanned her head again. "She's hemorrhaging. I can't stop this brain bleed."

"And you won't, Doctor," she managed to say. "My body long ago lost the ability to heal itself. Such is the price of dependance on the gifts of the Valarisi."

Proctor edged closer. "What do you mean?"

"With the touch of the Valarisi comes control, but also healing. It has been in my blood for a very long time, healing me, unnaturally extending my life, such that my body has lost all natural ability to heal itself. Over time, one becomes entirely dependent on it."

"How long have you been under their influence?" Granger edged closer. Krull looked pale. He worried she was on her last leg. Judging from the frantic chorus of the Children, they were worried about it too. Terrified, was a more appropriate word.

"I was one of the first. At the very beginning. As I spend more time outside their influence, my memory is coming back. Slowly. But I was there. Over ten thousand years ago when the Valarisi first exerted their dominance over us."

Ten thousand years ago?

"I thought you said you were seven hundred and fifty?"

A weak smile. "I told you, we've learned much from the Adanasi. I lied. I did not trust you. I did not know you." She coughed again. "It was the very first cycle of the Valarisi. I was a young matriarch, sent by our Bonded Council of Seven to settle a new planet. We had been there a few years, building a small city and taming the environment. But we did not know that the Valarisi's cycle was soon to begin anew. One hundred and fifty of your years. Like clockwork, as you say. And we were in the wrong place, at the wrong time."

"Where were you?"

"Penumbra Three. The very first cycle. For us, at least. But the Skiohra were the first race to fall."

Penumbra Three. It was right there in our grasp, and the Russians scared us off. Unbelievable.

She continued. "We were aware of the Valarisi. They were kind, but enigmatic. As a liquid-based life form it was nearly impossible to communicate with them. But we knew they were there. We knew they were intelligent. But then came the quickening. The moment when the Valarisi were truly born. When the *others* came, we were powerless to stop them."

"Others? What others?"

"You know them as the Swarm, Captain."

"The Valarisi?"

"No. The *others* control the Valarisi."

Granger was confused. "Are you saying that the Swarm and the Valarisi are two separate races? Two different things?"

"Of course. The Valarisi are a beautiful, harmonious culture. Luminous beings of liquid and light. The Swarm corrupted them. Absorbed them. Just like they did to us. To the Dolmasi. To the Findiri and the Quiassi. And finally, the Adanasi. Seven peoples. One family."

"Then who *are* the Swarm?" Granger nearly shouted.

"We do not know. They are *other*. They came from beyond. We do not understand it. They are meta-space beings, Captain Granger. Beyond that, I know nothing, only that, through the Valarisi, they were able to dominate me. Control my thoughts and make me do ... unthinkable things."

A sick feeling came over Granger. He could tell from the look on Proctor's face that she felt the same. It seemed their enemy was even more deadly, more powerful, and more pervasive and untouchable than they'd ever dreamed.

There really was only one hope. They had to hide. Get enough of humanity out of the reach of the Swarm so that they could return and fight another day, many years in the future.

"When is the cycle over?"

"Granger—" Krull descended into a coughing fit, not calming down for half a minute. "I thought you understood that. The cycles are over. The Russians interrupted the cycle, and it is no more. The Swarm is here to stay."

She closed her eyes, and fell into unconsciousness. Through the Ligature, he could feel her slip away. The doctor sprang into action, pressing a meta-syringe into her, scanning her chest. "Her heart has stopped."

And from the chorus of Children, terror. Their mother was dead, and soon, they would be too. He supposed that, normally, when a Skiohra mother died, her body would usually release some calming agent to the Children, to ease their passage too. But Krull's normal body functions were corrupted from the millennia of dependance on Swarm matter.

And so they cried out in terror, until, one by one, by the dozens and hundreds, they too fell silent.

CHAPTER SIXTY-TWO

Executive Command Center, Russian Singularity Production Facility
High Orbit, Penumbra Three

ISAACSON RAN BACK DOWN the corridor. His only thought was to escape from the scene of the crime. What were the chances someone saw what he did?

And did it matter? He passed through the atrium where the elevator doors hung open to receive him, but after a brief moment of indecision, decided against it. Instead, he aimed for the observatory, thinking to use the comm system to call down to ... someone. His security detail? Maybe they could escort him to his ship without being detained.

No, that was stupid. He needed to act like it was an accident. And the only way for that to be believable was to report it. Quickly. He raced through the doors to the observatory, and scanned the walls for a commlink. The walls were bare, except for the doors that led into the medical station, the lab containing the singularity equipment, and what he supposed were other labs and support rooms.

Except for the far wall, where through the window the planet Penumbra Three turned slowly, serenely, far below, unaware of the maelstrom of fire that was about to hit it. As he passed the window, still looking for a commlink, he noticed something odd.

Or rather, he noticed the *lack* of something. The cloud of debris, and the miniature moon at its center, was gone.

He turned back to Penumbra, scanning its surface, its atmosphere, waiting for the fireball that would announce the beginning of the bombardment. But it never came. Penumbra merely rotated, unscathed, untouched.

And yet the ball of debris was gone.

"Thank you, Eamon. You've saved us."

He spun around. Volodin. Standing in the doorway.

"I—I—I—" stammered Isaacson. "I'm sorry, Yuri, there's been an accident. We were talking, and he tripped, and I tried to reach down and help him but—"

"Shh ... shh ... Eamon, it's ok." Volodin hushed Isaacson, holding a finger to his own lips. "I know what happened. Believe me, it's fine. You did us a great service."

Isaacson breathed a sigh of relief.

"You've always been a good friend, Eamon. A good friend."

Isaacson glanced back at the planet. "And the debris field? That small moon that Malakhov was going to hurl down there?"

Volodin approached, standing next to him in front of the viewport, looking down at the planet. "It's gone. Thanks to you, our friend."

"Where did it go?" Isaacson was started to be a little unnerved by Yuri's repeated use of the word *friend*. Malakhov had claimed the ambassador was corrupted, but Isaacson hadn't really believed him. He couldn't believe a word Malakhov ever told him. Volodin was clean—certainly that's what Isaacson had determined himself four months ago, in the command center outside Omaha, when he'd had the young commander scan the room for meta-space signals. At least, that's what Isaacson had convinced himself of.

"To Earth, of course."

Isaacson felt sick. "To—to Earth?"

Impossible.

"Yes, Eamon. Thanks to both you, and your President Avery. You see, I know what she did to you. Implanting all those devices. And when she sent you out here, she uploaded a new program into them. A program that reached out to any meta-space scramblers in the area, and disable them. And with the scramblers gone, the Concordat finally had access to the friends aboard the station. Ever since you stepped aboard, the Valarisi have been busy. And we've been listening, Eamon. We heard everything Malakhov said."

Isaacson stepped back in horror, realizing what he'd done. And for once, he was speechless.

"We've suspected his plans for awhile now, of course. But hearing it from his mouth confirmed it for us. He thinks he been using us for years, but in truth, we've been using him. And *you* Eamon! You saw through him! You saw how he was manipulating you, trying to use you to accomplish *his* goals. You realize you would have never left the *Constitution* alive, right? He would have used you to destroy the Skiohra—who are now in open rebellion against the Concordat—kill Avery, then use that as a propaganda victory, demonstrating to the surviving worlds that even the highest levels of United Earth government weren't to be trusted. That they needed to cast their lot with the Russian Confederation. To trust Malakhov, their savior. Once you'd served your purpose, Eamon, he would have killed you. Just like Avery wants to kill you.

"But now you're a hero, Eamon. The greatest hero Earth has even known. You stood up and cast off your oppressors. It is through you that your people will finally be made friends. And know an eternity of fellowship and communion with us. Once Earth is gone, we will call a ceasefire, and allow an orderly surrender of the rest of the Adanasi, and, finally, you will be united with us."

What the hell do I do now? thought Isaacson. And the only answer he had, the only thing he could even think of, was to run.

So he ran. He turned and bolted toward the door, flying through, desperately trying to make it into the elevator before—

To his surprise, he felt a burst of wind blow over him and when he blinked again, Volodin was standing in front of the elevator.

"Remember when I told you about the initial contact with the Swarm during the Khorsky incident? How those men that went into the Swarm carrier came back ... changed? Stronger? Faster? Smarter. Wiser. Better. I neglected to tell you, I was one of those men, Eamon. I was one of the first to know friendship with the Valari-si. And now, it is your turn."

Before Isaacson could jump back Volodin reached out and grasped his arm. The ambassador's hand was damp with sweat—even as the fingers closed around Isaacson wrist, he could feel it.

Oh my god, I can feel it.

The Swarm virus rushed through the pores of his skin, entered his blood, and immediately started reproducing themselves and targeting his spinal column, his brain stem, his cerebrum, his entire brain, all the automatic centers in his limbic system, his respiratory system, his gastrointestinal system....

He knew all this because the first thing he noticed after Volodin touched him was that he could *hear* the other man's thoughts, then he could *hear* the thoughts of the Swarm virus penetrating his body, targeting all his systems. He could hear them as they went about their work, faster than he ever expected. And as his eyes grew wider, he began to be aware of something else.

Isaacson was *happy*. Blissfully happy. The virus—hell, it shouldn't be called a virus.

It should be called deliverance.

But something was wrong. He was one with the Swarm. One with the deliverance circulating through his body, but his living link to the Valarisi was butting up against something it didn't understand. Something metallic. Something ... electronic. That was doing ... something.

The implants. Avery's implants.

The virus immediately began attacking the tiny pellets embedded in his flesh—*we can cure all disease, lengthen the natural lifespan of these mortal carriers, surely we can disable Avery's*—

All at once, the implants, all thirty of them, exploded. Even as the blast waves tore Isaacson's body apart, engulfing not only him but Volodin as well, ripping them both to shreds, the last conscious part of his Swarm-enlivened mind screamed out, cursing Avery.

There was more than one program uploaded, he knew, in that final moment. The program that disabled the meta-space scramblers had been very helpful. This program, the one that detonated the implants at the first sign of Valarisi communion, was less helpful.

Curse that woman. Out of reflex, what was remained of his left hand tapped out the defiant rhythm he'd grown so accustomed to repeating.

Tap, tap-tap, tap.

Earth will die, and Avery with it, within the hour. They will all be made friends. Or they will all die.

CHAPTER SIXTY-THREE

Sickbay, ISS Victory
Interstellar Space, 2.3 Lightyears From Sirius

GRANGER DIDN'T SPEAK for several minutes. The doctor pronounced the alien dead, and left, leaving Proctor and Granger alone with the body.

"We can't win, Shelby. How do you fight against incorporeal meta-space beings? Beings who can reach across the void of space-time and completely control another race? And through that race, control us all?"

"I don't know," she replied, quietly.

"If they're meta-space beings, then they're everywhere. It doesn't matter how far we run, they'll be there. Even if we wipe out every Swarm carrier, they'll still be there. If we go on a campaign to neutralize every single gram of Swarm matter, they'll still be there. We'll miss a few spots here or there, or maybe a stray Swarm fighter blown off course in a battle will land on a planet somewhere, and they'll multiply, and the Swarm will rise again. It's hopeless."

They sat in silence another minute before Proctor stirred. "Tim, it's never hopeless. It's just a puzzle to be solved. A science problem. A logic problem. And human beings, that's what we do. Figure out the solution to the logical quandary, and we defeat the Swarm."

Granger rolled his eyes, "Well, shit, why didn't I think of that?"

"I'm serious, Tim. Think about it. Krull said that the Russians broke the cycle. That the Swarm is here to stay? If they broke the cycle, then that means the cycle can be affected. It can be restored. Or it can be shut down completely. Whatever the Russians have done, it proves one thing. That the link to the *others*, the ones in meta-space, is a natural, physical thing. A thing we can affect, a thing we can touch, or the Russians never would have been able to interrupt the cycle and make it permanent. And if they can do it, we can do it too."

Granger was shaking his head. "How? We're out of ships. We're out of people to fly ships. And more importantly, we're out of will. Did you see the looks in the faces of the bridge crew when we left? It was a good speech, but it wasn't *that* good. Those are people on their last leg. Do you really think they're going to let us fly off, away from Norton and the brass and Avery, off on some implausible quest to stop boogey-men who don't even live in our universe? No. It's over."

More silence. The moans from the main floor of sickbay crept through the closed door. "The singularities. It has to be," she said.

"Excuse me?"

"How the Russians interrupted the cycle. Something about the singularities lets the *others* reach into our universe and re-exert their control over the Swarm—the liquid, the Valarisi. There's no other explanation. There was probably some natural cycle, somewhere, that let them into our universe every one hundred and fifty years. But with the singularities, they don't need that anymore."

Granger nodded. "So, shut down all the singularities, and we close all the doorways into our universe?"

"All the man-made ones, at least."

Granger stood up. "Right. I guess that's all we've got. Let me guess. Penumbra Three? The Russian singularity fabrication facility?"

"And it's where the Skiohra first came into contact with the Valarisi—the liquid. That's where I'd start. And maybe we'll even learn what exactly it was you did when you showed up there four months ago."

Granger grunted. "That's if we can even convince the *Victory's* crew to go along with it."

The door slid open, as if on cue. Commander Oppenheimer strode in. Two marines stood behind him.

Dammit.

"Captain Granger, sir," began Oppenheimer. The two marine guards looked tense, and they glanced behind themselves periodically into sickbay.

"You here to arrest me?"

Oppenheimer smiled. "No, sir. They're just here for protection. In case any among the crew don't think the same as I do."

"And what exactly do you think, Commander?"

"That you and Commander Proctor are the best shot we've got at winning this war. The *Victory* stands ready to serve, Captain. Just give the word."

Granger breathed a sigh of relief and reached out to shake his hand. "Commander, the word is given. Set q-jump coordinates for Penumbra Three. We've got an enemy to destroy."

CHAPTER SIXTY-FOUR

Bridge, ISS Lincoln
High Orbit, Earth

GENERAL NORTON COUNTED DOWN the seconds until the final q-jump toward Earth. Damage to his ship was significant—a repair and resupply was desperately needed and the IDF shipyard at the still-under-repair Valhalla Station stood ready to receive them.

But the thing that occupied his mind most was Granger's treachery. Avery's eyes would finally be opened. They'd finally be able to move on from this nonsense of trusting an openly-compromised Swarm asset. For hell's sake, the man practically admitted to being in open communication with their mortal enemy.

"Final q-jump now, sir," said the ensign at helm.

The viewscreen shifted, revealing their blue, cloud-speckled home, its moon hovering distant and white in the background.

"Comm, open a frequency to *Frigate One*. The president should be waiting for us."

"Aye, aye, sir."

Moments later, President Avery's glaring face filled the screen. "General? Report."

"Not good, Madam President. The operation failed. The dreadnought escaped."

She swore.

"And Madam President, I think you should know that the dreadnought escaped with the assistance of Captain Granger." Norton went on to recount the entire botched mission to take the dreadnought, finishing with the moment the ship disappeared with the *ISS Victory*. "And furthermore, shortly after they left, I received a brief meta-space message from someone on Colonel Barnard's team indicating they went in the direction of the Penumbra system."

Avery's eyes flashed wide for the briefest moment. "Interesting. It just so happens our most useful tool is there now as well."

"And his mission? Are you sure it will bear out? We can't afford to keep losing like this."

"I'm confident that no matter what action Mr. Isaacson chooses to take, a decisive blow will be struck against the Russian Confederation and the Swarm. The two programs I uploaded into his implants should ensure that."

Norton rubbed his eyes—it had been a long, long day, with too much loss. "Care to fill me in?"

Avery nodded, hesitantly at first, as if she were deciding whether he, the damn chairman of the friggin'

Joint Chiefs of Staff of IDF deserved to be let in on her secret plans. Bitch.

"Very well. The first program will compromise the system the Russians have in place to keep out Swarm influence from their highest levels of government. My intelligence reports indicate that the entire Penumbra station is filled with meta-space dampeners. Isaacson's implants will interfere with them. Mr. Malakhov is about to get a taste of his own medicine, and may soon regret playing with powers beyond his control."

"And what if that backfires on us, ma'am? Opening up Malakhov to total Swarm control could bite us in the ass."

"He deserves it, General. Any discord and confusion we can create on their side can only serve us."

"Fine," he said, not wanting to argue further. What was done was done. "And the second?"

"The second is just a failsafe. If the Swarm decides to make our Mr. Isaacson a *friend*, the implants are programmed to explode. Should take out anyone close by, too. Hopefully Volodin, if not Malakhov himself. If we're lucky, he'll be near a singularity containment system and destroy it. Who knows, maybe there'll be a chain reaction that will take out the whole damn station."

That's a big if, you friggin' petulant politician.

"Very well, ma'am. In that case, I recommend we—"

"Sir! New sensor contact!"

His head snapped toward the rattled officer at the sensor station. "What is it?"

"Unknown, sir. Whatever it is, it's big. Putting it onscreen now."

The image of Avery switched to a splitscreen view. Her face contorted to one of dread shock, while the other half of the screen showed something impossible.

A small moon, surrounded by a shroud of swirling dust and debris, had suddenly appeared several tens of thousands of kilometers away, surrounded by a fleet of Swarm carriers, moving incredibly fast in their direction.

Toward Earth.

CHAPTER SIXTY-FIVE

Bridge, ISS Victory
Interstellar Space, 2.3 Lightyears From Sirius

IT TURNED OUT the marine escort was not as necessary as Granger feared. When he stepped onto the bridge, he saw some friendly familiar faces mixed in with the *Victory*'s crew. Lieutenant Diaz conferred with the officers at the XO's station. Ensign Prince, head still bandaged, sat next to the *Victory*'s helmsman. Ensign Diamond had replaced one of the tactical officers who Granger remembered as bleeding from the forehead. For the most part, stern nods met him as he walked toward the captain's chair.

"Ship status?"

Commander Oppenheimer slid into the XO's chair next to Lieutenant Diaz. His eyes trailed over the array of status reports. "Engine three still out. Power plant is operating at twenty percent, but your chief engineer has taken over down there and promised me fifty percent within the hour—"

"We don't have an hour," he grumbled, then raised his head to the comm. "Rayna, this is Granger. I need q-jump capability. When can I have it?"

"Sorry, Cap'n, things are a mess down here. When do you need it?"

"Ten minutes ago."

She snorted. "Good luck with that, Cap'n."

"Rayna, our entire civilization hangs by a thread. We need to get to Penumbra Three right *now*, and if we don't, we may as well get really comfortable here on the *Victory* because it's going to be our home for a very long, long time, seeing how Earth will soon become a large ball of molten rock."

Silence on the other end, punctuated by colorful muttering under Commander Scott's breath.

"Commander?"

"I'll reroute power from engine two to the q-jump caps. We won't need much acceleration, will we? The power shunts will overheat, but they'll hold. I think. Give me a few minutes, Cap'n."

"Thank you, Commander. Granger out."

Oppenheimer shook his head. "Captain, what's the rush? We're safe for the moment. Shouldn't we be getting back to Earth and reporting in to CENTCOM?"

Granger debated telling the whole bridge crew what their mission had become, especially seeing how the likelihood of coming back from it alive was on the lower end of reasonable.

But they deserved to know. Whether they liked it or not, he was their captain now. And they were his crew. He'd likely be sending them all into battle again before this was all over, and they deserved to know what they were up against. "Commander, we're going to the Penumbra system because that is where the Russian Confederation has been producing the singularity devices for the Swarm."

"Do you think we can disable them if we go there? Won't they be guarded by the Russian fleet?"

"Most likely." He explained the rest of what he knew, going over most of what Krull had told him before she died, laying out the stakes, only withholding one key piece of information, namely, that he had no idea how to permanently end the meta-swarm's incursions into their universe. They'd have to figure that part out once they got there.

"Incredible," breathed Oppenheimer. The rest of the bridge crew looked stunned. They were trying to process the possibilities, the ramifications—how could incorporeal beings reach through meta-space and exert their influence in our universe? Granger could see the fear in their eyes as they realized they were up against not just a mortal threat, but an immortal one.

"Look," began Granger, swinging around to look at the entire bridge crew one by one. "I can tell you, from personal experience, that...."

That what? That he was the Hero of Earth? That he'd fly into a singularity, magically fix things, and come back as the triumphant hero and all would be well? That everything was going to be ok?

"I can tell you that things may seem bleak, but no matter what, I won't give up, and I know you won't either. We'll figure this out. Trust me. I pledge you my life, such as it is ... look, we don't have time for speeches. Just do your duty, I'll do mine, and at the end of the day, that's all we can do. Understood?"

Everyone nodded. *Good.* He pointed at the comm station. "Get me the Skiohra ship."

Moments later, a Skiohra crew member appeared on the screen. The same one that had appeared behind Krull before—perhaps one of her deputies. "Granger," she said, seeming to seethe. "Vice Imperator Scythia Krull is dead. Our ship is crippled, and over four hundred thousand of your soldiers still occupy our home. Explain yourself."

Granger held up his hands. "Treachery, my friend. The treachery and influence of the Valarisi runs deep. I suspect even up to our highest levels of command. I'm ... I'm sorry. For all the loss among your people. For Krull. She was an amazing example of leadership."

The Skiohra bowed her head. "She was. And all her Children." The tone of her voice, even though alien, spoke of unspeakable grief. "She was the eldest. The Matriarch of Matriarchs. Her story will be told throughout the generations." She spoke to someone out of view of the screen, giving a few orders, before turning back to Granger. "I am Vice Imperator Polrum Krull. Scythia was my grandmother. I lead the family aboard this ship now—I and my fifty thousand Children," she added, putting a hand on her chest, presumably to indicate her offspring who lived the Interior Life.

"Polrum Krull, I am on my way to the Penumbra system. I know it is too much to ask for assistance, but any advice you might have would be appreciated. Do you know the layout of the station there? The status of any fleets protecting it? Anything you know, anything at all, would help enormously."

Polrum Krull bowed again. "Scythia warned me you would ask about this." She looked to the side and gave more orders to someone off-camera. "Granger, Scythia told you she was charged by the Valarisi to manage their periods of rest, and to negotiate with the Adanasi. All of the matriarchs were involved in the effort, overseen by the Valarisi, of course. I, and most of my Children, are particularly skilled in the sciences, and I was one of the principles among my people to integrate the Adanasi technology aboard the Valarisi ships."

Granger did a double take. "Are you saying...?"

"You will need help understanding their technology, Captain, and understanding how they are using it to destroy your world. Scythia Krull told me through the Ligature that helping you would be essential to our people's survival. Though it pains me to offer it—your people's treachery has been ruinous for us—we will come with you to Penumbra Three, if you like."

If I like?

Granger smiled. "Polrum Krull, you will be most welcome."

CHAPTER SIXTY-SIX

Bridge, ISS Victory
High Orbit, Penumbra Three

IT TOOK SEVERAL HOURS to complete the series of q-jumps out toward the Penumbra system, as it was at the other end of Russian Confederation space. But during that time he coordinated with Colonel Barnard, still holed up on the Skiohra dreadnought *Benevolence*, who, once he heard they were about to attack the Russian base responsible for producing all the terrifying weapons of the enemy, was more than happy to assist in the invasion.

And an invasion it would be. Polrum Krull reported that the station was massive—a hollowed-out asteroid. And not like the asteroids that were used in the construction of the *Constitution* and the *Warrior* and the rest of the old Legacy Fleet. This one could easily swallow any one of them whole, with room to spare for a few Swarm carriers. Polrum Krull didn't know how many ships were patrolling the orbits of Penumbra Three, nor how many soldiers Malakhov kept stationed there, but Granger wasn't going to leave anything to chance.

Each marine boarding ship would detach from the *Benevolence* and line up at the docking ports of the station. Four hundred thousand soldiers was probably overkill, but Granger wanted to be ready for anything. The *Benevolence* and the *Victory* would have to handle whatever ships, or, god forbid, fleets, that were patrolling the area.

"We'll secure the station, Captain. Then come aboard and do what you need to do," said Colonel Barnard on the viewscreen. A large gash ran across his face—a wound sustained during the aborted battle for the dreadnought. He'd lost a lot of men in the attempted takeover, but he seemed willing to overlook the fact that they were now cooperating with the enemies that, up until a few hours ago, were putting up a spirited defense of their ship. Granger gave the man credit for his professionalism—after he'd explained the situation and given the order, Barnard simply grit his teeth, saluted, and asked what he could do to help. He figured the army man was just thankful for a chance to finally see some action in defense of Earth, and didn't care much whether he got to knock Skiohra heads, or Russian ones.

"Thank you, Colonel. Rules of engagement: shoot to kill on sight, unless you see they're a technician or scientist. Even then, if they don't immediately submit ... well, you know the drill. We have no time to waste. I need that station within ten minutes, if you can manage it."

"Ten? I'll have it in five sir," the colonel said with a salute. "Barnard out."

Granger turned to Ensign Prince. "Final q-jump ready?"

"Ready, sir."

"Initiate."

The viewscreen shifted from an angled perspective of the vast Skiohra ship, to a view that Granger recognized from two months earlier, when he'd arrived the first time at Penumbra with his erstwhile invasion fleet. That time, he'd been on a mission to engage in a guerrilla campaign against the Swarm—catch them off balance, distract them, draw their attention away from invading human worlds and toward defending their own.

Little did he know that he could have ended it all by bombarding the surface below, or taking out the station where the Russians were producing the singularities. Of course, he still had no idea if either of those things would end the Swarm. That was his new mission. End them permanently. Not only destroy their weapons, and their worlds, but kick them out of the universe for good.

"Any ships? Fleets?"

"Several dozen Russian cruisers docked at the station, and a handful more in the vicinity," came the reply from tactical.

"What is their posture?"

Ensign Diamond shook his head. "They're not mobilizing."

"They may not know we're a threat yet, since we're with the dreadnought. We need to take advantage of their ignorance quickly. Colonel Barnard, you're up. Commence operations," he said into his comm channel.

He watched as the IDF marines' boarding ships detached from the dreadnought and darted over to the station—a massive rock whose surface was interrupted here and there by gleaming metallic surfaces, viewports, docking ports, giant bay doors—large enough to admit passage of the *Victory* and possibly a Swarm carrier—and all sorts of antennae, dishes, and other sensor equipment peeking out from the rocky surface.

"Captain," said Ensign Diamond, "conducting routine scans of the solar system, sir. Turns out the star is a binary. It's companion is a black hole."

The words electrified him. "A black hole, you say?" He turned back to the science station where *Victory*'s new science officer sat. "Confirm, Ensign Roth?"

"Yes, sir. About thirty solar masses. The hole and the star both mutually orbit a barycenter, but they're far enough away from each other that the event horizon is pretty quiet. Virtually no x-rays or gamma rays coming from the poles."

A black hole. A singularity. The coincidence was too much. "Shelby?" he said. "What do you think?"

"Tim, there are millions of black holes in the galaxy. Binary systems like this are common."

"But ... you don't think it's a possibility?"

"Of course it's a possibility, and we should keep an open mind. But if this one has somehow become a meta-space link, why aren't all black holes meta-space links? Like I said, there are millions them—that we know about. There might be billions, for all we know—the galaxy's a big place."

"Fine." Still, it was an odd coincidence. "Diamond, status of the marines?"

"All troop transports have docked, sir. Sporadic fighting reported."

The wait was almost unbearable, though in reality, only fifteen minutes passed before Colonel Barnard called over from the station. "Captain Granger?"

"Yes, Colonel?"

The words he was hoping for. "The station is secure, sir. Minimal casualties." He almost sounded disappointed—it appeared this wasn't the battle he was hoping for.

"Thank you, Barnard."

Proctor looked up from the science station, where she'd been huddling with a few member of her team she'd brought over from the *Warrior*. "Tim, take a look at this."

"Can it wait? We need to get over there and figure out what's going on."

"This might help us do that." He walked over and glanced at her monitor. "Look," she said, pointing to a few readouts. "Last time we were here we detected some gravitational anomalies coming from the planet, but we couldn't stick around long enough to figure out what was up. But now that I know what I'm looking for," she looked up at him. "Tim, there are thousands, tens of thousands of primordial singularities in orbit around the planet. They seem to be concentrated in this area here, where there is also an unusually high concentration of debris."

"What kind of debris?" Granger suspected he knew the answer.

"Rocks, dirt, water ... and metallic debris, too. Pieces of ships. Buildings. I think we're seeing where everything went. Everything that went into the singularities came out here."

"But where's the rest of it? There should be a small moon's worth of material here."

Proctor shrugged. "Maybe it hasn't shown up yet?"

"Maybe," said Granger, stroking his stubbly chin. "Or maybe—"

"Sir!" shouted Ensign Diamond at tactical. "Something just showed up on our scopes. Out of nowhere."

"A ship?" Had something else come out of one of the singularities?

"A fighter." He looked up, like he'd seen a ghost. "One of ours."

CHAPTER SIXTY-SEVEN

Bridge, ISS Victory
High Orbit, Penumbra Three

"LIEUTENANT VOLZ, this is Captain Granger. Do you copy?" Granger watched the screen as the fighter tumbled through space, narrowly missing a large chunk of rock and ice.

"He could be knocked out from traversing the singularity. That would explain *our* Volz's memory problems. *And* yours, Tim," said Proctor.

"Well," he began, shrugging, "we know he made it back. So whatever happened—happens," he corrected himself. *Damn, this timeline stuff is hard to keep straight.* "Whatever Ballsy did out there, we know he pulled out of it. *With* Fishtail. Speaking of, where the hell is Fishtail?"

Ensign Diamond and the rest of the tactical crew scanned the area around the station, the debris field, every altitude of their current orbit. Nothing. "Sorry, sir. Looks like she hasn't shown up yet."

Granger muttered under his breath. "We don't have time for this. Shelby, we need to get over to the station and figure out what we're doing. Let's go." He started for the doors, glancing back to Lieutenant Diaz. "Lieutenant, monitor the area, keep an eye out for Fishtail. See what you can do to help. Send a shuttle out for Ballsy if he gets in trouble—"

Proctor cut him off. "Ballsy might think we're Swarm. In fact, he *will* think we're Swarm—I mean, here we are, cozying up to what he would think is a Swarm ship, at a Russian station, with a Russian fleet, all one big happy family. No matter what we say, given his disorientation, he's not going to trust us. Plus, we already *know* what he thinks. He's told us as much."

"Good point," said Granger. "Either way, Lieutenant Diaz, keep your eyes on what's going down out there. Call me if you need me. Hopefully we'll be back soon, with some answers."

He and Proctor rushed down to the shuttle bay and boarded the waiting craft. Escape pods from the *Warrior* were pushed off to the side of the bay, and it took some delicate flying to ease the shuttle out the doors, but soon they were cutting through the void of space that separated them from the station. It grew larger and larger in their cockpit window, until it filled their whole view.

"Polrum Krull says the main command deck can be reached through that docking port," said Granger, pointed toward a spot on the sensor monitor. Several kilometers away he saw another shuttle, this one from the dreadnought, approach a nearby port and latch on.

"That'll be Polrum," he said. Their own shuttle approached, slowed, and eased into position. The docking clamps latched into place and the distant hiss of air told him the airlock had engaged.

Granger sprang out of the airlock as soon as the hatch swung open. When he passed through the door into the hallway beyond, Colonel Barnard was waiting for him. The other man saluted. "Captain," he said in greeting. "This appears to be the executive complex. Looks like Malakhov himself and his senior commanders used this wing as their base of operations when they were in this sector."

"How do you know?"

Barnard waved his arm through another door, indicating they pass through. In the space beyond was what looked to be an atrium, with a fish tank, photographs of the Russian president hanging from the wall, and potted trees and hanging plants.

And lying against one of the granite walls, blood pooled up beneath him on the marble floor, a body. Or rather, what was left of it. Granger recognized the face of the late Vice President Isaacson. The rest of his body, what remained of it, was raw and gouged, with limbs twisted at odd angles. An arm was missing. Across the atrium, slumped against the far wall, lay what looked like Ambassador Volodin.

"What do you suppose happened here?" said Proctor. Her face was white with the sight of the gore, but to her credit she picked her way through the carnage, scouring the room for clues.

"Whatever it was, I suspect it came as somewhat of a shock to Mr. Isaacson," deadpanned Granger. He never liked the man, in spite of his recent closeness to Avery.

"Granger," said Polrum Krull, who came through the door to the docking port hallway. Several of the marines spun around and readied their assault rifles. Granger waved them off.

"You've been here before?"

She nodded. "Yes. Among my Children are experts at the Russian quantum singularity technology, and I helped integrate the systems into the Valarisi ships." She went toward one of the doors in the atrium. "I believe we can access the database and remote quantum-field control through here."

Granger followed closely behind, with Proctor in step. Beyond the door was a large room with one giant viewport on the other side, nearly filling the entire wall. Other doors lined the walls, including monitors, control stations, a large beautiful oak desk, and more pictures of Malakhov. The man clearly loved looking at himself.

"Through here," said Polrum Krull. In one of the rooms branching off from the office with the oak desk and giant viewport, she sat down at a control station. "I can access records of all quantum singularities from here, I believe."

Granger watched lines of information stream past on the monitor. All in Cyrillic letters, of course. "You read Russian?"

"Several of my Children do. They read and interpret for me."

"Is that how you're speaking to me now?"

Polrum Krull looked up in surprise. "Of course. I myself don't have time to learn everything. But there is always one or two of my Children willing to throw themselves at a task I do not have time or energy for." She looked down at the monitor. "Ah. Just as we suspected. One hour ago, singularity 5521b was launched at a large, moon-sized mass of material that was orbiting Penumbra Three at a slightly lower elevation than this station."

"And the other side?" He knew the answer, but wanted to hear it from the Skiohra herself.

"5521a is assigned to a Valarisi carrier, which is—" she studied the readout for a moment. "In the Terran system. Orbiting Earth."

"We've got to stop it," said Granger. "Can we somehow send a signal from here? Make the carrier reroute? Or disable the carrier's singularity control system?"

Polrum Krull shook her head. "The connection we had with the Valarisi is closed. We dare not open that door again. And even when we shared the Ligature, we had no control over them. Quite the reverse."

"Can't you feed them false information? Like the Dolmasi did with me? Maybe ... maybe send them an image of all six of your dreadnoughts coming here to Penumbra and laying waste to the surface?"

"They won't care, Captain. Remember, the Valarisi are not the Valarisi. The Swarm is not from our universe, as Scythia Krull told you. Why would they care if we kill some portion of the Valarisi down on the surface? There's no way we could eradicate all of them down there, not even with all of our combined strength. The Valarisi would slip through the cracks—

the literal cracks in the surface, seeping down deep into the crust. We'd never destroy all of them, and so the Swarm doesn't care what we do to the Valarisi as long as some of it survives. No, Granger, the solution is clear. We need to send a singularity to Earth, intercept the mass, send it back here through the singularity's sibling, and follow through with Malakhov's plan."

Granger shook his head. "No. No matter what we do to the surface of Penumbra, it won't change the fact that the Swarm can still reach across meta-space and control the Valarisi. We need to find that link, the one with the hundred and fifty year cycle, and destroy it."

Polrum Krull nodded. "Yes, but where is that link? Ever since our liberation from the Valarisi two days ago, our entire civilization has debated this, to no avail. We simply have no idea how they had been entering our universe before the Russians unleashed their singularities."

It was a problem. One they had to solve fast—the mass of debris was most likely approaching Earth even as they spoke. Depending on the time dilation or compression on its trip through the singularity, it could have already arrived by now, destroying humanity's home.

Proctor had stepped out for a minute, but now ran back through the door. "Tim, you need to come see this."

The look on her face was all he needed to rush out of the room, follow her past the giant viewport, past Malakhov's desk, and into what looked like a hospital room.

He couldn't believe it.

There he was. Captain Granger—old, sick, frail, white and gaunt with disease.

And most definitely not in the past, as Kharsa had led him to believe.

He'd come to the future.

CHAPTER SIXTY-EIGHT

Executive Command Center, Russian Singularity Production Facility
High Orbit, Penumbra Three

"SHELBY, AM I DREAMING?" he said. It was surreal, to stand above yourself, looking down, seeing you, your own body, sleeping. It was like a near-death experience. There he was, on an operating table after a failed attempt at resuscitation and now his spirit was rising up over his body, looking down. Except he really was there—he was both.

"It's really you, Tim." She examined the readouts on the monitors nearby. "And you're not doing too well. Cachexia is setting in—the cancer is wasting your tissues. Acidosis, sepsis, muscle wasting. I'm no doctor, but I'd expect your organs to start failing any day now. Maybe any hour."

"But Kharsa said that I'd been a friend before. That I'd been Swarm. Why haven't the Russians converted me over?"

"We'll have to ask Malakhov," she said.

"You're a little late for that." Colonel Barnard had entered the room. The look on his face told Granger that there was even more news. "Found him at the bottom of long drop over in the bay. And that's not all we found. Captain Granger, the Old Bird is here."

It made sense, of course—if the old Granger was here, then the *Constitution* was here, too. "Go aboard. Secure it," he said.

"Aye, aye, sir." Barnard stepped out the door, talking into his commlink to issue orders to his marines.

Granger turned back to Proctor. "Shelby, look. If we don't do something, I'm going to die. And, I may not be a scientist, but I've read my share of science fiction. Aren't we in for a world of headache-inducing timeline disruptions if we let that happen? It's like I'm killing my grandfather here—how can I be dead in the past, but alive now?"

"I—I don't know, Tim. All theoretical work on timeline disruption is just that—theory. Some theoretical physicists think that due to quantum effects, two universes branch off from each other every time a new quantum event happens, and given that a near-infinite number of quantum events happen just within our own bodies in any given second, they think that there are an infinity of universes parallel to ours, and that if our past timeline is disrupted it doesn't affect us because for *us*, you and me, right here, it's already happened. But *his* timeline," she indicated the sleeping Granger, "will be affected. Same with all the time traveling that's been going on lately, I suppose. You, Fishtail, Ballsy. Even all those chunks of rock sucked from the crust of Earth and all the other targeted worlds—they've all time traveled to a degree."

Granger shook his head. "So, if I die here, our universe is unaffected?"

"Well, other theoretical physicists disagree. They say there is only *one* universe. Ours. And if we disrupt our past timeline, well, there's disagreement even on that. Possibilities range from the timeline just resetting to the point at which the disruption happened—even though that sets up the possibility of temporal loops—or, well, I think the term is *cataclysmic resolution*."

"That doesn't sound pleasant." Granger watched the monitor. His heart beat weakly, his blood pressure hovered at a terrifyingly low range. And yet, he remembered waking up on Proctor's shoulder four months ago. Sure, he felt weak then, but in the days following he'd made a full recovery. He'd felt, well, amazing, compared to his final days with the cancer setting in. There was only one way that could happen. He turned to Proctor. "Inject me."

"Excuse me?"

"You heard me. I know you grabbed some of your research before we left the *Warrior*. You've got some Swarm matter, right? Inject me. Put me—put him—under Swarm control."

He thought she was going to protest, to attempt to convince him there was another way. Instead, she nodded. "It will cure the cancer. Bring you back from the brink of death, just like Fishtail. But we'll need to find the singularity pair that you came out of, and send you back through it. That should inactivate the virus." She pulled a meta-syringe out of her pocket.

"Do it."

She pressed the syringe up to the sleeping Granger's neck, and a soft puff of air indicated the contents had been injected. Proctor opened a drawer and shuffled through the contents, searching for something, while Granger watched himself react to the virus.

Slowly, the color returned to his face. His heart rate increased on the monitor. The blood pressure rose. The levels of acid in his system began plummeting to normal levels as the virus began its work.

Proctor pulled something out of the drawer. "A sedative. We can't just let you wake up now, can we? That would invite Swarm attention."

Granger nodded. And right as the Granger lying on the table started opening his eyes, Proctor pressed the second syringe to his neck.

He flashed back to his own memories of the scene. There was the room—just as he remembered in his dreams. The tall viewport looking down on the planet. He was on his back, looking up at the overhanging lights, and he remembered feeling the presence of someone there. Someone behind him, standing just out of sight. *Someone*—that someone was *him*.

The heart rate on the monitor slowed as the sedative took effect, and the old Granger's eyes fluttered shut.

"There. You'll be asleep for awhile," said Proctor. "Enough time for us to make some plans, at least."

"Let's get back to Polrum Krull. She can find the singularity pair that I came through, and we can see about sending me—him—back. And we still need to figure out what to do with the debris heading toward Earth—"

He paused, staring out the window. Now that he was *here*, where he'd been four months ago, the dreams—the memories—they were coming back more forcefully. He'd stood at *that* window, looking down at the planet. He remembered the feeling of nostalgia, that sense of home. With a start, he realized that Kharsa hadn't been manipulating that part. He couldn't create that feeling. He couldn't force Granger to feel longing when he looked down at that planet. Perhaps Kharsa misdirected the feeling, altered the memory of what the world below actually looked like, made him remember a different planet—Kharsa's planet.

But there was something else. The feeling was true—his homeworld, the Valarisi's homeworld, that was indeed down there through the window, far below—and yet ... that wasn't the whole story. Somewhere, somehow, close by, was his true homeworld. Well, "homeworld" was too precise a word. His—the Swarm's—origin, was close. Not the Valarisi—the liquid beings, but the actual Swarm. He remembered *feeling* that. Looking down on Penumbra, and simultaneously feeling longing for the surface, and longing for his *true* home, somewhere close by.

"What is it, Tim?"

"We're missing something," he muttered.

"What?"

"Just a feeling." Before he could explain himself, a marine stepped into the room.

"Sir, message from Lieutenant Diaz. He says more sensor contacts have appeared in the debris field."

Proctor and Granger looked at each other.

"Fishtail," they both said.

The marine shook his head. "He said there were two new fighters that appeared. Both with transponder prefixes that correspond to the *Constitution*."

Two fighters?

CHAPTER SIXTY-NINE

Executive Command Center, Russian Singularity Production Facility
High Orbit, Penumbra Three

GRANGER AND PROCTOR both left the old Granger, still knocked out from the tranquilizer, under the guard of two marines, and rushed back to where Polrum Krull was still rummaging around through the computer database. On another terminal nearby was a comm station. Proctor keyed in the appropriate frequency for the *Victory*'s bridge.

"Lieutenant Diaz, this is Granger. Report."

"Diaz here. Sir, we just picked up two new contacts. Fishtail and Hotbox. Came out of two latent singularities in the debris field at roughly the same time."

"Are they responding to hails?"

"Negative. Both fighter's system's are in bad shape—I doubt they even have life support. And they're both on a collision course with a dense cloud of debris."

"What's the status of Volz's fighter?"

Diaz paused, probably examining his sensor display. "Looks like he's punched his accelerator and is moving to intercept them. But he'll never save both. I don't even know what he'll do if he catches up with *one* of them."

Granger turned to Proctor. "Patch me through down to the fighter deck. Get me the CAG."

A moment later, she nodded, and he realized right at that moment what a surreal moment it was—he was about talk to the new CAG, Lieutenant Volz, while the old Lieutenant Volz was out there in his fighter, on his way to attempt rescue of both Fishtail and Hotbox. "Lieutenant, scramble fighters. Get out there and help ... you."

"The fighter deck is a mess, sir. It'll be a few minutes."

Proctor shook her head. "They'll never make it out there in time. Fishtail and Hotbox have less than two minutes before they run into that debris cloud."

Polrum Krull glanced over to them. "The *Benevolence* is closer. My people have several shuttles ready to launch. I can notify them through the Ligature and they can attempt rescue of the fighter your pilot won't be able to reach."

Granger nodded. "Do it." He turned to Proctor. "Get me Volz. The other Volz." She nodded when the comm link was established.

"Lieutenant Volz, this is Captain Granger. I'm sending help. You go grab Fishtail. Don't be alarmed when you see some shuttles that ... well, they're going to look like Swarm fighters, Ballsy. But they're not. They're coming to help."

A laugh came through the comm channel. "Right. You really expect me to believe you, you bastards? A big Swarm carrier with a whole Russian fleet, and the *ISS Constitution*, all next to a big friggin' Russian space station. Do you really think I'm that stupid?"

Proctor whispered in his ear. "He probably can't see that the ship out there is the *Victory*, not the *Constitution*. They look identical."

Polrum Krull brought up a video feed on the monitor. At least twenty Skiohra shuttles had launched, and were approaching the three fighters. Volz's craft was getting close to Fishtail's, but suddenly it swiveled toward Hotbox. "No, you bastards. You're not getting him. You're not making him a *friend*."

Granger grabbed the console with both hands in a tight grip. "Volz, you don't know what you're doing. We're not Swarm. Don't do something you're going to regret."

"You may have gotten Granger, but you're not getting Hotbox."

And before Granger could say anything else, Hotbox's fighter exploded into a brief fireball as Volz squeezed off a few dozen shots. "Dammit," he breathed, then waved over to Polrum Krull. "Call them off. Call them off!"

On the monitor, he saw the Skiohra shuttles move away, back toward the dreadnought. Volz's fighter had finally come within meters of Fishtail's, though they were both still sailing straight for the debris cloud, now less than a minute away.

The hatch blew, and Volz launched himself out of the cockpit. A safety cord was tied around his waist, and as he sailed past the open hatch, he grabbed it and pushed himself toward Fishtail's fighter. In a breath-taking twisting maneuver, he managed to catch one of her fighter's gun barrels in one hand, and swung himself up toward the hatch of her cockpit. He keyed in an emergency open command, and the hatch swung open, letting him reach in to pull her restraints loose.

But it was too late. They were in the debris cloud. And even as Volz pulled Fishtail loose, a chunk of rock struck her in the helmet, denting it, and a stream of smaller pellets showered them and the fighters.

CHAPTER SEVENTY

Executive Command Center, Russian Singularity Production Facility
High Orbit, Penumbra Three

VOLZ'S VOICE CAME through the comm—the Volz onboard the *Victory*. "Uh, sir, I don't think I'm pulling out of that."

Granger leaned forward toward the speaker. "Ballsy? Are you sure? I mean, you're here, right? You made it."

"I'm saying that my memories stop here. I either got hit on the head or passed out or maybe I just don't remember what happened, but after I reached Fishtail ... I don't remember anything past that. I got back in my fighter and then ... nothing. The next thing I remember was seeing the *Warrior* out my window, with Fishtail on my lap."

Even as Volz described it, they all watched the monitor as the old Volz dragged Fishtail behind him as he pulled his way back along the cord toward his own fighter, struggling through a shower of terrifyingly fast rocks and pellets. There was no way he was going to be able find the singularity he'd come out of. Hell, he wasn't even sure Proctor could find it even using the *Victory*'s sensors.

Granger spun around to Polrum Krull. "Quickly. Can you manipulate the singularities? Can you do it from here?"

Polrum Krull navigated through a series of submenus on the console. "Yes. All latent singularities can be accessed from here. All I have to do is send out a focused graviton beam coupled with phased meta-space—"

"Just do it. Open the one he came out of, and send it toward him. Can you do that? Can you move them?"

Polrum Krull didn't reply, but furiously worked the controls. "Beam initiated, and integrated into singularity 8013b. It's opening. I'm feeding it mass—it needs to be at least half the mass of the fighter if they want any hope of surviving the fall—"

The cloud of debris showering them was getting denser. Luckily they were inside the fighter by then, but one well-placed rock could fly right through their viewport at any moment. "Just move it into their path. They're out of time."

Proctor pointed to the monitor. "Tim, that chunk of ice is going to hit them. It's going almost one kilometer per second—they're not going to survive that."

"Polrum, now!" Granger yelled.

Polrum Krull touched a spot on the console, and moments later, the fighter disappeared with a brief flash of light.

Granger breathed a tentative sigh of relief. "Any way to tell if they made it through?"

Polrum Krull nodded. "The singularity did not collapse. I was able to grow it enough that they safely passed though."

Proctor eased up behind Polrum Krull's chair. "So if the singularity is too small in relation to the mass suddenly falling it, it collapses?"

"Catastrophically," said Polrum Krull, nodding. She was picking up human mannerisms. "And the effect is channeled up the graviton beam we use to control it. If the object going through is a small fraction of the singularity's mass, the beam—and the source of the beam—is relatively unaffected. But as the mass of the object increases up toward double the singularity's mass, the effect becomes catastrophic, and will destroy the source of the beam. That is how you destroyed those Valarisi ships over Earth four months ago. The *Constitution* was just a hair over double the singularity's mass, and because the three carriers were still linked to it when you went in, they didn't survive."

"Then how did we survive just now? Didn't the beam originate from somewhere here at the station?" Proctor was studying the data readouts, her brow furrowed.

"Because I shut it off right before impact," said Polrum Krull. "I have no death wish."

Before Granger could ask any more details, one of the marines came in. "Sir, I thought you should know. He's—you're ... awake again."

CHAPTER SEVENTY-ONE

Executive Command Center, Russian Singularity Production Facility
High Orbit, Penumbra Three

GRANGER RACED BACK across the common area, past the giant window, and came up to the doorway of the hospital room. Outside, two marines still stood guard, assault rifles at the ready, pointed into the room, keeping their sights trained on the patient inside.

He looked into the room. The other version of him was not in the bed, but standing up, right next to the window, looking down at the planet below. He wasn't making any provocative movements, not saying anything. Just watching through the window, calmly.

"Do you remember this?" whispered Proctor in his ear.

He nodded. The more time went by, and especially now that he was watching the situation unfold again, but from a different perspective, he *did* remember.

And so it was with confidence that he strode into the room, pulling the door shut behind himself. The two marines were probably have aneurisms watching him walk into danger like that without an escort. Screw 'em. He knew exactly what the other version of him was feeling at the moment.

Longing.

And he, current Granger, needed to grill himself, and the Swarm inhabiting his body.

"Nice view from up here," he said. The other Granger didn't even turn.

"It is. So peaceful. You'd never know that the Adanasi were up here planning our destruction the whole time. We see why you fight them."

Granger stayed by the door. No sense in endangering himself unnecessarily. "Frankly, I'd do the same. In fact, I'm still planning on it."

Old Granger chuckled. "What's the point, Tim? Soon, very soon, we'll have you back, as well as all of the Adanasi. We will all be one. We'll bring the Skiohra back into the fold—such a shame that they fell by the wayside. A flaw in the design of the virus flowing through their blood—a flaw we've already corrected. They'll be with us again soon. The Adanasi, the Skiohra, the Dolmasi, the Valarisi, the other two races you haven't even met yet—the Findiri and Quiassi. And us. Seven peoples. One family."

"Who is us?"

"All of us. Me. You. Everyone on this station. We are all us. We will all be family, friends, bound by unity and purpose." Old Granger finally turned around and took a few steps toward Granger.

He made a gambit. "You're so sure of yourselves. So cocky. Arrogant. It will be your undoing. Even now,

I've putting into motion the operation that will finally destroy you."

Old Granger chuckled again. "Believe me, that planet down there is completely safe from you. We have nothing to fear."

"That's not what I was referring to. I'm not attacking the planet. I'm attacking you. The link to our universe you come through."

Old Granger stopped. "Impossible."

"Don't believe me? Try me. You've got my body there. You can reach into his mind. Am I a gambler? Do I bluff? Come now, you know I never bluff, because you're me. I'm telling you, I'm warning you—leave our universe now, before it's too late."

Old Granger cocked his head. "I'll concede that you don't bluff. We've explored your mind thoroughly. So sad—so much potential. And yet you've wasted your entire career as a second-rate commander, always setting yourself up for failure, going against your senior commanders, making enemies where you should have been making friends, sabotaging your career because—" the other man smiled, "Oh, this is rich. You've been sabotaging yourself because you've got this self-conscious chip on your shoulder. You were an average student, with average evaluations from your superiors, and you've been an average officer. You're self conscious that you never rose to greater heights. And so you tried to self destruct by playing the rebel, the curmudgeon, the insubordinate bastard."

"You're stalling," said Granger. "You know we've found your link to your universe, that we're about to shut it. So all you can do is stall for time and hope I fail. I assure you, I won't."

Old Granger laughed. A cold, mirthless laugh. "You think you can close it? Really? You're delusional. There's no way you'd ever get that much mass out there."

"You think I'm bluffing?" said Granger.

"Then what are you doing here? You're here because you're unsure of yourself. You see yourself here, from the past, wondering what will happen if you don't get me back to my proper place, back there on a burning *Constitution* falling down toward Earth."

"Hardly. I'm only here to stall, and draw your attention away from what I'm doing to close your link."

Old Granger's smile faded. "Impossible. There's no way to close a naturally occurring black hole."

The black hole. Proctor was wrong.

He turned back to the door. "Thank you. That's the piece I was missing. You've been most helpful, *friends.*"

He pulled the door open and walked through. To his right were the two marines with rifles at the ready, to the left was Proctor, brandishing the meta-syringe filled with more sedative. He gave a quick nod to her, indicating she knock the other Granger out, who was now pursuing him through the doorway.

Old Granger passed the threshold, and before he could react, Proctor pressed the syringe up to his back. He collapsed almost instantly.

"And? I could only hear snippets," said Proctor. Polrum Krull emerged from the lab containing the meta-space control room.

"We were wrong. The black hole is it."

"But, there are millions of black holes just in our galaxy."

"This one could be special," he said, glancing over at Polrum Krull. Do your people have any ideas? What do your Children say?"

Polrum Krull paused for a few moments, as if considering the possibility. "We've been debating this point nonstop since our awakening two days ago. Our knowledge of quantum singularity science is rudimentary, but we suppose that since the Swarm is able to reach through into our universe, it's *possible* they could have been doing it through the black hole for the past ten thousand years. But what explains the one hundred and fifty year cycle?"

Proctor tapped her chin. "Ensign Roth was telling me that the fifth planet in the Penumbra system—a huge gas giant—has an orbital period of one hundred and fifty years. Could they be related?"

Polrum Krull closed her eyes. No one said anything for another few moments.

"Polrum?"

"My Children are performing simulations. Modeling the possibility the gas giant would have an effect."

"They can do that?" said Granger.

"The Interior Life is different than the Exterior Life, Captain. You learn to be more focused, to concentrate better, to model the world around you. Since they can't see it and experience it for themselves, they must model it." She opened her eyes. "And what they tell me, is that yes, it is possible. The gas giant orbits the star and black hole binary, or rather, their center of mass. The barycenter. But the gas giant's orbit is elliptical. That could disturb the corona of the star at the perihelion of the orbit, such that every one hundred and fifty years, more material than usual falls into the black hole."

Proctor nodded. "Perhaps the material falling in is inducing the black hole into emitting meta-space radiation. Not only into our universe, but into ... others. But this isn't the only black hole in our galaxy to have matter swirling into it. Why is this one special?"

Silence.

Granger swore. "Do we really need to understand it to destroy it?"

Proctor rolled her eyes. "You can't destroy a black hole."

He strode out toward the atrium, where Isaacson and Volodin still lay dead. "Watch me."

CHAPTER SEVENTY_TWO

Executive Command Center, Russian Singularity Production Facility
High Orbit, Penumbra Three

FINALLY, AFTER ALL THE TIME fighting the Swarm, after all the fleet engagements, last-ditch planetary defenses, suffering through political maneuvering and cloak and dagger tactics by both his own government, the Russian Confederation, and the Swarm itself, Granger knew what he had to do. The same thing he'd already done. And it liberated him. He'd done it once. He could do it again.

"Lieutenant Volz, this is Granger," he said through the comm.

"Volz here, sir."

"Ballsy, I want you to transfer all fighters currently on *Victory* to the Old Bird."

"Excuse me, sir?" Volz sounded confused.

"You heard me. The *Constitution* is currently inside a giant bay here in the asteroid. We'll open the bay doors, and you get all the fighters over here."

"Yes, sir."

"And Volz, make sure Fishtail gets over here, too. Next stop is Earth, and a trip through a singularity just might hit the spot for her. Granger out." He punched the button again and continued. "Commander Oppenheimer? Lieutenant Diaz?"

"Bridge here, Captain," came Oppenheimer's voice.

"I want you two to transfer all non-essential personnel to the *Constitution*. That's everyone, except for a few key people to help me pilot the *Victory*, and maybe fire the guns. That's it. Everyone else to the Old Bird. Send them over in escape pods—they can dock at the vacant escape pod ports—and they're to stay in the escape pods until directed otherwise by Commander Proctor. She'll then have them escape from the Old Bird right before it heads back to Earth in the past. And I want them gone in five minutes. Understood?"

"Understood, sir. Bridge out."

Granger motioned for Proctor and Polrum Krull to follow him as he started back toward the atrium. On the way he pointed at a marine. "Wrap the *other me* up in a few sheets, and carry him down to the *Constitution*." The marine saluted and marched back to the hospital room.

"Tim, what's going on?" Proctor had caught up with him.

"Shelby, you're going to take the old me, with a skeleton crew, and go back to Earth on the *Constitution*. Once you handle the debris ball heading toward Earth, you're going to send the Old Bird back to the past. Make sure everyone abandons ship before you send it back. Except *old me*, of course." He strode back through

the atrium, past the elevator. Polrum Krull trailed shortly behind him and Proctor. "Krull? Can you contain a
latent singularity and make it portable?"

"Yes, Granger. That is how they are all stored. They
are modular. Once they've been deployed, of course,
they either collapse or float freely and latent in space.

"I need the coordinates of the one the *Constitution*
went through four months ago. I assume it's still orbiting Earth, and its sibling is here near the station somewhere. Find it, please."

Polrum Krull bowed her head, and began to withdraw. "Wait," said Granger. "We'll need one more pair,
too. A latent singularity, and its sibling."

"They are kept down in a storage bay, near where
they are loaded onto ships. Close to where the *Constitution* is now. I will bring you a pair, if you'll be so kind
as to direct two of your soldiers to escort me. I don't
believe I'll make it down there with your entire ground
army in the way."

Granger smiled painfully. The mention of the army
was pointed, and obviously a reminder to him of the
grave injustices the Skiohra had endured in the past few
hours. "Yes. That. I can't express how sorry I am that it
happened. When this is all over, we'll help bring those
responsible to justice."

"It is not justice I seek, Captain." She started walking
toward the elevator. "It is survival."

Granger pointed toward two marines who were
standing guard near the elevator. "You two. Escort our
guest to where she needs to go. She's to have access
to any location on the station she needs. And help her

get the bay doors open to receive the escape pods and fighters that are on their way. Understood?"

"Yes, sir," they both said, and followed her into the elevator. Granger continued on toward the hallway leading to al the docking ports.

"Tim, I know what you're planning. It's ... there's no guarantee it's going to work."

"It'll work. I know it'll work."

"How, Tim?" Her voice elevated. "How can you be so damn sure? We've got no time. The ball of debris is about to hit Earth, and meanwhile the rest of the Swarm and Russian fleets are out there somewhere. We can't just be going out on some damn-fool mission because your gut says so."

He turned to her. She was right, of course, it was foolish. But this time, he really was sure. "Shelby, I know, because I *remember* this time. Kharsa manipulated me, true. But he manipulated memories that were already there. I really *did* stand there by that window and look down at Penumbra. I really *did* feel longing. Like it was home. All he did was alter my visual memory of it. Made it look like his own homeworld in my mind's eye. But he can't alter the feelings. The thoughts. And now that I've been on the other side of the conversation, the whole thing has come back to me."

"What do you mean?"

"When I talked to myself back there. I *remembered*. I can't tell you how unsettling it is to finally remember that. To remember seeing my own face looking back at me, talking to me, except in my memories I was ... not me. I was *them*. And when I bluffed back there and told them I knew where the link was, I *remember* feeling terrified. Worried that Granger was telling the truth. The black hole *is* the link—I remember now—and we *can* destroy it, because they were terrified that I was going to. All we need now are two singularities, and send enough mass into the damn thing to keep it occupied for a few million years."

She grit her teeth. "Yes, Tim, that may work, but how can we hope to send enough mass into that thing? We've got nothing here but the planet. And from experience we know that one singularity is only going to gobble up so much mass from the planet's crust. We'd need a thousand times that much to have any affect. And, we're not affecting the black hole itself—it's quadrillions of times as massive as anything we could ever throw at it. The most we can hope for is to somehow disrupt the meta-space link coming through the black hole."

"Exactly." He boarded the shuttle through the hatch. "That's why you're going to take *two* singularities with you. One will be the sibling of the one the *Constitution* came through. You'll need to get the ship—and me—back to Earth in the past. The second is for the ball of debris. I'm going to take the sibling with me on *Victory*, and shove it down that black hole myself."

She finally understood his intentions, shaking her head. "No. Unacceptable. We're not going to lose you again. Not this time."

He grabbed her arm and looked her in the eye. "It's the only way, Shelby." He forced a smile before turning back into the shuttle. "Besides, I've died once. It ain't so bad."

"Tim," began Proctor, but she was cut off by emergency klaxons. They both instinctively glanced at the shuttle's viewport, out toward the *Victory* and the dreadnought beyond.

Ships were q-jumping in. Lots of them. Swarm carriers, Russian cruisers, even a few dozen ships that neither of them recognized, possibly from the remaining two families of the Concordat of Seven that still remained shrouded in mystery. Whoever they were, the space around the station quickly filled up with more capital ships than Granger had ever seen at once. Hundreds. Possibly thousands. There was a good chance this was the entire Swarm fleet. And the entire Russian fleet.

Against the *ISS Victory*, and one severely damaged Skiohra dreadnought.

Should be quite a fight.

CHAPTER SEVENTY-THREE

Docking Hatch 142, Russian Singularity Production Facility-High Orbit, Penumbra Three

"LOOKS LIKE THE CAVALRY is here," Granger muttered, adding, "Now I know we're doing the right thing." Before he could shut the hatch, a marine ran up to them, rifle slung over his shoulder and a large container in his hands.

"Sir, the alien told me to give this to you," he said, placing it in Granger's hands outstretched through the hatch. "And she said the sibling is already aboard the *Constitution*."

"Thank you, soldier. Shelby," he pointed down toward where the Old Bird would be moored in the giant bay underneath the deck. "Take care of her. Good luck."

She nodded curtly, her face suggesting she was about to say something else, but the hatch closed, leaving Granger alone with his thoughts, and half of the singularity pair that would be key to destroying the Swarm for good.

The shuttle's pilot pulled them away from the hatch. "Fly hard, Ensign," said Granger, eyeing the approaching fleet. "We've got no time to spare."

Extreme g forces thrust him down into his seat, draining the blood from his face. He almost yelled out for the pilot to decrease their acceleration, but a few moments later the ensign reversed thrust and came in hot into the shuttle bay. They landed with an ungraceful clunk.

By the time he raced to the bridge, the crew was in full battle mode. Commander Oppenheimer and Lieutenant Diaz were shouting orders to the bridge crew, the red klaxon lights were blaring, and Granger shook his head at the futility of it. One glance at the tactical display on his console told him all he needed to know. One hundred and fifty Swarm carriers. Four hundred Russian cruisers. Four hundred other ships of unknown design. The *Victory* didn't stand even a glimmer of a chance, even with the *Benevolence* standing between them and the newcomers.

We stand with you, Granger.

He recognized the voice. *Polrum Krull*, he thought toward her, *this is hopeless. Even your ship can't make a difference.*

No, she said. *But all of our ships will.*

Another flicker on the screen announced the arrival of a few more ships. Five more ships. Each as large as the Skiohra dreadnought, each bristling with weapons turrets and hordes of billions of Skiohra shouting out in a great civilizational battle song, singing for revenge. His mind reeled from the growing clamor of voices—millions of matriarchs and their consorts, hundreds of billions of interior Skiohra. All unified in a great battle song of an entire race.

It took enormous effort to shut them out of his mind, and by the time he did, the space between the dreadnoughts and the approaching enormous Swarm fleet lit up with weapons fire.

Go, Granger. We won't get another shot at this.

He nodded, still holding his pounding head. "Ensign Prince. Set a course for the black hole orbiting Penumbra's star. Maximum acceleration."

CHAPTER SEVENTY-FOUR

Docking Hatch 229, Russian Singularity Production Facility-High Orbit, Penumbra Three

POLRUM KRULL WAS WAITING for her outside the entrance to the hatch leading to the *Constitution*. She held up a hand indicating to her marine escort to halt—one of them carried the blanket-wrapped figure of the old Captain Granger. "Polrum Krull? Are the appropriate singularities ready?"

"They are, Commander."

"Then I guess this is goodbye, then. Thank you for your help."

"I'm coming with you, Commander. The singularities are highly time-dependent, as you and Captain Granger are well-familiar with by now. They require exact input parameters to teleport mass over any distance, if you want the mass to arrive at the *time* you want. Any error in the graviton polarization or the meta-space input and you could end up arriving early by a month, or late by a year."

Proctor nodded. "Very well." She motioned forward. "Shall we?"

It was like stepping back in time, which, she supposed, was literally what she was doing. The corridors of the *Constitution* were filled with battle debris, rips in the bulkheads where the strains and stresses on the hull had torn the ship apart, blood stains on the walls. Luckily, the Russians had cleared any dead from the ship.

Except for one. She nearly tripped over him—a young technician who was propped up against a wall in a corridor leading to engineering. With a jarring realization, she remembered tripping over this very same body, four months ago, when she was racing through the ship trying to find Granger, while the *Constitution* blazed through the upper atmosphere.

She nearly ran straight into a few fighter pilots in the hallway. "Ballsy?" she said, recognizing one of them. "Are all the fighters over?"

"Yes ma'am. And Fishtail is safe in an escape pod near the fighter deck—she fits right in down there what with her old flight suit still on. And she's got her own nurse and everything."

"Good work, Ballsy. Get back down there and prepare for imminent engagement with the Swarm. All fighters, no bricks, and we give it all we got. I'll relay instructions down there once you're all set."

"Yes, ma'am." He jogged off, leaving Proctor and Polrum Krull to resume their march to the deep interior of the lower decks of the *Constitution*.

Once in engineering, she found the familiar equipment installed by the Russians—the same singularity generation and manipulation equipment she'd had transferred to the *Warrior* from the crashed *Constitution*.

"I've loaded singularity 121b into the launch mechanism. That is the one that will take the *Constitution* to Earth in the past when the time is right. I've also loaded singularity 9098a. This is the one we will use to transport the ball of debris heading toward Earth to Granger's location at the meta-space link in Penumbra's black hole."

"Good. And you can precisely control the parameters using this equipment the Russians installed.?"

"Yes," Polrum Krull said. "And I've taken the liberty of loading a third singularity. 51b. Its sibling is currently heading to Earth right now, in a Swarm carrier that is escorting the debris field in toward Earth."

"What good will that do us? I thought we were going to q-jump our way in," said Proctor, slightly confused.

"Just watch."

CHAPTER SEVENTY-FIVE

Bridge, ISS Lincoln
High Orbit, Earth

GENERAL NORTON sat uneasily in the captain's chair of the *Lincoln*, staring at the screen with a sense of foreboding and dread.

The asteroid—or debris ball, or whatever the appropriate word was—had appeared suddenly about halfway to the moon, and was speeding toward the Earth. When it struck, their planet would die. The crust would be sloughed off, the oceans boiled, the mantle rising up in a tide of lava to overcome any remaining solid land.

But with it was a more immediate concern. One hundred Swarm carriers, positioned all around the ball of debris, as if escorting the civilization-ending mass. It wasn't just a random asteroid or moon. It was a weapon. The Swarm's final play against Earth, and it was a play that Norton knew in his gut they'd never counter.

"General, I've got you a few dozen more ships," said President Avery through the comm on his armrest. "The Caliphate finally came through—seems a large civilization-ending ball of dirt was enough to convince them that their prophet wants them to finally help us. And the Russian Confederation has fractured. Seems Malakhov is dead, and the ships not under Swarm control have come to their senses and decided to cast their lot with us."

"Thank you, ma'am," he said.

"Will it be enough?"

"It'll have to." On the split-screen he watched the Earth turn slowly, serving as a backdrop to the rag-tag fleet he'd assembled. In spite of their heavy losses, he'd managed to pull together the remnants of Zingano's fleet based at Britannia, and as many outlying cruisers from the secondary defense fleets based at the other major United Earth worlds. All told, nearly a hundred heavy cruisers.

Against over a hundred Swarm cruisers, it just wouldn't be enough.

"Any word from Granger?" said Avery, solemnly.

"None. The traitor bastard can rot in hell, for all I care."

Avery didn't reply. He knew her feelings on the matter—she couldn't, wouldn't believe that Granger had finally turned on them. That he'd been under Swarm influence this whole time. But now that Zingano was gone, there was no one to apologize for him. And his actions at the battle for the dreadnought convicted him, in Norton's eyes.

"Good luck, General. The entire Earth will be watching. And praying," said Avery.

"Thank you, ma'am. We'll do our best—"

The sensor officer interrupted him with a shout. "Sir! Massive power fluctuations from one of the Swarm carriers!"

General Norton snapped his head back to the screen, which had zoomed in to the carrier in question.

His jaw hung open. "Impossible!"

The carrier had exploded, and, emerging from the glowing wreckage, streams of debris from the unlucky Swarm carrier trailing from its ten-meter-thick tungsten hull, came the *ISS Constitution*.

CHAPTER SEVENTY-SIX

Bridge, ISS Victory
Near Penumbran Black Hole

THE SPACE AROUND the *Victory* was a firestorm. Granger could barely see the empty space out beyond the dreadnoughts and the incoming Swarm carriers. It was just a sea of green as both sides lit into each other with antimatter beams. Soon, purple beams joined the mix as the alien newcomers dove into the fray, and, not to be outdone, red streaks shot out from the Russian cruisers. Every so often the *Victory* would shudder from the weapons fire, but most of the destruction was targeting the dreadnoughts, which, in spite of their gargantuan size, were spewing great gouts of debris and fire.

The chorus called to him. *Granger, go. Faster. Get to the link. We'll cover for you.*

I'm going as fast as I can, he said. He clutched the container holding the singularity—his death and Earth's salvation.

Go faster. We won't make it otherwise. The chorus in his mind, billions strong, was almost too much to bear. Especially as he felt the deaths of millions at a time, as explosions ripped across the hulls of the dreadnoughts.

"Ensign Prince, another burst of speed."

"Aye, sir. But Captain, we're approaching critical velocity. Much faster and it will be impossible for us to avoid crossing the event horizon."

"Thank you, Ensign. Let's hope it doesn't come to that." He turned to Commander Oppenheimer. "See if we can't help them out a bit. Full mag-rail and laser spread."

The tactical crew sprang into motion, ordering up the mag-rail crews and feeding targeting parameters to the laser turrets. Due to the influx of the *Warrior* crew, the *Victory*'s weapons banks were once again fully-manned.

Thousands of slugs erupted from the *Victory*'s hull and joined the chorus of weapons fire lighting up the space between all the ships, all hurtling along at dozens of kilometers per second.

It was a scene of destruction. Sheer, utter destruction. Every other second, a Swarm carrier erupted in a massive fireball. But three more would take its place. The alien ships from the other two races of the Concordat, seemed particularly vulnerable to the antimatter beams leaping off the dreadnoughts, but their own purple plasma-based weapons were wreaking terrible havoc on the Skiohra vessels.

With a cry, Granger dropped the singularity container and held his head in his hands, leaning forward, nearly falling off his chair. What must have been ten billion voices all cried out at once, and then disappeared.

He forced his eyes open, and to his horror, one of the dreadnoughts exploded, raining thousands of chunks of glowing debris onto the surrounding ships.

"Faster," he breathed. "Faster, Ensign Prince."

"But sir, we're right at the limit now."

Granger gripped his armrests. His knuckles were white. And old.

He forced a grim smile. He'd had a good run. And he'd sacrificed himself once before. This was old hat. "Abandon ship. Get the hell out of here, everybody."

Everyone turned toward him, aghast. "Sir?" said Lieutenant Diaz. "Begging your pardon, but we're staying with you until the end."

"Like hell you are. I can pilot this thing by myself. Get out. Now. That's an order."

Lieutenant Diaz approached Granger's chair. "But—"

"No arguments, Lieutenant." He stood up, and placed a hand on his loyal deputy XO's shoulder. "It's been an honor serving with you. With you all," adding, looking around the bridge. "But now is the time to save yourselves. I cheated death once before, but I can't outrun it this time. I'm not dragging you all with me. Leave. Please," he added.

Diaz nodded slowly. He tapped the shipped commlink on Granger's console. "All hands to escape pods. Abandon ship. As soon as you're out, steer clear of the battle."

Granger held his head in pain as another terrified chorus of billions of voices screamed out. Another Ski-ohra ship, gone. Of the original seven, three had now been destroyed, with the *Benevolence* on her last leg as well. Easily over half of the entire Skiohra civilization was now gone.

But Diaz had brought up a good point. The escape pods were flying through a gauntlet of weapons fire. He projected his thoughts out, almost ashamed at what he was asking. *Please protect my people as they escape.*

The bridge crew was out. He monitored their progress as the escape pods started launching, hoping for a confirmation from the Skiohra that they'd provide cover for them. Given that they were sacrificing billions of their own lives in this final stab at the heart of the Swarm, he doubted they'd care about a few hundred humans.

We're coming, Granger.

The voice felt familiar. It wasn't coming from the *Benevolence.*

He glanced at the screen, searching for what he already knew was coming. And there it was—dozens of flickers. What must have been half the entire Dolmasi fleet.

Vishgane Kharsa's voice blared through his mind. *We're here, Granger. Do what you must.*

I thought you only cared about your own people, he thought toward the Dolmasi, with contempt. *You lied to me. About where I went in that singularity. And about the Skiohra. You lied, and millions of my people died.*

Yes. I lied, replied Kharsa. *Your people have done the same. Lying and backstabbing and scheming. We are no different from you. But we know what is at stake here, now. The final chance. Our chance to end the Valarisi forever. If we fail at this, we fail for all time.*

As much as it pained him to accept the help, he had no choice. *Fine*, he said. *Escort my people out, relieve the pressure on the Skiohra ships, and destroy as many Swarm carriers as you can. Once the link is destroyed, we need to make sure every last artificial singularity is gone, too.*

Yes, Granger. I shall send my fleets against the Swarm at Earth. If what you say is true, every carrier must be destroyed. Thank you. And farewell.

On the viewscreen he watched as the Dolmasi fleet entered the fray. The *Victory's* escape pods leapt away, and the Vishgane's ships surged in, targeting the carriers, raking them with a fresh wave of antimatter beams. He stooped to pick up the singularity's container. Inside, the tiny point of light occasionally flared. It seemed alive to him, like something waiting, expectantly and greedily, for its last meal.

His console beeped, indicating the last escape pod had launched. With grim determination, he slid into the helmsman's chair, set the container on the console, and pushed the acceleration back to full. In a moment he would initiate the singularity controls that would inexorably increase its mass to permit passage of the debris ball.

He was committed. He'd crossed the line of no return. Within minutes, he'd pass the event horizon, bringing with him the artificial singularity—the one paired with the sibling soon to be launched at the debris ball bearing down on Earth. In the back of his mind, he could just barely feel Polrum Krull's reassuring presence, lightyears away. She was projecting to him: they were close. *Expect the package any minute now. Initiate singularity mass increase in preparation.*

The next moment he found himself flying across the room, his head exploding with pain and stars. He landed in a heap, moaning from the sharp ache behind his ear.

"Granger," said a voice behind him. He slowly lifted his head.

Fishtail, holding the container for the singularity. Smirking at him. "Missing something?" she said, her fingers poised over the control panel on the side.

CHAPTER SEVENTY-SEVEN

Bridge, ISS Victory
Near Penumbran Black Hole

"NO," HE WHISPERED. "Fishtail, put it down."

"Shall I deactivate it? I wonder what will happen." Fishtail chuckled. A mirthless laugh, cold and jeering. "You've failed, Granger. And not only have you failed, you've been our most valuable tool. We've played you, right up until the end."

"How?" said Granger. "We're here. At the link. And any moment now about a quadrillion tons of shit is about to come out of that thing you're holding, and your precious link to your shit-hole of a dimension will be closed forever."

She smiled again, balancing the box with her fingers, tossing it from one hand to the other. She was still dressed in her flight suit, and trailing from one arm was the tube used to administer the sedative in sickbay. In the rush of the crew transfer to the *Constitution* she

must have been overlooked. "No, it won't. It would
have been quite the explosion." With a few taps of
her finger she manipulated the controls on the container. The occasional pulses and flashes from the box
became dimmer and less frequent. "There," she said,
"I've locked its mass. Nothing larger than a brick will be
coming through it now, human or otherwise."

No.

"Yes," she replied.

"Fishtail, I know you're in there. I've been there
myself. Under Swarm control. I remember what it was
like. It was overpowering, but I was still in there, somewhere. So are you. I could still think. Still remember
who I was and what was important to me."

The cold smirk. "Nice try, Granger. We assure you,
she has no control over this body."

"Even so, I know you're there, Fishtail. Fight them.
This is the moment. Our world is on the line. Fight them.
Fight them for your husband. Your parents. Fight them
for your son, back there on Earth. We can still win this."

She laughed again. "Granger, don't you understand?
It's over, no matter what you or this pilot does. The
board has been set, the die cast. There is nothing you
can do to stop our victory. Nothing but antimatter
could plug this hole, and fortunately, the only source of
antimatter is currently destroying the traitor Skiohra out
there, beyond your reach. We were very, very careful not
to give antimatter weapons technology to the Adanasi,
the Dolmasi, the Quiassi or Findiri. Only the Skiohra
and the Valarisi have it, and of them one is about to

be destroyed and the other we control utterly, and will control until the end of time."

Antimatter?

His mind darted to the storage bays down near engineering. The *Warrior* had been stocked with thousands of antimatter torpedoes on Avery's orders, ostensibly for carpet bombing any Swarm worlds they came across, and most likely a few Russian worlds as well in retaliation for their treachery. And if the *Warrior* had them perhaps the *Victory* had them, too. But they would need to be activated. He glanced to the side of the bridge and recognized the new antimatter weapons control station installed near tactical just as it had been on the *Warrior*.

In the instant he thought it, Fishtail's eyes grew wide. But he was too fast for her. He sprang out of his seat and lunged for the antimatter torpedo control panel. Before he could move more than a meter something struck his head, making him see stars again as he tumbled to the ground.

The container holding the latent singularity fell to the deck nearby, its corner tinged with his own blood. Before he could react or dodge, a foot caught him in the stomach and he felt himself fly halfway across the room.

The air had been knocked out of his chest, and he struggled to breathe. He rolled onto his back, just in time to see Fishtail close the last few meters between them. She kicked again, but this time he was ready. He caught her foot in his hands, which did little to stop the force—he winced as he heard a rib crack.

But holding her foot, he pulled, rolling over to his other side in the process. She fell over him, and he used the scant seconds to crawl toward the singularity container.

From lightyears away he felt Polrum Krull project a thought to him. *It's coming.* He felt her mind, and knew that the other end of the singularity pair would absorb the debris cloud at any moment. What would happen at his end now was anyone's guess.

There was no time to lose. He grabbed the container and fumbled with the controls. They were in Russian, dammit. But, thankfully, there were pictograms showing what each button did. He pressed the one that unmistakably said, *eject*, and with a powered click, the door to the chamber opened.

Inside, the singularity floated, invisible except when encountering a random air molecule that strayed too close, snapping when enough mass fell in, bound on all six sides by the gravity-plate walls—except now the sixth wall was missing, and the shimmering light began to rise up inside the box.

"What are you doing...?" began Fishtail.

But he didn't give her any time to react. Treating the container as if it were a bucket of water, he whipped it toward Fishtail, and in the absence of the sixth wall, the singularity flew out toward her, caught her square in the chest—

Making her disappear in a blinding flash.

CHAPTER SEVENTY-EIGHT

X-25 Fighter Cockpit
High Orbit, Earth

VOLZ CIRCLED AROUND the shimmering singularity again, scanning the vicinity for any more bogeys. The hundred-odd carriers had launched thousands of them, but between the remains of the IDF fleet, the *Constitution*, and the newly arrived Dolmasi warships, they'd managed to ward them off. The carriers were now focused on attacking the *Constitution* herself, apparently intent on destroying the source of the singularity rather than try to take out the singularity itself.

"Pew Pew, stay sharp. There's another cloud of fighters headed this way. Spacechamp, on me. All fighters, form a perimeter around the singularity, Nothing gets through. Nothing."

"Sure thing, boss," said Pew Pew. He'd been almost completely silent since Fodder took out the Swarm carrier earlier in the day.

"We've got your back, Ballsy," said Spacechamp. "We're not losing this one."

They swooped around again, heading toward the side of the approaching Swarm fighter cloud. Every second that passed, the singularity got closer to the giant ball of debris, a vast cloud of dust, dirt, and ice swirling around the central mass like a great maelstrom.

And below them, Earth brooded like a hapless, helpless, target, unable to do a single thing about the destruction about to rain down from above.

Suddenly, the singularity flared, then dimmed dramatically.

"What the hell happened? Is it gone?" he shouted into his comm.

"No," said Commander Proctor. "But we're reading that something came out of it. And it's readings have all shifted, somehow. Polrum?"

Polrum Krull's voice sounded through Volz's headset. "The other side—the sibling. It is gone."

"So you're telling me when we suck all this shit up, it's not going to hit the Penumbra black hole on the other side?" Proctor yelled.

"No," said Polrum Krull. "The link is closed. But if we launch the singularity into the debris field, the singularity itself will collapse, resulting in an explosion that should be enough to disintegrate the debris ball and knock the whole thing off course. It is well over escape velocity, so Earth should be spared."

"You're *sure* about that? What about the black hole? The Swarm's link?"

"My Children are sure, Commander. They've been running simulations for this eventuality just in case. But we must launch it soon. We will have to deal with the black hole later—right now Earth is the priority."

Something tumbled by Volz's cockpit window.

Impossible.

The unmistakable light gray and blue of a fighter pilot's uniform caught his eye, and the tumbling, splayed hair told him all he needed to know.

Without even thinking, he pressed the compression button on his flight suit, sealing it shut and filling his helmet with oxygen, and, making sure the safety-line was tied securely around his torso, he pounded hard on the hatch control button.

The cockpit hatch burst open, and he swung the bird around to match the velocity of the tumbling figure, and pulled up as close as he could. Then he released his seat restraint and bounded out of the cockpit, flying toward his target with arms outstretched.

When he reached her, he could tell she was awake. But just barely, and not for long. Without a thought for himself, he took several deep breaths, wrapped his legs around her torso so she wouldn't tumble away, then ripped his helmet off. The force of the escaping air nearly tore the helmet out of his hands, and it took some fumbling but he shoved the helmet onto her head and clicked the seal button, pressurizing her suit.

The pressure inside his head and lungs was overpowering. He felt capillaries burst on the surface of his eyes, and the urge to exhale was almost irresistible. But somehow, he managed to pull them both along the safety line and back into the cockpit. Distant, hazy memories flashed through his mind. But he knew it wasn't simply déjà vu. He'd watched himself do this before, just hours earlier.

His vision was fading. Flailing with his hands, he tried to close the door. To repressurize the cockpit. To finally, and irrevocably, save Fishtail once and for all. To finally make good on his promise to the kid.

But the safety line was caught in the hatch.

He felt his lungs erupt as the air escaped his throat, and blackness overcame him.

CHAPTER SEVENTY-NINE

Engineering, ISS Constitution
High Orbit, Earth

"COMMANDER, THIS is your last chance to save your world," said Polrum Krull.

She watched the sensor readout. Ballsy and the unknown pilot had entered the fighter, but were still drifting. On the other screen, the serene, blue planet turned slowly, unable to defend itself against what was coming. Slowly, she nodded her head. "Do it."

Whooping and yelling through the comm grabbed her attention. "Got them, Commander. Let's blow this joint!" Pew Pew's voice cut through the chatter of all the pilots as they blazed their way from the doomed ball of debris. The surviving IDF cruisers had pulled to a safe distance, and the Dolmasi, presumably warned by Polrum Krull through the Ligature, were corralling and luring the remaining Swarm carriers into what Proctor guessed would be the blast zone, on a tangent perpendicular to the direction of Earth.

"Now, Polrum."

Polrum Krull nodded, and pressed a button on the singularity control station. The shimmering light disappeared. An instant later, the giant ball of debris erupted. A massive piece of the ball shot off to the left at a terrifying speed, but to the right, the remainder of the ball disintegrated in a colossal explosion.

The rapidly expanding fireball started overtaking the fleeing Swarm carriers. The Dolmasi, whose propulsion systems were faster, managed to outrun the explosion, and after only ten seconds, the last remaining carrier was swept up in the blast. It almost reminded her of a supernova seen from lightyears away, but sped up a billion times. It was actually beautiful, and she wanted to stay and appreciate the scene.

Someone groaned behind her. Granger. Lying on the floor, starting to come out of the shock of being controlled by the Swarm and passing through the singularity.

She still had one last job to do. "All hands, to escape pods or shuttles. Now. You have five minutes. Proctor out." There was only a skeleton crew, and it should only take them a few minutes to evacuate. "Are you going to project it somewhere in front of the *Constitution*?"

Polrum Krull shook her head. "There's no direct port to get it out of here. All the carriers and our dreadnoughts were retrofitted with equipment to allow quick transport past the hull. The *Constitution* lacks such equipment."

"Then how the hell are we going to launch the *Constitution* into that damn thing?"

Polrum Krull looked miffed, as if she'd expected Proctor to understand this whole time, or read her mind. Proctor supposed Polrum had been growing used to doing just that with Granger. "Commander, it will work just fine in here."

"In engineering?"

"Of course. It does not matter which point of the *Constitution* touches the singularity first. At the moment of contact, the spacetime occupied by the whole ship will distort, contract, and finally collapse in on itself, re-emerging from the other side. By my Children's calculations, it should arrive back where it started no more than fifteen seconds after it left, just like you observed. Though, I would move Captain Granger from this area. The curvature of spacetime in the vicinity of the singularity will be ... extreme, to put it mildly, especially with so much mass moving through. To be safe, move him from here."

It clicked—she remembered, and she felt foolish for even bringing him down to Engineering in the first place. Afterburners—the bar—was a deck above them and down the hall, right where she'd found him four months ago.

Proctor lifted him onto her shoulders. He was mumbling under his breath, still unconscious, but slowly coming out of it.

"Wait, what about the black hole? The link? We've failed our mission."

Polrum Krull closed her eyes for a moment, before opening them, looking at the slumped form of Granger on her shoulders. "No. We have not failed. Granger

seals it now. Sealed with his own blood. It is an omen—
the Swarm shall never rise again."

Proctor shook her head at the mumbo jumbo, and
strode toward the exit. Granger was light—just like
she remembered from last time. His body still freshly
ravaged by cancer, his muscles and tissue wasted away,
he lay limp as a rag doll. She ran up the stairs away
from engineering, turned left down the long hall, and
emerged in Afterburners. She grabbed a chair from near
the wall and dragged it behind her, placing it right in the
middle of the room, facing the window, just as when
she'd found him before.

"Might as well give you a hell of a view, Tim."

She started to walk away, toward Polrum Krull waiting for her in the hallway, toward the escape pod, but
stopped in her tracks when she heard a low mumble.

"Tim?"

"Goodbye, Shelby."

Polrum Krull's cryptic words came back to her about
Granger sealing the black hole with his blood, and she
turned back with a start. "Tim?"

His eyes were open to slits. She reached down for his
hand, and another mumble escaped his lips. "Goodbye,
Shelby. Thank you."

Polrum Krull clapped impatiently. "Commander.
The singularity's chamber will open in less than two
minutes. My Children and I must leave."

"Coming," she said. She squeezed the hand harder.
"Goodbye, Tim. See you in a few."

He fell back into unconsciousness, and as she ran
down the hallway with Polrum Krull, she wondered.

Was that old Tim, or current Tim, reaching across the lightyears through the Ligature to bid her goodbye? She had half a mind to ask the Skiohra matriarch, but soon they were scrambling into the escape pod and strapping their restraints. With seconds to spare, she launched the pod, and it shot away from the *Constitution*.

A moment later, the Old Bird disappeared with a familiar, blinding flash.

CHAPTER EIGHTY

Bridge, ISS Victory
Near Penumbran Black Hole

GRANGER STOOD at the antimatter torpedo station on the bridge of the *Victory*. On the viewscreen, the event horizon loomed large, taking up over half the viewable area. The stars all around it seemed warped and contorted near the edges, flickering and shifting rapidly as he approached the black hole.

Fishtail was gone—the Swarm with her—and the singularity she fell into seemed to have collapsed, since it disappeared in a flash as soon as she vanished.

All that remained was the final act. His last stab at the Swarm, the beings reaching across the ages and incomprehensible distances between universes, connected by the tenuous link of the singularities—natural or otherwise.

But how to do it? He supposed that, whatever happened, the antimatter needed to go in first, before any reaction with regular matter had occurred. It seemed to make sense in his mind. As Fishtail had said the words, he'd reached out through the Ligature and tried to comprehend, to read the Swarm's collective mind, and the answer seemed to lie in unreacted antimatter.

So he loaded up as many antimatter torpedoes as he could, keying in the commands to have the warheads launch from the torpedoes without initiating. As such, they would fall into the black hole unactivated. The antimatter of the warheads and the matter of the torpedoes might eventually touch as they fell, but he hoped against hope that, long before then, the antimatter would somehow poison the link.

The torpedoes launched with the press of a button. Watching the viewscreen, he saw he still had time to launch another few volleys, so he set himself to work, sending out hundreds of torpedoes from the bow of the *Victory*, which split apart and sent their antimatter warheads tumbling into the abyss ahead of the great warship.

On the sensor readout, he watched something strange. The ships he'd left behind—the Skiohra dreadnoughts and the Dolmasi fleet still engaged in mortal space combat with the remnants of the vast Swarm and Russian fleet—they seemed to speed up. The battle increased in pace and intensity, and Granger marveled at how fast the ships were darting around, until he realized that time all throughout the universe was speeding up relative to him. As he approached the event horizon, time for him, as viewed from the outside, would slow down to an almost incomprehensible crawl. Lifetimes and whole ages of civilization would pass as the kilometers separating him from the curtain of the universe eventually shrunk to zero.

Before it was too late, he reached out across the Ligature, searching for Polrum Krull, attempting to let her know what he was doing. If he failed, then she at least needed to be aware of what he'd tried. He needed to make that contact before time had sped up so fast for the outside universe that all the relevant events were long since past. Soon, he supposed, everyone he knew would be long dead. And a few minutes after that, Earth's sun would go nova. Eventually, he supposed he'd get to watch the Andromeda galaxy slam into the Milky Way, and he'd have a front row seat to the creation of billions of more stars as the collision stirred up latent clouds of interstellar hydrogen. He'd get to watch civilizations rise and fall. Galaxies birth and die.

He found her, and the feeling in reply suggested the Skiohra understood. Then he turned his attention to a sensation that felt familiar. Something close by Polrum Krull.

It was himself. Now freed from the Swarm. He reached through the Ligature, as hard as he could, and thought he could feel himself open his heavy, tired eyes.

She was there. Looking at him. He could feel it. He projected a farewell, wanting nothing more than to somehow reach out, and hold her hand, and tell her that everything was going to be ok, that Earth was saved, that it was up to her now, that she'd be the Hero of Earth, that next time—if there was a next time—she'd be the one to step up and save their civilization from the next threat, when it came.

But he stopped himself. She'd already stepped up. She was the Hero of Earth. Just like him. Just like his whole crew, and the crew of the *Victory*, and the *Lincoln*, and the marine task force that executed the ill-advised mission to the *Benevolence*, and Scythia Krull—she was another Hero of Earth. And Polrum Krull. And the entire Skiohra civilization. And for that matter, the Dolmasi, for all their self-serving flaws.

Malakhov? Isaacson? Avery? Norton? He supposed even they had their parts to play, for good or ill. Even self-interested maneuvering could eventually be twisted and redeemed and made to serve the common good. *Shit, except Isaacson, that bastard.*

And then she was gone. Escaped, he hoped, but for him, gone forever.

And now he was alone. A moment later, he watched the stars blueshift until they were no longer on the viewscreen. With a quick alteration to the sensors, the view appeared again as the screen adjusted to show ultraviolet light, then x-rays. The event horizon loomed ahead. He wondered if he'd notice when he passed.

He wondered if the universe would end as he fell in, time sped up so fast on the outside that he could simultaneously witness both the beginning and final moments of reality.

He wondered why he had never let himself love. Could he have loved Shelby? Someone else? Only another life, another time, could tell him the answer. *His* time was gone.

He wondered if he'd still be awake when he crossed the horizon, if he'd survive the brief fall to the singularity—not some tiny, artificial thing that the Russian equipment could produce, but a raw, incomprehensibly dense point, where time and space and matter became one.

He wondered if he'd pop out the other side, like he had with the smaller singularities. Perhaps he'd meet the actual beings that controlled the Valarisi. The true Swarm. If he did, he hoped they had bodies, and that he still had a few torpedoes handy, and if not, a hefty assault rifle.

He wondered if it was all worth it. If he'd done everything he could.

He wondered if they'd still call him the Hero of Earth.

He wondered.

He wondered....

CHAPTER EIGHTY-ONE

Omaha, North America, Earth
Sally Danforth Veterans Memorial Medical Center

BALLSY THOUGHT he was dreaming. His dreams had been so vivid lately, ever since his own *vacation*. He wondered if he'd ever fully remember what happened. Floating through space, weightless, safety line wrapped painfully around his waist, reaching ... reaching ... reaching out for her, always just a hair too far away.

"Ballsy," said the voice.

His eyelids felt incredibly heavy. But he knew that voice.

"Ballsy, wake up."

He opened his eyes. She was there. But ... not the *she* he was expecting.

"Spacechamp?"

The pilot beamed down at him and slapped him on the shoulder. Pain shot down his arm and he cried out.

"Oh, sorry, bud. Your shoulder was dislocated when Pew Pew grabbed your fighter with a tow cable. And a concussion. And ... four broken bones on your left side. And ... well, let's just say you'll be in that bed for awhile."

Another voice from behind him was so loud that he wanted to stuff his ears full of gauze and shut his brain off—his head pounded with groggy pain. "Is he awake? Finally, Ballsy, we were beginning to think you didn't like us or something."

Pew Pew finally came into view, circling around his bed. Half his face was covered with thick bandages, and his own arm was in a sling.

"You've looked better," Volz said groggily. It hurt to talk.

"Things got a bit rough there when that singularity took out the debris field. But, as usual, I threaded my way through. Dragging not just my sorry ass, but your sorry ass out of the way. Was touch and go there for awhile."

Pew Pew lifted a bottle up to his mouth and chugged his beer. "You can't drink in a hospital, man, what the hell are you thinking?" said Spacechamp, but with a wide grin.

"Screw that," said Pew Pew, taking another swig. "We saved Earth. We deserve a god-damned medal. At the very least I deserve to get drunk off my ass. Besides," he swallowed a few more times, before wiping his mouth on his good shoulder. "I'm drinking for two now."

At first Volz didn't understand, thinking Pew Pew was making a pregnancy joke, but that made zero sense. Then he remembered Fodder. They all fell silent for a moment, remembering the lost brother.

Ballsy's gaze drifted out the window. Wherever he was, it was sunny, with late-winter rays lighting up the

windows. Luckily, a nurse interrupted the uncomfortable silence, setting a meal tray on Volz's lap. She didn't
even stop to ask if he was doing ok—she seemed quite
rushed, in fact, and Volz finally realized she was probably attending to dozens, if not hundreds of people in
the aftermath of the battle.

With effort, he grabbed the juice box on the tray and
punched the top open, and dumped out the fruit from
the fruit cup, holding it out the Pew Pew, who dutifully
poured in a few inches. Volz passed the beer-filled fruit
cup off to Spacechamp, then lifted his own juice box in
the air.

"To Fodder," he said. Spacechamp repeated him.

Pew Pew raised his bottle, and held it there for several moments, before composing himself. "To Fodder.
Don't fly like my brother."

They touched their containers together, Ballsy's juice
box, Spacechamp's fruit cup, and Pew Pew's bottle, and
they drank.

The question was burning inside of him. He didn't
want to distract from Pew Pew's moment, and disrespect his brother, but he had to know.

"So..." he began.

"Yes?" Spacechamp set the empty cup back onto
his tray.

"Where is she?"

Spacechamp and Pew Pew exchanged knowing,
heavy looks.

"Guys?"

Spacechamp fumbled in her pocket for something,
looking solemn.

"Guys? Please tell me. After all that, I deserve to know."

Out of her pocket, Spacechamp pulled a small folding electronic pad and tossed it at him. He examined it—it was an average video screen comm device. Spacechamp smiled when he shot her a questioning look. "She left a few hours ago. Right when she woke up. She insisted— had to go to Sacramento and surprise her kid."

Volz breathed a heavy sigh of relief. Pew Pew pointed at the device. "She said she'd be expecting your call."

With a touch of his finger, the screen turned on, and initiated a call to a preset location. He unfolded the device and rested it on his lap, and moments later, there they were.

Fishtail. Her eyes bloodshot from exposure to vacuum and bandages on her head. But she was smiling. And Zack Zack bounced next to her.

"BALLSY! YOU FOUND HER!" said the kid, in his too-loud kid voice.

"We sure did, Zack." He still couldn't believe he was looking at Fishtail, her cold smirk replaced by warmth. Control and corruption replaced by life.

"DID YOU FLY FAST?"

Volz nodded, and, watching the kid bounce out of his chair from pent-up excitement and run around the room behind his mom, all he could do was laugh.

CHAPTER EIGHTY-TWO

Senate Hearing Room, Old Supreme Court Building
Washington D.C., Earth

"Do you, Shelby A. Proctor, promise to tell the entire truth, and nothing but the truth to this committee, on penalty of perjury?"

"I do, sir." She held her hand high for all the cameras to see.

"You may be seated," said the senator. She couldn't remember his name, and she didn't care.

On the raised dais before her sat the armed services committee of United Earth's senate—sixteen men and women from across the surviving worlds that formed the core of the government. Behind her, filling the giant hall, thousands of congresspeople, journalists, celebrities, government officials, and regular citizens hushed as she sat down.

"Thank you again, Commander Proctor, for your service, and for your stellar performance during the war that has so devastated our civilization," began the long-winded senator. She could tell by his expression that he didn't like her, that he was putting on a good show for the crowd. But he was a nameless face to her. Soon, she'd fly off to Britannia, where her brother, and his wife and kids were waiting for her.

She was retiring. She couldn't bear the thought of being a pawn again. After reading the senate reports of the previous months, as the armed services committee grilled admiral after admiral, general after general, and finally the president herself, it became clear that there was far more to the story than was being made public. Inconsistencies, aberrations between people's stories, gaping holes in the computer records. She didn't know exactly how, but it was clear to her that Granger, herself, and countless others in the military had been led on by shadowy figures in the government.

Avery professed her outrage, of course, and demanded that the senate get to the bottom of it. But, at least for now, Proctor didn't care anymore. She had a cushy professorship waiting for her on Britannia, and a cozy mother-in-law studio with her family. She'd get to play with her nieces and nephews. Go out to eat. Lay on the pristine Britannia beaches.

"—So for the record, Commander Proctor, you have no knowledge of how or when the antimatter torpedoes were loaded into that storage bay on the *Warrior*, is that correct?"

"Yes, sir. I was on a brief one-day leave at IDF Science at the time."

"Ah, yes. So it says in your report," huffed the senator. "That's when you expanded your science team to include half a dozen IDF scientists."

"Yes, sir. Ensign Brendan Roth, Ensign Fayle, Lieutenant Kurt—"

"Yes, yes, I have their names here," interrupted the senator, waving some papers in his hand. "What I'm wondering, Commander, is why we have no record of those service members at IDF Science. It's like you came in and picked up some ghosts. Did you have ghosts on your science team, Commander Proctor?"

"I—no, sir. These were real people I worked with."

"Then where are they, Commander?"

Silence in the great marble hall. Although she couldn't hear anything, she knew that dozens of photographers were crouched nearby, taking her picture.

"I don't know, Senator—" Her eyes darted quickly to the nameplate. "Quimby. As I said in my report, they probably were lost in the escape pods when we came under Swarm fire as we fled the *Warrior.*"

"Well surely you would have remembered at least *one* of their faces during your short stay aboard the *Victory?* Surely, you and Granger, having lost not one, not two, but *three* Legacy Fleet heavy cruisers in the space of less than five hours, might have thought to, I don't know, check to see if at least some of the crew made it out alive before you sauntered off to the next ship?"

The crowd erupted in jeers behind her. She knew the crowd was on her side, that everyone practically worshipped Captain Granger and anyone that had served with him. Still, the question unnerved her. Because in truth, she didn't know. So many unanswered questions.

And yet, they'd won. Against all odds, against all hope, they'd won. For now, that was all she cared about. That, and getting back into a classroom, seeing her family, and resting.

The senator held up a hand, and the crowd settled down. "I'm sorry, Commander Proctor. I'm sure it was a harrowing time. Losing the *Warrior* like that, then seeing the *Constitution* used like a brick against that dreadnought, and then escaping to the *Victory*, only to see it get swallowed by a black hole while at the same time you sent the time-travelled Old Bird back through another Russian singularity, all the while losing crew member after crew member ... I'm sure it was terribly hard on you. You've been a good sport."

His paternalistic tone and attitude grated on her. If she wasn't under oath and under the tight thumb of dozens of video cameras, she had half a mind to vault over the table and punch the senator in the face. As it was, she held a saccharine smile glued to her own.

"Will that be all, senator?"

He vaguely waved a hand again as he examined his notes. "Yes, yes, I think we're done with you," he said. She started to get up. "Actually, hold on a minute. One more question, if you don't mind, Commander Proctor."

She lowered herself slowly back into her seat. "Yes, Senator Quimby?"

"Your graduate dissertation. On Swarm Periodicity and Refractory Processes. It was never taken seriously by the academy. Neither the broader academy, nor IDF Science. It was, for all intents and purposes, completely ignored. And yet, it turned out to be remarkably prescient on many issues related to the Swarm. Not perfect—no dissertation is, of course. But remarkably accurate, given what little we knew at the time. Why do you suppose it was not taken seriously?"

She shook her head. Why the hell was he bringing *that* up? She'd spent years on her research, living and breathing cyclical Swarm theory and breaking ground on what she thought would be convincing new directions in Swarm research. And then, she'd given it up. Command had caught her eye, and her imagination. Traveling to so many former worlds devastated by the Swarm—that had given her the wanderlust. The hope for adventure and exploration. And so she made her choice to give up the science and pursue command.

Now she was turning her back on IDF, and heading back into the classroom. What was she running from?

"I—I couldn't say, Senator," she said, inexplicably flustered.

"Do you think it was intentionally suppressed?"

Chattering broke out amongst the crowd. The nutjob conspiracy theorists had been having a heyday with all the events of the last six months, finding multiply-nested conspiracies amongst multiple government entities, colluding with Russians, with anarchists, with oligarchs and plutocrats from dozens of worlds, with the Swarm itself. The idea that true knowledge about the Swarm had been suppressed was one of the more popular theories, making Proctor, much to her extreme discomfort, something of a hero to the tinfoil-hatted nut-jobs. If she had her politics right, Senator Quimby was somewhat of a nut-job himself.

"I couldn't say, Senator. The idea of widespread suppression, coupled with a clear lack of evidence of said suppression, has never sat well with me. As you know, I'm a woman of science, and until you show me the proof that backs the idea up, the data that proves the hypothesis, then I'm afraid I can't subscribe to such theories."

More chattering. Another raised hand quieting the crowd. "Commander Proctor. Your credentials are impeccable. Your performance the past few months equally so. And so it boggles my mind that you were not taken more seriously before this whole fiasco began. Don't the aggregated circumstances and clues point to something deeper here? That perhaps, the Swarm was coming, and someone or some*ones* deep undercover *knew* they were coming, and prepared the way for them? Suppressing dangerous knowledge and ensuring that when the Swarm struck, we would fall before them like chaff before the wind? That we would be sifted, weighed, and found wanting?"

Senator Quimby was a religious man, and Proctor recognized the dog-whistles in his monologue. He was trying to stir up his base among those who were watching. And as far as she knew, *everyone* was watching. Hundreds of billions. All of United Earth, the Caliphate, the Chinese Intersolar Republic, and even the Russian Confederation.

But she wasn't taking the bait.

"No, sir."

He threw his notes down in a huff, and waved her away. "No further questions, Mr. Chairman."

The rest of the questioning was more subdued, though the fireworks flew again when the final senator grilled her on the possibility that perhaps Captain Granger would return again, out of the abyss, like he had before. It was the most popular, but most benign of the conspiracy theories, because, at least in Proctor's opinion, it came from a place of hope, rather than fear. She assured the committee that, no, Granger was gone. That, in fact, a scout ship had ventured as close to the Penumbran black hole as it safely could, and made optical observations of the event horizon, and confirmed that, at least from the outside universe's perspective, Granger was inexorably passing through the horizon itself, and would appear to do so for the next hundred thousand years. Or, at least until his image was so redshifted that the wavelength of the light leaving him became as large as the event horizon itself, at which point, all information about his journey toward the center of the black hole would be lost to the universe forever.

The hearing adjourned, and Lieutenant Diaz met her outside the Senate Hall. "Lunch?" he asked.

"Famished," she said.

They walked five blocks to the commercial district and Diaz led her up to a small hole-in-the-wall restaurant. "Sandwiches ok?"

"Fine." She followed him in. To her surprise, the place was packed.

Except she recognized everyone there. Ensigns Prince, Diamond, and Prucha. Rayna Scott. Several fighter pilots including Volz and his remaining Untouchable crew. Most of the surviving bridge crew from the *Warrior*, including Commander Oppenheimer from the *Victory* and several of his people.

They were all looking at her, solemnly.

"What the hell is this, an intervention?"

"In a sense," said Diaz. "Look, Proctor, I know you've turned them down. I know you've got that cushy professorship waiting for you on Britannia. I know we can't really compete against that and your family and warm Britannia beaches. But, in our defense...." He trailed off.

Ballsy finished for him. "We're pretty kick-ass." Everyone laughed. He seemed a lot happier than he'd been in awhile.

She laughed too, putting her arm around Rayna. "Look, guys. I think I need to stop while I'm ahead. They always say, quit at the top of your game, and you'll always be remembered kindly. Stay too long and, well, you know what they say about guests overstaying their welcome. Rotten fish and all that."

Diaz nodded. "Fine. We understand." He turned to one of the bridge crew members and pointed. "But, before we go, we wanted to show you this. One last pathetic effort to get you to change your mind."

The lights dimmed, and on the wall appeared the image of a ship, projected from some handheld device.

It looked exactly like the *Constitution*. With a few modifications.

"The ISS *Chesapeake*. We're her crew. Every one of us here. I asked the top brass, and no one could tell *us* no." He turned to Proctor. "All she needs is a captain."

Her hand covered her mouth.

Rayna added, in a low voice, "We kept the seat warm for you, Cap'n. IDF was about to name another captain, since you turned them down. But we convinced them to wait a few more weeks. To give you time, you see."

She wanted this. She didn't realize how much she'd been wanting this. The grilling by the senators only confirmed it—she had no desire to sit at a desk, to deal with bureaucrats. And, *damn*, if the academy wasn't chock-full of bureaucrats.

"On one condition," she said. The tiny restaurant fell silent. "We change her name. From now on, she's the *Granger*."

No one spoke. But everyone nodded.

"She's the *Granger*," repeated Rayna.

Pew Pew snorted, and laughed out loud. "*She's*? *She's* the *Granger*?"

Commander Scott rolled her eyes. "Ships are girls, Lieutenant. Get over it," she said, to more laughter.

They sat down to eat, and as the hour passed, Proctor became more and more comfortable with her decision. Her brother would be hurt, of course, as would the kids—they were opening their home to her. Giving her a well-earned respite from the rigors of command and IDF and ships and space and battle, and everything uncomfortable and unpleasant about living in close quarters with a thousand other misfits aboard a floating hunk of metal.

But the Old Bird, and the *Warrior*, they were her home. And this was her family. And the *Chesapeake*—the *Granger*—she couldn't imagine a better home than that.

CHAPTER EIGHTY-THREE
EPILOGUE

President's Stateroom, Frigate One
High Orbit, Britannia

PRESIDENT AVERY PUFFED on her cigar, her feet kicked up on the desk. A whiskey bottle fell off with a crash as her calf brushed up against it, but she shrugged. There were plenty more bottles. All the time in the world now to get drunk and dally with the cabana boys as she saw fit. A woman had needs, after all.

"I think we've got things tied up on my end. What I still can't believe, is how damn lucky we were with Granger. That a man should pop up out of nowhere and rise to the occasion—boggles my mind. We should have had something more concrete in place."

Avery nodded at her companion. "He was pretty amazing, I admit. One big-damn-hero moment after another. But, you know, if he hadn't been there, some-one else would have. That's the thing about us west-erners. Everyone thinks they're the hero. But when the time comes, most people scatter. They wilt. But not Granger. He had spine. And if it wasn't him, it would have been Proctor. Or Zingano. Or *someone*."

"After all our plans, Avery, it unnerves me to think it all rested on chance. If he hadn't pulled off what he did, if he hadn't been susceptible to the clues we sent his way, sent Proctor's way ... I shudder to think. I mean, what if Granger had denied her science team to board?"

"He wouldn't have done that. There was no time for him to pore over personnel backgrounds. He trusted Proctor. And *she* had no time to pore over personnel backgrounds. Believe me, Mr. Malakhov, no matter who was there, I'm confident we would have pulled it off."

The Russian shook his head, and slammed back an-other shot. "Whatever. I'm done. My end is clean, and, if I'm not mistaken, I'm dead. No thanks to you." He winked at her with his new eye—the surgery scars were healing fast.

"Yes, terribly sorry about that."

"Did you really have to send Isaacson after me like that? Sloppy."

"Honestly, I didn't know he'd actually try to kill you. But either way, we both know the Swarm had to be absolutely convinced we were at each other's throats. They had to be completely and utterly distracted by our little civil war. I think we accomplished that, wouldn't you say?"

He poured himself another glass. "Yes, well ... next time tell your puppets not to aim for my eye. That hurt."

"What are your plans?" Avery puffed another ring of smoke into the air.

"Vacation. One, long, thirty-year vacation. I've been president for, what, sixteen years now?"

"Come now, Mr. Malakhov, something tells me you could pull some strings in the Duma, and you'd be president for life."

"I'm *dead*, remember? Went through a great deal of hassle to get to this point. If I were to suddenly come back to life, that would be a fearsome amount of wasted effort." He poured himself another shot from the whiskey bottle. "No, Madam President, I'll be quite content to disappear into the countryside of the Caucusus. Or maybe a little island on New Petersburg."

They smoked their cigars and drank in silence for awhile longer, before Malakhov finally stood up to leave. "Well, Madam President, it's been a pleasure. A fruitful and profitable thirteen year relationship. The fact that humanity is still here—well, I think that says a lot about what we've accomplished."

She tapped her shot glass with a finger. "There's one last thing I'm still not understanding."

"Yes?" He stopped at the door.

"The antimatter. All my clandestine programs developing that shit. The manpower, the expense—all of it. We loaded it up on all those ships at your insistence, waiting for our chance to shove it down the cumrats' throats. And then at the end, of course, it worked. We shut down the Link. But my question is—well, two questions, actually."

"Shoot."

"Why didn't you just give us the damn antimatter technology to begin with? I never understood that."

"Appearances, Madam President, as you know all too well. It would have raised suspicions."

She rolled her eyes. "Yes, yes. Whatever. I'm sure we could have arranged something. But no matter. The bigger question is this. And I have the feeling you don't have an answer for me."

"Try me."

"The antimatter pods. From the torpedoes Granger launched. They're still on their way to the target. He hasn't even finished crossing the event horizon yet, from our perspective, and won't for another hundred thousand years at least. From his perspective, my scientists tell me that he'll witness the end of our galaxy before the tidal forces get strong enough to finally rip him to shreds. How can the Link be truly destroyed if we can sit outside that infernal thing, point a sensitive scope at the horizon, and still *see* the damn antimatter falling in? Nothing's been destroyed. No antimatter has reacted with a single molecule of that black hole yet."

He paused with the door halfway open, nodding. "You're right. Makes no sense. All I knew was that, in my interrogations with the Swarm subjects, that point came across loud and clear, though they never said a word. They tried to hide it from me. They were terrified of the idea of antimatter falling into that thing. It's why they never gave us the antimatter beam technology. Just think what we could have done with *that*. Fly a hundred ships out to the little bugger and beam a few tons of antimatter straight into the hole itself. No fuss, no muss."

She shrugged. "Anyway. It's over." She puffed another ring. "What do you make of the reports from the Octarous cluster about possible ship movements in Findiri and Quiassi space?"

He walked out the door. Before it closed, he called back, "Not my problem anymore, Barb. And if you'll take my advice, you'd get out before it becomes your problem too."

Thank you for reading *Victory*.

Sign up to find out when *Independence*, book 1 of *The Legacy Ship Trilogy*, is released: smarturl.it/nickwebblist

CONTACT INFORMATION

www.nickwebbwrites.com
facebook.com/authornickwebb
authornickwebb@gmail.com

DISCARD

31998345R00253

Made in the USA
Lexington, KY
26 February 2019